Hannah's Wharf

Connie Monk, who comes from a family of musicians, is married and lives in Devon, where *Hannah's Wharf* is set. Her previous novels are *Fortune's Daughter* and *Jessica*, which are also available in Fontana, and *Seasons of Change*. *Jessica* was shortlisted for the 1987 Romantic Novelists Association Award.

Also by Connie Monk

CONNIE MONK

Hannah's Wharf

FONTANA/Collins

First published by Judy Piatkus (Publishers) Ltd 1987
First published by Fontana Paperbacks 1989

Copyright © 1987 by Connie Monk

Printed and made in Great Britain by
William Collins Sons & Co. Ltd, Glasgow

CHAPTER ONE

It wasn't the first time she'd come upon him like it. She felt herself freeze. He was sitting with his back to the doorway, bent forward, his head on the table, his pen fallen from his hand. She knew what she would hear, she'd heard it before. The sound of his sobs haunted her.

'Father?' It took all Hannah's courage.

No reply. Not a flicker of movement, not a sound. He must be asleep. Perhaps she ought to leave him, he had such bad nights. Then she pictured the results of her morning's work keeping warm on the end of the kitchen range.

'Father.' Louder this time and still he didn't seem to hear. Panic overwhelmed her, fear that stripped her of the maturity she strived for. In the silence she longed for any kind of sound. The tears she'd dreaded would be welcome. She crossed to his side with no idea of what her next move should be, clinging to the belief that she could wake him.

'Father! Didn't you hear me?' Her voice was shrill, the sound of it unfamiliar. 'Wake up.' She shook his shoulder.

Hannah had known misery and loss but she wasn't prepared for this. With her hand still resting on her father, the fright she felt was a physical thing. It seemed to close her throat and made her heart fill her chest. If only he'd give some sign, if only he'd cry so that she could hold him and comfort him.

Gripping his shoulders, she tried to raise him, seeing that where his head had hit the wooden tabletop one lens of his spectacles had broken. Saliva dribbled from his open mouth, his eyes stared unseeing. Frantically she looked round the small dining room where he'd been working.

Help, that was it. She must get help. 'Please . . . please . . .' she rasped. But please what?

Her mind rejected what her heart already knew. It was too late for help.

Outside, the October sun sent a shaft of light across the brick wall of the back yard, the same sunlight that had fallen on Hannah as she'd stood by the stone sink in the kitchen just a few minutes ago. Through the wall that divided their house from their neighbours' she could hear sounds – a table being dragged across the floor, a broom knocking against the skirting as Mrs Tonks cleaned.

'I'm going to get the doctor.' She knew he didn't hear but, child as she still was, she needed to tell him. Carefully, she lowered his shoulders back to rest against the table. Even in this moment it struck her that his sheet of paper was still blank in front of him. This morning, like so many of these last months, he'd written nothing.

She would leave the front door unlocked. Doctor Harris would come in his trap. He'd get here before she could, running. That he might bring her back with him didn't enter Hannah's head. She'd seen him often enough the previous winter when he'd visited her mother in her last illness. She'd answered the door to him, fetched warm water; always he'd treated her as though she didn't exist. It hadn't surprised her, she'd been brought up to expect it. It was an age when children kept to their place, were expected to be seen and not heard.

Supposing he was out! Supposing she ran all the way to Craven Place and no one knew where she could find him! She'd have to leave the message and come back. Her father would be in the same position, the afternoon light would fade, she'd still be there with him, trying to wake him, trying . . . Hannah felt sick with fear. Her mind focused on just one thing: she must find the doctor, not for his powers of healing – it was too late for them – but because she was so alone. When her mother had been ill, she and

6

her father had had each other. Yet, even then, Hannah had known it was nearer the truth to say that she had had him, for he'd found no comfort in her. He found none in anyone since his wife's death.

The front door of their terrace house, number four Albany Street, opened directly on to the footpath, and only inches from it was the front door of number six. In the way that children understand things, Hannah had always known without being told that her parents disapproved of their neighbours, Mr and Mrs Tonks. But Alice Tonks was kind, no one had needed to tell her that either. A second's hesitation then Hannah overcame her fright and hurried past their door.

'Nothing wrong is there, dearie?' Alice appeared in the dark entrance hall. She must have been watching round the edge of the lace curtain like she often did.

'It's Father, I can't wake him. I'm running to get Dr Harris.'

'Best we come in duckie, take a peep at what's amiss.' Then, calling back down the hallway: 'Jo! You there, Jo? Mr Ruddick, next door – young Hannah here says she can't rouse him. Best we go in with her, then you can run and bring the doctor.'

Together they trooped into number four, Alice leading the way. How strange to see them here. In all the years they'd been neighbours, they'd never before been invited in. Whether or not they'd actually been invited this time was an academic point, but the sight of them there stabbed at Hannah's conscience. She could almost sense her mother's silent disapproval of their coming in, and picture her father retreating with no more than a cool nod of his head. The Tonks weren't the sort of people her parents expected to mix with. She'd sensed their feelings for the first time when, years ago, Alice Tonks had given her a mince tart – 'Just warm from my oven, duckie.'

Adele Ruddick had smiled coolly, almost too politely,

7

and told her young daughter to: 'Say thank you nicely, Hannah, then take it indoors and put it on the dresser for your tea.' Hannah had known, small though she'd been, that what Mrs Tonks had wanted was for her to eat it there in the street, where she and Jo could watch the child enjoying her treat. Then there'd been occasions when her ball had gone over the wall. 'Knock on the door and ask politely – and mind you apologize. Then come straight back.' Alice and Jo had never borne any malice that she'd not stayed. Without being told they too had understood the situation.

Crowding into the narrow passageway with her neighbours, Hannah felt guilty, sure that her mother must be looking down and disapproving.

'Where is he, duckie?'

'In the dining room.'

'And which would that be?'

How funny, not knowing. All the houses in Albany Street were the same. 'This one.' Hannah put out her hand to open the door.

'Best you cut along back to the kitchen. Me and Jo'll see if he's got his senses back yet. Come on, Jo, in here, in the middle best.'

To the Tonks the kitchen, at the back, was the heart of the house. The 'front best' was the holy of the holies, coming into its own on occasions of importance – weddings, funerals, Christmas. The 'middle best' was one stage down, it gave a special air to Sunday afternoons after the dinner had been cleared away and Alice had changed into her best frock.

Alone in the kitchen Hannah listened and waited. Smut, their rusty black cat, mewed at the window so she pushed it up far enough for him to get in. He dropped from the sill on to the side of the stone sink and daintily balanced his way along until he could leap on to the arm of the wooden fireside chair where he stood purring, his tail

8

pointing to the ceiling. He appreciated the golden wonder of her piecrust, seemed as surprised by it as she had been herself. His whiskers twitched in anticipation. Hannah took him on to her knee, her long fingers caressing his neck and under his chin and ears just as he liked her to. The smell of food and this unexpected attention, was almost too much for him. He stood up, he sat down, he stood up, he turned round, digging his claws into her as he chose the perfect spot to settle. And before he found it the door opened and there was Alice.

Even after the reception her overtures had always met with from the Ruddicks it wasn't in this portly, round-faced woman's nature to bear malice. She was certainly ill at ease, though, Hannah could tell it from the way she fingered the material of her apron.

'Now then, duckie, you get and eat some of that dinner. Jo's run for Dr Harris.'

'I'm not hungry. I'll keep it for later. Perhaps Father might be able to eat some.' She had to say it, she had to hang on to the pretence of hope even though now there was no shape to the future. Her fingers moved on Smut's throat, she could feel the vibration as he purred. The sound seemed to fill the room.

'Let me give a spoonful to Smut. Look at 'im, you'd think he was starving. See the way his nose is going.' And so saying Alice took one of the plates that Hannah had put on the rack above the range and lavished a large helping of dinner on the delighted Smut. 'Now what about you? Smells a treat.'

Hannah shook her head, tears taking away her voice. Such a little while ago she'd put out the knives and forks. It hurt to remember her pride as her gaze had gone time and again in disbelief to the golden glory of the meat pie. She'd imagined the look of pleasure on her father's face, his words of praise as he sat to the table. Now he wouldn't . . . he wouldn't . . . A sob broke in her throat.

9

'Now then, duckie, your Pa wouldn't want you to be crying.'

'. . . dead . . . Father too . . .'

'Poor little soul.' The kindly Alice balanced uncomfortably on the wooden arm of Hannah's chair. 'He'll be with your Ma, try and think of that, duckie. Couldn't have been no heaven for her till he came, I wouldn't wonder.'

Satisfied that the plate was well polished, Smut started his after-meal wash and brush up, turning a disdainful green-eyed glare on Hannah as he was swept back into her arms. Only Smut held reality for her. He was all she had.

Alice, one work-roughened hand on Hannah's shoulder, went on: 'Never seen such a change as there was in him after your Ma was taken, poor soul.'

'But he had me!' Hannah gulped helplessly. She remembered his gentle smile, his 'Good girl, good girl' when she'd brought their food to the table. Never a word of criticism for her many failures. Yet hearing Mrs Tonks' words she knew that criticism would have needed an awareness that he'd no longer had. She held Smut against her face, feeling his long silky fur. It was no use. Shock and panic were being replaced by something else, realization of the scale of her loss.

'What'll I do now? Mrs Tonks, I don't know what to do!' For all these months since her mother had died at the beginning of the year she'd struggled to stretch the meagre few shillings she'd been given each week, battled to make a home for them. 'I'll get a job. We'll manage, Smut and me'll manage. They won't send me away, will they?' The 'they' of authority was as far as her imagination would stretch.

'Have you any family, duckie? Grandparents, aunts, uncles?' But in all these years Alice had never seen anything she might have taken to be a family visit, and she didn't miss anything for the want of looking.

'Father has a sister. I've never seen her. She lives a long way away.'

'Hark!' Alice cocked her head and listened. 'That'll be Jo, he's found the doctor.'

They heard the men go into the dining room. Silently they waited. It took but a minute for Dr Harris to confirm what they already knew and then Jo brought him out to the kitchen. He was a short, wizened man. His ratlike face held too high a colour and he had thin, tight lips. The parting in his wispy ginger hair was only just above his right ear, then the lank strands were coaxed to the left of his head in a vain attempt to camouflage his bald patch. He wore a black frock coat and carried a tall stove pipe hat.

Hannah pulled herself to her full height, shoulders well back even though the bodice of her outgrown dress took the strain and her bony knees showed beneath the hem. She meant to let him see that she wasn't a child. She would be fourteen at her next birthday. She'd find work, she wasn't something to be 'disposed' of like he seemed to be disposing of her father. It was hard to keep the corners of her mouth steady, so she held them between her teeth. Bravely, she met his gaze. No one could call Hannah a beauty with her straight honey brown hair falling to her waist and held off her forehead with a brown band, her snub nose and generous mouth. But her teeth were strong and very white, her dark blue eyes fringed with long, dark lashes in contrast to the lighter shade of her hair and her brows were clearly defined. Her face had a look of courage and of character. No beauty perhaps yet there was about her something arresting. Hannah would never be overlooked.

Dr Harris viewed her with a stab of irritation. He considered that with a patient's last breath his own responsibilities should come to an end. Not so easily could he shut the door on this case, though, even if Humphrey

11

Ruddick hadn't called on his services until it was too late. He'd visited often enough to see the wife and he knew there was only this one gawky child. He hoped she had relatives to come and see to things otherwise it would fall to him to arrange for her to be taken in at the Home.

'Who is the next of kin . . . er . . . child?'

'My father has a sister.'

'And may I ask where?'

'She's not near here. She lives in Devonshire.'

'There, fancy that.' Alice looked from Hannah to Jo. 'Fancy, there is family after all. And we never knew.'

'Write down her name and address for me,' the doctor ordered Hannah.

'He calls her Louise and she lives in Devon – that's all I know.'

At the doctor's impatient tut-tutting, it was Jo who suggested she should look to see if her father might have kept an old letter that would give them a clue, or at least an address.

'She never wrote, I'm sure she didn't.' But even so Hannah led the way along the passage to the front room to look in the bureau. 'Your father's bureau' her mother had always called it, and it had been out of bounds. Now here she was rummaging through it contents, not only her but Alice and Jo Tonks too! Newspaper cuttings about Humphrey Ruddick's poetry readings, an envelope containing a golden curl (undoubtedly her mother's), a demand for rent, bottles of ink, boxes of nibs, a bag of receipts. Ah, here was something! What was this? Right at the back behind the receipts was a long parchment envelope. She took from it a foolscap document and started to read.

'I'll have that.' The doctor held out his claw-like hand and she was still child enough to obey.

'Humph.' Then: 'I'd better get a cable to her straight away.'

'What does it say?'

'Say?' He seemed surprised that she should hinder him with enquiries. 'This aunt of yours, Louise Netherton, lives at The Hall, Deremouth, Devonshire. Your father had the foresight it seems to arrange that in the event of your being orphaned you should be put in her care. I'll send a cablegram. No doubt she's in service at this Hall. Perhaps she'll be able to find you a position there, it may well be a large establishment judging by the address.' He put the envelope in his bag and turned to leave. 'I'll have the body removed for autopsy,' he told Jo, 'and I'll call again in the morning regarding the child.'

'We'll see Hannah's not alone, don't you worry your head about her.' The kindly Alice took control. And as good as her word, before the horse drawn ambulance had turned the corner bearing Humphrey Ruddick's body away, she arrived to take up residence until this Louise Netherton person came to look after the child.

So, late in the evening when a cablegram was delivered she and Hannah read it together. 'Unable to travel. Sending Thurlston to attend. Arrive Hastings 5.40. Louise Netherton.'

'This aunt must be married, duckie. Thurlston, she says. Must be her hubby.'

'Am sending.' It hardly seemed the way to speak of a husband. What sort of a woman could she be? Whatever she was like she'd never been interested in her brother or his family. The cablegram did nothing to reassure Hannah, only added to the unreality of everything about these last hours.

Until today Alice had never been inside the house. Now here she was sleeping in the dead man's bed. 'Best take my own sheets,' she told Jo. But she was determined to stay awake and listen. At the first sound from Hannah she'd be into the room, her matronly bosom ready to cushion her.

13

She listened and listened, her breathing growing deeper, her eyelids heavier, and listened and slept.

It was the sound of her soft snores that brought Hannah face to face with what had happened. 'That Tonks woman', as her mother had called her, asleep in their own bed! Mother gone, and now Father too. Smut sensed her restlessness and moved closer, lying against her legs. She put her hands up and behind her and lay clinging to the iron rail of her bed-head, feeling the place where the paint had chipped off. The cold metal was familiar just as everything in her small room was familiar, even in the darkness. The speckled mirror on the chest of drawers, the silver-backed hair brush that used to be her mother's but had been given to her for her twelfth birthday, the wobbly chair by the side of her bed with the worn rush seat and the spar that kept coming out. 'Next time I have something to heat the gluepot for, remind me and I'll stick it,' her father had promised. Now he would never mend it. She felt the sting of unshed tears. She'd never hear that 'Good girl, good girl' or see the gentle, vague smile in his light blue eyes.

She reached to pull Smut, her anchor, towards her. But he had a mind of his own. His luminous eyes pierced the darkness in a haughty glare, his fur bristled with indignation, and like a shot he was on her chest of drawers, from there to balance for a second on the open window then a safe landing on the kitchen roof before dropping lightly to the ground. Hannah stretched her legs. The bed was still warm from his body. Ahead of her the night was long and lonely.

But daylight, even the first hint of dawn, brought a new resolve. She'd run away without seeing this man Thurlston who was being 'sent'. Then another thought: if she did that they'd think she was frightened. She'd stay and meet him, let them see her as calm, dignified, grown-up, someone Father would be proud of. But after that she'd go. She

14

wouldn't wait for this aunt who'd never cared about them to tell her what she had to do. So first thing in the morning she packed a grip and hid it under her bed in readiness. Then, taking her mother's chain purse from the top drawer of her father's dressing table, she counted up what money she could muster. A shilling and some pennies in her housekeeping tin, and she knew Father's savings would be in a box in his wardrobe. There might not be anything in it, or there might be a lot, sovereigns. She didn't know how much he made from his poetry, but it had never allowed for luxuries. Her mother had always saved what she could for a rainy day, knowing even when things were flush that any time the weather could break. And a good thing she had, for over the months since her death it had been her foresight that had kept them fed and paid the rent.

The box yielded up two sovereigns, one crown, three half crowns and two florins. Hannah had never handled such wealth. It gave her new confidence. She couldn't see what was ahead, where she'd find work. If she'd been a boy she would have had no doubts. She would have gone to sea, found a job on one of the fishing boats that came in and out of Hastings. She imagined it now as she climbed on to a chair and craned her neck so that she could see the far horizon. She imagined the smack of the sails, the thrown spray . . . But she was a girl and the pictures in her mind would go no further. Her fingers caressed the chain purse. Back in her own room she hid it with the grip, then shut the door carefully behind her and went downstairs.

Smut was at the kitchen window scratching at the glass. As soon as she let him in he jumped to the ground, rubbing around her legs as she poured him a saucer of milk. Smut! What would become of him if she wasn't here? She pictured the kitchen dark and empty, the coals dead in the range, him mewing at the window looking for her . . . She clenched her teeth.

Necessity made her cunning. She gave no hint that she had plans of her own when later on she said to Alice: 'Mrs Tonks, what will happen to Smut if my aunt says I have to go to live there?'

'Never you worry your head about Smut. He's in my place half his life as it is. It's the fish, you know. Get's a whiff of my Jo coming home from his cart and round e' comes with his tail in the air. You don't need to fret about Smut, he'll have a good home with Jo and me and never know the difference.' She meant it kindly but Hannah found it hard to force herself to smile. Not notice the difference.

By evening the unknown Thurlston had arrived and already Hannah's future was changing. Jo Tonks met the train and brought him home. A giant of a man with a florid face, that was Hannah's first impression as she watched them coming along Albany Street. The lump in her throat seemed to be choking her.

'This is Mr Thurlston,' Jo told them. 'We got the wrong picture, Alice. I was saying to him, we thought this aunt of Hannah's, Mrs Netherton, was sending her husband – Thurlston Netherton we thought it'd be. But it seems he works for her. She's got a fine place there in Devon, servants carriages . . .'

'Fancy, now! But then poor Mr Ruddick was always a gentleman.'

It wasn't the thought of a fine house and servants that stopped Hannah taking her grip and her purse and going in search of freedom. So what was it? Perhaps it was Harold Thurlston's bluff heartiness that held her here – or perhaps she was too numbed with misery to fight.

Harold Thurlston dealt with the landlord, settled any outstanding bills, and she felt herself being swept along with the tide. His instructions must have been to deal with the house, the furniture and the child, in that order. Upstairs she listened as a furniture dealer was shown

16

round. She bit hard on her knuckles as she heard: 'Nothing of great value – but I'll clear the lot for you.' The table where her father had worked, her mother's favourite beaded chair . . . it was her home.

Two days later they were on their way westward. From Hastings to London, then on to Deremouth.

Harold had girls of his own. He knew if his Kath was miserable she was always hungry. Something to eat might put a bit of colour back in the poor child's face. 'Here,' he said heartily, 'see what Mrs Tonks gave us. What would you say to a fish cake?'

'I'd say "thank you",' Hannah made herself rally to his call.

So they bit into their fish cakes and swigged at the same stone bottle of ginger beer with complete disregard for the other passengers. Harold studied the girl sympathetically, wanting to help. Not like Kath in looks, but looks weren't everything.

At Reading another passenger joined the compartment and at Newbury two got off. It wasn't until the train steamed out of Taunton that they finally found themselves on their own. With no one to overhear she asked him: 'Mr Thurlston, can you tell me about my aunt? What's she like?'

Two days ago she wouldn't have let herself believe that she could find herself travelling westward in the company of the unknown 'Thurlston'. Had he been different, perhaps she wouldn't have been. But there was something about this genial giant that reassured her, and if there was one thing she needed it was reassurance.

'I'll say this, she's a good mistress. A man couldn't ask for better.'

'You mean she's nice?' That wasn't easy to believe. 'You see, Father never talked about her. She never had anything to do with us. Not even when Mother died. No one ever mentioned her. I think they couldn't have got on.' Even speaking of it gave her an uneasy feeling of disloyalty to her parents.

'It happens like that in families sometimes, my dear, often no more than some small thing sets them against each other. Not for us to judge the ins and outs of it. And perhaps you're imagining it, eh? It could be no more than the distance that set them apart. 'Tis a long way, you can see that.'

'And she's nice?'

'Like I say, I couldn't ask for fairer. Must be upward of fifteen years since the master died and she's never altered. Be a change for there to be a young lady like yourself in the Hall. Never had a family, she and the master.'

'Tell me about the Hall.'

'Netherton Hall. The house was built towards the end of the last century – 'twas the master's father, old Mr Netherton, who built it. That was before I remember, of course, I went there as a jobbing lad to help in the garden, and I've been there ever since.'

'You live in the Hall?'

'Bless you, no. I live in the gatehouse, have for many a year. The head gardener has always had the gatehouse and it was when I was wanting to marry the missus that the job fell empty. The master offered it to me, along with the house.'

That still didn't tell Hannah what she wanted to know. What was she going to? What sort of a home?

'Is it big, the Hall I mean?'

'Not one of the great houses but a fine place for all that. It's the gardens I take charge of. A lovely rolling lawn – if you walk to the top it gives you a view that fair takes your breath away. Orchards, rose gardens, and near the house a real suntrap where we grow all the fruit and veg. Out beyond the orchard there's a copse you could lose yourself in. 'Tis a bit of a jungle, and except for taking some of the wood for burning it's left to run wild. The times I've said

18

to my missus, 'twas a good day when the master set us up in our place there.' He beamed contentedly. 'Not much we can't grow. Reckon if you planted your umbrella it'd take root.' He would happily have talked about the garden for the rest of the journey.

'How far is it from the sea?'

'I suppose a mile or two. No, less than two down the hill to the quay. That's where the company is, the wharf.'

'Company?'

'Ah, Netherton's. Netherton Shipping Company.'

Was he telling her she'd inherited a whole family, and not just an aunt? Then he explained and the future suddenly had a meaning, a shape at last: Netherton Shipping Company, set up by her aunt's father-in-law, trading to the furthermost corners of the world.

'Since the master died it's been managed for her, of course, the mistress doesn't go there these days. No family, you see. Great shame, no son to follow on. Means a lot to have a son.' And from his voice it was evident he counted himself amongst the lucky ones.

Exeter came and went. Dusk was already falling, Hannah would see little of Deremouth this evening. She looked out over the misty country, the Exe estuary and the sea beyond. The sea, Hastings, home . . . memories that drove away her newly awakened interest in what lay ahead. That tight-lipped doctor would be surprised to see her now. Aunt Louise in service, indeed!

Daylight was nearly gone as they finally climbed into the one and only hansom waiting outside the station at Deremouth. She peered around her, seeing all she could of the little town. A muffin man walked past, balancing his tray on his head and ringing his bell to attract customers. She saw a little boy chasing after him, a dish in his hand. Under the gaslamp opposite two women stood gossiping. Then the pony moved off and she was on the last stage of her journey. They passed an inn called the 'Jolly Sailor' where one or two men were gathered in the doorway, then another called the 'New Quay Inn'. No men here, just a group of children playing 'five stones' as they waited outside. She had her first glimpse of the shipping offices and of the masts of the ships moored at the wharf, and leant out wanting to absorb it all. If only it weren't so dark! Clearly she could see the masts of the ships tied up at the quay, on the wharf the gaslight threw its glow on them; then in the mouth of the estuary she recognized the sails of a schooner, ghostly grey, its lamp heralding its approach. Journey's end as night fell. She saw all of it for a fleeting moment as they climbed the hill above the harbour, just long enough to boost her optimism. The memory of it lasted.

The hill from town was steep, the even rhythm of the pony's hooves slowing as the incline grew steeper, onward and upward to Netherton Hall and the moor beyond. As they turned in at the great iron gates that had been left open for their arrival she saw what must be Mr Thurlston's gatehouse, the single lamp in one room throwing a dim light to the window. Very different from the shafts of light that streamed out from the Hall at the end of the drive.

The door was opened to them by a middle-aged maid-servant, a colourless woman with hair pulled up and pinned under her mob cap and an expression neither hostile nor friendly. Wordlessly she ushered them into the large, square hall where a fire burnt brightly in the fireplace on the far wall.

'They've arrived ma'am,' she announced to someone unseen in the room to the right. Hannah expected she'd have to wait while her aunt talked to Mr Thurlston; this was the usual order of things, grown-ups first, children after.

But her aunt's voice carried out to them, clear and firm. It was not the ring of the fair-minded, good mistress Harold Thurlston had described but a domineering voice.

Hannah turned to her kindly friend, filled with shame to hear him summarily dismissed. 'Show the child in on her own. Send Thurlston home, and tell him I'll see him at eleven in the morning.'

No thank you for all he'd done, for his kindness, for being her friend. No interest in what had happened in Hastings. As Harold gently pushed her towards the door of the room where her aunt waited, her hand went to the chain purse. She'd never felt so alone, but her head was high.

'Come along in and shut the door behind you. Let me see what I've been sent.

Standing very straight, shoulders well back, Hannah faced her aunt. She was a tall woman, held erect by two silver-knobbed sticks, dignified, austere and unsmiling. That was the first impression. Only as the seconds went by did Hannah notice the long, heavily ringed fingers, white-knuckled as they gripped the sticks for support.

'Humph! Nothing of your father about you. Nothing! Turn round. Take your cape off. Slowly, girl, slowly.' Louise sniffed, if from anyone so haughty it could be termed a sniff. 'And is that the best you could find to travel in?'

It was a blow below the belt. Dressing for her journey Hannah had put on her Sunday frock. It was too short and too tight, but hearing her aunt's caustic remark she felt herself back in the kitchen in Albion Street, her mother kneeling on the rug in front of her range making the final adjustment to the hem. 'It's going to be so pretty, Hannah. You've never had such a pretty dress!' Two years ago nearly, just before the beginning of the long illness that had taken her from them.

But she wouldn't let this hateful old woman know the misery that ached inside her. 'Father has been very busy,' she lied, her voice tight and controlled, 'he's had no time to worry about new clothes for me.'

'Hah!' It might have meant anything. 'Busy with his rhymes, I suppose.' The scrutiny continued. 'Well, if there's nothing of him in you, there's nothing of her either, I'll give you that. If ever a man needed a woman with a bit of stamina it was Humphrey. Never could understand what he could see in her – and I told him so. Feathery little piece, with those great eyes. Never took them off him. Poor simpleton, he didn't stand a chance.'

Even misery was forgotten. Anger got the upper hand. 'You've no business to talk like that!'

Louise was pulled up short. 'Humph! Suppose you're right, I shouldn't say it, at least to you. Always speak my mind, always have.' She eyed this new-found niece as if she were an item for sale, an item it was doubtful if it was worth purchasing. Then: 'Well, you've been dropped in my lap so there's nothing for it but to make what I can of you.'

Hannah's jaw ached from the effort of holding it steady. The ache reached right down to beneath her ribs; her tummy might have been made of jelly. But she'd not have this arrogant old woman know it.

'I'm sorry you've been troubled with me, Aunt Louise. But you can see I'm not a child. A lot of girls of my age find work.'

'Work!' You think I'd have a niece of mind work! At, what is it, fourteen years old you can talk such tommy nonsense? Just put it right out of your head, you hear me, before we go a step further.

'Certainly you've not the shape of a child. Not decent at your age going around showing your figure like that, Humphrey never did have the sense to . . . Oh well, never mind him.'

For a second Hannah's shoulders rounded. She folded her arms self-consciously across the budding bosom that had earned her aunt's displeasure.

'If that's the best get-up you have then it's time you were

22

found something else. I'll not have any niece of mine seen out looking such a scarecrow, as if all your things had shrunk in the wash-tub.'

For months Hannah had known she'd far outgrown her wardrobe. With each step her boots reminded her of it; her long boney wrists protruded beyond her cuffs; her skirt was only just to the top of her knees. It was only now, seeing her aunt's expression, that she realized just how the outside world must see her. At home people were used to her bedraggled appearance, and none of their neighbours had much anyway.

It seemed Louise Netherton was used to giving orders and having them obeyed instantly. Patience wasn't one of her virtues – if, indeed she had any. Without further ado the bell-rope was pulled to summon Gladys, the colourless servant who had ushered Hannah in.

'Gladys, I want word sent right away to Phyllis Bentley. Tell her to come here this evening, straight away, and to bring her measure.' Good mistress, Mr Thurlston had said time and again. Certainly not one to let the grass grow under her feet.

Only now did Hannah take stock of the room. In the first shock of meeting her aunt it had been no more than an opulent background, somewhere she felt a stranger. It was a large room, high ceiling elaborately carved as was the wooden mantelpiece. A four-tier what-not stood in one corner, laden with china and bronze that without knowing why, Hannah was sure must have come from the Orient. The walls were covered with heavy red and gold embossed paper and hung with gilt-framed paintings, too many to count at a glance. It was fashionable to display an abundance of paintings but Hannah felt that these weren't displayed for reasons of fashion nor yet for ornamentation but were a symbol of real wealth. The house's design reflected the tastes of the previous century as did the furnishings of graceful Chippendale and Heppelwhite.

23

Louise Netherton loved beautiful things around her and had no use for fashionable dust-harbouring fretwork or covers fringed with bobbles. If the line was good, the colour clear and true, decoration wasn't necessary. That was her option and at Netherton Hall her opinion was law.

Hannah's impression of the drawing room was of richness, order and beauty. It was alien to all she'd known, just as Louise was with her critical eye and sharp tongue.

Humphrey Ruddick had been many years younger than his sister, an afterthought and a shock to his middle-aged parents, born a few months after Louise had married Charles Netherton and left home. Her seniority, coupled with an affluence unknown to the respectable shop-keeping Ruddicks, had kept him in awe of her as he'd grown into unconfident youth. They'd seen each other but seldom and, when they had, she'd voiced her views on what she thought of a young man who was intent on earning his living by writing 'rhymes' instead of taking over the book shop when their father was ready to give up. 'All that flowery nonsense' she'd swept his poems aside. Then, when he'd been old enough to have learnt more sense, he'd fallen in love with Adele, a girl no more than half his age. 'Flipperty', 'namby-pamby', 'feathery' were but a few of the scornful adjectives she'd used to describe her new sister-in-law. It had been long ago now, and the last time she and Humphrey had seen each other. They had never been close and their mutual lack of interest had easily turned into an unhealable rift.

Now, as the door closed on Gladys, Louise turned back to Hannah. 'What you'll find to do with yourself here I don't know. I'm old enough to be your grandmother, and the servants aren't far behind me. If you'd been a year or two younger I'd have sent you off to lessons.'

'I've finished school. Since Mother died I've kept house. I tell you, I'm not a child.'

'Humph.' Not in so many words did Louise say that she disliked the thought of a young person in the house but Hannah didn't need telling. Behind her back her fingers locked tightly together. Only about an hour ago she'd been looking at the masts of the ships, her spirits lifting. Now the memory of those same ships, so much a part of her aunt's life, all belonging to her like everything and everyone in the grand house, brought the sting of tears to Hannah's eyes. But she wouldn't give way to them. She wouldn't. She was afraid to breathe too deeply, only short, shallow breaths were safe; anything more and a sob might break in her throat.

'I hate her. I hate her. He said she was nice, but she's hateful. She needn't have brought me here, I didn't want to come.' But she wasn't going to give her aunt the satisfaction of knowing how near to breaking Hannah was. She clenched her teeth together, her chin high.

Work from the Hall meant a good deal to Phyllis Bentley, the local seamstress, and gladly she came straight away.

Two skirts, two blouses and a dress were to be made for this leggy young girl. 'And about time too. Disgusting a girl of her height showing her legs like it.' But she kept her thoughts to herself, allowing no more than a hushed tut-tut as she slipped the tape measure around Hannah's bust over the strained bodice of her erstwhile best frock.

'Plain but well-fitting, that's what she needs,' Louise ordered.

'I've a length of green wool, enough for a dress. I could start on it tonight if you think green would be suitable.'

They discussed Hannah, talked over her but never to her. She held her arms up, she held her arms out, she turned this way and that. But how could she fail to be excited at the prospect of new clothes?

Then at last the day that had seen such changes came to an end. Her few clothes had been unpacked and folded away in the mahogany chest of drawers. She opened the drawers thinking how smoothly they ran, and thinking too how different her things looked in their vast depth. The gaslight hissed in the silence. Everything here was quiet, she couldn't even hear her steps as she walked across the floor. At home her bedroom had had linoleum underfoot; here the carpet stretched almost to the walls, patterned in red and blue and green. She remembered what Mr Thurlston had told her: how when he was a young man her aunt's husband used to sail to faraway places, how the Hall was full of treasures he'd brought home. Silly to wish he'd still been here, he would probably have been as beastly as she was, but Hannah felt that she might have come near to him. Charles Netherton, a man who'd sailed the world then come home to manage the company, to build it up into what it was today.

She pulled the bedroom curtain to one side and looked out, down the length of the drive to the gatehouse where a dim light still burned. Mr Thurlston was her friend, the thought of him was her only comfort.

Then she took her purse out of the pocket of her cape and hid it carefully in her handkerchief sachet.

'You'll have to make your own amusement.' Louise looked at Hannah down the length of the breakfast table. Hannah heard it as meaning: 'Make sure you keep out of my way.'

'I'm used to being on my own Aunt Louise.' With morning light some of her optimism had bounced back. Aunt Louise wasn't what she'd hoped as she'd listened to Mr Thurlston – but Aunt Louise wasn't everything. She thought of the schooner putting in to harbour last night and the row of masts in the late dusk. 'It's not very far to the town. I thought I'd go and –'

'Then best you think again! You'll do no such thing! A niece of mine seen about the streets of Deremouth looking like a scarecrow! You'll keep yourself out of sight if you please, miss, until you are fit to be seen. Didn't I make myself clear last night?'

Hannah wanted to argue, wanted to say just what she thought of anyone who judged a person by the clothes on their back. But she couldn't. She was afraid to trust her voice.

They continued breakfast in silence. A week ago kidneys, mushrooms and gammon would have been a feast beyond her wildest dreams, but now she chewed and chewed yet she couldn't seem to swallow.

But later, once outside in the autumn sunshine, she began to look around her with interest. She remembered Harold Thurlston's description of the gardens and felt she already knew her way across the lawn, between the rhododendron bushes where already next year's buds were formed in promise of spring, and to the orchard beyond. She could see people working there. The habit of obedience had been thoroughly instilled in her all her life; she knew she must keep herself out of sight until she was better dressed. As the two men worked, picking the crop, they talked; neither of them noticed Hannah. She ventured as far as the edge where the lawn gave way to rougher grass, picked up a couple of windfalls and turned to the slope leading to the top of the garden. This must be where she'd find the view Mr Thurlston had told her about. 'Fair takes your breath away,' he'd said, and so it did.

Like a jewel the sea sparkled beyond the estuary. On the Deremouth side of the river the land was green, beyond the town were rolling hills; on the other side the tall headland of Braggs Point, its red sandstone cliff a rich contrast to the grassy slope on the landward side, and the bank of trees beyond dressed in their autumn glory. Louise was forgotten. Hannah climbed on to the gate that led to the lane beyond the boundary of the Hall and sat astride it, biting into the first of the apples. This was the next best thing to the quay, and perhaps in a few days she'd have her smart clothes and with them her freedom to explore further.

'And what did you find to do with yourself?' Louise asked her at lunch time, her tone not so much showing interest as hinting that she was ready to find some fault with whatever Hannah's pastime had been.

But after the morning she'd had she was prepared to try again. 'I've been in the garden. Mr Thurlston had described it so well I felt I almost knew it. I've been watching the estuary from the gate at the top.'

'Humph.' Not very encouraging.

'Aunt Louise, do you often go to the wharf?'

'Never. I've not been there for years. I've a very good manager. What would I want with meddling? They have work enough to do without me going there hindering.'

'I'm looking forward to seeing it all. I'll be glad when my new clothes are ready and I can go out.'

'You can just think again! If I'd be wasting their time, I don't know what good you think a visit from you would do. The wharf is no place for a child – and a girl at that!'

'I wouldn't be any trouble, honestly. I'd not even talk to them if you say so. I just want to see it. From the hill this morning I watched the ships waiting in the bay for high water so that they could come in. A clipper and a brig.'

'Oh, and who told you what they were? Thurlston, I suppose. I doubt he knows a clipper from a coal scuttle.'

'No one told me. I know a ship's rig – as well, I'm sure, as Mr Thurlston knows a Blenheim from a Bramley.' Children should be seen and not heard indeed! She wasn't going to let her friend be spoken about like that and not come to his defence. She spoke with her eyes downcast, only allowing herself one quick upward look when her glance immediately met her aunt's, dark blue eyes and light blue held in a battle of will.

'I'll not have cheek. Get along with your meal, if you

28

please, miss.' But Louise was thrown off balance. Her none too sure grasp of her fork was lost and it fell to the floor. Without a word Gladys stooped and picked it up then gave her a clean one from the drawer. Without a word she took it. As if to make up for the old woman's bad grace Hannah tried to catch Gladys' eye in sympathy, but her glance was ignored. It seemed no 'thank you' had been expected.

'Keen on ships, are you?' Louise picked up the conversation again.

'At home I used to watch them. Father had a telescope he let me use . . .' Home. Less than a week ago everything had been normal. She'd cooked fish for their lunch a week ago today. It stuck to the bottom of the pan, was black and unappetizing. Even Smut hadn't been too certain about his dinner. Smut, was he missing her? Was he still looking in at the window to see if she'd come back? Damson pie for dessert took a lot of swallowing.

Again Louise spoke, but what she said did nothing to bridge the gap between them. 'Ships! The sea! Hah! Now there's a proper life for a man.' Had she left it at that the first link might have been forged but she went on; 'Charles – your uncle I suppose you'd call him – my Charles, ships were his life. And a good life too. None better. He offered young Humphrey a place in the company. Did you know that? Before he got tangled up with that girl, your mother. It was when he was just a lad still but determined not to settle down in the bookshop. His head always full of his silly rhyming, even then. As well he didn't accept. Can't think he had a business head on his shoulders, can't think he'd have earned his way.'

'Father wrote very fine poetry.' Again Hannah's dark blue eyes glared into her aunt's faded ones.

'Ah, well, to each his own.' Louise gave up the battle of grappling with fork and spoon. 'Just remember what I say. Children are no use down in that yard. You're to keep out

29

of their way. Not that you can go anywhere until you get some decent rags to your back.'

Alone at the top of the garden Hannah refused to let herself cry. She'd not give her aunt the satisfaction of seeing her with reddened eyes. For months she'd wanted her mother, had needed to share her unhappiness with her father, yet because she knew he had more than he could bear already she'd tried to bottle it up. She still tried, but with every breath it got harder. There was nobody, nobody. Even Smut ... Her thoughts were disjointed. There was no avenue they could go down without this strangling misery choking her. Biting hard on her thumb she heard her own hiccoughing sobs. Then she gave up the struggle and sank to her knees by the gate.

She no longer cared about the view, nor did she realize that someone was climbing the grassy slope behind her. It wasn't until she heard the voice that she knew she wasn't alone.

CHAPTER TWO

Hannah had reached rock bottom. At that moment she was beyond caring if the voice belonged to Louise herself. But it didn't. It belonged to a girl of about her own age, a girl with a round, freckly face, sandy coloured hair too wiry to be called curly and, when she smiled, wide apart front teeth. Not a pretty girl by any stretch of imagination, but one who radiated good humour.

'Things'll seem better soon, honestly they will.' She knelt by Hannah's side. 'I'll go away if you tell me to – I'm not much good at helping, I don't expect, but I wish I could be. It'll be all right here, honestly it will, when you get used to it.'

Hannah sniffed and wiped her hand across eyes and nose in one swoop. The surprise of finding herself not alone had stemmed the flow, only dry rasping sobs still caught her breath.

'Where did you come from?' she hiccoughed.

'From the gatehouse. I'm Kath Thurlston. There's me and Beatrice and Algy. Didn't Pa say?'

Hannah shook her head. 'Don't say anything,' she hiccoughed, 'about me – being like this. I don't want her to know.'

'I won't tell. But there's no shame in crying, Hannah. I'd cry.'

'She says I'm a disgrace, a scarecrow.' She clutched at the most recent straw that had finally broken the back of her courage. Even that was hard enough to put into words, but the rest – her home, her parents, Smut, the losses which had torn her world apart – she couldn't talk about.

31

'"I'll not have a niece of mine seen looking such a scarecrow", that's what she said.'

'Then she's stupid. She ought to be jolly glad to have a niece at all.'

'She's ordered some things for me to wear. You see Father had been busy – and I've grown so fast.'

Kath nodded. 'Anyway, clothes don't matter too much around here. You don't need a smart dress to walk on the moor. That's were I'm just going, to get some blackberries. Why don't you come with me?' She stood up, picking up a basin from the ground. Hannah could see now that she was a short girl, plump but healthily so. Kath looked as sturdy as an oak; even her nails were cut square to her chunky fingers. Again that smile that lit her face. 'Come on, why don't you? All you need for the moor is a stout pair of boots, the rest doesn't matter a jot.'

Good stout boots, she'd said. Hannah was conscious of her feet crushed into boots far too tight and aching to relax into at least the next size. Kath's dark flannel skirt reached to a few inches higher than her ankles, her white blouse was plain, far from new, but well laundered. Automatically Hannah pulled her knee-length dress as low as she could. But the autumn sunshine seemed warmer than it had before, the sky bluer, her out-grown clothes mattered less. The two girls looked at each other, laughing spontaneously.

'Come on. If we go out of the gate here it's no distance.' Side by side they strode off, along the lane that ran towards the open country. Ahead of them they could see for miles, for although they were near the coast the land had risen sharply. The far distance was lost in a haze, and behind them lay the estuary and the sea. The air was full of the pungent smell of autumn. The afternoon took Hannah from one extreme to the other, from utter misery to a wild joy born of the unexpectedness of the sudden reawakening of hope. Neither she nor Kath were really children, Kath was actually her senior by nearing a year, yet there in the freedom of the lonely moor, they might have been any age. They had youth and energy and, more than that, they were both excited by the unforeseen way the afternoon had turned out. Kath was always quick to make friends, but there was no one outside the family around these parts of her own age. She had friends in Deremouth, and she enjoyed the three days a week she helped look after the children at Miss Sherwood's school. To Kath life was a happy affair; Hannah felt the joy in her and responded.

'There are huge berries on those bushes over there,' Kath told her. 'Come on, I'll race you!' She knew where the best bushes were, but Hannah ran the faster.

By the time they got back to the gate into Netherton Hall garden the sun was already going down, a misty red ball sliding out of sight over the distant moorland. Their fingers and lips were stained with purple juice after a successful afternoon.

'I was thinking,' Kath said, surveying Hannah with what she hoped was a well-disguised worried look, 'Ma and Beatrice have gone to market, so there's no one in. You could come home with me if you like and wash your face.'

'Do I look awful? Can you see – that I cried, I mean?'

Kath was always honest. 'Just a bit. Well, I can. But then I know, so that makes a difference. By the time you've had a good rinse and tidied your hair you'll be as good as new.'

So they went to the gatehouse to carry out repairs.

'There's hot water in the kettle on the range,' Kath told her.

'Cold would be better. Can I just splash at the sink?'

A stone sink, not unlike the one she'd been used to except that it had no tap and the water drained away into a bucket that stood outside and rain or shine had to be emptied in the ditch at the back of the little garden.

'Just a jiffy, then, I'll get some water,' and Kath took the bowl from the sink and went outside to the pump.

Alone in the kitchen Hannah looked around her. It was a room that seemed to tell her all about Harold Thurlston's family, a kitchen that was lived in, their retreat from the world. She looked at the scrubbed wooden table, five chairs neatly pushed in place around it; at the dresser where their cups hung and their saucers and plates were kept. They didn't all match, but they all shone. So did the range. It was clear to Hannah, who'd had just such a one to battle with herself, that this one had a daily dose of black lead. Above it on the mantelpiece was a tea caddy, a tin where home made biscuits would be kept, and a faded water colour of an ivy-clad cottage. On the wall was a wooden clock, its loud tick the only sound until she heard the squeak of the pump outside. On the wall facing the fire was a high shelf where they kept a long row of stone jam jars, each neatly labelled: Raspberry '52, Gooseberry and Rhubarb '51 (only one jar of that left), Plum '52, Damson '52, Loganberry '50. No time to ponder why no one liked loganberries. Hannah's inspection ranged past the dresser to the pewter dish covers hung on the wall, probably never used but glowing with a gloss that comes from frequent and regular polishing.

'Here it is,' Kath returned with the cold water, 'and the roller towel's there, on the larder door.'

Hannah threw cold water on her face, cupping it in her hands and douching her stiff eyelids. Then, vigorously, she rubbed her face in the rough towel. If her cheeks were pink her eyelids might not look so red. She would have given a lot not to have let herself cry like that. Just imagine that voice when she got back to the Hall. "What's this I see? Been blubbing like a baby, have you!"

'That looks lots better. Now I'll take you upstairs and you can tidy your hair.'

'It's a big bed,' was Hannah's first reaction – but in fact

34

it was a normal double bed pretty well filling a small room. It left space enough for a narrow chest of drawers and one wooden chair. Fortunately there was a built in cupboard, as minute in proportion as the rest of the room, so no wardrobe was needed.

'We both sleep in here, Beatrice and me. Then there's the little room next door, that's Algy's.' If this was the double room, Algy's could be little more than a cupboard!

On the first afternoon Hannah didn't stay long at the gatehouse. They'd been out for two hours or more, there was much to be thought about and digested. And she wanted to be away before Mrs Thurlston and Beatrice came home. The afternoon had brought so much unexpected happiness, in some inexplicable way she knew she wanted to save the rest of the family for another time.

'Do I look all right now, honestly?' she asked on parting.

'Honestly, you're smart again.'

'Smart! Whoever heard of a smart scarecrow.' Two hours ago she couldn't have said it. Now it was easy.

'Silly old chump she is,' was Kath's laughing reply.

Hannah went back up the drive, full of good intentions, courage and determination. Tonight she'd face Aunt Louise again and if the old lady responded to her friendliness all well and good. But if she didn't . . . "She can please herself. Silly old chump!" And silently she giggled, remembering Kath's voice.

That evening, like any other, the Thurlstons' kitchen was alive with activity. They crowded into it, for in such a confined space five was a crowd. At the stone sink stood Harold, his face covered with lather, his tongue firming his cheek as he scraped with his cut-throat razor, peering into the small wooden-framed mirror that hung by a string on the wall behind the sink. Algy was busy, trying his hand at re-stuffing a wooden chair that had been given him. The frame had nothing wrong with it, but the seat sagged in a depressing fashion and he was determined to make it worthy of the home he would share with his Sylvia as soon as they had enough behind them to wed. No longer did Algy go to the Rose and Crown – further along the lane that led from Deremouth at the neighbouring hamlet of Lumley. He used to enjoy a glass of cider and a game of shove-ha'penny, but since love had assailed him he put his money in a tin box under his socks and worked towards the day Sylvia could give up her job as under-housemaid at the vicarage. He was seventeen and had been working with his father in the gardens of the Hall since he'd been old enough to give up school. He'd started with odd jobs just as Harold had, but already there wasn't a man more useful than he. If he'd inherited his father's love of the garden, his looks came from his mother; slight, with a stoop to his shoulders, and a thin face that wore a worried frown far more often than circumstances merited.

Then there was Beatrice. She was the eldest, older than Algy by just over eleven months. To describe her as slight might conjure up an image of daintiness; to call her thin, one of frailty. Beatrice was neither of these things despite her lack of stature. Slight and thin, yes; dainty and frail, never. She too had the same stooping shoulders, but hers were narrow, and even and when she stood to her tallest she could barely top an inch more than five foot. Her wrists and ankles were no bigger than a child's. Fine, dark hair, parted in the centre then wound around her head in a single plait; a pale, sallow complexion. No two sisters could have been less alike than the Thurlstons, in appearance or personality. Kath's mouth seemed to be more comfortable when it smiled, but not Beatrice's. If she could be said to have any single claim to beauty it would have been her mouth, the perfect rose bud so loved by fashion. But did it smile? Almost never. Yet when it did her whole face was transformed.

Tonight as the family congregated in the kitchen Beatrice sat close to the lamp, carefully putting a heel back in Algy's sock, while at the table Kath was busy cutting out what would be a new skirt from a length of material her mother had bought for her in the market. And at the range stood Sarah Thurlston who, even silent, was the obvious pivot on which the household turned. She took the lid off the large iron saucepan and stirred the vegetable soup that guaranteed none of the Thurlstons would go to bed hungry.

'I met your Hannah today, Pa,' Kath said. 'We went blackberrying.'

Before Harold could stop the rhythmic movement of his razor and take his tongue from his cheek, Sarah jumped in: 'That's no way to speak of her. Just remember she comes from the Hall.'

'She'd rather be just Hannah, Ma.'

'Best heed your mother, m'dear,' said Harold the peace-maker. 'The child has had sadness enough. Let her find her feet with the missus. You don't want to get her into trouble for the company she keeps.'

'What's wrong with – ' Kath was prepared to argue, but Beatrice interrupted her.

'What's she like, Kath?'

'We got on ever so well. Had great fun on the moor.'

Harold wiped his face on the towel in the roller, the sight of him conjuring up the memory of Hannah as Kath watched. "Fun on the moor"? Well, so they had. She wasn't going to tell them about the other part.

'Fun or no, you don't want to get her into the missus's bad books.' Sarah had the last word while Beatrice watched them, looking from one to the other, keeping her thoughts to herself.

'The soup's all ready. If you've done with cutting that skirt, Kath, get it rolled away. And you, Beatrice, put that darning up now and see to the table. Look at all those shavings, young Algy. If you don't tidy up your ways I don't know what Sylvia will do with you. Get and empty the bucket for me, there's a good boy, as soon as your father lets his water go, then get the broom and clean up your mess from my floor. Oh, and fill the second kettle while you're outside or we'll not have enough with the chill off for our washes in the morning.' Her voice was quick and sharp, her eyes darting from one to the other, missing nothing. Small she may be, but it was plain to see who ruled at the gatehouse.

Like a well-trained army they did her bidding.

'That's better.' Harold's ruddy face emerged from the roller towel. He was far too used to Sarah to be upset by her sharp tongue. One thing he'd learnt over the years was that it was when she was quiet that trouble was brewing. Beatrice spread the cloth and started to put the things on the table and he sat at his place ready. As soon as she put down the loaf he pulled it towards him, cutting a thick slice to be going on with while he waited.

The soup smelt wonderful. Kath sat at her place too, saying no more about the afternoon. 'Cut me a hunk too, Pa. I'm ravenous.' As soon as her soup was put in front of her she dipped her bread into it with gusto.

Only Beatrice couldn't forget. She'd not seen the girl her father had brought from Hastings, but she'd heard what he'd said about the home he'd had to close up. And she remembered his: 'Poor lass, looked not much better than a waif.' Of them all it was Beatrice who understood what Hannah must be suffering there at the Hall where she had no real place.

Later, lying by her sister's side, she whispered: 'Kath, what's she like, this Hannah? Is she pretty?'

'I didn't think much about her looks. I just knew we'd be friends. I suppose she's a gawky sort of girl – quite tall – but of course what she wore made her look worse.'

For a long time Beatrice lay awake, her eyes wide open

in the darkness. How big and quiet the Hall must seem. Old Mrs Netherton was enough to frighten any young girl. Hannah, poor gawky Hannah – she must know she wasn't wanted there. The servants would all be saying just as Pa had: 'Looks like a waif', and Hannah would know.

Kath had already dropped into her first heavy sleep. "Easy enough for her. What idea does she have of being lonely? Hannah, poor gawky Hannah. I'll be your friend, your real friend. Not like her, just thinking of having fun. I'll understand you . . . it'll be different for us. She goes dashing off to that school – I'm always here – you'll always have me."

Although Beatrice was three years older than her sister, it was she who stayed at home to help Sarah. She always had. Even when she'd been young her schooling had been intermittent, and to be honest she'd much preferred looking after the others to doing sums or learning to read. When she'd said she, too, wanted to find a job, she'd been told: 'And what do you think you can do except housework? And if that's what you're doing, there's more than enough of it here looking after your own family without being at the beck and call of strangers.'

Thinking of Hannah, she was determined to find a way of meeting her before Kath's new friendship developed. 'The Lord helps those who help themselves' Sarah was often heard to say. And the following morning it did look as though she might be right.

'The missus says I could take any windfalls you want, Sarah,' Harold said at breakfast time. 'If I get a chance I'll gather them up.'

'Time for jamming, the blackberries are at their best. I'll be glad of them. You'll have to get out on the moor today and go brambling, Beatrice. Yes, Harold, get the apples, get all you can. I'll put up some mint in them too if I've enough.'

Beatrice seized her opportunity. 'If you're busy, pa, I could collect up the windfalls.'

'That's the best thing, you've got more time than I have.' He got up from the table, collecting the mid-morning snack Sarah had put up ready for he and Algy to share. Then, turning to go, he added: 'No touching the trees, mind, you're only to have those on the ground.'

So that was how Beatrice came to be in the orchard where there was a view of the Hall. On such a glorious morning the unknown Hannah must surely appear. Shy as she usually was, on this occasion Beatrice was more concerned for the gawky girl who had lost her parents and her home.

Then it happened. The conservatory door opened and out came Hannah. Beatrice stood very still, watching her. 'But she's beautiful!' It had to do with those scarecrow clothes. To Kath they hadn't mattered one way or the other; to Beatrice they made of Hannah a kindred spirit. Mrs Netherton's niece wearing a fashionable gown would have been out of her reach. To such a girl she could never have called out as she did to Hannah as she skirted the orchard on her way to the top gate.

'Hello, I've been watching for you.'

'For me? Did Kath tell you about me?' For no one else had talked to her.

'Yes – and I knew Pa had brought you here. Mrs Netherton said we could have the windfalls, I've been picking them up.'

'I could help you if you like.' And with a backward glance at the house, she went on: 'I've just been having another sermon on keeping myself out of sight until I'm fit to be seen.'

'I think you look nice. Truly I do.'

She must have taken giant strides in the healing process, for this morning Hannah could laugh. Nice! She picked up a bruised apple and bit into the good side.

'You must be Beatrice, Kath's sister. She told me about you.'

Beatrice's blue-grey eyes were immediately wary. 'Told you? Told you what?'

'That you were Beatrice, and that she has a brother too, Algy.' Still biting into her apple Hannah bent to help pick up the windfalls. 'I was so glad she found me yesterday. We went on the moor, had a lovely afternoon. Did she tell you? Got blackberries.'

'Oh, those few. Yes, Ma's making a pie for dinner. This afternoon I've got to do the proper picking. The few Kath got wouldn't be any use for jam.'

Hannah took stock of this sister of her new friend. There was something touching about her. Perhaps it was what she wore, a black dress that had seen a lot of wear and been ironed until the cotton shone. Beatrice would never have a problem with bodices straining at the buttons and hemlines too far from the ground. At eighteen she could wear what she had four years ago, could and did. The white overall could never have been made for her, most likely it was a hand-me-down of Kath's. It had been washed, worn thin, patched in one place, and although she had tied it as tightly as she could around her tiny waist it still hung shapelessly loose. She could feel Hannah's scrutiny. Her moment had come, and bravely she seized it.

'We're not a bit alike, Kath and me. She's jolly company, I know that, but I'm always here. If you get lonely . . . if you want to talk, properly talk . . .' She'd never made such a long speech and even now her words drifted into silence. She believed she was offering friendship, but Hannah knew it was more than that, it was a cry for help.

'I'd like that Beatrice.' Hannah was responding at least as much to the pathos of her appearance as to the kindness of her offer. Beatrice's thin arms struck out like two pale sticks where she'd rolled back the sleeves of her dress.

'Bring an extra basket and I'll help you with the black-berries,' Hannah said, wanting to help her.

Phyllis Bentley worked fast, sitting up well into the nights and straining her eyes as she stitched. Commissions from the Hall were valuable, especially if this young girl were to live there. It was clear she had nothing to her name and was growing fast.

So Friday morning found Hannah alone in her room, the soft woollen material of her first long gown transforming her from child to woman. Wide-eyed, she looked at her reflection. For a moment the ghost of her mother hovered near her. In all her life she'd never had a dress made by anyone else. She turned slowly round, full circle, as if showing herself off for her mother's approval. The excitement helped to restore her, that and the natural hopefulness of youth.

Only one thing spoilt her appearance – the long hair still held off her face with a ribbon band. In the little drawer on the dressing table she'd seen some pins, left by someone who had stayed here at some time she supposed. She'd put her hair up. Fourteen was the very earliest a girl would be expected to do that – "But I'll soon be fourteen and I'm tall. She won't be able to treat me like a child any more. Just wait until she sees this!" She brushed each strand, twisted and coiled it just as she'd seen her mother do. And so the chrysalis gave way to the butterfly, tall, with a newfound grace and assurance. Hannah turned this way and that to examine herself in the pier glass. Her spirits rose. Really, it was impossible not to smile at what she saw. Only the pinching of her boots was a reminder of the way she'd looked before.

'The Missus says you're to come.' Gladys knocked and opened the door in one movement but stopped in her tracks at what she saw. 'Lordy me, I'd not have known you!' Length of service, coupled with the suspicion that young Miss Hannah's father had been something of a skeleton in the family cupboard, lent terseness to her voice. 'She's in the morning room, and she don't like to be kept waiting. Buck up, now.'

Impervious in her newfound dignity, Hannah walked down the flight of shallow stairs. Oh joy! Just feel how the material of the long skirt trailed on the stairs behind her. It was Miss Ruddick who went to find her aunt in the morning room, curious and eager for her comments.

But there was none, not so much as a flicker of an eyelid, for Louise wasn't alone. With her was a woman of tidy but drab appearance, clad in grey with the exception of her black bonnet, and by her side were two wicker clothes hampers.

'This is my niece, Miss Ruddick.' Louise rose to the occasion as if the girl's ladylike appearance was nothing out of the ordinary. 'Hannah, I sent an order to my clothier in Exeter. You're to go through these boxes. Miss – er – Humphreys, isn't it? will help you. I'll leave you to it. I don't need to concern myself with all these fripperies.' Then, turning to Miss Humphreys, the lady in grey, she added: 'Everything that fits we'll keep; the rest you may take back. Good morning to you.'

Hannah found herself alone with the visitor who was busily unstrapping the first of the hampers. Outdoor garments, coats, jackets, a cape, bonnets, a muff, and, joy of joys, boots! Spencers, chemises, drawers with legs nearly to her ankles and trimmed with lace, stockings, garters, still whale-boned corsets, wired underskirts ... there seemed no end.

Finally hampers and grey lady were gone. The morning room had taken on the appearance of a clothes shop. Hannah went in search of her aunt.

'Aunt Louise, I don't know how to say thank you. I never dreamed of having so much. I didn't expect – '

43

'Never mind all that. Turn round and let me have a look at what Phyllis Bentley has made of you. Hah!' Approval? Satisfaction? 'Well, don't stand there, Pull the bell for Gladys. Tell her to have Lizzie carry all the clutter up to your room and stow it away. At least now I don't have to worry if you put your nose out of the gate.' And as if to put an end to the conversation she lowered herself into her fireside chair and jabbed at the burning coals with her stick to set the flames dancing up the chimney.

With new clothes came new freedom but, more important, an end to Hannah's childhood.

This afternoon she knew exactly what she meant to do. How strange it was to have to keep her intentions secret. At home such a thing would have been unheard of; her father would have listened with that quiet, tolerant smile. Now, even though she was sure Louise had no real interest in her whereabouts, she knew instinctively it would not be wise to say 'I went to the moors with Kath', or 'Beatrice and I went blackberrying'. Whatever it might be, her action would be sure to bring some criticism. And certainly this afternoon's plans must be kept to herself. 'Won't have you hindering them. Can't be doing with you asking silly questions' Oh yes, she knew Louise's views well enough. But she wouldn't hinder them, she'd stand right out of the way. She just wanted to see, to watch the men at work, to get the feeling of it, the smell of it . . .

'I thought I'd give my new clothes an airing and walk to town. Can I fetch you anything back, Aunt Louise?'

'A new set of bones! Walk to Deremouth, eh? Used to do it myself. Do I want anything? Yes, peace and quiet, that's about all I want.'

Ten minutes later Hannah shut the door on Netherton Hall. She was sure that at her going mistress and servants breathed a sigh of relief, and, for her own part she couldn't get away fast enough. There was no sign of life as she passed the gatehouse and she didn't know whether to be

44

pleased or sorry. She didn't want anyone to come with her today, she had to go alone, but in her new dress and coat she felt a stranger to herself. She wished she could have shown her outfit to Kath and Beatrice, been reassured about it. One thing was certain and, stepping out, her confidence grew with each stride – comfortable feet can put an entirely new complexion on life. Her toes stretched into the soft leather of her boots; at one stage she stopped walking just for the pleasure of flexing and stretching them. Then on down the hill, almost at a run now, her newfound dignity forgotten.

The harbour was busy. The smell from the fishing smacks reminded her of home. She shut her eyes and breathed deeply, letting the voices of the men wash over her. All her life she'd known it, the way they called the weights of their loaded baskets, the sight of those baskets being lifted on to the waiting dray to be taken to the Fish Market. She sniffed, loving it. Fish, tar, jute . . .

Beyond the few fishing boats a barque was tied up and alongside it an old hulk no longer seaworthy on which two or three men were working. This part of the wharf was public. Only at the end did she come to a wide seven-barred gate bearing the sign: 'Netherton Shipping Company. No Admittance Except on Business'. Her aunt's voice echoed in her memory. Certainly she had no business to be there.

Even so, she didn't hesitate. She went in, closing the gate firmly behind her. The water was low, nothing could enter or leave the estuary, but there was plenty of work going on. "Alexander", a brig, was moored, her square sails furled, gangplank in place and the cargo being carried off.

She watched, fascinated.

'Something you're wanting, missie?' "Missie" he'd called her! The man who came across the cobblestoned quay wasn't for a moment fooled by her new adult image. She felt uncomfortably like a child being caught trying on

45

her mother's clothes. She wished she hadn't pinned her hair up.

'I just came to watch.'

'Then best you nip off back round t'other side o'the gate, missie. 'Tis private in this part. Won't do to let Mr Webster catch you – ah, 'specially not 's afternoon.' And as if to emphasize his point he nodded his head in the direction of the upper windows of a shed-like building, listening.

Hannah, too, could hear the raised voices.

'Yes, I do know it's private.' Then she gave him a wide smile. 'I don't know who Mr Webster is, but I don't think I want him to catch me, not from the sound of him. Is he the manager? You see I've come to live at Netherton Hall with my aunt.'

'Well now, that paints a different picture, if you belong to Mrs Netherton, if she sent you.'

'Oh, but she didn't. She said I'd be in the way. I'd better not let Mr Webster catch me, had I?' Then, just as he had, she nodded her head towards the building. 'Not today.' But still she didn't go back to the other side of the gate. 'Can you pretend you haven't seen me, Mr . . .?'

'Ben Brooks is the name, miss.'

'I'm Hannah Ruddick. This morning from the garden I watched this brig come in. Where has she come from, Mr Brooks?'

'Just Ben'll do me, miss.'

Just Ben he might be but there was nothing servile about Ben Brooks who was a mountain of a man. Just to see the breadth of his shoulders, the size of his hands, was an indication of his strength. His auburn beard was wiry, the hair on his head a shade or two lighter and just as thick and curly now as it had been more than forty years ago when he'd first been engaged by Charles Netherton to help in the yard. His complexion was weathered, his blue eyes

46

clear, as though he were used to scanning far horizons. Hannah liked what she saw.

Unaware of her scrutiny he answered her question. '"Alexander", she's in from Spain.'

'What do we take to Spain?' The 'we' didn't go unnoticed by Ben.

'She won't be in Spain yet awhile. A round trip ahead of her first. About nine months she'll be away once she leaves Deremouth again.'

'Tell me about her, Ben. Aunt Louise hasn't said much – except that women and children have no place here.' But this time she said it with a laugh; she knew instinctively that Ben was her ally.

'The master used to run his place himself, you know. Mr Webster, he was here, but it was the master's show. Back in those days, years back I'm going now, she used to come here. Seemed to want to interest herself in it all. I think he used to like her in there. I mind how when she came he used to put a seat for her by the window so that she could look out at what was going on down here. Never comes near the place now though, hasn't since he's been gone. Leaves it all to Mr Webster.'

'And the brig? Why will she be away so long?'

'She'll go off from here with a full load of clay, take it up to Liverpool. For the potteries, you understand. Then in Liverpool she'll take on salt – salt goes to Liverpool from Cheshire, from the salt mines, I dare say you know that. 'Tis after that that her real journey starts. Out across the Atlantic, six weeks or more it'll take her, can be up to eight, out to Newfoundland.'

'Taking salt? Nothing else?'

'Aye, just salt. Most of it will be sold when she gets there, that's nought to us, we do but carry it for the most part. But the skipper'll have enough kept back for the cargo she'll take on – cod. That has to be salted, keeps it sweet. Big industry in Newfoundland waters, cod. We've worked that route as long as I can remember. Many a ship brings the catch back here to England – salts it first, you understand. But "Alexander", she does the round trip. The fish'll be taken to the Mediterranean ports. Then, that job done, she takes on fruit for the home market. She'll come back to Bristol, that's where it gets off-loaded, then taken by railway to London I dare say. Like I told you, that's nought to us, we do but carry the goods. Then back to Deremouth and a right royal welcome, I'll wager, for she'll have been away nine months or more. Be about July by the time she ties up here next.'

'But they're bringing the cargo off here. I thought you said Bristol.'

'Oh, aye, she put in there first. Best part was put off there. What the humpers are carrying now is what we call "broken remains" – fish and fruit. Not the top quality; that'll be in London afore this.'

'Fish and fruit,' Hannah chuckled, 'it doesn't sound a very good mix.'

'Kept well apart, they'll have been.' He laughed too.

"Humpers" – the men who carried the cargoes ashore; "broken remains" – second-rate and inferior. The language was new and exciting.

All around was the jostle of men at work, the rattle of barrows being trundled over the cobblestones. Further along the wharf sacks of corn were hooked on to a pulley and raised to be stacked on to a waiting dray; from the siding where a single railway track came to an end at the dock there was the sound of shovelling as a load of coal was thrown into trucks. Liverpool ... Bristol ... the Mediterranean.

Hannah felt she was standing at the hub of the universe on that afternoon of hazy October sunshine. So enthralled was she that she'd completely forgotten the angry voices she'd heard coming from the manager's office.

* * *

48

Alan Webster faced his son across the leather-topped desk.

'You expect me to believe that this'll be any better than any other of your hare-brained schemes? I give you half a year. And then how do you think I can come to your aid? Out there you'll be on your own.'

'This time it's quite different.' Compared to his father's Tommy's voice was low and even. 'Father, do you realize, they're literally bringing gold out of the ground? Gold! Here, see for yourself, read what Rodney says – '

'Bloody Rodney McGee! Can't you see it, son?' His tone changed as he tried to advance a different angle. 'Every time you've got mixed up with that fellow, it's meant trouble. And how can I help you if you're the other side of the world?' Memories stirred and some of the venom returned. 'Look at that fiasco in Bristol. Twenty guineas it cost me to get that trollop off your back.'

'She had nothing to do with Rodney – nor with this. Anyway I told you at the time I never promised her marriage, I only – '

Alan's glower silenced him, the excuses drifted into silence. Before his father's look Tommy's gaze shifted.

A week past his twenty-first birthday he was a handsome young man with dark well-cut hair, gingery brown eyes, and a habit of pressing his lips tightly closed. When Tommy smiled he didn't show his even, white teeth; his face took on the look of a child's drawing of a happy man, his mouth in a neat upturned bow.

'Can't you see the selfishness?' Alan tried another tack. 'How are we going to break it to your mother? It'll be enough to kill her.'

But he was facing defeat and he knew it.

'Mother will have faith in me. And, Father, it's too late to try to persuade me against going.'

Alan had no other weapon left to him but cajolery. In these days of large families Tommy had been their only child, coming to them after twelve years of disappointment. He'd brought them worries and heartaches but he was dear to both his parents, the reason for their existence, or at any rate giving colour to it. The thought of him far away in Australia was past contemplating. Alan was prepared to try anything.

'Look son, think of it this way. The old lady would welcome you into the firm, she's always had a soft spot for you.' Then as Tommy opened his mouth to interrupt: 'No, hear me out. Give it a try, son. I promise you I'd teach you my job and I'd not hang on, I'd step down and make room for you. Now what do you say to that? Chasing across the world in the hope of finding a nugget or two in the ground! Here it would be handed to you. A good future, yours for the taking.' Surely that must be his trump card. The company had been Alan's life but he was prepared to make the ultimate sacrifice if it would hold on to their beloved Tommy.

'Don't you ever look beyond this footling little harbour? I tell you there's wealth, riches, and you compare it to the safety of this day-to-day grind. I'll never stay in this one-eyed hole. Never!'

Disappointment, hurt and anger all combined in Alan as his fist came crashing down on the desk top. 'Then go to the devil! But don't come to me for your passage money — or to bale you out at the next sign of trouble.'

'I'm working my passage. Sailing out of Liverpool next week on the "Orion".'

Blue eyes glared into gingery brown ones. It was a silent battle and only for a second did their glances lock and hold; that was all it took. Into Alan's mind flooded a thousand memories: himself and Emily gazing proudly into the basinet; Tommy trotting after him, staggering on podgy baby legs; Tommy lisping his first sentences; Tommy on the moor with his butterfly net and on the

50

green by the shore with his cricket bat; Tommy at seventeen arguing just as he was now, his mind set on making his fortune in London; then with no fortune made, refusing to come home, instead going north to the potteries; then south to the Cornish tin mines; from there to a troop of touring players; his last venture had been with the *Deremouth Gazette* where for nearly eighteen months he'd tried to inject drama and interest into the local happenings of the little town.

Tommy had his own memories. How after each failure his parents had come to his rescue. Each time his father had brought out the same bait – 'Mrs Netherton would find a place for you. Come and work with me.' The corners of his mouth turned up but there was no smile in the gingery eyes. He knew he had won again. And he knew too that his parents would never let him set out emptyhanded.

'It won't be forever, Father. I shall come home again, you'll see. You'll be glad later that I had the courage to do it.' Outside the window the late afternoon mist was rising over the sea. He imagined the promised land on the other side of the world, a land of sunshine and gold. At twenty one life has so much to offer.

Hannah hadn't been much interested in the angry voices, there was so much else to take her attention.

'Sounds like he's coming down.' Ben cocked his head as the door upstairs closed. 'Just draw back down the passageway, missie, if you don't want to be copped.'

Footsteps on the stairs. One person descending. It must be the caller leaving.

Hannah might not have noticed the argument but she did notice the young man. Whatever it was Mr Webster had been shouting at him it didn't seem to have upset him, he was smiling to himself as he passed the end of the passageway. He didn't glance their way but his image impressed itself on Hannah's mind. So far her life had had no place for young men, she'd known none to compare with him.

The upstairs window was thrown open and Alan roared an order to the humpers at the end of the quay.

'What's that they're loading?' she whispered her question instinctively. With the manager in his present mood she didn't want to land her friend in trouble for spending his time with her.

'That's granite, miss. Comes from the moor. Got their own tramway, they have, to take it to the river, then it's brought down stream to the dock. This lot'll be shipped out in a day or two, round to London it'll go. Won'erful trade there is for granite. Won'erful stone.'

The upstairs window slammed shut.

Just one more question and she'd go. 'Who was the man Mr Webster was quarrelling with? Do we ship goods for him?'

'Bless you, no, miss,' Ben chuckled. 'That's his lad, young Tommy. Don't see him here often – and when we do it usually means trouble.'

'Wait for me!' Heavy steps pounded up the hill behind her. 'I wonder I recognized you in your finery. You've got rid of the scarecrow then?' Kath caught her up, clutching at Hannah's hand to hold her still. 'Let's have a good look. Turn around. My, but you do look nice. Aren't you thrilled?'

Hannah nodded. 'I've had such a wonderful afternoon I'd almost forgotten. But, yes, I am, of course I am. Especially as now I have the freedom of the town. Kath, I've been to the quay! There was a boat from Spain, and Mr Brooks, Ben, he's been explaining – '

'I never go there. It's funny, isn't it, we've lived here all

52

our lives but I don't think any of us ever bother with the boats. It's Friday, one of my days at the school, that's where I've been.' There was no doubt she considered her afternoon had been better spent than her friend's. For a moment Hannah was disappointed, she would like to have talked about all she'd seen. But she was glad of Kath's honesty. To talk about the dock and find she'd been boring her audience would have been dreadful.

So she said: 'Tell me about it. What do you do at the school? You're awfully young to be a teacher.'

'Oh, I'm nothing so clever. I help look after the little ones, take them into the garden to do drill, clear up the mess when they've been painting, wash them if they fall over, cuddle them if they cry, sometimes help them make things with paper shapes, all that sort of thing.'

She puffed as they strode up the hill but shortness of breath didn't stop her chattering. As they came to the gates of the Hall there was a movement in the garden of the gatehouse. Hannah could have sworn it was Beatrice and surely she must have seen them? But whoever it was went inside and shut the door.

'Got company in the drawing room.' Gladys was crossing the hall as Hannah came in. 'She didn't say she wanted you in there, expect you better keep yourself out of the way. She'll send if she wants you.'

Hannah caught a glimpse of her reflection in the mirror, her 'new look' coming as a surprise. But for all her grown-up clothes she was still more child than adult, young enough to accept that her presence wouldn't be wanted. Even so, Gladys had cast a shadow on her afternoon.

'I shall be in the library,' she answered with what she hoped was dignity.

'Up to you but it's cold in there. No fire in there today.

The missus said she'd not be using it, especially with an old friend for company.'

This was the first time Hannah had actually been inside the room. She'd only seen the book-lined walls through a half open door. Now she looked around her. Row upon row of books, some very old, some in Latin. Books of charts, books on navigation, on shipping. Works of Jane Austen, of William Shakespeare, John Milton, Shelley, Wordsworth, Coleridge, then, more up-to-date, of the new Poet Laureate Alfred Tennyson. Then, at the very end of the same shelf, four slim volumes – the works of Humphrey Ruddick. 'Rhyming nonsense' his sister had called it. Yet his books had been read, the fingered pages were evidence of that. In one there was still a bookmark. Hannah opened it at that page.

> 'To love but once and once for all,
> In unity and truth delight;
> Where'er that love's long shadow fall
> Is blessed in His sight.'

Her father had often read aloud. Hannah was instantly back again by the hearth in the parlour, her father on one side of the fire, her mother on the other, she on the 'humpty' between them. Much that he'd written she'd not understood; this, like so many more, she didn't even remember. Her long fingers caressed the red leather binding. Here amongst so much that was strange was something of her own, like her father's voice speaking to her. *'Where'er that love's long shadow fall is blessed in His sight.'* The love had enveloped all three of them, the shadow of it reached out to her now. Yet at the time she'd accepted, not questioned. If the shadow still reached out to her, must it not have touched Aunt Louise as she'd read it? She'd bought his books, kept them, read them . . .

'Oh, I do beg your pardon.' Her reverie was shattered when the door opened and a young man stepped into the room. 'I'd no idea there was anyone in here. You must be Mrs Netherton's niece.'

'That's right. I'm Hannah Ruddick.'

'And I'm Daniel Lowden.'

'You're not Aunt Louise's visitor?' It was so utterly unlikely. What would a young man like this be doing choosing to spend his afternoon visiting Louise?

'That's me.' He was in his late twenties, of medium height and build, with brown hair that was neither straight nor yet really wavy and blue eyes. It was a good face with even features; a neat face, yet not a weak one. She took in his appearance, vaguely surprised. She'd expected her aunt's friend to be someone very different. But she was far more interested in her discovery of the poems.

'Mrs Netherton says there are some books of charts I might borrow.' Then noticing the slim volumes in her hand, 'Am I disturbing your reading?'

'No, I've only been in here a few minutes. I was looking at these.'

He glanced at the titles. 'Humphrey Ruddick. Of course – your father.'

She nodded.

'May I see?'

Humphrey had written two long works, story poems. On these had been based any reputation he had made for himself. But it wasn't to these that Daniel turned. Just as Hannah had, he opened the book where the silk ribbon marked the page. Silently he read. There was no self-consciousness as he did so, not a trace of affection. As he closed the book he said: 'You're lucky, Hannah. In the words he left behind you'll always be able to find him.'

He spoke as if she were grown-up but she felt inadequate, gauche. She knew just what he was telling her though not how to reply. But she answered with honesty.

'He used to read to Mother and me, but usually I didn't understand. I liked it though, the feeling it brought. The

55

poetry was a kind of background music, it didn't matter that I didn't know what he was talking about.' Then, putting the books back where she'd found them, she turned to him with a directness not at all in keeping with her grown-up dress and unswept hair. 'Are you really an old friend of Aunt Louise's? That's what Gladys said.'

'I've known her as long as I can remember.' He laughed softly at the question. 'Your Uncle Charles was my God-father, a friend of the family. Father's in the same line of business, works out of Liverpool. I always come to see Mrs Netherton when I put in at Deremouth.'

'Put in?' She frowned, puzzled. Anyone less like the men she'd seen on the quay she couldn't imagine. 'Do you mean that you're a seaman? You don't look a bit like one.'

'Ah,' he teased her, 'but that's because I bathed and shaved and put on a good suit to come a-visiting your Aunt Louise. Twelve hours time and I'll have reverted to type and be on my way to London dock.' His blue eyes were laughing. 'It's wonderful what a suit of clothes can do for a man.'

She chuckled. 'And for a girl! If you'd come a few hours sooner we'd not have met, I'd have been kept hidden in the closet. But with my new frock I'm let loose.'

'Then I'm grateful for the timing of the tides.'

'I noticed some books of charts over there on the top shelf,' she told him, trying to cover the fact that for the second time in five minutes she'd not known how to answer. And just as she spoke the door burst open and in came Louise, bearing down heavily on her sticks.

'Have you found what you want, Daniel?' Then, seeing Hannah: 'So this is where you've been hiding yourself.'

The memory of the leatherbound books, the silk ribbon marking her place, seemed to make of Louise something akin to a friend, or so Hannah thought. This was her moment, in here with father's books on the shelf just behind her. 'No, Aunt Louise, I was just telling Mr

Lowden, I don't have to be hidden anymore. So I went to Deremouth – you remember I told you I was going to? And, Aunt Louise, honestly I wasn't a nuisance – I went to the quay. It was so exciting. I told Ben who I was. You know Ben?

'I know Ben – and I know I told you I'd not have you there wasting their time and getting in the way.' Louise's voice cut like a knife. 'And when I give an order I'll be obeyed. It seems I'm to give you a roof, feed and clothe you. So remember please, miss, she who pays the piper calls the tune.' She seemed to have forgotten Daniel's presence but Hannah hadn't. She was humiliated. He'd spoken to her as an equal, as if she mattered here. Now he'd know that she didn't. She was a burden on her aunt. Hannah felt her face flood with colour as the voice went relentlessly on: 'It's no place for women there, and certainly not for children, so just keep away.'

Just as long as her own voice didn't betray her, there was still fight in Hannah. 'There were women there,' she answered defiantly, 'girls on the quayside. Not in *your* yard, on the public quay.'

'And if you were less of an ignorant child you'd know better than to talk about them, waiting there as the boats come in. Is that what you want people to think of you?'

'I don't understand – '

'Well, I do, and that's an end of it! Now try and remember I have a guest in the house. And since at last you have a change of clothes to your name, I suggest you go and make yourself presentable before coming to the table.' Then to Daniel, dismissing Hannah as though she didn't exist: 'That chart you were after is in the big book at the far end of the top shelf. But you must take everything else you want. Charles had all these drawn up, you know. He'd want you to have them.' And she didn't even glance as Hannah went out of the room, head high but spirits at

57

rock bottom. The depths were all the lower because only a few minutes ago she'd allowed herself to hope.

She didn't have to stay here; she still had her purse. All her life until now she'd known just where her piece in the jig-saw had fitted into the pattern that made up her home. Here she was nothing; a burden, an ignorant child. The new gown mocked her as she stared at her reflection. It was charity, cold charity. She had to be clothed, she had to be fed, not because Aunt Louise cared but for the impression it created. 'I'll not have a niece of mine wandering like a beggar,' that's what she'd say.

Off came the dress. 'I don't need her beastly charity, I'll be glad to go.' Of course she would. She had to believe it. One after another she took off her new things, dress, underwear, boots . . .

Back in her outgrown dress and tight boots, her cape around her shoulders and her long hair brushed and hanging loose, she was ready. Strangely it was those familiar 'scarecrow' clothes that re-kindled hope, those and the chain purse tucked safely in her pocket.

Defiantly she looked at her reflection. This was Hannah Ruddick, she was as she was. She'd make her own way.

CHAPTER THREE

Coming to the head of the stairs Hannah stopped and listened. All was quiet. She crept down, across the hall, along a side passage and out, closing the door silently behind her. For a few seconds she stood quite still, struck by the unfamiliar country smell of the October evening. Like everything else it was strange to her. A tic pulsed nervously in her cheek. Until now she'd never been on her own, not really on her own. There had been Mr and Mrs Tonks, Smut, Mr Thurlston . . . 'Fair and just' he'd called her aunt. But she wasn't, she was hateful! From Harold Thurlston it was only a short step to memories of their journey together. London! That's where she'd go. There would be work to be had in London, and amongst all those people no one would find her. Not that they'd look. Aunt Louise didn't want her and there was no one else.

Stealthily she moved across the strip of grass that divided this side of the Hall from a narrow copse. She must get away from the house. The servants might see her and take word to her aunt. Another hurdle was the gatehouse. She mustn't go out through the main gates or someone might hear her step and look out. Kath and Beatrice, she didn't want to think of the hours she'd spent with them, of their friendship. Once in the shelter of the trees she paused to get her bearings. It was very dark, but with the lights of the house behind her she knew she must make off to the right then she ought to come to the lane. Each step held a pitfall, fallen branches, exposed roots, twigs that brushed her cheek or caught on her cape. There was a moment when she came near to turning back. What was she doing here, alone in the night, with nowhere to run to, nowhere

59

to hide? But even while her confidence faltered, in an illogical childish way she knew she couldn't turn back, she'd got her old clothes on, she'd be seen.

Her sense of direction hadn't failed. She finally came out of the trees on to the stoney and uneven surface of the lane that would lead her to town. Now it was just a question of putting her feet down carefully so that she didn't twist an ankle in one of the many potholes, taking step after step until she got there. The station was somewhere beyond the main street of shops.

When she'd left the yard a few hours ago dusk and mist had been falling together, like a blanket. Now the wind had got up, the air was clear. Soon her eyes were attuned to the darkness and ahead of her down the hill she would come to the gas lamps of Deremouth. Once or twice she stumbled on the rough surface but at last she reached the cobblestoned hill, the gas standards each throwing out its island of light. On her right was a wall, she could just see over it to the dock below and 'Alexander', one of the four ships tied up in Netherton's Quay. She bit her lip, remembering the afternoon. Netherton's yard, the public quay . . .

Then the thought burst in on her, bringing her to a standstill as she looked at the ships. Daniel Lowden! He'd told her he was going to London dock. He must have been tied up on the quay this afternoon. Already in her mind she was reviewing the fishing smacks, the barque, then an old hulk where men worked. The barque, that must be Mr Lowden's! The railway station was forgotten as she turned round the corner into Quay Hill.

She must walk steadily not run, attracting attention. On the quay luck was with her. There were no lamps near the barque which lay in shadow and, what was more, the gangplank was in place. For a moment she stood back in the shelter of the wall then, sure no one was about, she walked towards it, head up, just as if she had every right to be here. No one seeing her would have guessed how her heart was thumping. 'Prince Rupert' the barque was called; she saw the name painted on the side as she went up the gangway. The ship was silent. With only one night in port – and hardly that, for water was high at about midnight – the crew wouldn't be wasting their time on board. Coming down the hill to town she'd heard the singing coming from the Jolly Sailor.

Once on board she peered from left to right. Where to now? In the dim, shadowy light from the quayside lamp she could see the dome of the paddle housing, the single funnel. Steam would take 'Prince Rupert' out of harbour, the sails from fore and aft masts wouldn't be raised until she was well out to sea. Steam meant there must be a boiler, and a stoker. Somewhere in the bowels of the ship she could see now a lamp was burning, that must be the engine room. No use standing here, she'd grope her way to the cargo hold. Down the ladder Hannah went, then again she waited and listened. She was getting her bearings. The sound she could hear must be from the engine room, down and forward of where she stood. That decided her; the cargo must be down and aft. She prided herself on her 'fores' and 'afts', for until this moment she'd never been aboard so much as a row boat! She needed to pride herself on something, for her tummy was full of butterflies.

'I'm hungry, that's all it is,' she told herself. She had to hang on to her belief that what she was doing was right. 'I'm lucky to have heard about Mr Lowdon going to London, I'm lucky to have known this must be his ship, I'm lucky no one saw me come on board, I'm lucky – oh, please let me be lucky, please let me find somewhere to go, please help me!' That was as near as she'd go to facing just how frightened she was.

Down the next ladder. By now it was quite dark, the air thick with the stench of cargoes old and new, stale and lingering. Fish, over-ripe and rotting fruit, oil, jute – a combination of things recognized and strange. The butter-flies rose in her throat.

She knew she must get used to it. It was only coming in from the clear night air that made it seem so strong. Inch by inch she felt her way forward, her hands touching on sacks though of what she had no idea. But they'd be somewhere to sit, somewhere to lie down, for she'd be there in this dark hold for hours. Hours? Days? Her tummy rumbled, she could feel it churning, hear it, the only sound in the stillness around her. If she could lie down and go to sleep her body would get used to this putrid atmosphere. She curled up on the sacks, her eyes tight shut.

What was that? She held her breath, listening. Some-thing was scratching. It seemed to be some distance away, but in the dark how could she know just where? In a single movement she was on her knees, bolt upright on the sacks. Fear of being found on deck was nothing compared to this, yet she was incapable of movement. Across the hold two bright luminous eyes glared at her. A cat! The blinding terror eased, but in its place came a sick fear of where she was, what she'd done, what was ahead of her. Those eyes were her undoing. They might have belonged to Smut. How many times had his gaze pierced the darkness if she'd disturbed his night time slumbers?

There were heavy footsteps overhead, then without warning a vibration shuddered through the hull. The cat rushed past her and shot through the hatchway, while she remained frozen and still. The engine had started. Any minute now the paddle would be turning, and they'd pull away from the wharf. The gentle rocking motion told her they were under weigh. She must be still, she *had* to try to sleep, she wanted oblivion until the voyage was over. She looked no further. She didn't even try to form a plan of what to do on shore. Minute by minute, hour by hour, she couldn't do better . . .

How they rocked! With each wave her dark world rose then was tipped back down ... up ... down ... up ... down. Yet her stomach seemed to go up with the 'down' and down with the 'up'. She tried to take deep breaths, but the stench choked her. They'd hardly started, she couldn't feel like this! Not yet. Not at all.

From the voices overhead she knew the crew were on deck. The buffeting got worse. They must be coming to the mouth of the estuary, out on to the open sea. She clung precariously to her couch of sacks as she was thrown from side to side. Then, just as suddenly as the throbbing engine had started, something else happened. What it was that changed the motion she didn't know, but now the rolling of the ship was gentle. She was no longer thrown from side to side; now her world rose and fell, gently, steadily. She felt the change but didn't recognize it as a sign that the sails had been hoisted. Soon the engine cut. 'Prince Rupert' rode the waves on sail alone.

Sleep must have come to her. She was woken by the feeling of something running across her arm! Or had she dreamt it? In a second she was on her feet, too frightened to move. Swaying with the ship's motion she stood in the blackness, her mouth dry, the butterflies fluttering through her whole body, arms, legs, stomach. Across the sacks where she'd been lying she heard the scuffle of something running. She wanted to scream and it wasn't fear of being heard that stopped her, that was nothing compared to the horror of where she was now. But she daren't scream, she daren't open her mouth in her struggle to hold down the nausea that tore at her. Blindly, she groped for the ladder, then out of the hold, up the second ladder. Air. She had to find air. That the deck was alive with activity meant nothing. Retching, crying, she had to get to the rail.

'Gawdstruth! Where'd she come from?'

'Young Bert – ' for he was the youngest amongst them, the only one likely to have enticed a floozie of her age to follow him aboard — 'who's the moll? You'll be in for it when the skipper finds her.'

'I never seen 'er afore. Nought to do with me, honest.'

Hannah heard them but, her head over the rail, she cared nothing for any of them. The spray was cold on her face, she tasted the salt of it. Whether it was seconds or minutes later she felt a hand on her shoulder she had no idea.

'It'll pass. Everyone goes through it.'

At the same moment her stomach lurched uncontrollably. She heard herself retch. Her mouth was sour with vomit and her eyes watered with the strain — and with relief at hearing a voice she recognized.

'It's all right. It's all right, Hannah, I'll look after you.'

She wiped her shaking fist across her mouth but couldn't stop crying.

'Take a swig of this,' Daniel Lowden unscrewed the top of his brandy flask. She gulped it down, breath-taking, burning. In shame she heard herself belch.

'. . . sorry . . .'

'Another sip. Gently now.'

Like an obedient child she did as he said.

'Straight ahead now, Mr Bailey,' he shouted to his mate. 'I shall be below.'

'Aye aye, Cap'n Lowden.'

He took her down to his cabin, a square low-ceilinged room. It housed a large table, with a lamp hanging from the hook over it. There were three round-backed chairs, a cabinet, a couch where she supposed he must sleep, and a wash basin. There was no tap but a pipe to carry away the water that came from a large enamel jug. It seemed the captain had a certain amount of comfort; a far cry from a stowaway in the hold!

He poured water into the basin for her. 'Here's my towel. You'll feel better when you've rinsed your face.'

She nodded, not quite looking at him, ashamed of her

64

appearance, ashamed of the smell of vomit that seemed everywhere, ashamed that she couldn't stop crying now. She felt empty, drained, without even the strength to try to control herself.

'I'll leave you for a while. When you feel better try and rest on my bed.' Daniel spoke kindly and asked no questions. But gone was that feeling of equality she'd had this afternoon. Now she was a child, he a man. She nodded in answer to his instructions, expecting him to go. But still he lingered. 'We'll work something out Hannah. When I come back we'll talk about it.' The rolling of the ship didn't seem to worry him. It was only she who clung to the basin to try to hold the world steady.

But he was calling on her resolution, and she'd not let herself be seen to be beaten.

'Thank you, Mr Lowden.'

When he'd gone she splashed cold water over her face, cupped her hands then rinsed her mouth, gargled, spat. All in all she began to feel more like herself – or she would have if only the floor would stay still just for a moment.

He was gone some time and when he came back she was asleep on his couch, 'Prince Rupert' lying at anchor five miles from Deremouth.

'You can tell she doesn't want me there.' Her blue eyes pleaded 'Please take me, Mr Lowden. I couldn't stay there, you must see I couldn't.' It was an hour or two later. She'd woken to find Daniel Lowden seated at the table, watching her.

'My friends call me Dan.'

She repeated it, 'Dan', her mouth showing the first hint of a smile, even her smarting eyes losing their guarded expression. He was more than twice her age.

'If you'll take me I won't be any trouble, and I'll be all right once we get there. See.' And she dug in her pocket for her purse, opening it to show him. 'I've got money. I took what Father had in his box. I don't need to stay there.'

To her the few coins spelt security. The look of trust on her face touched him. That miserable bit of money, all she had left of what had been her home, was her anchor. How could he explain to her that it would be gone in no time, that London was no place for a child on her own?

'I was going to go on the railway, then I remembered what you'd said. I thought if I hid in the hold I'd still have all my money left.'

'Who is there in London, Hannah?'

'No one, but there must be work. That must be the best place to find work. I told her I could get a job, that I was sorry I'd been dropped in her lap. That's what she said I was: dropped in her lap, and she'd have to make the best of it. Well, I've gone. And I'm not going back. I'm not! Not ever.'

'Your father wanted you to be with her, it was he who arranged it. I can see it's been hard for you.' Just how hard he'd realized that evening when the third place had been left empty at the table.

'Stupid child,' he could almost hear Mrs Netherton's voice, 'making a scene when she knows I have a visitor. I shall leave her to sulk. An empty belly will bring her to her senses.'

'But think about your parents, Hannah,' Daniel pressed. 'What would they have felt knowing you to be alone in London?' He had to help her find the courage to go back. If she could hang on to the memory of her father she might do it for his sake. 'Your father made this arrangement so that you'd never be wandering on your own.'

'I won't wander. I'll find a room, I can work. Kath works – Kath lives at the gatehouse. She helps at a school. I could do something like that . . . or . . . or something. I'd do anything. I'm not a good stitcher and I don't cook very well, but I'd try anything.' She talked fast, words tumbling out. Was she telling him or reassuring herself? Of one thing Dan was certain, he couldn't take her with him and turn her loose in London.

'Your father wanted you to be with his sister, Hannah.'

'Well, he wouldn't have if he'd seen what she's like. Anyway, Father never expected it to actually happen.' Her throat was tight, she had to keep talking. 'She hates him, sneers every time she mentions him. Says he was a simpleton and Mother feathery.'

His brows puckered in a worried frown. 'Then it has to be up to you to prove her wrong. A simpleton and a feather could never have brought you up to have courage, now could they?'

'That's what I've been telling myself. All the time when I was frightened on those sacks down there, I kept telling myself it was for them as well as for me that I wasn't going to stay there and let her say the things she did.'

'I do understand. Honestly I do.' Dan came over to the couch where by now she was sitting with her knees drawn up. He sat on the edge, turning to face her. 'And I know that what you've done must have taken courage. But so too would staying there, staying and showing her how wrong she is. I've known her all my life, Hannah. She wasn't always like this.'

'Humph!' Hardly more than a grunt, but it might have been Louise's voice.

'So many things have changed her. I used to love coming to Netherton Hall when I was a child. Then, I suppose I must have been about the age you are now, one day we found her having to use sticks to walk. It couldn't have come on her that quickly, I suppose, but until I saw the sticks I hadn't realized. Perhaps I hadn't been there for some months, I don't remember. She used to be so lively, and would play cricket with us on the lawn. Then, in such a short time, she seemed to seize up. It couldn't have been

67

more than weeks after that that her husband died. A short illness and he was gone. First one thing then another. She must have felt her world had fallen apart. After that she seemed to turn in on herself, hold a grudge against life. Underneath she's just the same as she always was, every now and again I catch a glimpse of it. Whenever I'm this way I come to the Hall: sometimes no more than once a year, sometimes twice in a month. Sometimes she seems glad to see me; sometimes she snaps and snarls like a bad-tempered hound. But I wonder if any of us would do any better if we couldn't manage to do up our own buttons, and barely keep a grip on our knife and fork.'

Hannah sat very still, her arms folded around her drawn up knees.

'You're on her side,' she mumbled. And she'd thought he was her friend.

'Partly I am, and partly I'm on yours, Hannah.'

'She's full of hate, she's warped with it. You only see her when she's glad to have you there. She's not glad to have me.'

'Then why do you think she brought you there? Do you think you're being fair? She needn't have consented to the guardianship, you know. And when you lost your father, she could have sent you off to school. But she didn't. She brought you into her home. And if you say she's made you miserable, think about it and be honest: have you brought her any happiness since you've been there? Have you tried to see things from her side?'

Hannah chewed her lip and didn't answer. She'd expected understanding. She should have gone to the railway station not the 'Prince Rupert'.

'What is it you hope for in London?'

'I said – I shall find work.'

'Then, Hannah, earn your keep at Netherton Hall. It may not be the sort of job you like the thought of, but truly it's one worth doing. Bring some interest and hope into her life again. She wasn't always like this. She's cocooned herself in her unhappiness, that's why you can't get through to her. If you run away you'll regret it. You'll always know you let yourself be beaten before you'd really had time to try. What do you say? Let's go back together, eh?'

She turned her head away from him, biting on her bent thumb. Did he have any idea of what he was suggesting? He didn't have to stay. Just an hour or two and he'd be away from it. She'd be back to all she'd run away from – and once Aunt Louise knew she'd tried to escape it would be worse. She'd sneer, she'd say cruel sarcastic things . . .

'Fancy you recognizing me. You'd only seen me in my new gown.' When Hannah did speak it had nothing to do with what they'd been discussing.

'I dare say I looked at *you*, not your smart clothes. Anyway – ' he laughed softly – 'you'd told me about having been kept in the closet, remember?' Now she did look at him, saw the smile in his eyes. Yes, of course he was her friend. She knew she could trust him.

She nodded.

'Can I tell them to haul in the anchor, Hannah? We could get in on the mid-day tide. What do you say?'

'If I say I won't go back?'

'Then we'll head straight for London.'

He waited.

'All right. I'll try again.' Her voice was flat. He knew the courage it took her to say it.

'Good girl.'

'Dan . . .' Her hand moved hardly at all, yet she desperately needed to touch someone, not to be alone. She felt it taken in his and her fingers clung. 'You will come back soon? How long's it going to be? Sometimes a year, you said.'

'I'm putting down my cargo in London, then taking on

another for Gibraltar. I'll not go straight back to Liverpool, I'll come in to Deremouth, I promise.'

'And if – if it's been dreadful – suppose it really is – then promise you'll still help me get away?'

He nodded. 'I promise I will. Give it those few weeks until I come back. And, Hannah, for your own sake and for hers, try to remember what I've told you. The person she used to be is still there somewhere. It's not hate she's full of, it's pain and hopelessness.'

Hannah didn't answer. She knew all about hopelessness.

The 'Prince Rupert' changed course and headed back to Deremouth. It was a pale-faced Hannah who walked unsteadily down the gangplank, the solid ground under her feet feeling as strange as had the rolling of the ship. She'd been offered breakfast on board but had refused it, escaping to the fresh air while Dan ate his. Even the smell of the coffee turned her stomach. Walking uncertainly along the quay she felt empty, defeated, dreading the scene that must await her at the Hall.

The door was opened to them by Gladys, and had Hannah been alone the maidservant would have given vent to her sense of outrage. As it was she eyed them up with no hint of expression on her colourless face.

'I'd like to talk to Mrs Netherton, Gladys, if you'd tell her I'm here,' Dan said. Then to Hannah: 'I'll see her alone, there's a good girl.'

Gratefully she escaped upstairs. She washed, changed into her green dress, brushed and pinned her hair. What were they saying downstairs? She knew she'd been some time trying to overcome the traces of her night, surely she'd be sent for soon. But why wait to be sent for? She viewed the tall girl in the pier glass, a girl who'd travelled a long way since she'd put on her new frock yesterday. She wouldn't wait to be sent for like a child. If they were talking about her, then she wanted to hear what was said.

70

'Head up, shoulders back and down you go,' she told her reflection.

She gave a soft knock at the door of the morning room.

'You may come in.' Her resolve took a momentary dip at her aunt's voice, but she wasn't going to let anyone know it.

As she went in she looked for Dan, he would bolster her confidence. But Louise was alone, sitting very straight in her armchair, a silver-headed stick gripped in either hand for support. What had passed between Dan and her, Hannah would never know.

'So! Don't stand there as if you've come face to face with the Day of Judgment, child. I understand from young Daniel that you and I have little to be proud of in our behaviour.'

'He said that?'

'Never you mind what he said. Weren't his words, but – well, it's a long year since anyone has spoken to Louise Netherton so straight. Hah! And to you I don't doubt. Told you too, did he?'

Hannah nodded.

'And what about it?' Louise leant forward on her sticks.

'What about it, I say? Can we do better? Dare say you're ignorant of the old – and I know nothing of children.'

'Aunt Louise, I'm not a child.'

'Seems you've behaved like one. Running off rather than telling me what you thought. Well, and now that you're back, what have you to say for yourself?'

Such a short while ago if Louise had spoken to her like it Hannah wouldn't have been able to say anything, she would have been frightened to trust her voice. Now she remembered Dan, the way he'd listened and understood, the way he'd talked to her and what he'd told her.

'I behaved badly, I should have stayed. But it's not easy to be where you know you're a burden. This is your own home, you wouldn't know what that's like.'

Louise pushed a log further on to the fire with the end of her stick. Then, brusquely, she spoke.

'I'll say this just once then we'll talk no more about it. When I heard from the solicitor that young Humphrey wanted to name me to be responsible for you, I was – sounds namby-pampby, not what you'd expect, not what *I'd* expect, but I said I'd tell the truth, then no more about it – I was moved. Hah! I was moved – touched.' She glared, seemed to expect some sort of rebuke. 'There! Now I've told you! I prided myself nothing could touch me anymore, but that did. Not that I expected him to die before me, mind you, leaving me with his child to provide for.'

'Well I've said it! Now, no more about it. Just pull that bell and we'll tell Gladys to bring a tray of tea. Been sick, so Daniel tells me. No food inside you since you ran off.'

'It was the smell of the hold.'

'Turned your interest away from the ships, has it?' And from her laugh it was evident she thought she'd scored a point.

'That it hasn't! Aunt Louise, about what you just said –'

'Let it go. I told you, no more about it.'

'No. That's not fair. You know how I've been feeling. We've got to be honest or we'll not do any better.'

'I told you to pull that bell cord. Get along and do as I say.'

'Just one more thing – and tell me truly. Would you still have been . . . moved, touched you said . . . if you'd known you were to have me dropped in your lap!'

' "Truly", you ask me. I'd have been frightened to death! Hah! Frightened to death.' Then, with another piercing look: 'Not frightened now though, not now I've got your measure, so don't get any ideas that I am. I'll just have to get used to you. Hah! If you learn to do as I say and pull that bell when I tell you.'

Hannah wanted to ask why Dan had gone so soon but with new perception she realized that 'Why didn't Dan stay any longer?' would be interpreted as 'I wish I wasn't alone with just you'. So she said nothing, just pulled the bell cord and carried the gateleg table to the fireside.

It was hard to be sure just where the difference lay, but from that day the relationship between Hannah and Louise moved forward. Whatever it was that Daniel had said it must have the laid the foundations for a bridge that could bring them together. Not that they crossed it. They moved a step or two nearer, they each eyed the other warily, guardedly, but with interest. There would be no going back to where they'd been before.

And something else changed for Hannah too. She started visiting the gatehouse.

Sarah answered the door to her knock, an uncertain frown quickly chasing away her look of surprise. She'd caught a glimpse of Hannah before, and recognized who the caller was.

'Does the mistress know you're coming here? She may not think it's right for you. Or did she send you down with a message, is that it?'

Behind her back Hannah crossed her fingers. 'Yes, she knows. It's not a message, I just wanted to come. You don't mind do you, Mrs Thurlston?'

'Bless you, no. But Kath's not home, she's at the school on Wednesdays. Monday, Wednesday and Friday, that's when she's out.'

'Isn't Beatrice in?'

'Oh yes, she's back there in the kitchen.' But she wasn't. Beatrice came into the tiny hallway, her thin face transformed by a rare smile. Hannah was *her* friend. Purposely she'd come today when Kath was out, it was Beatrice she'd come to see.

73

Later when Louise asked what Hannah had found to do with herself on a wet day such as it had been she was told: 'I spent the morning at the gatehouse. I told Mrs Thurlston a lie, I said you knew I was going there. I had to, she looked so worried in case you'd not given permission.' Hannah was learning guile, seeing the way to steer her aunt.

'Humph. No nonsense about Sarah Thurlston. Always keeps to her place, no nonsense about her. You'll come to no harm under her roof. Can't say I know much about those girls but the lad, Algy, is a good worker.' She took a spoonful of soup, gave Hannah a long and thoughtful stare, muttered another 'Humph,' then: 'A good enough woman Sarah Thurlston, got her own sort of pride.'

After that Hannah went often to the gatehouse, sometimes with Beatrice, sometimes with Kath.

October gave way to November. Many a morning the estuary was shrouded in mist. It hung low over the river, leaving the Hall, set high on the hill, hanging in the clear air above it. It wasn't simply a morning mist; often it would linger all day, and Deremouth with the green hills beyond would be lost to view. On Mondays, Wednesday and Fridays Kath was as removed from them as the rest of the unseen town where she worked. Those were Beatrice's days.

The sisters were as different in personality as they were in appearance and, added to that, Kath's Tuesdays and Thursdays were free. 'A working girl is entitled to enjoy herself when she's at home,' was Sarah's opinion, and it was she who made the rules. Beatrice hadn't the luxury of days off. 'Can't call hers work, she never has to turn out on a wet morning,' was another of Sarah's opinions.

In the first week or two it didn't strike Hannah as strange that when she called for Kath on Tuesdays and Thursdays there was never any sign of Beatrice. Kath would be ready for whatever they'd arranged to do – long

74

tramps on the moor, trips into town. Days with Kath were active, always with a little more packed into them than they had time for, meaning a race for home at the end.

Hannah looked on this new era as beginning when Dan went away. He'd told her that when he came back, if she'd found it hopeless at the Hall, he would help her. But she had to be fair, she had to try to keep her bargain and make it work. He'd been gone almost three weeks on the Thursday that she called for Kath and, for once, found Beatrice downstairs with the others. Kath and Hannah had arranged to go to the beach this morning, shell hunting. Kath wanted the shells for school. Miss Sherwood had told her that on Monday afternoons she could have the children to herself. Her mind was buzzing with ideas for things she could teach the children to make with shells.

'You'll need the big round basket,' Sarah was telling Beatrice as Kath brought Hannah into the kitchen.

'Morning, Mrs Thurlston. Hello, Bea'.

'Good morning? Cold morning more likely,' Sarah answered. She gave a quick look at Beatrice. She was uneasy, Hannah could sense it.

Beatrice mumbled something that might have been meant as a greeting but didn't look up. It was a moment that Hannah wouldn't forget. Yet why? What was different? What was wrong? Kath, her coat on, was tying her bonnet. Nothing unusual about her, she was the same as usual, and she took no notice of Beatrice's withdrawn expression. But Sarah was aware of it, Hannah was sure of that. Beatrice's shoulders were hunched. She didn't look at Hannah at all. In fact, she kept her eyes lowered.

'Now remember all you have to get Beatrice. I've written it down, but I know what you are.' Sarah got a huge, round basket from the cupboard under the stairs.

'I'll remember,' she growled.

'I wonder if you'll get everything in just the one.' Her mother hesitated then, despite the size of the first, brought a second and smaller basket out. 'Better take the two. Get a move on now or Bill Giles will have sold out of sheeps' heads.'

'Are you going to market?' Hannah asked the obvious. 'We'll all walk in together.'

'You don't have to.' Still Beatrice didn't look at anyone. 'It's Kath's day off, go off and enjoy it.'

For a second Kath hesitated, then agreed. 'We could walk down the hill together, we're all going the same way. Look, Hannah, I've got this box for the shells. I thought we could share the one.'

It was plain something was upsetting Beatrice and, as if to make up for it, Kath chatted almost non-stop. At the bottom of the hill into town they parted, the shell hunters going off to the beach and Beatrice to the market. Hannah couldn't get the thought of her out of her mind.

'Kath, why was Beatrice so quiet? Is something wrong with her?'

'Oh, she'll be all right. Look at this one, these are my favourites.' And determined to change the subject she squatted down to sift the stones in her search.

But it was no use, the memory was there all the time. Beatrice, laden down with two baskets. Beatrice miserable.

'Kath,' Hannah called along the beach after half an hour or so, 'we can't leave Bea to carry all that load of shopping home on her own. I'll come shelling again Saturday if you like, but let's go and find her.'

'You don't want to worry. She often carries both baskets. Anyway I can't come Saturday – I've been asked to visit Sylvia's home. You remember Sylvia, she's Algy's sweetheart.'

'Oh, come on, Kath, it's mean to leave her to do it. I'll get some for you on my own tomorrow then.'

'No. I shall stay here.' It seemed there was a side to Kath too that Hannah hadn't seen.

Alone she went to the market. The misty morning was

well suited to the mood of the outing. Why couldn't they have all come to the beach, all hunted for the shells, all gone to the market? But she was learning that with the Thurlston girls it could never be like that.

'Hannah! Hannah!' There was a radiant smile on the face that had been so withdrawn. 'I've been trying to will you to come. Do you believe it's possible to do that? I've nearly finished, I don't think there was anything else.'

'Your mother gave you a list, have you checked it?'

'Here it is. You call it out to me. It's easier that way.'

And now that there was a smile on her face again Hannah wasn't going to argue although she seemed to bemaking much of a small job. All checked, they turned for home.

'I'll take the big one, you take the other.' Hannah relieved her of one basket and felt her free hand taken in Beatrice's.

'Did she mind you leaving her? You didn't have to. But she'll soon find someone else to help her.' Whatever had upset Beatrice earlier, misty morning or no, there were no clouds in her sky now.

When they reached the gatehouse she didn't suggest Hannah should come in, any more than Kath had said 'What are you doing this afternoon?' But at the Hall the fire was burning in the library, and one thing Hannah had had encouraged in her all her childhood was a love of books. There was something between her new friends she didn't understand, and had she been able to look in at the gatehouse as the day went on, she would have been even more puzzled.

A silent dinner, at least silent as far as Beatrice and Kath were concerned. Then Sarah heard them upstairs in their bedroom, talking. 'What'll it be now, I wonder?' as they came downstairs. Ah, still talking, Kath laughing. 'Either daggers drawn or thick as thieves, like a couple of dogs over a bone.' But as the afternoon went on, the two of them working together on the finishing touches to the skirt Kath had been making, Sarah still wasn't happy about them. 'Like a pair of lovers who've just made up after a tiff. Why they can't behave like other people I'll never know.'

As long as the day lasted they were able to put the events of the morning to the back of their minds. It was only later when they lay side by side in the darkness that it forced a wedge between them. Neither spoke; the room was still. Then a sniff from Kath.

Beatrice listened. 'It isn't you who should be crying.' Even though she spoke softly Kath heard the accusation in her tone.

'I'd looked forward to it – she's my friend! We always have fun.'

'Fun! You've got other friends, all the people at school, and you're always coming home saying who you've been talking to.' By now Beatrice was crying too. If Sarah could have heard them she would have despaired. A long silence, then Beatrice mumbled: 'I've never had a friend before – '

'Yes, you have. You've had me. You've always had me.'

Beatrice turned around, moving closer to her sister. 'But I'm only a bit of your life, don't you see? All your friends at school – '

'They're all either old or young.'

'Yes, but you like it there. It's not like me, here. I've got nothing, not a proper life.' As Kath had recovered some of her composure, it seemed Beatrice's was beyond recall.

'Everyone has a proper life if only they can see it.'

'Well, I can't see it. Until Hannah came I had no one, nothing.' She felt under her pillow for her handkerchief, blew her nose and was partially restored. 'Anyway, when she had to choose it was me she wanted. She didn't stay with you, fun or no.'

'She was just sorry for you, that's why.'

They turned their backs on each other with flounce. It

was as if they needed the drama as well as the heartache. Once sleep took over they moved to each other again and when they woke it was in the same position as every morning, Kath's broad hips against Beatrice's lap, Beatrice's thin arms around her.

In the morning room of the Hall was a silver calender. Each morning Lizzie, the housemaid, turned the knobs on either side of it to alter the date, the day and, when the time came, the month. November was well gone and Hannah was still scanning the horizon for sight of the 'Prince Rupert'.

'I wonder you're so keen to see him again,' Kath said as from the lane by the top end of the garden they looked out beyond the estuary. 'If I were you I'd want to try and forget the whole miserable business.'

'He'll want to know how I've got on.'

'You've never really told me what he's like. Is he handsome? Dashing?'

'What do you call handsome? I've never really thought about it. He's – I don't know really – sure, certain. And he looks nice, I suppose.'

'But what does that mean, nice? I'll tell you what I call handsome. Tall, broad, strong, dark, rippling muscles.' Kath giggled, delighted in her make-believe hero. 'You know the kind, Hannah. Looks right into you, makes your knees turn to jelly.'

'My knees were jelly anyway, and my stomach too.'

'Oh, Hannah! Where's your sense of romance! Describe him properly. Is he swashbuckling? A young sea captain – why it's the sort of thing romances are made of.'

'Kath, you are a chump,' Hannah chuckled. 'He's nice and he looks nice too – but he's not so very young. Yet even though he isn't, he must remember what it felt like. I

79

could tell he understood me. He knows things without being told.'

'Doesn't sound very exciting to me. I say, Hannah, do you know the manager at your aunt's yard? Mr Webster, I think they call him.'

'I've never seen him, but of course I know about him. Aunt Louise always speaks about him as if he's the height of respectability. Are you telling me Mr Webster is swashbuckling?'

'Gracious, no. A dry old stick I'd think from the look of him. But his son is! He works for the newspaper. Just to watch him walk down the road makes a girl's knees turn to jelly and her toes curl!'

Hannah laughed, but then with Kath she so often did. Never with anyone else had she had this feeling that just ahead life was waiting, full of promise.

'Mr Webster's son isn't with the paper anymore. Aunt Louise told me about him after Mr Webster had been to see her the other day. He's gone to Australia to find his fortune. They're taking gold from the ground, digging it out. He's going to get rich.'

'Gracious! Didn't I say he was romantic and swashbuckling? Heigh-ho!' But Kath laughed despite the exaggerated sigh. 'To think of the times I've fluttered my eyelashes in his direction — like a hussy, Ma would have said. What a waste!'

'Look! Look, Kath! that's 'Prince Rupert', see her, just coming round the headland. Dan's come, I'm sure of it.'

'The tide's low, she won't get in. Do you suppose he'll come to see your aunt this evening?'

'He promised me.'

'Well, if you want a chance to talk to him properly you won't get it there, with polite table talk all around.'

Of course Kath was right. Hannah made up her mind what she'd do. By about two o'clock there would be enough water for 'Prince Rupert' to get into the estuary.

As soon as lunch was over she'd go as fast as she could to the dock and meet him when he came ashore.

Today Louise was less than agreeable, meal table conversation was the last thing she wanted. If it weren't for the bright-eyed child at the other end of the table she'd not have to force herself into the pretence of eating lunch. Will power and concentration were needed to carry her fork to her mouth with her crippled hands. When Hannah disappeared as soon as Gladys had carried away the dishes, Louise neither knew nor cared where she'd gone.

Had the leaves not been making a carpet of gold to dance on the lane in the winter sunshine, it might have been spring. There was a feeling of promise in the air. Or so Hannah thought as she half walked, half ran, down the hill to Deremouth. She mustn't be late, she must be there when he tied up. Today she didn't care who saw her going towards the quay, but threw discretion to the wind.

'Prince Rupert' was nearly in, her sails furled, paddles turning slowly as she inched her way to the quay. And Dan was on deck. He saw Hannah and waved. She shouted. Then the gangplank was down and after a last word with Mr Bailey he came ashore.

'Hannah! How did you know we were in?'

'I've been watching for you. From the top of the garden, you remember, you can see the ships come.'

Remembering his promise he prompted: 'I've thought about you, Hannah. I've tried to will things to go well.' He was leading her towards Quay Hill and the town. His voice was anxious and he seemed to be expecting the worst.

'I know. I could tell. Every time I felt – well, anyway – I'd remember all you'd told me and knowing you were coming back was a sort of prop.'

'And have you often felt like that?'

'That I needed a prop?' She considered the question, then answered honestly: 'Not as often as I would if I'd not

81

had one. Really I've been quite strong,' she added with pride.

He squeezed her hand. It was her childish honesty that touched him. In a few more years she would have learnt to show only as much as she chose of the truth. Now she threw herself wide open.

'Good girl.'

'In a funny sort of way I believe I *am* beginning to know her. Can't imagine her ever being fun, like you said, but it's as if every now and then the fog clears and I can see – someone kinder – someone not so crotchety.'

'I hope it's clearing for her too?'

'For Aunt Louise? Don't be silly. I'm always the same.'

He laughed. 'I believe you truly believe that.'

She frowned. How silly. Of course she was always the same.

As they walked she stole a glance at him. She'd told him things weren't beyond bearing – yet there was something in his face, something anxious.

'Truly I've managed, Dan, I think we'll get used to each other, Aunt Louise and me, one of these days. I'll go on trying, you don't have to look so worried.' She was rewarded by a smile. 'Are you coming straight home with me now?'

'Not this time. I would have had I not had the chance to talk to you, but now that I have I'll get away on this tide. I want to get to Liverpool as soon as I can. My brother is ill.'

'I didn't know you had a brother.'

'There's a lot you don't know. Time for all that. Yes, I have a brother, older than me. Peter, he's in banking. Rosalind, that's his wife, wrote to me asking me to get home as soon as I could. I found the letter waiting in Gibraltar.'

'Is he very ill?'

'I'm afraid so. He's been sick a long time, he gets no

better. Rosalind is worn out. She sounded . . . well, she's never been strong. Then there are the boys, their two sons.'

'And you wasted time coming here just because of me! Dan, I'm so sorry. I didn't know.' She felt like an intruder.

'I wanted to come, Hannah. I've been worried about you.'

'And I shall worry about you, Dan.' She'd had neither brother nor sister, but she'd often thought about what it must be like to have one, someone who understood, who shared a home and a background. Dan had had it and it seemed he was losing it. 'Let's go straight back to the ship.'

'Don't you come. There's a lot of truth in what your aunt said. A dock is no place for a young girl to wait about, the seamen get the wrong idea. Promise me you'll go straight home? You'll be there before it starts to get dark if you hurry.'

'That's just silly . . . All right, I'll do as you say. But I still think its silly. I'm not scared of the dark.'

'To please me, then, Hannah.'

'Yes, I promised. Dan, next time, you'll stay longer? You will come back again soon?'

Hearing her he realized how important that prop had been. 'I will, truly.'

'I won't say anything to Aunt Louise about meeting you. She'd think I've made you my friend now instead of hers.' She put it badly, but Hannah was learning.

'Good girl.' She felt the pressure of his fingers on hers, then he was gone back down the hill to the quay.

It was three or four days later that a letter was delivered to Louise. 'From Hilary,' she muttered to herself as she broke the seal and took out the single sheet, closely written on both sides. Hannah was silent. Who was Hilary? The 'seen and not heard' dictum prevented her asking. 'Hilary,' Louise repeated, 'Daniel's father. Oh dear . . . gone has he . . . umph . . . umph . . .' as she read and digested the news. Then, to Hannah: 'Peter – that's Daniel's brother. *Is*, I say.

was his brother. Now what's to be done with the young woman?'

'Peter's wife?'

'Widow. I just told you, Peter's dead. Feathery weakling she always was even at best. Ah,' as she read on, 'to make her home with Hilary it seems. Well, at least the boys will have someone with a ha'porth of sense to look to them. How she bore two sons I'll never know. And what she'll do with her life without Peter is beyond imagining, doubt she knows how to wipe her own nose.' Memories enveloped her. 'Hah! Feeble . . . feathery . . . I told you.' And a glare as if the fault for it all lay with Hannah.

Feathery . . . feeble. But she'd said that before, and Hannah knew how wrong she'd been. Today Louise was in an expansive frame of mind; it was Hannah who was tight-lipped, Hannah who believed herself 'always the same'.

Sometimes Dan docked in Deremouth twice in a month, sometimes no more than twice a year. He arrived unexpectedly one morning in January and Hannah knew when she heard where he was going that it must be a long while before she would see him again. He was bound for Buenos Aires and then Auckland, going out round the Horn and home from the east, making a round the world trip. He'd be in Deremouth twenty four hours. Hannah thought he'd come to pick up a cargo and he let her go on thinking it. But his new ship, 'Europa', was fully loaded. He'd come simply to put his mind at rest, to let her know that her prop wouldn't fail her even though half the world came between them.

'Let me take you down to see "Europa",' he said to Louise. 'She's a fine vessel – iron hull, screw type propellor. She drives more power than any vessel I've sailed.'

'Power! What rubbish you fill your head with, you and

your steam!' Louise snapped. 'What sort of engine could give you the power of the wind? That's nature's way, sent by the Almighty. And you, you with your arrogance, think you can do better. I've heard it all before. Remember the to-do when the "Sirius" crossed the Atlantic? Had to chop up the tables and doors in the end to fuel the fire to keep her going. How will you earn your keep, just tell me that, if the cargo you carry has to be fuel for the boiler? Hah! Trust the Good Lord, He'll send the wind to fill your sails, my boy. You and all your newfangled nonsense!'

'You're right, Mrs Netherton. We can't do without our sails.' Then he grinned at her disarmingly. 'But give us time, and we will. It's fourteen years since the "Sirius" had to burn her tables and chairs. It must come, you know. With each decade there are advances. We must move with the times, a company can't stay viable if it refuses to accept change.'

'Hah!' She wasn't going to admit defeat. 'Well, Mr Webster sees to things these days in the yard. If my Charles were here he'd know what it is you're blathering about.'

'Wrap yourself up against the cold and let me show you.'

'Come to that dock? You'd be pushed to get me there in July, you'll certainly not do it in January.'

'Then we can't go?' Hannah saw hope of the trip fading.

'And what would be the good of you going there, getting in everyone's way? The dock's no place for women or children either. I've said so often enough.' Then with a smile that showed a wicked triumph: 'Being tied up in dock doesn't hold a ship stable, my girl. They can do without the exhibition you'd very soon make of yourself.'

Hannah felt her neck grow hot. If he hadn't known it already, Dan would have been able to imagine now what she had to suffer at Louise's hands. He kept his thoughts to himself though and came to the rescue with a laugh, 'Remarks like that aren't worthy of you, and well you know it.' His tone took any sting from his words. It seemed he was adept at pouring oil on troubled waters. 'I'm sorry you won't come Mrs Netherton, I would have enjoyed taking you. But at least, let me have the pleasure of showing the "Europa" off to Hannah.'

It was a day that left a lasting mark on her, just as that visit to the yard when she'd talked to Ben. 'Europa' was tied up on the public quay so she saw Ben only at a distance today, recognizing him by his auburn hair. She waved to him and his answering 'af'ernoon, missie' carried back to her on the wind. He'd not forgotten her; he'd recognised her. The knowledge seemed to complete her joy as she preceded Dan up the gangplank to go aboard 'Europa'.

There was so much she wanted to see on his great ship, yet Dan led her first of all to the engine room. 'This is where the excitement lies, Hannah.'

'Down here, in this dark, smelly chamber! Oh, but, Dan, how can this compare with the smack of the wind in the canvas?' She hated to appear backward looking, remembering what he'd said to Aunt Louise. And she remembered something else – her one and only sea trip. She was ashamed.

'The challenge isn't just what man can endure from the elements. There's something else – what man can design. The better the boiler, the more steam pressure, the greater the speed.'

'But what about the poor seaman down here in this dark hole, stoking the boiler?'

'He has pride in what he does, and so he should. You can see it in his gleaming brasses. And there's more to running on steam than stoking a boiler, you know. On this engine there are more than twenty points that have to be kept lubricated constantly, to make sure they move easily. If he doesn't oil them the whole thing would seize up. It's a constant job, the whole progress depends on the man down here.' He paused, his mind on what he'd said. 'But more, far above, it depends on the man who designs, the man who understands . . .'

That might be true, but still Louise's arguments carried weight with Hannah. Dan sensed her doubts.

'We're winning, Hannah, this must be the way forward. Here, come into my cabin and I'll try and explain how it works.'

At his desk he made sketches, taught her for the first time the rudiments of the workings of an engine. She learnt how steam poured into the cylinder, pushed the piston, moved the rod, passed into a second cylinder to work again, giving extra power to the propellor's drive.

'You see, that in itself is a great stride forward. All that power used to be wasted when we had a single cylinder, blown away in the exhaust; that's why we have the second cylinder. It's what we call a compound engine, it uses the steam more than once.' He sat back in his chair looking at her, his eyes bright. This was a new Dan. His feet might be firmly on the ground but Hannah knew, even though she might not fully understand them, that Dan too had his dreams. 'This is only the beginning! For centuries men have relied on just the wind for propulsion. But not now. Never again. We're lucky, Hannah, to have been born when we were. There's never been such an age for advancement.'

How could she help but be infected by his belief? She wanted to learn, wanted to understand. 'Can I go below again now that I've seen the drawings. It would mean more now.'

No place for women, Louise had said. But she was wrong.

From the engine room they went to the crew's quarters; cramped they were, too. 'Europa' was built for speed, her lines fine and sleek, she had nothing like the cargo space of the slower bulk carriers. So every available foot had to be given to the goods they transported, even though it was the crew who suffered for it. They had their home in the fo'c'sle. This was to be no pleasure cruise. Dan, Mr Bailey, a boatswain, a carpenter, a sailmaker, a cook, a steward, seven apprentices and seven seamen were to man 'Europa'.

Hannah had to see it all, hold the coarse rope in her hands, touch the canvas; she needed to absorb the feel and the smell. Dan stood back and watched her. He'd come to Deremouth to reassure her before he went so far away. She was a child. Not for a second did he think of her as anything more, a lanky colt-like child. Just as Peter and Rosalind's two boys did, so Hannah tugged at his heartstrings. All of them young, all of them vulnerable. Dressed as she was now or as he'd found her that night on 'Prince Rupert' back in October, her honesty, her eagerness, the way she turned to him so trustfully, didn't alter.

'Dan, all the spring and all the summer! You won't be back until the blackberries are ripe again. It'll be autumn.'

'I must go, Hannah. I'll ship letters to you whenever I can. And you know where I'll be putting in, I hope you'll write to me too.'

No one had ever sent Hannah a letter, actually addressed it to her. At the prospect she brightened visibly. But it was small comfort the next day as from her viewpoint at the top of the garden she watched 'Europa' putting out from the estuary. The single tall funnel belched forth its smoke, the wash from the screw propellor Dan was so proud of left a trail in its wake.

The wind was bitingly cold, blowing from the north-east on a February day, but despite that Beatrice was in the garden gathering the first of the snowdrops from a sheltered corner.

'Bea, look what I've had.' Hannah called to her as she

88

let herself in through the little wooden gate from the main drive, waving what looked like a letter.

Beatrice ignored the paper but came to meet her. 'Come inside where it's warm. Ma's gone to see a friend in town, there's no one here but me. Look aren't these beautiful? A promise that winter's almost gone.' She held her posy towards Hannah. Her fingers were swollen and cracked with chilblains.

'Your poor hands!'

'They get like this every year, they always have. None of the others ever get chilblains, yet Pa and Algy are out in all weathers.'

'Let's go in the warm.' Instinctively Hannah put an arm around her friend's narrow shoulders.

'That paper you've got – it's a letter, is it? I suppose it's from that friend of Mrs Netherton's.'

'Yes, from Dan. But he's not just her friend, he's mine too. He put in at Oporto before setting out for Buenos Aires, so he sent a letter to me from there. See!' Time and again her eyes had gone back to it, addressed to 'Miss Hannah Ruddick.'

Beatrice didn't answer. She unfolded the closely written parchment and frowned over it. Then passing it back: 'To be truthful, Hannah – though you'll think me ignorant – I'm not much for reading. I didn't get a lot of schooling and we don't have any books in the house, except just the Bible on the table in the parlour. As for reading, there's too much else to do. Anyway, you say he's your friend but I don't see how he can be, you hardly know him. You sound like Kath, always looking out expecting to find Prince Charming.'

'Indeed I'm no such thing!' Hannah spoke crossly.

'No, I know you're not. It was a silly thing to say.' Beatrice knelt in front of the range, poking at the coals. 'Men! You'd think women were put on this earth for their pleasure. Well, I never will be!'

Holding her hands towards the bars of the fire she rubbed her fingers together. How they tingled and itched! Kneeling at her side Hannah took them into her own.

'Don't put them so close to the heat when you come in from the cold.' She examined them, the skin red and cracked. 'Oh, Bea, you poor thing.' Lifting them to her mouth, she gently blew on them.

Perhaps it was what had gone before – the letter, the talk of Dan – that upset Beatrice, or perhaps it was Hannah's sudden gentleness. Her face looked pinched with cold and her mouth trembled.

'Beatrice, what is it? Tell me.' And still Hannah held her hands.

'Expect it's the chilblains.'

'No it isn't. You can tell *me*, surely.'

'S'pose it's the letter. What he tells you must be exciting – faraway places and all. I never have anything to tell you, nothing interesting.'

Hannah's arms were strong. She held the little body against her and rocked Beatrice as though she were a child. She was shaken by the unexpected tenderness she felt. After a while Beatrice sat back on her heels. There was a stillness about her, even a hint of a smile.

'Put your letter away, Hannah. Let's not talk about it any more.'

Hannah didn't understand why, but she was glad Beatrice seemed happy again. Next time she had a letter she wouldn't mention it. Once Dan had been home again and Beatrice had had a chance to get to know him, she'd feel different.

But right from that first time Kath wanted to hear what he'd written. His talk of faraway places encouraged her in her wild talk of swashbuckling sea captains and dark-eyed romantics. Hannah smiled to hear such daydreams. Dan was Dan, he was reality.

* * *

That July there was a heatwave. Day after day the sky was cloudless, the sun beat down relentlessly. One of the girls' favourite places was a deep ravine cutting through Mann's Wood, the woodland belonging to the Hall. At the bottom of the ravine the stream flowed on its way to join the river in the estuary, its clear water breaking over rocks and large boulders. The Fairy Glen the girls called it. No one ever came here but them.

On this particular hot day as Kath drilled the children on the lawn of Miss Sherwood's school she looked longingly at the clear sky and imagined the Fairy Glen, silent except for the rippling of the water over the boulders and the song of the birds. But there she was wrong! At the bottom of the steep slope, kneeling on a smooth flat rock and trailing their hands in the water, were Hannah and Beatrice.

'Let's dabble our feet.' Hannah was the one to suggest it. Off came their stockings and they stepped into the clear, shallow water. Long skirts were bulky to hold and seemed to make them even warmer.

'No one comes here. We could take them off.' Beatrice watched keenly as she waited for Hannah's reaction.

'Let's! Just imagine how lovely to feel the sun on us.'

Dresses, petticoats, one garment after another, off they came. Hannah laughed as she pulled her chemise over her head. 'Like Salome!' If Beatrice had no idea what she was talking about it didn't matter, she laughed too.

Beatrice was naked now except for her bloomers, white cotton, held with elastic at mid-calf, with no sigh of lace or frill. Her underwear was as plain and well-worn as everything else she wore. How tiny she was. The firm, hardly perceptible swelling of her breasts, shoulder blades so pronounced, arms like sticks. Stripped to their bloomers they looked at each other.

'Can't matter. No one can see us.' Hannah made the first move.

Beatrice's rose bud mouth was slightly open. She ran her tongue around her lips. She wanted to say something, but didn't know what.

'Come on, let's paddle again.' Hannah turned back into the water. 'Feel the sun on your back, Bea. Isn't it bliss?'

Oh, but she was so beautiful, Beatrice couldn't take her eyes off her. The curve of her breasts, the rounded hips, her long slender legs. As Hannah stepped further into the stream, Beatrice followed. Her hands longed to reach out, to touch the dimple above the crack of Hannah's bottom, to feel the –

'Oh, this is much better!' Quite unaware of Beatrice's thoughts Hannah bent forward, cupping water in her hands and letting it trickle over her. A second later she felt it on her shoulders, dribbling down her back.

The day was so hot by contrast the stream felt like ice. It wasn't long before they were back on the warm, smooth boulder, lying side by side, the sun beating down on them.

'I'm glad we're like this.' Beatrice turned on her side towards Hannah. 'I knew you'd look like you do. You're so beautiful. Strong, warm, perfect.'

For a moment Hannah wished she had her clothes back on. 'A great lump like me, perfect!' She tried to change it into a joke.

'I don't expect anyone but me knows that you have a mole on your tummy.' Beatrice bent forward to lay her lips on it. Hannah sensed the need in her to have someone to love, to be loved. Dear Beatrice. Undressed she seemed so vulnerable, almost pathetic. Hannah's fleeting embarrassment vanished, her hand on her friend's narrow back was gentle.

'I'm all bones,' Beatrice whispered. She lay back on the boulder drawing the hand to her. 'Feel me. I want you to know what I am.'

Then, side by side, they lay quite still. The moment was over. Thus far, and no further.

CHAPTER FOUR

Perhaps it was her inability to keep pace that made Louise doggedly try to hold time still, to put off change. Hannah knew she'd have a fight on her hands when, on her seventeenth birthday, she made her pronouncement.

'Aunt Louise you said I was too young, so I waited. All this time I've waited but I'm not young now, and I can't spend my life drifting. Kath does a job of work – '

'The gardener's girl! Are you likening your mode of life to what's expected for the servants?'

'I'm not likening it to anyone's.' The battle was on. 'I don't know anyone so useless and that's the truth.'

It was more than two years since Dan had shown her over 'Europa', even then fostering her dreams. In that time she'd acquired a confidence she'd lacked as a newcomer. But how she'd come by it who could guess? Certainly Louise had done little to instil it in her. Some of it must have come from the new knowledge she'd gained, the hours she'd spent amongst her uncle's books in the library.

'And what, may I be so bold as to ask, do you suggest doing with this aimless life of yours? Could it be that your girlfriend has found you some sort of caretaking job like hers at the school? Looking after the offspring of local tradespeople, wiping their noses for the shopkeepers' brats! Well, I'll not have it! You hear me? I'll not have it!'

Hannah opened her mouth to rise to the bait, then thought better of it. That was something else she'd learnt, and a difficult lesson it had been too. Aunt Louise said things for the pleasure of making her angry. Well, she wouldn't give her that pleasure, not today. Today was too important for games.

'No, of course I'm not wanting to look after children. Can you imagine I'd be any good at that? Aunt Louise, there's only one thing I want to do, only one place I want to work.' And now Louise was listening. Hannah spoke with such intensity she *had* to listen.

'In the yard you mean? Webster sees to that side of things, you know he does.'

'You mean it's Mr Webster I should speak to? But you're head of the company.'

'Back on that tack again! Wanting to get down there with the ships. Those Webster takes on aren't girls and well you know it! If you'd been a boy then you'd have been there all right. And I'll give you your due, I believe you'd have been worth the teaching. But you weren't a boy, more's the pity.'

'What difference does it make whether I wear a skirt or a pair of breeches? I'd not be going to sea. My gender doesn't make any difference to what's between my ears, now does it? It's brain I'd be using, not brawn.'

'Why Humphrey had to sire a girl I'll never know. Couldn't even do that right! And what do you suppose they'd do with you underfoot down there? What use would you be? Doing a job instead of some local lad, taking orders from Webster, from everyone, for family or no everyone has to start at the bottom. Why can't you be content to stitch and paint like any other girl, to go calling, to find yourself a beau?' She poked at the coals with her stick, a sure sign of irritation. 'Use your brain, you say. What do you know of tonnage, of costing, of equipping a ship, of ordering stores, of –'

'How shall I ever know anything if I go on wasting my time like this?'

Hannah dropped to her knees on the hearthrug in front of her aunt, her eyes wide and earnest. Somehow she had to make her understand.

'Aunt Louise, how would you feel if you were in my

place? You'd not want time to slip by without you, you'd want to be living, learning, trying to make your mark. I know you would.'

'The wharf is no place for a woman. I ought to know.' She sighed, seeming to shed some of her certainty. 'Ah, I ought to know if anyone does. Used to go there with Charles – as keen as you to start off with, sure I could make my mark. But I was never useful. He used to put a chair by the window so that I could look out, he seemed to like me to be there – but they worked around me. I was never useful, never anything on my own.' She sniffed, pulling herself up straight on her sticks as she sat forward in her chair. 'Is that what you're wanting? To be allowed down there to watch people? That's how it was. I'm telling you, I felt myself to be no more useful than the comfortable chair Charles used to set for me to sit in.'

'But if they'd let you, you could have been useful.' Hannah rested her hand on her aunt's. 'You knew that, didn't you? You always knew it. And it's different now. No one can say a woman can't do a proper job. The most important job in the land is done by a woman – our Queen. Aunt Louise, I want to be able to contribute to what goes on. There must be something I could do. I'd work as hard as anyone you could engage – harder, I swear I would. I'm not asking favours because I'm family.'

A knock on the door and in came Gladys. 'Excuse me, Ma'am, got that Mr Webster out here. Come unexpected he has, asking to talk to you.'

'Webster? Tell him to wait a minute.'

'It seems like fate, Aunt Louise – Mr Webster coming.'

'Fate, nothing! Lot of nonsense. Must be something wrong to bring him here at this time of the month. If it's business brings him we shan't be needing you in here. Just send him in as you go across the hall.' But Hannah gone and Alan Webster facing her, Louise's tone changed 'Hah,

95

Webster. Must be fate sent you here this afternoon. Saves me having to call you out.'

'Indeed, ma'am?'

'You may sit down. Now tell me, have you all the staff you need at the yard? In the offices I mean, I've no interest in what outside men you take on.'

'How strange that you should ask me. It's that very reason I've come to talk to you.'

'Hah! Then speak up, man.'

'Albert Tyzack has a responsible task, he's done it for years as well you know. But he'll not go through another winter. It's time we took on a young man to learn so that he can fill his place when he goes.'

'Tyzack. I remember him well. Bertie Tyzack. You say he's throwing in the sponge?

'Not yet – and never from choice. But his eyes are failing, it's been painful to watch him peering at the ledgers in the lamplight. Through the summer months he'll carry on, but he'll never face up to the short days again.' A rare thing for Webster to be so expansive. And why the urgency? The short days were months away, they were only in April. But Louise nodded her head as she listened, giving no hint that she'd guessed there was another reason for this request. 'Mrs Netherton, I have a proposition.'

'Hah! And I'll hear it. But first I'll have my say, tell you why I was sending for you. 'Tis this girl who lives with me. Miss Ruddick, my niece. She may wear a skirt but she's none the less able for that. Skirt or breeches, it's what's between the ears that counts. Our dear Queen is an example of what a woman can be worth – and you can't gainsay me there. I mean her – my niece I mean, not Her Majesty – to come into the company. And I want a place for her, a job she feels to be her own. Bertie Tyzack will teach her his trade, there's no reason why she shouldn't furnish a ship with its victuals as well as any man. No point in waiting, she's to start tomorrow.'

'And what am I to pay her, ma'am?'

'Whatever you'd pay any lad you engaged to do the same job.'

Alan Webster's face had taken on its habitual closed in look. 'Any lad' she'd said. A lad from the town. 'In the first year – and more if he showed himself slow to learn – no more than a guinea and a half each month.'

'That's the figures then. She's to have no special treatment. She's to learn the business, Webster, not just Tyzack's part of it; she's to get the feel of the company. I want you to see to it that she gets the chance. But no special favours mind. It's right that she knows and understands – I've no one else. Hah! Well, that's settled. Now, tell me, what brings you here?'

'What we've just agreed puts a different complexion on things, ma'am. 'Twas about Albert Tyzack, someone learning his job, that I came.'

'Fancy that, and on the very day I decide it's time young Hannah – Miss Ruddick – stopped idling her days away. Fate! Didn't I say so?'

'Mrs Netherton,' Webster plunged on, 'we've had news of my boy.'

'Hah! Bright lad is Tommy.' Louise beamed, though whether remembering Tommy or at the satisfactory way she'd dealt with the problem of Hannah it was impossible to tell. 'Plucky one too. Must be a real pride to you, a son with the courage to leave all his security to seek his fortune. Great pride!'

'Indeed he is that, ma'am. And a great joy too, for he writes that he's coming home. By now he'll be well on his way, his letter can't have travelled far ahead of him.'

Louise was quick to understand what was left unsaid. A replacement to take over from Tyzack, a special visit from Webster, Tommy on his way home. She believed in straight talking. 'So! And you want the lad to settle down in the company, is that it? Is that what brings you?'

'There is nothing I want more. Netherton's has been my life, more to me than a job of work done for a wage. You know that, ma'am. The guv'nor knew it. To have my son learning to be part of it, to feel that one of these days he might be able to take not just Tyzack's job but mine . . .'
Louise had thought Webster a dry old stick even in his youth, for 'old' often has nothing to do with years. But for Tommy he bared his soul, to get the boy home, safe and prospering with the company.

'You can't do that to a young man, you know – expect him to try on his father's shoes and want nothing more than to grow into them. He has to find his own way, to prove his manhood. And quite right too. Well, Webster, your Tommy's never been one to take the well-lit, safe path. He's strayed along many an unknown track looking for his road to success.'

'He'll settle, ma'am. Just youthful restlessness.'

'Am I criticizing him for it? Indeed, I'm not. But what makes you so sure that he'll arrive home this time to drop permanent anchor at the wharf?'

Alan shook his head. 'I just hope, Mrs Netherton. It's what I want for him, what his mother and I both want above all else. If there had been an opening, something to offer him – '

'Hah! And so you have. If he's worth his salt of course you have. We can afford to pay him – if he's ready for us.' Her bright eyes pierced him. 'And what makes you suppose you'll go on forever? Time you took someone on to learn the ropes as manager. Tell the boy that. I don't mind admitting it, I've always had a soft spot for Tommy. Give him a try, teach him all you know.' Then she chuckled. 'If he'll come, that is. Rascally young scamp – but bright. Channel his mind and he'd be a useful man.'

Had she been able to she would have stood up. The interview was over, Webster read his dismissal in the way she straightened herself in her chair, the slight inclination of her head.

'You're very good, ma'am. I'm deeply indebted.'

'He hasn't come yet. May be nibbling at the bait, but you've still got to land him. Hah!' And again that chuckle. 'Young scamp, worth a fortune, is he? Well, never mind. We shall see, we shall see. Just send Miss Ruddick back to me on your way out, she'll be in the library.'

Fate, the girl had said. As if there was any such thing! Fate wasn't going to tell Louise Netherton how to run her life. The truth was it was time Hannah found something else to do except moon about with those Thurlston girls.

'Ah, there you are,' she said as Hannah came in. 'Well, miss, you say you're worth the teaching so you're to report to Albert Tyzack. He's getting beyond his job – not a word of that to him, mind you. Can't blame a man if his sight fails. Sight – bones – if it's not one it's another. You're to help him, learn from him, and do as he tells you. And just remember, as long as he's there he's at the helm. You understand me?'

'What does he do?'

'He stocks the ships, victuals for the crew. More to it than you think. Do your sums wrong and you'll have them short of water and food before journey's end. And, remember, not a hint to him that we expect he'll soon be going, that's something just between you and me. He has a daughter, as I recall, somewhere along the coast Brixham way. She'll see he's taken care of when the time comes. In the meanwhile, just learn all you can from him. You tell me you're so clever – well, time'll show.'

As long as she'd been at the Hall, Hannah had taken every oportunity to go to the quay. Not to Netherton's Yard, she couldn't disobey her aunt as flagrantly as that, and even the public quay had been spoilt for her by the warnings about why girls hung around there. Her vantage point had been the wall at the top of Quay Hill, and here she'd spent many hours looking down on the activity below, watching the ships come in, watching cargoes being loaded. And always she'd been alone, for ships held no attraction for either of the Thurlston girls.

She knew that Kath would be delighted with the news she carried to the gatehouse. But Beatrice? The only one of them to be left behind, how would she react? Lately Kath's interest had been centered on a young man named Richard Slade, an apprentice cabinet maker. For both of them it was first love and for weeks he'd filled her mind to the exclusion of all else.

This evening before dinner Hannah hurried to the gatehouse, excited to bear the tidings of her aunt's change of heart.

'You'd better come inside, if you can find an inch to put yourself,' Sarah said as she opened the door to her knock. 'Two of them courting and still all underfoot!'

'Not for much longer, Mrs Thurlston,' Hannah laughed. 'This time next month Algy will be a married man.' For he and Sylvia had found a cottage to rent, one of a terrace a mile or so away and, at last, they had collected together enough for the start of their home.

'And that's not all!' Kath heard the remark. She was over the moon with excitement, her words tumbling out almost before Hannah was in the room. 'I wanted to come up to the Hall to tell you but Pa said I wasn't to, it wasn't the thing. You must have known I wanted to see you!'

'Tell me what?' But she hardly need ask, one look at Kath and Richard told her – and one look at Beatrice too, standing apart from the others, her face a mask, giving nothing away.

'About me and Richard! We're to be married too. He's asked Pa.'

In the confusion of congratulations and well-wishing no one took any notice of Harold's mutterings. 'Hardly more

100

than children. Be promised, all well and good, but wait a year or two for marriage, that's what I say.'

The little room was alive with the buzz of voices. A large stone jar of Sarah's parsnip wine stood on the dresser. It seemed Hannah had arrived at the moment of celebration.

'There's a house in Merchant Place, quite near Mr Coleridge's where Richard works. One of his mates lives there but he's moving out in the summer. It's a rent we could afford, Hannah. We could make a nice home of it to start off with.' Kath was deaf to her father's mutterings. He'd given his consent so the rest would fall into place naturally. She'd always been able to wheedle him any way she wanted.

In the midst of all the excitement Hannah's own news made but a small ripple. But the only reaction she'd worried about was Beatrice's, and her expression remained inscrutable.

'You'll be wanting your meal and I must go,' Hannah said when she'd finished her parsnip wine. 'Walk back with me, Bea?'

'Don't you be long.' Harold was determined that one person at least should obey him. 'Five minutes, no more. Your Ma will want a hand.'

'Well?' Hannah asked as, instead of going back up the drive, they climbed the slope to the top of the garden.

'What do you mean? About Kath or about you?'

'Both, I suppose.'

'It's right that you should be part of the business. If you'd been a boy you would have gone there before this, everyone would have expected it.'

'That's what I told Aunt Louise.'

'I'll miss you dreadfully – but you've hankered after it for ages, I've known that.'

'And Kath? Are you glad about that? Or do you think like your father does that they're too young?'

101

Hannah watched. At mention of Kath, Beatrice's expression altered. As she'd talked of the yard, of Hannah hankering after it, she had looked woeful but now she didn't. When she answered her voice was hard.

'It wouldn't make any difference, she'd still do the same thing. She's changed, Hannah. Her thoughts are only for him. Oh, you've seen her, she hardly takes her eyes off him, seems to be willing him to look at her, and touch her. And he does, at every chance he does. He lusts after her and she loves it. It's revolting!'

'But, Beatrice, don't you think they'll be happy?'

Beatrice shrugged her shoulders. 'How would I know. She'll think she holds the world in her hands, I dare say, running around waiting on him, begging his favours. I wish . . . I wish . . .' It was clear she was upset.

'What do you wish? Just look at that sunset on the river, see how red the light is on the headland. You can almost believe a Fairy Godmother might appear to grant a wish on an evening like this.'

For a long time Beatrice was silent. Hannah thought she'd put her wish behind her whatever it might have been. Then: 'I wish I could be lifted right away, somewhere beyond that shaft of golden light. Not just me, you too, Hannah. Shall we shut our eyes and wish, just you and me?'

'Life is real, life is earnest,' Hannah quoted, words her father had read to her when she'd been too young to understand.

Beatrice turned her back on the view and started down the slope. 'Well,' she said, 'at any rate I shall get a bed to myself at last.

She said she minded neither Hannah going to work nor the prospect of Kath getting married. Yet inside her there was something that imprisoned her in unhappiness.

* * *

The next morning found Hannah at the quay and her life with a new purpose. She was to share a room with Albert Tyzack. The offices were on the upper floor, reached by a wooden stairway from the storage area. Alan Webster had the largest room, overlooking the wharf – Hannah had known that from her first visit when she'd heard him shouting at his son – and next to his was the smaller room where she and Albert were to work together. Years ago, when Ben Brooks had told her about the voyages the ships made, the cargoes they carried, she had thought Netherton's Yard the centre of the universe. And that morning as she hung her bonnet and cloak on the peg next to Albert's, she thought so still.

Never before had a woman worked at Netherton's. Alan saw no reason for one now either, but he kept his opinions to himself.

'"Queen Adelaide" to Valparaiso. Master and twenty two crew,' he said as he came into their room, passing written details of the voyage across the desk to Albert.

Hannah remembered what Kath had said about him. 'Looks a dry old stick.' And so he did. So he probably had even when he'd had youth on his side. His face was long, his mouth thin, his hair receding from a widow's peak. There was no smile as he came in, no 'Good morning'. At least, to Albert Tyzack there wasn't. Then he turned to Hannah, his mouth stretching into what he imagined would be construed as a smile.

'I trust Tyzack is seeing you are comfortable, Miss Hannah. Can you manage on that table?'

'Just "Hannah" will do me very well.'

'Indeed no. It wouldn't be correct.'

'Then I prefer Miss Ruddick. And I'm not here to be made comfortable, Mr Webster. I'm here to learn to be useful. And so I intend.'

'Quite, quite. Well, just see to it Miss Ruddick has everything she needs, Tyzack. Umph ... yes ...' A lad from the town would have presented no problem, but the guv'nor's niece seemed to have rendered him tongue-tied. For a moment more he hovered, undecided, then with a bow of his head in her direction he turned to go. But halfway through the door he looked back, the grimace he supposed passed for a smile so forced it was embarrassing to look at him. 'Don't let any of it worry you. If you find it too much . . . Well, let's just see how things go.'

She told herself that he meant it kindly, but the inference that being a girl she wouldn't be capable only made her more determined.

Albert chuckled as the door closed. 'Don't 'ee take any notice. Dare say he's frightened at the sight o' a pretty young lassie about the place. Now then, m'dear, jus' you draw your chair up over here 'long o' me and I'll show you how we set about stocking out a ship.'

So she had her first lesson. And for Hannah there was no looking back.

Not until he got home that evening did Alan Webster speak his mind. 'She may learn to do Tyzack's job, but we don't need her there. I don't like it, Emily. "I've no one but her", the old lady says, "teach her all she wants to know". We can do without a woman, it's a man's place to run the company. Given the chance Mrs Netherton might have been much the same herself as I recall, always there at one time. The gov'nor never let her meddle though. No place for a woman.'

'It'll be no more than a nine day's wonder. She'll soon miss her freedom. Don't worry your head, Alan. Now, tell me – what's she like? Is she comely?'

'Oh, aye, looks well enough. And she's nobody's fool, I could tell that. I suppose that's what bothers me, truth to tell. To you I don't mind saying it, although I'd not to anyone else, that's what it does, Em, it bothers me.'

'Then don't let it.' Emily Webster's mind worked faster

than her husband's. 'Looks well enough, you say. Handsome? Pretty?'

'Tall girl. Handsome I dare say you'd call her.'

Emily settled herself comfortably in her armchair and took up her sewing. The smile that played around the corners of her mouth was anything but forced and her brown eyes were laughing as she looked at Alan.

'Handsome, is she? And certainly with prospects, there's no question of that. Now, Alan, just you think about it. Isn't Tommy on his way home? And weren't you looking for something that would encourage him into the company?'

It took another moment for Alan to catch up with her reasoning, but when he did the smile that creased his thin face chased away his worried frown. That night he went to bed a happy man. For a week or two after that their faith in their plan held. Then it was dashed by a letter in Tommy's hand and posted in London. He had come to England, but not to Deremouth.

The same evening as Alan and Emily shaped their hopes for Tommy's future, Louise took up position by the window to watch for Hannah to get home. Not that she meant to let herself be seen looking out. She was ready to move back to the fireside at the first sign of the pony and trap.

'Hah! Here she is. Well, miss, we'll see what you think of being a worker. Not all excitement, you'll have found that out. Hah! To be seventeen, to have all the learning before you, ah, and all the living . . . Now, what's the girl up to? Little minx, keeping me waiting while she calls to see those Thurlston girls. I won't have it!' But she had no choice.

When, some twenty minutes later, Hannah arrived to find her aunt sitting beside the fire, there was no hint of how anxiously she'd watched the hours of the day drag by until this moment. Nothing in the old lady's manner suggested how many times she'd hobbled to the window.

'Well, miss, so it's time for you to come home already. And are you still intent on being a working girl?' Her eyes were bright as a bird's. She wasn't going to ask the details, but looking down at her Hannah had never been so conscious as now of what it must be like to sit alone and wait.

'Aunt Lou,' she dropped to her knees in front of Louise's chair, 'I know I'm only at the beginning, but I felt I was a part of it there. Oh, I wish you could have been there – '

'Lou. You called me Lou.'

'I'm sorry. Don't you like it?'

'Not been Lou since Charles died. Aunt Lou. Fancy that, now.'

'It must be because of the wharf, his wharf.'

'Well, get along, tell me how you did. Did you earn your passage? Did you make yourself useful to poor Tyzack?'

'I hope so. I tried to. He's a dear. We got along very well. I don't think he minded at all about me not being a boy.'

'Minded? Not for him – or any of them – to have objections. You're my niece aren't you! That's sufficient.'

'But even apart from my being your neice, Mr Tyzack was nice. We got on right from the start. That was what I liked, he didn't make a fuss of me because I live at the Hall.' From where she knelt she and Louise were level. Neither was a demonstrative person, but now her hand reached out and covered the ringed fingers. 'Aunt Lou, I *am* grateful, really I am. And you'll be glad I'm there, I promise.'

One of the sticks clattered to the ground. 'Hah! Silly child. Grateful! What nonsense. Just pick that cane up, then ring the bell. We'll take a glass of something before we go in to dinner. Grateful indeed. Such nonsense.' So

106

many things had been nonsense over the years. Even now her tone didn't alter.

Without a word Hannah picked up the cane. She'd come a long way to seeing what was behind that crotchety façade.

'We'll drink a toast, Aunt Lou, shall we, to Netherton's.'

'Hah!'

As the evening went on Hannah told her about her day. Each month on the third Thursday Alan Webster came to the Hall, gave his report on the business, put facts and figures in front of Louise. But this was different. In Hannah's words she almost heard the crack of the wind in the canvas as a sail was hoisted, the rattle of the wagon wheels on the wet cobblestones of the quay, the men calling to each other as they worked.

Much later, after Louise had been helped to bed by the ever-faithful Gladys, Hannah raked life back into the coals then took paper and pen from the writing desk.

'*Dear Dan,*' she wrote 'with so much to tell you I hardly know where to start . . .'

That was in April. By summer Algy and Sylvia had settled into their mid-terrace cottage in Lumley, Kath's thoughts were turned to the bottom drawer she was collecting, Richard using all his spare time making furniture, Hannah absorbing every new thing that would add to her understanding of Netherton's. Only Beatrice's days passed unchanged.

'Can't make that girl out,' Harold grumbled to Sarah as he tied his boots ready to set off for a day's work. This morning he needed to grumble about something. Nothing was the same since Algy had left home, and soon Kath would be off too. 'Can't wonder she doesn't find herself an admirer. She'd run a mile if a young man so much as smiled at her.'

'Well, you don't need to worry on that account, it's not likely one will,' Sarah snapped. 'About as sunny as a foggy November teatime.'

They were on dangerous ground. There were things they were both tempted to say but commonsense prevailed. She poured tea from the pot into his can then screwed the lid on. Starting work before eight in the morning he always took something to have at about eleven. Today it was a slab of bread pudding and, to wash it down, cold tea.

'Here,' she banged the can down in front of him, 'take your tea.'

Footsteps on the stairs. One of the girls was coming. They both turned to the door expectantly. When they snarled at each other as they did this morning they needed Kathy's sunny presence. The thought of so soon losing her had a good deal to do with their ill humour.

'Oh, it's you,' Sarah greeted Beatrice.

'I'm off then.' Harold opened the back door. 'Just see you help your mother, Beatrice. She's already got the copper going.'

And that was the start of the day. Not a good one.

Soon Kath had gone of to school and Hannah passed in the trap on her way to the wharf. Monday morning, steam pouring from the copper, the washboard ready in one zinc bath, next to it a second full of blue water to rinse the 'whites', the mangle pulled into the middle of the floor of the larder where it was housed. Monday morning, just the same as any other.

A knock on the door, and there was a postman with a letter.

'Get over to the garden and find your father,' Sarah said as she read. 'Tell him his old man's been taken ill. We've been sent for, and quickly too according to this. Tell him he must go and see Mrs Netherton. Family has to come first.'

'Will you have to stay there? How ill is he?'

'On his way I'd say from this. No good giving it to you, you'd not have the wit to read it. Just do as I say. Tell him I'm putting out things in a bag now and changing my dress ready. Hurry! The Exeter train goes about mid-day, we'll have no time to waste if we're to get that one.'

Louise set great store by Harold Thurlston. On hearing that he had trouble in the family she naturally helped, like the good mistress he thought her. She sent instructions to Higgins, her coachman, to get the carriage ready and Harold and Sarah were driven off in style in time for the mid-day train.

They found that old Mr Thurlston was, indeed, 'on his way' as Sarah had said. On Wednesday came news of his death. This time Algy found himself face to face with Louise.

'Of course you must all go,' she agreed to his request for time from work to attend the funeral on Friday.

'That's the funny thing, ma'am. This letter I've got here, Beatrice just brought it across to me to read, she couldn't get the gist of it ...' With a puzzled frown he brought it from his pocket. 'Do you think Pa's not put it clearly? Do you think he means what he says, or is it a mistake? See, ma'am, he says for me to bring Sylvia, and Kath is to come, but not a word about Beatrice. What do you think? He can't mean her not to come with us, can he?'

'What does she say?'

'Nothing. Just looked – that sort of tight look she's got. You know Beatrice.'

'No, I don't. I dare say he thinks one of you ought to stay at home to see to things. It doesn't give a man a better seat in heaven, you know, just because he has a crowd around his grave.'

Louise had never given much thought to the family at the gatehouse as the children had grown up, at least not until Hannah had come into the picture. Now, for the first time, she felt sympathy for the solemn-faced, round-shouldered slip of a girl, Beatrice. And for the first time she saw a side to Harold Thurlston's character she'd never suspected.

That evening Hannah arrived home later than usual. Louise knew she must have stopped at the gatehouse and was already half prepared for what she would hear. Beatrice was nervous at the thought of staying in the house alone, so Hannah intended to stay there with her while Kath and her parents were away.

'I'm sure the family expect her to go with them, but she says "no". Mr Thurlston wouldn't have meant her to stay at home alone, though. What do you think Aunt Lou?'

'Me? What would I know about it? If the girl thinks she's expected to stay at home, then I expect she's right.' And that was as far as Louise intended to be drawn.

Kath, Algy and Sylvia went on Thursday afternoon, so that evening Hannah moved in with Beatrice.

'I still think it's just a muddle. He probably just didn't make himself clear. After all, you're the eldest. You of all of them should be there.'

Beatrice didn't answer her straight away, didn't quite meet her eyes. There was a stillness about her that added emphasis to what she finally said.

'He was always beastly to me.' Her words fell into the quiet room. One quick, direct glance at Hannah then away again.

'Your grandfather? But why? How could he have been?'

'It's always been the same for me.' Beatrice's mouth trembled. 'It would have been better if I'd never been born – better for all of them, better for me. You don't know what it's like to have no one to care.' Still that faraway look, her chin high, two great tears rolling unheeded down her cheeks to her chin.

'Bea, don't talk like that. Of course people care. I care.' Hannah took the little hands in hers. Bea was obviously upset at what had happened but not for a moment did Hannah take her outburst seriously.

'You truly do, don't you? Promise me you do. You're my only friend.' By now her face was contorted with misery. Hannah was no stranger to tears, more than one night in those first months at the Hall they'd beaten her in the solitude of her bedroom. But tears should be something private, something to be fought against. Yet Beatrice didn't hide her face, didn't even turn it away or make any effort to regain control of herself.

'Wipe your eyes, Bea. Of course I care. You're my dearest friend.'

'You've got so much! Me, of course, you've got me. Then there's Kath, she's your friend too, and all the people you enjoy being with on the quay, there's your aunt, and that Mr Lowden. It's not like that for me.'

'Bea, you're upset today. Tomorrow you'll feel differently, when they come home.'

Beatrice shook her head. 'I'll never be one of them. I told you, Pa's father was always horrid to me, even when we were little. He used to give things to the others – "Here's a nice red apple, lad" to Algy, I remember he said one day in their garden. "Now I'll reach one down for you Kathy." I was standing there just by the tree and he pushed me out of the way. "Can't you find something to do?"' She almost choked. 'Not just him, all Pa's family. Ma hasn't any, not now. She did have but not now – because of me. That's why she hates me.' Hannah had never seen such despair.

Her arms were strong around her friend. 'Hush, Bea. How could it be because of you? You're imagining things. Do you remember her people? Were you there when they quarrelled?'

'Never saw them.' With Hannah's hand she wiped her tears. 'Didn't want me, Ma, Pa, none of them. Never have.

111

Sins of the fathers, that's what they say. And of the mothers. He isn't my father, you know.'

'Mr Thurlston? But, Bea – '

'I found out years ago. They don't know I heard, they've never told me. It was very late one night, I felt it was the middle of the night but that's because I'd been to sleep. I woke up to hear them quarrelling. Kath was sound asleep and I expect Algy was too, he never seemed to know any of it. I couldn't really understand but I knew they were hurting each other as much as they knew how. I must have been about six, perhaps seven. I didn't know what "bastard" meant, but I knew it was me. He seemed to spit his words at her. She did too. "Do you think I wanted her? Do you think this is what I planned for my life? Slaving in a hovel like this, turned out by my family. And you expect me to be grateful!" I can still hear her, each thing she shouted seemed to – to – stamp itself on me. Can you understand? Probably not, not even you, Hannah. No one can know . . .'

Only the last sentences stemmed Hannah's flow of pity, the consciously tragic expression of Beatrice's face. 'You were only young. You might have heard a row about – oh, I don't know, something quite different.'

'I told you what I heard.'

'But you might have misunderstood, Beatrice. Of course he's your father.'

'He isn't! Ma screamed at him: "You expect me to be grateful, to be here for your amusement, and I have to stand it – all because of her. Good kind Harold Thurlston made an honest woman of her, gave a home to her child." No, at the time I didn't know what it all meant, but I knew it was me, it was my fault. She said people whispered about the child, me, "a reminder of my sin" she said. I lay there in bed, frightened to breathe. I knew I was her sin, it was my fault she was unhappy. It was me they didn't want.'

112

Picturing the little girl Beatrice must have been, Hannah put her arms around her.

After a minute or so Bea pulled away and moved to the window. The glow of the evening sun emphasized the swollen, reddened eyelids in her white face. Unexpectedly she smiled, or made what Hannah supposed was a brave attempt at a smile. 'I feel new, different, just sharing it.' Her fluttering touch on Hannah's cheek was gentle. 'I'm a bastard.' She spoke the words clearly, almost proudly. 'There I've said it!' In sharing her secret the stigma of it seemed to be lessened. But more than that: she'd spoken of Hannah's other friends but she was sure that there wasn't one of them who'd shared a confidence such as this with her.

Suddenly Beatrice was happy, wildly happy. Not that she gave any sign of it, her smile was sad.

Until that night Hannah had never slept in the same bed as another person. How tiny Beatrice was, snuggling close as if she needed protection from life's hard knocks. Hannah wanted to shield her. But in fact within minutes she was asleep.

For a long while Beatrice still lay awake. She felt cleansed, she wanted the night to last forever, afraid that the wonder of what she so nearly understood would vanish like a rainbow with the brightening sky.

'Good, you've come. I'd been watching for you.' Kath's face beamed its welcome as she opened the front door of number eleven Merchant Place. Already the furniture was in place. Less than a week now and she'd be mistress of her own home.

'Wait a year or two' had been Harold's advice, but even when he'd said it no one had listened. Now that he'd brought his mother to live with them there was nowhere for her furniture, and she'd always been especially fond of

Kath, 'Sunshine' as she'd called her. So within months of receiving permission for her engagement, Kath had wheedled him into consenting to the marriage. In all her eighteen years he'd never denied her anything she'd really wanted, and now what she wanted was to be Mrs Richard Slade, mistress of this tiny terrace cottage with its door opening to the cobblestone pavement of Merchant Place.

'We don't need anything bigger, not for ages.' Proudly she preceded Hannah up the steep narrow flight of stairs that led off the front room. 'Even with a family we can manage for a while, we've got two rooms up here.' The top stair brought them to a door which opened on to the larger of the two then, through that, they went into another, hardly worthy of the name. This one was still empty. 'As soon as we're actually living here Richard can make a start on things for it.' And in her mind Kath already pictured the crib which would stand against the wall.

Hannah admired each thing she was shown; her pleasure came from watching Kath.

'I can't believe it, Hannah. We're so lucky.'

'You'll be really snug, Kath.'

'I know.' She folded her plump arms across the already matronly bosom. 'It's almost frightening to have been chosen to be so lucky. You know, Grandpa dying like that has been such a help to us – I don't mean to be unkind but if it had to happen, well, wasn't it just the right time? Grandma having to give up her home and go to live with Pa and Ma ... If that hadn't happened I wouldn't have had all these things.' And as she spoke she altered the position of one or two ornaments on the mantelpiece, trinkets that had been part of her grandparents' lives and now were hers, in her own home. And probably by this time next year there'd be a baby in that second room. Kath's happiness knew no bounds.

What had become of the eager girl always so ready for

fun, who'd looked on every outing as an adventure, whose dream lover turned her knees to jelly and made her toes curl? Walking back to the quay Hannah was conscious of a sense of loss.

But it was short-lived, pushed from her mind by the sight that confronted her as she hurried back along the public quay. 'Europa' was in! Dan was home! With the same unaffected excitement as ever she ran up the gangplank.

'Dan! she shouted and made for the ladder to go down to his cabin.

'Gone ashore, miss,' Mr Bailey told her, 'along to the yard. Gone to look for you, I expect – not often we tie up here and don't find you waiting ready for the gangway.'

'Thanks, Mr Bailey. I'll go and find him. Oh – and welcome home!' Then she was back on the wharf, through the gate into Netherton's yard and running towards the sheds.

'Dan! Dan! Are you up there, Dan?' Two steps at a time was no way for a young lady to climb the stairs. From the doorway of her room he watched her coming. Her greeting was the same bearlike hug that she'd given him for years. And then he held her at arms' length, looking at her. It was nine months since he'd seen her last, and in that time she'd come a long way.

'Well?' she laughed, conscious of his scrutiny.

'So, Hannah is a working girl.' While he'd waited for her he'd glanced at the papers she'd left on her desk, been impressed by the way she was tackling her job. 'I found a letter from you waiting in Oporto. You said Mr Tyzack was finishing. I suppose you're working on your own by now?'

'Yes. He's been gone about six weeks, he finished at the end of September. He was a dear, Dan, I do hope he's not fretting. See, this is what I've been doing, this is for the "Merry Monarch". She'll be at sea about one hundred and

115

twenty days, twenty six men on board. To start with, even for short trips, I did my sums, then did them again. Checked and re-checked. But it's getting easier.' Together they bent over her papers, both doing a little of that re-checking even now.

'I allow three-quarters of a gallon of water a day for each man, then I add three percent for emergencies. They take salt water soap in case the ration doesn't hold out for any reason but Mr Tyzack said three-quarters allows enough for drinking, cooking and washing. Unless, of course,' she added with a twinkle, 'the master over indulges himself. Give a man a basin and perhaps he'll go wild.'

Rather than use salt water they plugged the scuppers to collect rain; salt water gave rise to boils and other skin trouble. Twice a week a ration of lime juice was doled out, believed to alleviate this and to help prevent scurvy, loss of teeth, swollen legs, loss of hair, all the maladies thought to be brought about by cramped and poor conditions coupled with a monotonous diet.

Dan read her long list of stores to be put aboard:

> One half barrel of pork
> One half barrel salt pork
> One barrel of beef
> One half barrel salt beef
> One half barrel butter
> Half barrel dried peas
> One barrel and one half barrel of flour
> One barrel sugar
> One barrel coffee
> Quarter barrel Green Tea
> One keg rum
> Hard biscuits
> One barrel rice
> Half barrel lime juice

116

Four pans bread
3100 gallons fresh water
One barrel tar one-third full
One half bolt of canvas
One coil 1 inch rope
Ball canvas thread
One coil 2 inch rope
30 pairs boots – spare
One case of candles
10 pairs stockings – spare
Five waterproof coats – spare
Bandages

He turned the page. The list was comprehensive, he could think of nothing forgotten. By his side he was conscious of her waiting, standing like a child with her hands clasped behind her back, hoping for his approval.

'There's nothing I've forgotten is there, Dan? I'm sure I haven't – but I need to be more than sure. This is the first long voyage I've done alone, Mr Tyzack tried to look ahead before he went, to watch out for me as far as he could. Have I done all right, Dan?'

'I'd entrust "Europa" to you, Hannah. Does that show my faith? Yes, I'm proud of you, my Hannah.'

She coloured with pleasure. There could be no greater way of showing his faith than that. He would entrust 'Europa' to her. Her glowing cheeks had nothing to do with what he'd called her. As long as she'd known him he had inspired her, encouraged her dreams of ships and cargoes. What she had become was in a large part what he'd made of her. She beamed with gratification at his praise.

On this visit he was to be in Deremouth for three days and, as he always did, he stayed at the Hall. 'Europa' had wine to be off-loaded and ball clay to go aboard before the final leg of her journey home to Liverpool.

That evening after dinner Louise took her usual place by the hearth, indicating she expected Dan and Hannah to do the same.

'Draw up your chairs. Hah! A good many months since you've known the comfort of a fireside, Daniel. Now then, tell me, what do you make of Hannah, eh? That's what I want to hear. You've been to the yard, seen how she's shaping. So, tell me.'

'I have already told Hannah herself. You must be very proud of her, Mrs Netherton.'

'Just as long as she's earning her passage there.'

'You're doing that all right, aren't you, Hannah?' There was laughter in his voice. Louise had spoken as if she weren't even there. Not for the first time Dan poured oil on troubled waters, his tone more than his words restoring peace before it had quite been lost.

Louise seemed satisfied. The glance that rested on Hannah even held a suspicion of humour. 'So now we'll hear about you, young man. Nine months and more you've been away, and must have a story or two to bring home to us.'

Where was the difference between this evening and the many others when he'd stayed here? Hannah supposed it to stem from her; now that she was part of the business she felt involved with their talk of ships. That may have had something to do with it, at least as far as she and Louise were concerned.

But to Dan it was something more. His Hannah, the child he'd come to love, had grown up. She was the same, yet that very sameness only emphasized to him that something between them had changed. Or was the difference not in her but in him?

He'd arrived on Monday. By Thursday morning 'Europa' was loaded and ready to go out on high water. His days in Deremouth had been busy; they'd gone fast.

118

It was time for him to go aboard and, on the quayside, Hannah said goodbye to him just as she always did.

Her arms around him she touched her lips against his cheek. 'God bless you, Dan, and carry you safely.'

'God bless you, Hannah.' He dropped a light kiss on her brow. The same words each time they parted.

Then he went up the gangplank. At the top he turned to look at her. His Hannah grown to be a beautiful young woman, waving goodbye to him with the same trust, the same open friendship of the child who'd made of him her prop four years ago.

CHAPTER FIVE

Tommy had been in London for more than six months. Whatever he'd found in Australia, it hadn't been gold. But this time he'd made up his mind that he wouldn't let himself be seen as a failure. He wrote to his parents of the gay life he was leading in London; let Deremouth believe that he was frittering away his fortune.

In truth he'd arrived with little more behind him than Hannah had had in that purse of her mother's. He'd found himself a job with a silversmith, a room to live in. But for Tommy life was never dull. Money or no, he had no intention that it should be now. It was the week before Christmas when he found himself suddenly without work and with hardly more in his pocket than the price of a railway ticket to Deremouth. The reason for his sudden change of fortune was something between himself and the silversmiths.

To see him no one would have guessed his plight. Tommy faced the world with an air of assurance. He always had. Arriving at the station he walked straight to the quay, and came face to face with a tall girl, dressed in a tartan gown, no hat, no cape, and carrying a sheaf of papers in her hand. Now what could she be doing coming down the gangplank of a schooner that lay tied up? It was more than enough to arouse Tommy's interest.

He raised his hat, stood still and waited. It was obvious he meant her to stop and speak to him. What did surprise him was what she said.

'You're Mr Webster's son. I recognize you.' A statement, not a question. 'Your father's out, would you like to go in and wait for him?'

'Yes. I'm Tommy Webster. And you? You can't be a humper, nor yet a part of the cargo they've brought in. I know! You're a mermaid they picked up on the way.'

She laughed. 'I'm a humble worker. Hannah Ruddick is my name. It's my job to see none of the crew goes hungry or thirsty.'

'Are you telling me that Father is taking women on the staff?'

'I'm the only one. And I think the idea wasn't his own. It came from my aunt, Mrs Netherton.'

Just for a second he was lost for an answer. But his: 'Let's go inside and wait for Father, shall we? I'll come and hinder you until he gets back' sounded natural enough. It gave no hint of the way his mind was working.

So Tommy came home for Christmas, at least that was what he told his parents. Alan was no fool, but he'd learnt his lesson. This time he'd move slowly, let Tommy work things out for himself. So he did no more than let a casual sentence or two drop into the conversation: 'Miss Ruddick seems interested in the firm. And a good thing if she is, as the old lady says there's no one else to follow on' or, on another occasion, 'She gets on well with the staff. No easy thing for a woman to head a business, and the day'll come when I shan't be there. It's to be hoped when she takes a husband it'll be a man whose heart's in shipping. Bad thing else for the company and it'll be his in all but name.' He let fall these seeds, hoping the ground was fertile. And for good measure he added a plea to the Almighty as he made his nightly homage.

And which it was that tipped the scales he didn't question. Enough that on the 1st January 1856 Tommy sat at his side as he bowled along in the trap heading for the office on the quay.

Then came the day when he said: 'Isn't it your afternoon to go to the Hall, Father? I'd like to come too, I've not seen Mrs Netherton since I came home.'

'I say, yes! That's a grand idea. She's got a soft spot for you, m'boy, always has had. She'll like to think you've asked to meet her again.'

That was on the Third Thursday of February.

On the third Thursday of March Louise received Alan's report just as she did each month then, when the time came to dismiss him, she suggested: 'I'm not a nincompoop you know, Webster. I'm quite capable of reading your figures, and your report speaks for itself. Next time don't waste your afternoon riding out here, send young Tommy. It'd be a tonic to talk with the boy. Hah! A tonic! And my days are dull enough to need one.'

If Alan Webster's gaunt face could be said to lighten with pleasure it came near to it then. He set his pony at a brisk trot back down the hill to town, keen to pass the invitation on to Tommy. Nothing more, no added pressure, no suggestions of where it might lead. Just the message. But Tommy didn't wait the four weeks until the third Thursday of April, he found an excuse to ride out to the Hall before that. He took with him a paper that needed Louise's signature, and she was so delighted at his unexpected visit that she didn't point out Hannah could easily have brought it home with her in the evening. Then, once the paper was folded away, it took little to coax him into pulling a chair to the hearth. He settled comfortably, he made her laugh – a rare thing – with stories of the gold prospectors. When she told him to pull the bell cord for tea to be brought to them he didn't need twice asking. Galdys carried in the tray then was dismissed. Today Tommy would pour from the heavy silver tea pot.

A red letter day for Louise, and not a bad one for Tommy either. Back at the yard he whistled softly to himself as he took the stairs two at a time. Life was unexpectedly pleasant.

'You look busy.' He stopped at Hannah's half open door.

122

'Yes, I am. But not too busy if there's something you want me for.' Her tone was controlled, she knew it was, she knew the effort it took to keep it even, disciplined. Not for a second must he guess how her heart was thumping. 'Come in. Is it something you want me to do?'

'Ah,' he laughed softly, moving idly into the room, 'you could say that.'

'Yes?'

'Oh, nothing to do with the company. Put your pen down for five minutes, Hannah. There's more to life than equipping ships, you know.'

She laughed, doing as he said. 'You might not think so if you ran short of flour half way to Newfoundland.'

He sat down on the second chair, the one which had been hers until Bert Tyzack had vacated his desk. His lips turned upwards in the smile so characteristically his, the smile that fascinated her.

'I've been taking tea with your aunt.'

'Today? Surely it's not the usual day?'

'Her signature was needed. Then she kindly suggested I should stay for a while.'

'If Aunt Lou suggested you should stay it wasn't from kindness, be sure of that. She asked you because she wanted your company.'

'You and your Aunt Lou are very alike.' The way he said it, 'your Aunt Lou', seemed to make him one with them. 'Your Aunt Lou', not 'Mrs Netherton'. Hannah thought of her aunt's caustic tongue and wondered whether or not she was meant to take it as a compliment. 'But I didn't come in here to talk about elderly aunts, even though I enjoyed my hour with her.'

'I thought you said it wasn't about business.' And as if to protect herself she took up her pen.

'And neither is it. Hannah, in my pocket I have two tickets for an evening of sea songs at the Town Hall tomorrow. I wish you'd let me take you. We could go to the Charlton Supper Room first and I'd drive you safely home afterwards. What do you say? Will you come with me?'

Wild excitement surged through her. Her face gave no sign of it, only the tightening of her grip on the pen.

'I'd be delighted. I – ' But she checked herself. "I've never been to a concert before" was what she'd been about to say, but she had no intention of letting him know that. The beam of pleasure was something she couldn't hope to control, her dark blue eyes were alive with joy. It was a rare thing for Hannah to be tongue-tied. For weeks she'd dreamed of just such a moment as this and now that it had happened she was rendered speechless by the unexpected wonder of it. She felt gauche, quite unworthy of the attention of handsome and sophisticated Tommy.

He was used to girls being flattered by any sign of his interest, he'd come to know the tell-tale signs. Did his gingery eyes smile at her? Or did they laugh?

The next evening Alan walked home alone, leaving his pony and trap for his son. It was an uphill climb but he stepped out willingly enough for such a cause. Emily was watching for him, he knew from the movement of the lace curtain as he came through the gate to the short front path.

'Well?' She had the door open ready for him.

'Well enough,' he confirmed. 'I left them all ready to set out.'

It wasn't Alan's habit to kiss his wife in greeting but this was no ordinary evening. Hannah ('Miss Ruddick' for so long, but somehow since Tommy had been there she'd become 'Hannah') had looked like a child off to her first party.

'Mustn't push the boy, Em, but . . .' He said no more; he didn't need to. Their thoughts moved silently along the same path. Tommy, their dear Tommy, escorting Netherton's heir, escorting . . . courting . . .

'I've brought out a bottle of rhubarb wine,' Emily told him. Like him, she knew this was no ordinary evening.

Had Louise Netherton herself been Tommy's companion his behaviour couldn't have been more circumspect. Supper then the front row of the balcony of the Town Hall, a foot-tapping hour of music and the drive back to the Hall, keeping the pony trotting at a steady pace. Louise invited him inside to take a glass of wine. Invited? Ordered was nearer the truth.

'It was splendid, Aunt Lou.' Hannah's eyes still shone with excitement just to remember it all. 'Four men all dressed up like sailors, and Miss Miles from the drapery shop – do you remember her? – at the piano. We knew all the tunes, didn't we, Tommy! You'd have loved it, Aunt Lou.'

'I'm afraid, Mrs Netherton, you'd have found the stairs too much in that crowd. But, if there's another evening like it, I could get tickets for the front downstairs. Would you come with Hannah and me?'

Old Louise beamed. Hah! What a boy he was! Made her feel like a person again!

After he'd gone and the ever faithful Gladys had helped Louise to bed, Hannah went to the writing table.

'Dear Dan,
It's been such a day! I can't go to bed without telling someone – and that means you. Do you remember I wrote that Tommy Webster had come to work at the yard? He's learning his father's job, I suppose one day he'll take over. But that won't be for ages. Tommy is keen and very interested, though. Aunt Lou says it's because he's travelled the world, done lots of other things before he decided. You remember he went to seek his fortune in Australia. When he came back he was in London for months. He says fortunes are for spending! This evening he took me to a glorious

concert at the Town Hall, lots of songs, sea songs, I knew them all. We went out to supper first then he brought me home. You should have seen me!

We sat in the front row of the balcony! I didn't tell him it was my first concert – well, how could I when he's lived such a gay life? He would have thought me dreadfully dull wouldn't he?'

Dan found her letter waiting for him when he docked in Calcutta. '*The orchard is carpeted with daffodils*' he read, for she'd written it in March. By then it was July; daffodils would have given way to borders of pinks and lupins. In his imagination the noisy Calcutta waterside, alive with native dock workers, gave way to the gentle English countryside, the garden at Netherton Hall. And Hannah? Four months had passed since her début into Deremouth's night life.

On that sultry July day Dan felt a great sense of loss. He knew himself for a fool that he'd blindly believed 'his Hannah' would stay unchanged.

From Calcutta they would be sailing home. To write to her now would be no quicker than waiting to see her himself. Either way it must be months away. The apples would be gathered in, leaves blowing from the trees of that orchard where the daffodils had danced in the spring gales. He read the first part of her letter again, feeling her excitement. Even the bold uneven writing showed it. '*Tommy Webster . . . gay life . . .* ' Just let him hurt her! Dan bit hard on the stem of his pipe, cut off from her by time and distance.

Tommy was enjoying himself. There was his father, frightened to do more than drop the occasional hint; there was Hannah, too inexperienced to hide that innocent anticipation; there was old Mrs Netherton, openly revelling in his attention. He'd had plenty of girl friends. Hannah wasn't really his type. But, damn it all, any girl with her expectations was his type! Time was on his side. He meant to make haste slowly, keep her on her toes.

Here was something Hannah couldn't talk to anyone about. Certainly not to Beatrice, instinctively she knew that. Nor yet with Kath, Mrs Richard Slade, her mind full of turning herself into a 'good wife' and before long a 'good mother' too. Tommy Webster, swashbuckling, romantic, the sort that 'made her toes curl and her knees turn to jelly' had been a part of Kath's childhood. In those days it would have been easy to tell her about that first evening, and then as time went on about how he would put his head round the office door as he passed by, make some remark as he went on to his own room. The Kath of old would have understood exactly the disappointment that he hadn't lingered. But there were the other times, Kath would have wanted to hear about those too, when he'd come in, sit on that second chair, smile that special smile . . . From her Hannah would have had no secrets, not even the way her heart banged right into her throat when, occasionally, he'd let his hand rest for a moment on her shoulder as he moved behind her to the door on the way out, leaving her not knowing whether the brief contact excited him as much as it did her or whether he'd not so much as noticed what he did.

The months of summer passed and by August Alan was losing some of his certainty. It seemed to him that Tommy was no nearer paying serious court to Hannah. Often enough they could be heard together in her office and yet . . . Alan was puzzled. But then father and son were so different, he couldn't even begin to understand the workings of Tommy's mind; he had no knowledge of the game he played.

An occasional veiled hint, a word of encouragement, just enough to make her want more — Tommy was enjoying himself. Had it been solely ambition that spurred him on he would have wooed and won before this. Hannah was an enigma to him; he delighted in her mixture of aloofness, friendliness and, he suspected, passion waiting for a spark to ignite it. 'Handsome' Alan had said of her that first day. 'A pretty lassie' had been Bert Tyzack's opinion. Neither was the whole truth. The gawky child had developed into a tall woman, slim, with a confidence that Tommy saw as being a legacy from Netherton Hall. Yet she was no real beauty with her tip-tilted nose and generous mouth. Time enough to find the answer, the puzzle was pleasure in itself.

He was sure of her. The longer he held her at arms' length, kept her waiting, the keener she'd be.

It was a Saturday morning early in October. The humpers' day was in full swing when Hannah drove her trap along the wharf towards Netherton's yard. The water was low. On the public wharf men were rolling barrels of wine down the gangplank to the cobblestoned quay from 'Marie Louise' tied up during the night when the tide was up. The 'Hercules', a small brig that plied a regular service between Deremouth and Cardiff, was alongside.

''morning, Miss Ruddick,' the skipper shouted as Hannah passed by, certain of the ready answering smile.

'Hello, Mr Chedzey. Are you off again today?'

'Aye. Soon as there's the water.'

Tomorrow was Sunday, a day of rest. And that meant as much as possible, then a bit more, had to be squeezed into Saturday. Once inside Hannah went up the steps and along the passage to her room. Alan's door was shut. Tommy's door was shut. Everywhere was silent except for her tread on the bare boards of the floor. She knew they — by which she really meant Tommy — must hear that she'd arrived. With a smart click she shut her door behind her,

128

then took off her hat and coat and waited. Tommy always came to say good morning; even if it were one of his more distant days he'd put his head round the door.

Silence. Resolutely she pulled her papers across the desk and took up her pen. When she heard the wheels of the Websters' carriage she didn't let herself look out, he mustn't imagine she'd been listening for him! Instead she crossed to her door and opened it, then hurried back to take up her pen again.

'Ah, I see you're ahead of me this morning. Dear me, I've never arrived so late in all my years.' It was Alan who stopped by the open door.

'There's nothing wrong is there, Mr Webster?'

'No, no. Not wrong. By the evening post yesterday a letter arrived for Tommy – from London. It seems a friend of his – someone he stayed with when he was there last year, you know – is ill. Of course the boy felt he should go to see him, the poor fellow is alone, no family.'

'Of course he had to go.'

'It wasn't until this morning that I knew what the letter had brought. He had an engagement locally last evening, I'd retired before he came home. Visiting old friends, I believe.' He gave that smile that wasn't a smile. 'I said he should wait, try and make the journey in a day tomorrow. On Saturday his duty is to be here.'

'But if his friend had sent for him.'

'A cry for help, he called it.' Then, with a flash of inspiration; '"Tell Hannah what's happened", he said "Hannah will understand that I'm doing the right thing."'

'Indeed he is!'

After Alan left her she went back to her sums. A crew of twenty men to be at sea an estimated seventy days with enough food and water to allow for delays, enough medical supplies to allow for an epidemic of sickness. Flour, salt beef, potatoes, lamp oil, water . . . with a light heart she worked. 'Tell Hannah ... Hannah will understand.'

It was mid-day, the morning had melted. She saw the water had risen, 'Hercules' was already moving towards the mouth of the estuary on her way to Cardiff. But it wasn't 'Hercules' she was staring at, it was a ship she recognized at a glance. 'Europa' was home. Dan was home.

He was on deck. From the first sight of the quay he had been watching for her. And there she was, her arm waving furiously. Hannah, waiting for him just as she always did.

'Dan!' he heard her shout.

She hadn't changed. She was still 'his Hannah'. And the moment the gangplank was in position she was hurrying aboard, her hug as fierce as it always had been. Relief flooded through him. He was shaken by it and by the need he had to hold her.

'I knew today was special, I felt it in my bones,' she said, laughing. 'How long have you got, Dan? How many days?'

'No days at all, Hannah. I've only put in to see you. I can't keep my fellows from their homes while I enjoy myself.'

'No days? You mean – '

'A couple of crates have to be put off, but we'll be away on the tide.' Already the crates were being dragged up from the hold. 'Now tell me about you, Hannah. The last letter I had you'd been sampling Deremouth's night life. A concert.'

'That was ages ago, more than half a year. It's so hard to keep you up to date with the news when letters take so long. Kath's having a baby ever so soon now and you wouldn't even have heard she was expecting.'

'And the others? How's your aunt?'

'She's just the same. Tired of her stupid bones, you know.'

'And Beatrice? And young Webster, the fellow who took you to the concert?'

'Tommy's away today. He's in London.'

Dan was watching her closely but her expression told nothing.

'And have you been leading a very gay life since your evening at the concert?' He had to know, it mattered above all else. There could be few lonelier lives than that of a ship's master. The crew were knit together by shared experience, only the master was alone. Dan had told himself that his need of Hannah was born of that isolation. Of course he loved her, she'd been dear to him ever since she'd fled to the 'Prince Rupert' knowing he was a friend she could trust. He'd felt a personal pride in her development as the butterfly emerged from its chrysalis, he knew he'd been partly responsible for her interest in the trade of the company. It must be because he was cut off from female company that his thoughts turned so constantly to her. Now here she was, close by his side, just as warm in her welcome – her trust and her friendship hadn't altered. He wanted to reach out his hand to her, there were a thousand things he wanted to tell her. But he'd be gone on the tide. A wrong word, a move too quick, and there could be a barrier between them. She'd told him nothing more of Tommy. The evening out couldn't have been as important as he'd thought. For today, that had to be enough.

Hardly more than an hour later the gangplank was pulled back onboard and from the wharf she waved him goodbye.

Up Quay Hill, a turn to the right for a hundred yards or so along Waterloo Street, then one came to Merchant Place. Here the children from the cottages played, hopscotch, skipping, leap frog, vying with each other to see how long they could keep a top spinning as they whipped it along the street; and here, too, the women hung their washing, clothes lines stretching across the thoroughfare.

'You're coming along nicely, Mrs Slade dear,' Mrs Shackleford from number thirteen said as she pegged her husband's nightshirt next to Kath's sheet. 'Not much longer to wait now.'

'I've always been lucky. I'm never ill.' And, her washing securely anchored against the wind, Kath beamed at her neighbour. Her smile was as spontaneous as it always had been, but there was a solidness about her now that wasn't entirely due to pregnancy. She looked with satisfaction at the whiteness of the sheet – "Not like that Eva Burton's from number two. I'd be ashamed" – then turned to go indoors.

'Here, just a second. I wanted to ask you -- don't look now, but coming out of old Ada Syms' place, up there at the end of the street. Do you know who he is?'

Kath look puzzled. 'Yes. But whatever would he be doing calling on Mrs Syms? That's Tommy Webster. His father manages Netherton's.'

'That's just what I said to Harry last night. I've seen him about since he was a boy. Harry said I must be mistaken. I told him: "I'll ask Mrs Slade", I said, "she'll know. Right friendly she is with the girl from Netherton's." Well, come from the Hall yourself before you were married, isn't that so?'

'Have you seen him before, then?'

'Ah, over these last few weeks, since old Ada Syms' granddaughter moved in. You must 'a seen her. Harry hears the talk down at the 'Jolly Sailor' where the men from the boats go and he says she's no better than – ' she looked about her as if she wanted to make sure what she said couldn't be overheard; she'd not like young Mrs Slade to run away with the idea she played fast and loose with words like it – 'no better than a whore,' she whispered. 'Harry's heard that they all know her down on the quay where she waits for the boats. That's what I hear. True or not I couldn't swear but not the sort of person I'd want to know, if you understand me. Hush, here 'e comes, don't let 'im think we're talking about them.'

Without a glance at the women with their washing, not even at Eva Burton's dingy sheet, Tommy turned out of Merchant Place and back towards Quay Hill.

Gloria Shackleford picked up her tale where she'd put it down. ''Spose like all of them, he needs his creature comforts. He's keen, that I'll vouch. I've seen him of an evening, oh, five or six times lately. Coming up here sniffing after her, hardly waits till the door closes on old Mrs Syms. She goes off to the pub most nights, you'll have noticed.'

'Oh dear.' Kath's freckled face pucked with concern. 'Isn't it sad what dreadful lives some people lead? Nothing but drinking in the pubs or picking up with strangers. I said to Richard, "We're so lucky. A nice bright home, a baby nearly here . . ." '

'That's it, dear. Well, I tell you, it's a relief to me and Mr Shackleford to know what good neighbours we've got in you and your Mr Slade. And don't you forget, I'm always just through the wall. I've had three of my own. If you feel poorly or a bit down just you give me a knock, come in for a pot of tea and a chat. Any time, dear. Nothing like a bit of company.'

After that morning Kath watched for the comings and goings from the house at the end of the road. She didn't stray far from Merchant Place, usually not beyond the shops in Waterloo Street. Once or twice lately Hannah had taken her to the gatehouse in the trap, but she'd rather be here in her own home. Nice to see Ma and the others but . . . She felt guilty as she told Richard: 'There's always an atmosphere there. Grandma is a dear, well of course she is, look at the nice things she gave us, but she never seems to smile. Not at Ma at any rate, nor at Beatrice neither, but then she never did at her. Just Pa she fusses over. I feel like a stranger there, not comfortable.'

So looking out for the pretty, dark haired girl from the end house, and for Tommy Webster, became a game to her. And the next time Hannah came she told her: 'Mr Webster's son comes visiting along here.'

'Where to?'

'The end house, on the other side of the street. There's a girl there, people say she's a bad lot – a whore.'

Hannah walked to the window. Any excuse to keep her back towards Kath. 'People like to say the worst of anyone.' She spoke lightly enough, despite the effort it cost her.

'You know, Hannah, I used to expect you and Tommy Webster would fall in love. Remember all the nonsense we used to talk when we were young?'

'Oh, you poor old lady.' Hannah laughed. 'And when did you finish with being young?'

Kath chuckled. 'It is funny, isn't it? But I'm not the same, not a bit the same. Perhaps it's because of the baby coming. I feel so differently about things. Remember how we used to dream of romance – well, I did anyway, I'm not so sure about you. What a goose!' And again she laughed, her hand moving protectively over the bump that had changed her life.

'You'll be the same again, Kath, once you've got your body to yourself again.'

'Of course I shan't! How can anyone grow backwards? Do look at the time, I must get on. I'm going to make a cottage pie for our supper. I like to have everything ready for the table when Richard gets home. But, Hannah, the Syms girl – that's her name, Susie Syms – keep a watch out. I've heard that even before she came to live with old Ada Syms she used to hang around waiting for the boats to come in. Wouldn't you expect Mr Webster's son would aim a bit higher than a tart off the streets?'

134

Hannah pretended, even to Kath, that the gossip was of no importance. But she couldn't pretend to herself. To her love was a gentle thing. It had to do with memories of her childhood, her parents, the Aunt Lou she'd come only slowly to know; it had to do with Dan too, with the certain knowledge that come what may nothing would alter him, he would always listen and understand. It had to do with Beatrice – and with Kath. She wanted to believe that she and Tommy were building a love like that, like and yet different. Never before had she been *in* love. She felt longing for something un-named and out of reach; yearning she didn't understand; a need she hadn't known she had. All were alive in her and all were a part of what she felt for Tommy. At his smile she wanted to shout for joy, but if he passed her door without a glance she felt rejected. Never until now had anyone had the power to show her heaven or hell.

With determination she threw herself into her work, not just the job Bert Tyzack had taught her but the cargoes and voyages that were the pounds, shillings and pence of Netherton's. She watched for pretty Susie Syms on the quay, noticed how sometimes Tommy would speak to her, just a word or two in passing. Had it not been for what Kath had said she wouldn't have given it a thought. She was in the grip of so many emotions that were new to her and jealousy was one of them. Her body was awakened, those half-understood yearnings took shape. Susie was a whore Kath had said, a woman who earned her living by letting a man make love to her. To Hannah, Tommy's need of a prostitute was strangely exciting.

Just thirteen months after her wedding, Kath gave birth to a son, Timothy Harold. The three girls, Hannah, Beatrice and Kath, were together in the bedroom of number eleven Merchant Place. Sitting up in bed, comfortable against well-plumped pillows, the proud mother had all the appearance of one giving a royal audience. Unlike the other two, she was a wife, a good wife; and now she was a mother, she'd be a good mother. Her infant son gazed blankly towards the ceiling, sneezed, snorted, then nuzzled against her abundant breast. Like her, he had all he desired.

Beatrice moved nearer to her sister, pulled a chair close to her side, 'Ah,' she breathed, 'the little love. Oh, Kath, the little love.' Her hand gently cupped the tiny head that lay at her sister's breast.

Kath beamed. 'Ma says he looks like Algy did when he was born.'

'Algy?' Beatrice frowned. She wouldn't think of him as anything but as he was now, helpless and perfect. 'What nonsense.'

'Who wants to hold him? Which one first? You, Hannah?'

But it was Beatrice who took him, her small frame hunched over him as she rocked him in her arms.

'Fancy!' Hannah spoke her thoughts aloud, taking in the sight of the two sisters. 'Us with a baby.'

'Us, indeed! *Me*. You two don't know what you're missing.' Then, picking up her knitting, Kath settled to work. 'If you'll hold the baby, I'll be able to get on with this. I'm making socks for Richard.' There seemed no end to the attributes necessary to the making of a good wife. Kath was barely nineteen years old. Where was the girl who'd loved to hold up her skirts and run laughing across the moor?

Hannah walked to the window. Two grubby kneed boys were playing leapfrog outside, but then Merchant Place was never free of children, even as late as this with the lamps lit. Perhaps it was Kath's smug satisfaction, perhaps it was Beatrice's starry-eyed tenderness as she held the baby, that gave Hannah this hollow empty feeling. Or was it the November evening, the winter mist that swirled in from the sea?

'I ought to go.' She turned back to the others. 'It'll be late by the time I've been back to the quay to collect the trap and then driven home.'

Beatrice wouldn't be coming with her. Just as she had in the old days she would be sharing a bed with her sister, while Richard had been moved out to sleep as best he could on a couch in the tiny adjoining room. The Slades couldn't afford the luxury of a laying-in nurse, and Beatrice was glad. Kath and the baby were hers to care for.

"Don't come down to the door, Bea, it's cold out there.' Hannah wrapped her long fur cloak around her.

'No. I won't. I mustn't bring foggy air to the babe.'

The bedroom was warm, a bright fire burning in the grate. Outside the night was damp with mist. Every house sent a column of smoke from its chimney, the smell hung in the dank air.

It was at the end of Waterloo Street that she bumped into him, literally bumped into him as he turned the corner from Quay Hill.

'Hannah! What are you doing walking the streets alone at this time of evening?'

'I've just been visiting a friend.' Then, watching the effect her words would have on Tommy: 'She lives in Merchant Place, just down the street here.'

No effect at all.

'I'll walk back to the yard with you. I don't like you to be alone on the quay at night.' Her momentary fit of gloom was dispelled. And if her thoughts were anywhere in Merchant Place they weren't at number eleven, but at the end house where she was sure Susie must be waiting.

'I wouldn't want to take you out of your way if you were going somewhere.'

'I wasn't. My evening is free and I'll not think of you

going through that mêlée on your own. There's a ship just in from the east, it's no place for a young lady.'

'Then, if your evening is free, I have a better idea! Ride home with me. Take supper with Aunt Lou and me. She'd be delighted, I know.'

So battle commenced. It was a fair fight, she told herself. Susie was a prostitute, a plaything, not a girl to take seriously. Hannah pictured her waiting, watching – then probably finding company somewhere else, most likely down there on the quay where the brig had come in from the east. Yes, the fight was on. And tonight the score was in Hannah's favour.

The pony and trap collected, they drove up the hill out of town. The mist was no longer melancholy, heavy with smoke. Now the night smell and fog isolated them, the hazy pool of light from the lamp on the trap barely reaching as far as the sides of the lane. The sound of the wheels rattling on the uneven surface was muffled, unfamiliar, adding a magic of its own.

Just as Hannah had known she would be, Louise was delighted at the unexpected company, especially company in the shape of Tommy. Tonight she needed cheering. This was the third Thursday in November and this month's figures had been such that Alan had felt it was his responsibility to present them himself.

'Well, young man, I'm glad to see you. Missed your company this afternoon. Webster – your father – was full of gloom, concerned about the slump in trade.' She glowered from one of them to the other. 'You young people, always so sure of yourselves, what's the solution? Hah? Tell me that?'

'It's not just us, Mrs Netherton, it's the same with other shippers. I have heard it suggested – I dare say my father has put the proposition to you himself – we should join forces with other companies, pool our resources according to the voyages and freight, lay off some of the – '

'Netherton's! Indeed he suggested no such thing! He'd have had more sense than to voice the thought. We're an independent company, levy our own charges, make our own routes. The very idea! Other companies!'

'You know, Aunt Lou, it isn't as sudden as you're saying. The coastal trade has been steadily falling ever since I've known it,' Hannah said. 'The railway is quicker. And the railway is here to stay.'

'Quicker it may be, but dearer. You can't tell me the freight goes cheaper by rail.'

'No, it doesn't. It costs eighteen shillings and fourpence a ton from Deremouth to Paddington. We can take a ton of freight to London dock for ten shillings. But by sea the insurance is high. With the winter storms ahead it would be foolish to suppose that the next few months will be better than the last.'

'So, miss, are we supposed to sit back and watch the yard face ruination?'

'Not that, Mrs Netherton,' Tommy reassured her. He'd been looking forward to a pleasant evening here at the Hall, the old lady always made him welcome, enjoyed his tales, made no secret of that 'soft spot' his father said she had for him. 'This month we took a knock when we lost "Hunters' Moon" in Dover Strait.'

'There!' Louise beamed at her guest. 'What did I say! Didn't I know you'd been sent to bring me cheer?'

But it was Hannah who spoke. It seemed an evening of pleasantries wasn't what she was after. 'I've thought a lot about it, Aunt Lou, about what we can do to inject new life into the company. Times change. We shan't remain viable if we run the business forever on the lines Uncle Charles laid down half a century ago.'

'Change, you say? Webster said nothing to me of change.'

'Aunt Lou, I've been thinking about the "Oberon".'

'Ah, she'll add something to the coffers. As you say,

times change. You're right. I remember when your uncle had her built. She was the pride of his heart, was the "Oberon".'

'She needs some work. I've done drawings – not very good ones, I know – but if you sent her to Oliver and Hawkins to be re-furbished – '

'Back to the shipwright? Whatever nonsense will you think of next!'

'It's a much better idea than putting her under the hammer. Oh, I wish I could show you, I wish I had my sketches here! Aunt Lou, the cargo hold could be converted. We'd make it into cabin accommodation, a stateroom. We could have a new boiler built, a compound engine. Winds wouldn't dictate to us, we could run "Oberon" to a schedule whatever the weather – well, almost whatever the weather. We'd carry fuel enough to power us round the coast, or to the Continent. People take much less room than freight.'

'Passengers? You mean "Oberon" to carry passengers?'

'We have to be able to offer something the railway can't. Not everyone wants to be rocked and jolted on a dirty railway train. Soot, smuts, smoke. Who could possibly want that when they could be breathing in the pure sea air? Luxury! That has to be our selling point.'

'Passengers . . . engines . . .' Louise was out of her depth. 'Whoever heard of luxury on a ship? Haven't you read what they write about the conditions? An account in *The Times* only the other day – cabin passengers I'm talking about, not those poor immigrants huddled together not much better than cattle as they set out to find a new life.'

'But that's on the long voyages, the Atlantic crossings. I don't mean anything like that. This is where we'd be different. I *do* mean luxury, comfort, and we'd feed them well. I've been working it out. I've even talked to Mr Hawkins when he was in the yard.'

'You have, miss, have you! Hah! And you, Tommy, I

suppose you're behind all this? You'll have seen her drawings. What's your opinion of m'lady here's high flown ideas?'

'I've not seen the drawings. I had no idea Hannah was considering it. But, Mrs Netherton, it's something I've had in mind myself. Not with "Oberon", I can't claim to have thought of adapting her for our purpose, but certainly the idea of a passenger service. If you would give us your blessing to work on it, to give concrete form to our ideas and lay them before you, I believe you'd not regret it.' He looked at Hannah, the corners of his lips turning up into a smile. 'I think we see it as a way forward, to make the future secure.'

Hannah couldn't hold his gaze. She felt everyone must know how her heart was racing. Certainly, looking from one to the other, Louise thought: "Hah! So that's the way the wind blows. Well, and if it is, it's nothing to grieve over. A way to the future, the boy says. Their future. Netherton's future. No, nothing to grieve over."

'Do your sums then, the pair of you. And, Webster – your father, Tommy – he has enough on his plate to worry about. This is something for the three of us for the time being. I'm not promising I'll give it my blessing – but we'll see, ah, we'll see. Way to the future, you say. Hah!' Louise's spirits were raised. They still looked to her for her support, these young people. Even her silly blessed bones couldn't spoil this evening. And when Tommy left it was she who said: 'Just see to it that you come again, Tommy, come often. I'll not be left out of your plans. Bring your drawings; bring your figures. We'll have some fine evenings wrestling with this. Arrange it with Hannah. Take supper here again – and soon.'

'I shall look forward to it, Mrs Netherton. Your interest means a great deal – to both of us.'

CHAPTER SIX

'Netherton's has always carried freight.' Instinctively Alan suspected change. He'd become used to the idea of a steam driven paddle wheel – many of their boats came in and out of harbour under steam – but screw propellor was new to Netherton's, and therefore not to be trusted. And as for pandering to the comforts of passengers . . . words failed him. 'I don't like it, Em. And they're going right over my head with their plans. The old lady is worse than the young one, hardly spares the time to glance at my report. "Oberon" this, "Oberon" that. I tell you, Em, I don't like it.'

'Then, Alan my dear, you *should* like it. Isn't it more than we ever dared to hope for our boy? Three evenings this week he's had supper at the Hall – and not just this week either, all the winter he's been visiting. By now he's no stranger to the way they live there. Of course you should like it, Alan! And you tell me you believe Hannah is taken with him – it doesn't surprise me, she's not the first – I just wish he'd bring her home, let us start to know her as his sweetheart. But you'll see, he will. Be sure of that. And you quibble over whether the old lady bothers with your report!'

Over Tommy's future Alan was as confident as his wife. It wasn't that that gave him his misgivings. It was something in Tommy's attitude. Even now, with no hint of a betrothal, he was no longer the apprentice learning to step into his father's shoes. A frequent and welcome visitor at the Hall, the future he seemed set for had nothing to do with being his father's son.

Those winter months found Kath with less time to

watch the comings and goings at the house at the end of the road. With her thoughts full of the miracle of her tiny son she no longer wondered how often Tommy visited. Now it was Beatrice who noticed. She watched for him at the Hall and she watched for him in Merchant Place.

Coming home in the early darkness of a March evening Hannah recognized the little figure toiling up the steep slope out of town.

'Whoa, there.' She drew in the reins as she came alongside. 'Climb up, Bea. Why didn't you come to the yard and meet me? Fancy attempting to walk in the dark when you know I bring the trap about this time.'

'I know you do, but you might not have wanted me. You so often have that man with you.'

'Tommy.' Even saying his name gave her pleasure. 'He's working on the plans for the "Oberon" with me, I told you. Aunt Lou likes to hear all about it.'

Beatrice climbed up into the trap. It seemed to Hannah she sat as far away as she could, her cape pulled tightly around her. 'I've spent the whole day at Kath's.' It was evident she wasn't going to talk about Tommy. 'Richard didn't come home for his dinner, she'd made him up a box of food. It was just us and little Timothy.' Quite clearly that was the way she liked it.

'You enjoyed yourself.' It wasn't a question.

'Hannah, I wish we could make time stand still. I thought that today. Little Timmy will grow up to be like those boys out there in the street, dirty hands, grazed knees . . .' They drove on, the only sound the wooden wheels on the stoney lane. 'Does he tell you about his sweetheart?'

'Does who? What sweetheart?'

'Then you don't know! That man you bring home, Tommy Webster. There's a girl living near Kath, as pretty as a picture she is. They say she goes with lots of men, but she doesn't look like that. She's beautiful.'

'Kath told me – about Tommy and her. Yes, I've seen

her, she's lovely.' Hannah's voice was calm, hardly interested at all.

Beatrice didn't actually change her position, yet Hannah
felt her relax, it was as if she'd come closer. 'You mean he
doesn't pretend to you that he's in love with you? I've been
worried about you, Hannah. He's here so often, yet time
and again I've seen him at Merchant Place. I was frightened
he was turning your head, using you . . . Men! There's
Kath slaving after Richard, scrimping and making do on
what he brings home yet trying to make the place like a
palace just so that he'll be pleased.' Beatrice's quiet voice
was hard. 'And pretty Susie Syms making herself available,
letting herself be used to satisfy the lust of that Tommy
person – and others too I dare say from what Kath tells
me. Is that the only place for a woman, the only use?'

'Of course it isn't.'

Now Beatrice did slide along the seat nearer to her.
Again a long silence as they jogged along the rutted lane.

'Nearly home,' and this time Beatrice's tone was flat.
'It's been such a nice day away from it all. Ma carping, Pa
never coming home with a smile now that Kath and Algy
have gone – and the old lady sitting there like a spider in
the corner, never a word yet watching, not missing a thing,
and full of hate.'

'Bea, why don't you find yourself a job somewhere else,
get away from it?'

'I've told you before, Ma needs me. And, Hannah, if I
went away to work somewhere else when would I see you?
I'd have no one.'

They came to a halt outside the gatehouse.

'It was nice coming home together.' Beatrice leant
towards Hannah and kissed her cheek. 'I'm glad your
Tommy didn't come this evening. I was trying to get home
ahead of you, I didn't want to see you go by with him
while I was walking. I expect he's gone to Susie Syms.'

Hannah took up the reins. Ahead of her the lights of the

144

Hall sent welcoming shafts into the night, but they did nothing to lift her spirits. She was eighteen, she was in love, she was alone. Pretty Susie Syms. Was Beatrice right? Was he with pretty Susie Syms?

Yet in the morning she'd hardly had time to hang up her hat and cloak on the hook when he appeared in her doorway. It seemed today wasn't to be one of his 'distant' days. He pulled the second chair close to hers and settled for a visit that seemed to have nothing to do with 'Oberon'. And just as quickly as her spirits had been cast down so now they recovered; first love was leaving Hannah powerless.

It was on a morning towards the end of May, Alan and Tommy arrived at the yard to find Hannah just ahead of them. No sooner had Ambrose, the lad who took charge of the ponies and traps, closed the gate behind her than he had to open it to let them drive through.

She turned to them, waving a copy of the *Deremouth News.*

'Have you seen the paper?'

'Only the front page. Is there something special?' Alan climbed down to join her.

'Just look at the splash they've given us! This should get us off to a good start.' She'd written out the notice herself and taken it to the newspaper office. They'd promised to print it but no more than that. Only items of paramount importance were given the bold lettering she showed to Alan and Tommy.

Netherton Shipping Company announce that from the beginning of July the "Oberon" will make regular weekly trips between Deremouth and London, putting in at Weymouth and Dover en route. The "Oberon" is a clipper screw type boat re-furbished to carry twenty cabin passengers in luxury, in addition to steerage and deck accommodation. The very latest in comfort will be afforded in spacious staterooms. The day of the stage coach is over! The railway train may be fast but why suffer noise and dirt when a sea trip can be a pleasurable experience? A voyage is healthy, invigorating and, on the "Oberon", it is above all luxurious.

Passenger fare to London	Saloon 20 shillings
– ditto –	Steerage 12s.6d.
– ditto –	On deck 6s.

A limited amount of freight will also be carried and may be off-loaded or collected at Weymouth or Dover if required.

'There! What do you think of that?' From her tone, Hannah might have been producing a white rabbit from a hat.

'They've indeed been generous with their space,' Alan managed.

'I hope we can do as well in London – and Weymouth and Dover too,' Tommy said.

'The posters have arrived too to put around the town here. Where do you think they should go Tommy?' Her smile was warm. The 'Oberon' belonged to both of them.

Alan went inside and left them. He heard them come up the stairs together and go to Hannah's room. Never a cloud without a silver lining. As Em said, what did it matter if this business with passengers was over his head? This 'Oberon' nonsense was Tommy's gateway to the Hall. A silver lining to be sure.

Tommy took the posters from Hannah and went off to choose prominent positions for them about the town. By now Alan was engrossed in his work or he might have changed his mind, the cloud might have appeared to be ominously grey.

As so often, Susie was outside Netherton's gate. She

didn't speak as Tommy came from the yard; she gave no sign that she'd noticed him. Yet she knew that he meant her to follow, and he knew she'd come. It was nobody's business who she spent her time with and, as a rule, she cared nothing for what people said about her. 'Susie Syms is setting her cap at the gov'nor's son' the men might whisper now, and this time it did matter. She'd never felt like this before; gossip mustn't soil what was between her and Tommy.

'I waited for you,' he greeted her as she hurried up Quay Hill to join him. 'I hoped you'd follow.'

'You jolly well knew I would.'

'And if I did? What's wrong with that? I'd follow you. You could lead me anywhere your fancy took.'

'And where has my fancy got to take now? What are you up to, out in the town in the morning and not in those dusty old sheds?'

'I'm putting these up. See, Susie. I didn't want anyone else to do it, I wanted to be sure they went where I wanted.' He unrolled a notice to show her. 'How about sailing to London on the "Oberon", eh? How would you fancy that?'

She read the notice. Her schooling had been sparse, what she knew was self-taught. But she could read as well as the next, it wasn't in her nature to be left on the outside, not understanding. Writing was more of a problem, it was the spelling she could never be sure of. This morning though she had no difficulty in getting the gist of the notice and replied smartly enough: 'I'd fancy it fine, Tom – if I had the twenty shillings for my fare and the sort of clothes to make a lady of me.'

'You will have, Susie. You know, I could run that company standing on my head. One of these days you'll have the things you want. We'll go to London again soon, eh, like we did before?"

'Honest, Tom? Like a dream that weekend, wasn't it?

147

What about these notices then, where are you going to pin them up?'

Side by side they walked. A handsome pair, both so dark. Tommy was elegant, even foppish. Susie's dress was poor yet she wore it with an air that many a lady might have envied.

'All right for this evening, Susie?'

''Course it is.'

When he slipped his arm around her waist she leant closer to him. And when he moved it so that his fingers caressed the curve of her breast, she covered his hand with hers, holding it against her. Her eyes smiled into his, her lips pursed, hardly a movement at all yet it stirred his memory and his excitement. He was a fool, all his reason told him so. But with Susie so close he was deaf to reason.

All too soon the last poster was pinned up.

'I must get back to the yard,' he told her. 'Don't come with me.'

'Just to the open wharf, Tom.'

'No, not even there. I hate leaving you standing outside there.'

Her cheeks flushed with joy. Tommy cared about her, wanted her to be respected! Men flocked to Susie, they always had. But she didn't give a fig for any of them . . . just Tommy . . . only Tommy.

'Come early, Tom. I'll see Gran goes off to the Sailor. Come as soon as you can get away from the yard. I'll cook your supper. Like last night, Tom,' she jogged his memory, as if it needed jogging.

They were just behind the railway station. An alleyway ran between the building and the back of sheds used for smoking fish. First he looked around making sure no one was about, then he steered her into the passageway. Morning or evening, it was all one to Susie. As he put his arms around her she pressed close against him. He felt her soft body moving, tempting him, pushing everything else from his mind. Her mouth opened to his kisses, her tongue teased.

'Susie, what you do to me . . .' And her fingers ran down his spine, her hand moving to his groin then caressing the evidence of just what she did to him, her own excitement keeping pace with his. Eleven o'clock in the morning! Somewhere across Station Approach a fish seller with his barrow shouted his wares. A dog barked. Her breath was warm. How could he wait until this evening?

'You gotta go to work, Tom.' Her mouth moved against his as she mumbled the words, her voice soft, the dialect endearing.

'. . . umph . . . what I could do to you . . .'

''s evening. Come as soon as you can, Tom.' Between each sentence her lips, pursed and open, moved on his, warm and damp. 'Straight from the yard. I'll wait for you at the top of the hill, where you waited for me 's morning. Then we'll go back to my place.' Her tongue teased in a final caress. 'I'll feed you.'

'And I'll feed you.' Closer and closer he pressed himself against her. 'I'll feed you,' through clenched teeth, 'Now, this minute I could feed you.'

'Gotta go to work, Tom. Dunno what ol' Gran'd say if I took you back now.' Her chuckle was tender. 'Come on, Tom, we'll make it worth the wait.'

'Damn and blast that bloody wharf! I wouldn't care if I never saw another ship.'

Not so easily could Tommy put his feet on the ground, nor get his passion under control. He watched Susie go then turned back to the wharf. Once there he went straight to his room, shutting the door behind him and looking around him with distaste. At that moment he came nearer to saying farewell to ambition than he'd ever been. He sat at his desk, his eyes closed. Almost he could feel the warmth of her, hear her laugh so full of love. Dear, sweet Susie. He knew if he could bring her nothing but himself it

149

wouldn't alter her. It wasn't what he had she loved, it was what he was. He could give this charade up, find a job somewhere else, marry Susie. Pictures of the life they'd have together chased through his mind, the sort of place they'd live in, the sort of people who would accept his darling Susie. Was that what he wanted? Yet could he face life without her? Tonight. He'd be with her tonight.

A door slammed. Hannah's. He drew a sheath of papers towards him, making a pretence at working. He heard her footsteps, running along the corridor. She must have heard him come back. The footsteps ran straight past his door, racing down the stairs and out on to the quay. His curiosity got the better of him, it even got the better of that burning need in him that had driven him to seek the solitude of his own office. As he went to his window he heard her steps still running away from the sheds and towards the public wharf.

A gangplank was being put ashore while she waited. He could almost feel her impatience as she stood there, waving to someone on deck.

Tommy had been so sure that time was on his side, but what he saw now brought his confidence to an end. Hannah didn't even seem aware of the crew all working furiously to bring the crates marked 'Deremouth' from the hold. She noticed no one but Dan as she hurled herself at him and was taken into his embrace.

'Europa' had come in as soon as the flowing tide had given enough depth to the estuary. The crew had been away from home since November, too long to have any interest in Deremouth when Liverpool was so near. They grudged even the time it took the humpers from the dock to carry off the crates.

In his cabin Dan attended to the paper work while Hannah perched on the edge of his bunk watching him.

'I can't believe it!' To think that he'd been out there on the channel, coming closer, and she'd not known, not even

150

had a suspicion that there was something extra special about the day. This morning her mind had been too taken up with the notice in the newspaper for her even to look out of the window. 'Every other time you've come, I've known. For days before you got here, I'd always watched on every tide. And now you're home, and I can't believe it.' She hadn't changed. His Hannah. 'Aunt Lou will be so pleased. You'll find a difference in her, Dan, even I see it and I'm with her all the time. Her "blessed bones" keep her anchored to her chair more and more.'

'This trip I must get away before the tide ebbs. Some of the men have wives and children waiting in Liverpool — watching each tide,' he repeated her expression.

Her disappointment was plain to see.

'I shan't be going back to sea for a while, Hannah, not for some weeks. I thought . . . ?'

'Yes?'

Could she possibly be guessing how much was behind his suggestion? 'While I'm in England, I'd like to come to Deremouth for a while.'

'To stay at the Hall? Oh, Dan, that would be wonderful! I've such a lot to tell you, things I want you to share. I want you to have time to come to the yard with me. Dan, have you had letters from me? I never know whether they can reach you. We're adapting "Oberon" for passenger service. I want you to see her. She's my special baby — well, not just mine, Tommy's too. Aunt Lou is keen and interested, it's been so good for her to be a part of it. I want you to see what we're doing, Dan.'

'Tommy?' he queried — as if he didn't know.

'Tommy Webster. Don't you remember, I've told you all about him.'

'You wrote that he'd taken you to a concert.'

'Oh, that. That was ages ago. This is different. We've worked it all out together when he comes to the Hall. Dan, I want you to meet him.'

'And so I shall. Your aunt thinks very highly of his father, I know.'

Hannah laughed, but how hard it was to meet his eyes. 'Good, steady, reliable Mr Webster! Tommy's not a bit like his father.'

He raised his brows in silent enquiry.

'I don't mean he isn't reliable, but he's different. Mr Webster's a dry old stick – I remember that was the first thing Kath said about him, and so he is. Tommy's not a bit the same. But you'll see – '

There was a knock at the door. ''Tis all off, Mr Lowden, sir.'

'Right you are Mr Bailey, thank you.' Dan stood up, gathering together the papers. 'I must take these ashore.' Lifting the crates to terra firma was only half the job, delivery notices had to be handed over for signature. 'Another half hour and the water will be going down.'

'Leave them with me, Dan, I'll have them signed and post them on to you. Sometimes you can be held up a long time waiting for signatures.'

This was the new Hannah, assured in the business, knowing what had to be done and capable of doing it. Just for a moment the ghost of that child he'd first loved seemed to stand between them, seasickness and misery plain to see, her small chain purse held out to him as proof that she could fend for herself. For so long he'd thought of himself as her prop. When was it that he'd realized he couldn't stand without her?

'I'd be grateful, Hannah.'

Today, for the first time, their parting was strained. Always it had been so natural to put her arms around him, bid God to carry him safely. But somehow these last minutes had driven a wedge between them. She took the papers he passed to her, laid her hand on his arm and felt it covered with his.

'Come as soon as you can, Dan. I'll tell Aunt Lou.'

He promised he would, sent greetings to her aunt. Both were aware of the void between them and the knowledge of it made it impossible to overcome. Only as she turned to go did he take her hand for a moment in his and touch it lightly with his lips.

A quarter of an hour later 'Europa' cast off her moorings.

At the top of Quay Hill Susie waited. Tom was late this evening. She watched over the stone wall, craning her neck to see whether the sheds were still open at Netherton's. On the quay the humpers were still working, a sloop being loaded. 'Come on, Tom boy, I got your supper all cooked ready. Come on, let's have a good long evening. Gran be gone ages ago.' Ah, here was a trap coming! That must be the old lady's niece going home, she must have kept Tom late. 'Going home on her own this evening.' Susie smiled to herself. All very fine the family taking an interest in him and all he was planning for this 'Oberon' he was always going to the Hall to see about, but when he'd worked hard all day he deserved his evenings. The smile lingered. She knew just how Tom liked his evenings to be spent. She wasn't jealous of the time he gave to Netherton's. That was the way it had to be when a man meant to get on. But in a minute he'd be with her and he'd put all thought of work out of his head. 'Not a ship sails the water could come between Tom and me.' Once Miss Ruddick had gone he'd come hurrying up the hill.

Then she saw them. He had the reins, Hannah was by his side. Even then she expected the trap to stop. He'd hand the reins over and get out, Miss Ruddick must have given him a ride up the hill. Surely he hadn't got to report to the old lady again, not this evening. He'd been there once already this week and it was only Wednesday now. Surely he wouldn't tell her he couldn't come this evening

. . . Up the hill came pony and trap at a steady pace, not slowing. Susie moved forward, half lifted her arm to wave, to attract his attention. Then something stopped her. He'd seen her, she knew he had, yet he looked at her as though she were a stranger.

'The bitch!' Susie's dark eyes blazed with rage. 'The thieving bitch! Tom's mine.' There was a sick fluttering sensation inside her. She bit hard on her knuckles to steady her trembling mouth. 'You got money, you got fine clothes, you got all the things a girl needs to fight with. But he doesn't love you, don't you think he does. Tom . . . Tom . . .'

And on her own she walked home along Waterloo Street and Merchant Place. His supper was waiting, keeping warm over a pan of hot water. Two fried herrings. Not like they'd be giving him at the Hall. Two herrings – and so much more. All Susie had she gave to Tom.

It was past seven, shadows were starting to lengthen and the western sky taking on a rosy hue that promised a red sunset. The air was still, it was the moment before dusk when the world was hushed. No sound but the unhurried clip-clop of the pony's hoofs.

'Whoa, there.' Tommy drew in the reins. Hannah turned towards him. She hardly dared breathe. She knew why he'd stopped – and yet she was frightened to acknowledge what she believed lest she was wrong.

Afterwards she looked back and tried to re-live those seconds, but she could never be sure how it happened, who'd made the first move. His mouth was on hers, he seemed starved for love as he kissed her. In Hannah's whole world there was no one but them. All those half-understood longings hadn't prepared her for what she felt now. Every nerve in her screamed to be nearer, nearer. His hands were firm, gently leading her, drawing her . . .

'Hannah,' he mumbled. She could feel his mouth move

154

on hers as he said her name, again and again. Then: 'I want you so much. Say you love me. Tell me.'

'Yes, yes, yes.' She strained to be closer to him. 'Yes, Tommy, you know I do.' Where now was the calm, practical girl they knew at the yard? This new Hannah was greedy for his touch. There was no finesse in her response; like a young animal she was driven by instinct. Cupping her breast he could feel her nipple harden against his hand. His fingers caressed knowingly. Her teeth clenched; part sigh, part moan, Hannah was lost. Other women had known how to excite him, how to use their hands. Hannah knew nothing. She didn't try to curb her passion, neither did she know where it might lead.

The promise of it excited him. In his mind he stripped her, and not for the first time. He'd watched her, wondered about her, mentally he'd made love to her. But he'd seen her as a cool receptacle for his own passion, quiescent, tolerant, dutiful. Even this afternoon he'd been prepared to accept that, for the sake of everything else she'd bring into his life. Tommy was a healthy, physical young man; Hannah was begging for more than she realized. But his moment hadn't come. This time, when reason prodded, he listened.

'I can't live without you, Hannah. Promise you'll marry me. Whatever hurdles there may be – and God knows I've no right even to ask – '

'I'll marry you. Yes, yes, Tommy. It's all I want, all I'll ever want.'

'Put your hat straight, I can't approach your aunt asking for your hand with you like that,' he said with the smile she loved. He realized there might well be hurdles, the son of the plodding Webster asking the hand of the old lady's only heir.

But he was wrong. There was no doubt in her pleasure as Louise stomped across the room to plant a kiss on the

155

proferred cheek of her soon-to-be nephew, almost forgetting her 'silly bones' as she did it.

'If you're to be Hannah's choice for a husband then I'm delighted.' she beamed. 'Delighted!' How her life had changed! Not so many years ago the dreary Webster had made his monthly reports, the pounds, shillings and pence of the yard no more than a means of making sufficient income for her vast expenses. Now here she was with Hannah, her natural heir, wanting to wed a man whose life was wrapped up with the yard, with all Charles had done. And more than that, Tommy put a sparkle back into her life again, made her feel she was part of things with all these plans for 'Oberon', deferring to her, making her feel she mattered. No wonder she beamed her pleasure on them both.

They took their places at the table. Gladys carried the joint of lamb to the sideboard to carve, Lily carried in the dishes of vegetables.

'We'll have the meat on the table tonight, Gladys. No, no, not in front of me. Give it to Mr Tommy. Hah! Now then, young sir, if you're to be the man of the house, we'll see what sort of slices you can get off that.'

It was fortunate for Tommy that he watched and remembered. Often enough he'd seen the precise Alan carve a leg of lamb. Now he took up the carvers and earned himself yet another mark of approval.

Hannah rode high on a bubble of happiness. Soon she'd be his wife, Mrs Tommy Webster. Their lives stretched ahead of them, always interwoven with Netherton's. Tommy loved her. All these months her dreams had been half formed but always woven around him. Never had she dared go as far as this. Mrs Tommy Webster. His smile across the table sent her spirits soaring. 'I can't live without you', he'd told her. All this time he must have been loving her just as she had him. She couldn't keep her eyes off him.

Later, alone in her room, other images couldn't be held

156

off any longer. She'd have to tell Beatrice. She'd be hurt, feel herself rejected, not understanding that marrying Tommy wouldn't make any difference between Hannah and herself. 'If only she could fall in love.' Yet, even as Hannah thought it she was ashamed, for she knew it was for her own sake she wanted it, for the freedom that would come if Beatrice gave her heart to a man, someone who could share her life. But it wouldn't happen. Hannah didn't ask herself how she knew it but she was certain, for Beatrice there would be no man. There in the stillness of the night Hannah felt the burden of Beatrice's love. A friendship, begun in adolescence, that had known no barriers. She'd accepted it naturally, it had been part of growing up. She'd assumed that it would change, develop as they did, so that they'd stay close as time went on, in marriage, in motherhood. Perhaps she was worrying unnecessarily. After all, Beatrice had accepted Kath marrying Richard. She'd felt no jealousy when Timothy was born, only tenderness for him. There'd been no jealousy in Hannah's interest in Netherton's.

Then she remembered her very first letter from Dan. That had been something she couldn't share with Beatrice. And now Hannah's thoughts turned in another direction. Dan. Today he'd come home, and in her excitement she'd forgotten to tell Aunt Lou. Then, habit and shame combining to prompt her, she closed her eyes tightly in the darkness as she silently said: 'Thank you for taking care of Dan and bringing him home safely.' Even her thanksgiving went off in another direction. Tonight there was so much to say thank you for.

Beatrice leant against the five bar gate and gazed unseeingly towards the horizon.

'Beatrice? Aren't you going to say you hope I'll be happy?'

'As if I need to tell you that. You know I do.' Beatrice turned towards Hannah, her eyes swimming, her nose already pink in her thin, white face. 'Fancy asking me a question like that! He won't love you like I do. He'll never understand you like I do. How can he?' Again she turned away but not before Hannah saw how her hands trembled as she tried to wipe away her tears.

'Don't. Bea, love, don't cry.' Her arms reached out. How boney the narrow shoulders were under her hands. Then, without turning, Beatrice moved backwards, close to Hannah, pulled her hands downwards until she held them against the barely perceptible swelling of her breasts. Backwards and forwards she rocked and, by now, the silent crying had become more than she could control. Through clenched teeth she sobbed. Hannah felt a tear fall on her hand.

'Bea, Bea.' She pulled the tiny form into her arms, turning her round as she did so, holding her tearstained face against her shoulder. She couldn't bear to see such misery, such anguish. It was her fault. She'd let this come as a shock when she ought to have been honest with Bea before, told her she was in love with Tommy. She could have cushioned her against this hurt. One thought after another crowded in on her. Anything but the one she wouldn't acknowledge. Shock! Revulsion! Beatrice's action had brought back to her those moments in the trap last night with Tommy, the desperate longing that had consumed her as she'd held his hand against her, felt his fingers caress.

The shadow of Beatrice was the only cloud on the next days. Hannah visited Emily Webster, was welcomed and approved; she visited Kath and was clasped enthusiastically in her solid embrace; Ben Brooks waylaid the happy pair to tell Tommy he was a lucky young man and that 'they don't often come like Miss Hannah here, that they don't!'

She knew Beatrice was avoiding her. Always she'd waved as Hannah passed by in the morning, but not now; always, if she'd been in the garden when the pony and trap came up the lane in the evening, she would come to speak, but not now.

So it went on for a week.

'Beatrice was here all the morning,' Kath told her.

'Did she say anything about me and Tommy?' But was Kath even listening? As they talked she was cleaning her spoons and forks, rubbing them as if her life depended on their shine. 'Kath – did she?' Hannah prompted.

'Just that she hoped you'd be happy. Where's my shammy? Just see if I left it in that drawer behind you Hannah. I wanted to get these done before I give Timmy his feed.' Kath chattered happily as she polished. 'I hope he's good and starving, I feel ready to burst. Honestly, Hannah, some women have trouble in making enough to feed a babe. I've so much he really ought to have been twins! I look forward to him taking it.' As if to prove that she could provide with such munificence she puffed out her chest, and the buttons strained. 'I'll be glad when he wakes up ready. What were you saying? Oh, yes, Beatrice wasn't it? Yes, she hoped you'd be happy. But she's a funny stick, quite hang-dog sometimes. When I said how grand it was to think of you with a husband – perhaps this time next year with a baby well on the way – she gave me such a look. Silly, I know, but it was almost pitying. Beatrice pitying *me*, as if I'm some sort of a fool. Comes over here fast enough to fuss over Timothy. Hannah, I do wish she'd find herself a sweetheart. It's not much of a life for her at home. Never was, I suppose, not that I gave it much thought at the time. But I can see it now, and with Grandma there too.'

Timothy stirred, Kath became all mother, and Hannah went back to the yard.

Dan's stay was short after all. He arrived by train in the afternoon, taking a cab straight to the Hall. He left the next morning on the pretext of business to attend to in London. The visit had not gone as he'd hoped, but then he'd not expected to see Hannah with that emerald ring on her finger. But as their single evening together wore on, he knew he was grateful even for what was still left to him.

It was late, Louise's bedroom was already in darkness. Together Dan and Hannah sat outside on the verandah. The garden was heavy with the scent of honeysuckle.

'You're happy? Truly happy, my Hannah?' His voice was low. He heard himself say it. Out here in the stillness of the summer night alone with her he could no longer keep up the charade he'd played all the evening. 'My Hannah'. After this evening would he ever be as near to her again? Would he ever have the right to ask her if she was truly happy?

For her too the evening had been a strain. It hadn't been Tommy's fault. He'd been introduced to Dan and had treated him with all the deference he would any family friend he might meet here at Netherton Hall. Dan was a man some ten years his senior, and a friend of Mrs Netherton's. They'd talked of ships, of trade, of the 'Oberon'; Dan had told them of his last trip, and of his next. Yet all the while Hannah had felt he was a stranger.

Now, with those quietly spoken words, he'd come back to her. In the darkness she smiled, settled an inch further back in her seat, content to be where she was.

'Happy? For me and for Tommy, yes Dan, I truly am. We've worked together for months. Sometimes I've thought he – well, I've thought he liked me, you know. Then sometimes I wasn't sure. Then it all happened so

160

suddenly, the very day you came home,' she told him with childish honesty. 'There is just one thing, though.'

'Yes?'

'It's Beatrice. It's so easy to talk to you, Dan.' She took his hand in hers. 'I love Beatrice dearly and I feel – I'm ashamed that I can make her so miserable, know I'm making her miserable, yet I can't help it. If only she had something in her life, someone. There's Kath's baby, she adores him. But you see, even there she'll get hurt. He won't look to her, it'll be Kath. Beatrice needs to come first. And I've told you before what it's like for her at home.'

He was quiet, but she knew he listened.

'Poor Hannah,' he said at last. 'But it had to happen, either for you or for her. If you hadn't fallen in love with Tommy it would have been someone else.'

'She's so alone.'

'Once you're married she'll realize that she hasn't really lost you.'

'If only I could tell him everything.' But even to Dan there were some things she couldn't say.

His voice broke into her thoughts. 'If it were a man, loving you, losing you to Tommy, now that would be different.' There was something in his voice that told her more than he'd intended. Her hand gripped his. Poor Dan. Had that happened to him with someone? Had he loved some girl and lost her? How strange that she'd never known. She'd believed she'd known him so well all these years, had there been some niggling regret in his life that he'd kept from her?

'Dan?' She leant towards him, and reached for his other hand. In touching him she felt she'd understand what he was telling her. Then what he'd said took on another meaning. Was he telling her that things must be different for them once she was married?

'Dan, it won't make any difference between us, between you and me?'

'Come now, Hannah.' And here was the Dan who'd talked so brightly at the dinner table with Tommy. 'What use will a happily married woman have for a prop?'

'I'll always have need of you, Dan.'

'Of course I'm your friend. Come, it's time you were in bed. Do you still go to the yard as early?'

'More or less.' What had gone wrong? Dan was already standing, pulling her to her feet to go indoors. It was as if it meant nothing to him that probably they'd never talk quite like this again.

'Wait here,' he told her. 'I'll go in and fetch the lamp.'

'Not for me. I could walk anywhere here blindfold. Anyway, it's not even dark now we've been out here so long. I can see you clearly.'

And he could see her. The frightened child so determined to make a place for herself anywhere just so long as it was away from Deremouth; the eager, loving girl who'd never failed to run to him with open arms, who'd never hidden from him how she'd scanned the horizon for sight of his coming; the woman, still his friend, always his friend. Was it her fault he'd let himself make of her his guiding star? Was it her fault he'd let himself be knocked from the very foundation stones of his life at what she was doing? No, of course it wasn't. He'd always been a friend she could rely on, come what may. And so it must be.

'Hannah,' he raised her chin, trying to read her expression but seeing little more than the pale shape of her face, 'more than anything I want your happiness. If it lies with Tommy then he's a lucky man.'

'It won't alter things for us, Dan. What you said just now, about Beatrice ... if she'd been a man ... Dan, we're proper deep-down friends, you and me. We won't alter because of this, promise me.'

'I won't alter, my Hannah.' Gently he kissed her forehead.

'And you will still come here, just the same, just as often?'

'I told you, I won't alter.'

Her lips touched his cheek. This was their farewell. They'd see each other in the morning at breakfast, but this was their goodbye.

'God bless you,' he whispered.

'And you. Bless you and carry you safely, Dan.'

The wedding was planned for the first week in January. Louise had spent this third Thursday of November closeted with Alan and Tommy, for this time a message had been sent that father and son should bring the report together. The outcome of their interview was a substantial rise in Tommy's salary from the commencement of the New Year. Hannah's interest in Netherton's wouldn't lessen, at least not immediately. But her life would change, and who knows how soon there would be babies. Babies or no, Louise considered that once the girl had a husband, it was his place to pay for the home, to provide, to pay servants. So it was Tommy's wage she adjusted. His father would still be manager but Tommy was to be married to her niece, his must be the higher salary. That was the way Louise wanted it and she was ready to slap down any objection Alan might raise.

'It may seem to you a rum arrangement,' she told him, poised for battle, 'but I'll not be told what I may or may not do. Hah!'

She needn't have worried. Alan smiled his approval. Her terms set the seal of security on Tommy's future.

So she went a step further. 'Number four Vicary Terrace is to be let. It's part of Lord Hunter's estate, you know. Yesterday I took tea at the Vicarage, and met Clive Tozer there, he's Lord Hunter's agent. I could have seen to things then and there, but it's a man's place to arrange his own affairs so you're to meet him at number four in the morning, Tommy – ten o'clock, I told him – to sign the lease. It's a fine house, the age of this one or thereabouts, in the middle of the terrace. You'll know the terrace, fronting the sea, within sight of the estuary and Braggs Head? Well-built, good accommodation ... Well, you'll see for yourself in the morning. Ten o'clock sharp, mind. I'll say nothing to Hannah, and there's no need for you to either until you've got it settled. A woman likes to know her husband is the master. A woman like Hannah *needs* to know it. Fair and just a man should be, but always the master. Just see to it you remember that, Tommy. And see you're not late in the morning.'

Certainly there were larger houses on the outskirts of Deremouth, but those in Vicary Terrace were the most substantial in town. It would be an address to be proud of. And his new salary would be more than enough to pay their way. Silently Tommy laughed to himself. No extra responsibility for the work of the yard was to come his way. The bountiful payment could only be attributed to stud fees! And thinking of Hannah, those hidden depths to be discovered, no wonder he smiled.

The betrothal to Hannah had made one difference. He could no longer afford to be seen with Susie. But the evenings were dark, and no one in Tanner's Row knew the pretty girl with the black curls who'd moved into the middle house on the left. If the neighbours had worked on the quay they would have been just as keen to gossip as Gloria Shackleford had been in Merchant Place, but Tanner's Row was the other end of town, not frequented by seamen or humpers.

Weeks ago Kath had told Hannah: 'That girl has moved away, left town, I suppose. Not that Tommy would visit her now, of course.'

Now, waiting for him to arrive, Susie combed her thick hair, lifted a curl here, tweaked one into place there. She pinched colour into her cheeks. Then she stood back to survey the results, pulling the neck of her dress a little lower, smoothing the material over her trim waist. In the kitchen the clock on the mantelpiece struck the hour, eight o'clock. Any minute he'd be here. For a few precious hours he'd be hers.

Pride told her she ought to have rejected him. He was to marry the girl from the Hall, one day Netherton's would be his. But Hannah Ruddick could never love him like she did. To have even the crumbs of his life must be better than to have nothing.

'Anyway,' she said to the girl in the looking glass, 'marriage, respectability, all that – she can keep it. Tom's not like that. For all her fine clothes and la-di-da ways, what I got of 'im can't ever be hers, never, never. Reckon only me comes near to the real Tom. Hark, there's 'is step. Tom's come. Tom's here.'

He had no illusions about Susie. He knew what the men on the wharf had said about her, and he knew they were right. But it made no difference. He'd never considered marriage to her, but he couldn't imagine life without her.

Alone with her in the cottage in Tanner's Row, Tommy believed the world and all his ambitions well lost just for the hours they spent together. His life was divided into two; the roles he played sharply contrasted, yet each adding to the excitement of the other. Yesterday evening he'd taken dinner at the Hall. Few young men could have looked more elegant than he in his evening suit and frilled shirt; few could have been more attentive or more charming to their ladies. Today he'd come straight from the yard, here to this little home he rented for Susie. She was waiting, loving, generous Susie. She made no secret of her need for him yet she never clung.

They pulled the table near to the kitchen range. Like

every other man coming home from a day's work to Tanner's Row, Tommy took off his cravat and stiff collar (in truth for most of them stiff collars and cravats were for Sundays, a muffler sufficed during the week for most of them), then he opened the top button of his shirt. This was part of the role he played. To act like a working man cut him off from that other life. Together he and Susie ate the mutton stew she'd cooked slowly all day.

'This is good, Susie.' He pushed his plate towards her and she ladled a second helping from the saucepan.

'Dip your bread. There's lots of gravy.'

Just for a moment he thought of the thin slices of beef he'd eaten last evening, rare and succulent. 'Dip your bread' Susie told him. There was an earthiness, a crude reality about her; the food she gave him was generous, to be eaten with relish. And later . . . He dipped his bread. Tonight he wanted no finesse, no affectation. Yet Susie was a beautiful girl by any standard, perhaps the most beautiful he'd ever seen.

'Let's pull the couch to the fire,' she said when at last they had wiped their plates clean with their crusty bread.

He was disappointed. Was she telling him she couldn't let him make love to her this evening?

'You mean you – ?'

'I mean it's better by the fire.'

A quickening of excitement. The blinds were drawn, occasionally there was the sound of footsteps just outside as someone walked past, but that only added to the feeling of isolation. To Susie lovemaking was something to be enjoyed. Her appetite for it was as a glutton's for food. Put a piled plate in front of him and he'll eat every morsel, savour flavours familiar and unfamiliar. So with Susie. Her body was a gift for pleasure – her own and Tommy's. He transported her to realms of fantasy. Here in the humble, shabby kitchen she was a princess. The fireside rug was all any sumptuous satin couch could have been. Willingly,

166

eagerly, she responded to his touch. She was both seducer and seduced.

So quickly the evening went. The clock on the mantel-piece struck midnight, not with the mellow tone of the 'grandfather' that stood in the drawing room of Netherton Hall, but with a tinny ring. Like everything else here it was cheap and tawdry. The sound of it, the sight of the dying ashes in the range, the lingering smell of mutton stew, all these things brought Tommy back to reality. And ahead of him was a cold walk home.

'You gotta go, Tom,' Susie whispered, her face against his neck. 'I'd like to stay cuddled up like this all night.'

'Soon get cold.' But he made no move.

'I'll give the fire a rake.' She knelt back on her heels and took the poker to rake life into the coals. He watched her. Grandfather clock, cold night, what did any of these things matter? She was so lovely, so loving. 'Buck up, Tom,' she said as the coals flamed in response.

'Buck up, you say. You're enough to make any man buck up. Come back here, Susie.'

Her black eyes were alive with laughter. She held her lips to the proof that he had indeed bucked up.

'You're a wicked woman, you know that?'

'Reckon I am, Tom. But when I'm with you I don't feel wicked. I feel – dunno – pure, somehow. Silly, I s'pose.'

He leant forward and kissed her as she knelt there. His other life might not have existed. 'No, Susie. It's not silly. You are pure. You're wonderful.'

But it wasn't the same as saying 'I love you'. And she knew it.

Dan had promised to come to Deremouth to give Hannah away. That year Christmas came and went in the shadow of the wedding, planned to take place less than a fortnight after. There was only one thing that marred Hannah's happiness – Beatrice. No matter how Hannah tried to persuade her she refused to be Maid of Honour.

'I couldn't! I don't know how you can expect it! Walking up the aisle behind you, people staring while I watch you being taken away. I thought you understood me, but you don't. You don't know what it's like, I should feel ill . . . Ask Kath. She'd take your wreath of flowers from you, she wouldn't mind. I could stay and care for Timmy – try not to think what was happening.'

'No, if you won't do it I'll manage without.'

Beatrice turned away. It took so little to upset her in those weeks before the wedding; she cried for nothing.

There was one afternoon when she seemed calmer, at least she did when Hannah brought her to the Hall to help set out the wedding presents to be displayed in the library. It was the first of January, less than a week to wait now.

'A new year starting, and so many changes ahead.' Beatrice took Hannah's hand and held it to her cheek. Such tenderness Hannah felt for her; with that one gesture she'd re-kindled all they'd felt for each other. 'Perhaps you'll have a baby. Perhaps by the time we begin next year there'll be a little one. I love babies. I shall love yours. For us to love and care for.' As she'd talked her eyes had filled. The tears rolled unchecked, her voice croaked and her mouth trembled. Hannah took her in her arms.

'Bea. Dear, dear, Bea. Please don't cry, dearest.'

'I'm not "dearest", not any more.'

'That's not true. You'll always be my dearest friend, you know you will.'

'. . .nothing left . . . nothing to look forward to . . .'

'You'll meet someone you'll love – some man, I mean. You'll find all this happens for you too, Bea. I didn't understand until Tommy came.'

Louise's step in the hall made them draw apart, Hannah to open the door for her and Beatrice to stand with her back to it, fumbling with the arrangement of presents on the table.

'Well now, you two, what sort of job have you been making of all these gifts. Hah! People have done you proud, Hannah. You'll set a fine table with this silverware.'

Louise hardly glanced at Beatrice, much too engrossed in the generosity of her friends at her niece's marriage. And the girl soon rallied from her bout of weeping, until the next.

Hannah and Tommy were married on the first Saturday of January at eleven o'clock. The times of the tide had been taken into account. Those from the yard who didn't come inside the church at least wanted to be able to watch the couple come out. Low water was at mid-day.

They came early, in time to see Alan and Emily Webster arrive and, of course, old Mrs Netherton. Then there was a second group, standing a little apart outside the iron railings of the churchyard. These didn't come from Netherton's, these were seamen. Had they not been putting out again by the end of the afternoon they might have been in the Jolly Sailor instead of hanging around in this icy wind. But the skipper had no mercy on anyone arriving on board the worse for ale.

Dan was a good master. Most of his crew had sailed with him on many voyages, enough to know the welcome that always awaited him when he put in at Deremouth. The girl must have no relatives of her own for today 'Europa' wasn't here to take on a cargo; they'd broken their journey to Trieste so that Dan could lead her up the aisle. Some of these seamen had been with Dan on the night that Hannah had stowed away on 'Prince Rupert'. There were few confidences they didn't share. Yet today, whatever they thought, they said nothing as the carriage arrived and they watched Dan help the bride alight.

The organ rang out. The congregation rose. The bride had arrived.

The church was full of acquaintances of Louise's, employees, those who'd come from curiosity, townsfolk who'd enjoyed a gossip over the escapades of 'Young Webster', tradespeople who'd known Alan and Emily for years. Towards the back sat Harold and Sarah Thurlston, Kath and Richard; no sign of Beatrice. She must have stayed at home to look after Timothy. Hannah felt a sense of relief. She was glad Beatrice wasn't here to watch and listen.

Back at Netherton Hall they sat round the large dining table. For a moment Hannah caught Louise's glance, a silent message that said more than ever their spoken words could have. All around was the hum of conversation but their wordless message cut through it. The years they'd shared, good moments and bad, crowded in on them. It was a day full of emotion. There was so much Hannah wished she could say to her aunt – but she couldn't, and did it matter that she couldn't, was there any need? 'Hah!' she seemed to hear.

Seated next to her was Dan. 'Who giveth this woman to be married to this man?' He was acting a charade, and only he knew the effort it cost him. He talked to Emily on his right then across the table to the vicar.

Then there were the Websters. Alan was ill at ease to be sitting side by side with Mrs Netherton, trying to assume the manner of her social equal. Emily didn't feel comfortable in a gown that had been so wildly extravagant under any other circumstances she would have considered it a waste of good guineas, but for Tommy nothing was too much. She hardly knew old Mrs Netherton and what little she did know made her tongue-tied. No, the Websters weren't at ease – but they looked on Tommy with loving pride.

The bride and groom were to catch the 4.50 London

train; Dan was to sail even before that; the Vicar had a sermon to finish; Louise longed for the guests to be gone so that she could give up the battle and find what comfort she could in her fireside chair; Emily longed to unlace her new and expensive corset so essential to the line of the new and expensive gown. So as soon as the meal was over the party broke up.

As Hannah moved to go upstairs to change for her journey Dan stopped her. 'I'll have left by the time you come down,' he told her, his voice level and quiet. The charade was over. The tic in his cheek told her this parting was as important to him as it was to her. Did he realize how tightly he was gripping her hands?

'Hannah . . .' It wasn't like Dan to be lost for words. He kissed her forehead. 'Bless you.'

It must have been the emotion of the day that made her jaw ache so, her throat feel closed and tight. 'And carry you safely, Dan.'

Emily and Alan went ahead of Hannah and Tommy to the railway station. At Netherton Hall their farewells would have taken second place to Louise's; on the platform the moment would be theirs alone.

'Now then, young man.' In the hall Louise stood tall and regal despite her sticks as Hannah came down the stairs. 'Just you see to it that you give her a honeymoon to remember. You know the city, it's the child's first visit, so mind you make it a memory worth keeping.'

'Indeed I will, Aunt Lou.' It wasn't the first time she'd spoken to him on the same lines. There had been a day just before Christmas when she'd sent for him. Her sermon had been much the same then except, with the two of them alone, reinforced by a bag of sovereigns to cover his expenses. 'And not a word to a soul' – as if he needed telling! Today's parting words were no more than a reminder.

171

'As soon as we get back I'll come and see you, Aunt Lou.' Hannah put her hands on her aunt's shoulders.

'Think I can't manage on my own I suppose!' Louise sniffed. 'Miss your chatter and noise about the place. Hah! Might get a bit of peace and quiet!'

'Then just make the most of it,' Hannah teased. 'We'll be back a week today. Tell Gladys we'll be here for dinner.'

'No need, no need at all. I'll not have you make a burden of me.'

'Oh, Aunt Lou.' It was that word 'burden', it brought with it a backdrop of memories that pointed up the affection that had grown between them. Hannah's strong young arms hugged the old lady, almost knocking her off balance.

'Bless the child. You'll be having me make a fool of myself. Get along now. Take this husband of yours and – and – ' Then, for the first time in all these years, Louise planted a kiss on Hannah's cheek, a firm, loud kiss. 'Now take her away, Tommy, and mind she behaves herself.'

All day the wind had howled, blowing from the west. Had it been from any other quarter the clanging of the bell rung to call out the crew to man the lifeboat might have carried to the Hall. As it was they knew nothing of it as their carriage set off to take them to the station in the winter dusk. By the time they reached town it was dark, their train was almost due. The people who'd come to wave them off were standing in little groups, each independent of the other. Harold and Sarah; Phyllis Bentley (who'd looked on with pride as Hannah had walked up the aisle this morning wearing the gown she'd stitched) with her her sister; Emily. But where was Alan?

The thought was hardly formed in Hannah's mind when it was forgotten, pushed aside by what happened. From the shadows at the back of the platform rushed a small figure in a too-large grey cape and black bonnet. 'Hannah! I had to come – couldn't not come.' And Beatrice was there, hugging Hannah, caring nothing that all eyes were on her. 'Be happy, always be happy.' Tears, but this time they were a safety valve for the emotion that burned inside her. A great wave of relief surged through Hannah. Beatrice had come!

'Where's Father?' Tommy shouted to his mother above the noise of the in-coming train. Her reply was lost to them. She had to wait until the engine had hissed itself into relative silence, then while the porter was putting their mountain of luggage in the guard's van she told them: 'Didn't you hear the lifeboat bell? He's afraid it might be something coming to Netherton's gone on to the rocks. He's gone to see.'

Doors were being slammed, Tommy was waiting for her to climb aboard, but Hannah stood rooted to the spot. The lifeboat! Dan sailing about an hour ago. She must go and see, she must be sure the 'Europa' was safe.

'In you hop, Hannah,' Tommy prompted, and as if to endorse what he said, Emily planted a farewell kiss on her cheek.

'Here's Father now. He'll tell us.'

By now they were both in the compartment with 'Reserved' on it. 'What was the trouble?'

'Nothing, son. I was afraid I'd miss you.' Alan panted up to them. 'Only a bit of a mishap, all over now. The lifeboat didn't waste any time.'

Hands were shaken, hands were waved. Hannah leant out to ask him what boat it had been but the train started with a jolt and her: 'It wasn't "Europa"?' seemed to be thrown back at her. Alan's answering wave, his 'Good luck' and his smile – a smile that was indeed a smile – was answer enough. She moved aside to let Tommy lean out. His parents would wave to him until the train rounded the bend or was lost in the night.

So it was that she didn't see Susie. Like Beatrice she'd waited in the shadows. Now, as the train pulled away, she

173

ran forward and the light fell on her. Tommy watched her there, standing alone, apart from everyone else, in an island of light cast by the lantern. His lovely Susie. He leant out of the window until she was lost to view.

CHAPTER SEVEN

From Paddington their carriage, its back step piled high with their mountain of luggage, took them to a hotel near Piccadilly.

Hannah had travelled across London just once before, on that day she'd first come to Netherton Hall. Then it had been daylight, the pavements thronged with people, the thoroughfares crowded. Now it was late evening when she'd expected it to be quiet. Her eyes were bright with excitement as she looked out on the scene. Night or day, London throbbed with life. It was like a dream to be here. Mr and Mrs Tommy Webster! As the carriage bowled along she wanted to absorb every sight, to live each minute as it came. For in truth she couldn't honestly look ahead, to the hotel room and the hours alone in it together.

It was already late and they were shown to their room where a table had been set up ready near the fire and a light supper would be brought to them. A good beginning. She looked around her, wide-eyed with delight in all she saw.

'I suppose it must be different for you, Tommy, you've travelled so far and done so much. But this is – oh, it's so *grand*.'

He smiled indulgently, happy to take responsibility for the choice of hotel, for he had no intention of letting her know Louise had told him where they should stay.

'Nothing is too grand for you.' He smiled. He hadn't expected to feel like this. He'd gone into marriage with his eyes wide open – yet the memory of that figure on the railway platform haunted him. He looked across the table at Hannah and imagined Susie in her place. Just one

175

weekend he and Susie had had in London, not at a hotel like this but in a room near Paddington. Nothing about that weekend had been like this . . .

They ate their meal then he told her: 'Pull the bell, sweetheart, it's just beside you. We'll have them take these things away. Then no one will disturb us.'

She did as he said. Everything was new, strange and exciting. Just themselves, the door shutting out the rest of the world, the mysterious spices in the mulled wine he poured warming her throat. A wave of joy surged through her. Whatever the next hours brought to her, she was ready. She wanted only to be one with Tommy. Even from Kath she'd heard no details of the intimacies of wedlock, but Hannah was an intelligent girl. She might never have seen the male form but she'd had a child's natural curiosity when she'd looked at the coloured pictures in her mother's Bible and what she'd learnt there had been coupled with what she'd seen in the park when the sculptor had disregarded the figleaf. She had confidence enough to believe herself ready. And in that moment before the fire when Tommy kissed her, more than ready, willing and eager too.

But later she found he bore little resemblance to the modestly figleafed figure, nor yet to the naked statue in the park. As he caressed her, titillated her, she wanted each minute to last and yet she longed to rush on to the mystery of what would follow.

'Take that off.' And as he said it he was divesting himself of his dressing robe. Just for an instant he seemed a stranger to her, the naked body in no way connected with the Tommy she knew. In the long mirror she saw herself, tall in her silk nightgown, a high frilly neck, tight frilly cuffs, her hair hanging to her waist. If he was strange to her, so must she be to him. A ghost from the past nudged her. She heard the echo of Beatrice's voice one hot summer's day by the stream: 'I want you to know what I am.'

176

She pulled her nightgown over head and turned to him. In that moment she felt she gave herself. Nothing was secret. She held her hands towards him.

Then his voice broke the spell. 'I won't let it hurt more than it has to – but it always hurts the woman if it's the first time.'

He sensed her withdrawal, recognized his mistake. And in that second they were separated by their own thoughts. Yet those thoughts were both of a dark eyed girl. It wasn't the first time for him. Hannah remembered how Kath and Beatrice had watched him go visiting – and he remembered his lovely Susie. He'd not wanted to think of her tonight, not meant to let the ghost of her come between him and Hannah, standing here like a lamb brought to slaughter. He must re-kindle the fire he knew to be there. She was standing facing him, her hands to her sides now, waiting for a cue.

He pushed her back on to the bed. 'I'll be gentle.'

If only he hadn't said it. If only he had let nature be her guide. If what he did hurt her then she would have rejoiced in the agony of it. And yet there was no un-saying those fatal words: 'It always hurts.' She tried to push them from her mind.

Long after he slept she lay awake, wide-eyed. Delicately she touched the outline of her body: her breasts, her flat stomach, hips, groin, vagina. Somehow she'd expected a change. But there was none. She stretched, feet to the bottom of the bed, arms behind her head. Her disappointment had vanished. As he'd brought himself to a climax she'd known a moment of supreme awe that she could do this to him. So much that had been a mystery she could understand now. Still there were things she didn't know, things she wondered about in the darkness. Would it hurt as much next time? Perhaps tomorrow night he'd do the same thing again, what would it be like then? Somewhere outside a clock struck two. Everything was quiet except for Tommy's deep, even breathing. Gradually she drifted into sleep.

When she woke she could hear the rattle of wheels on the road, the sound of shovels scraping as the thoroughfare was cleaned for the day.

'Tommy?' she whispered. 'Are you awake?' And, as he moved towards her: 'Good morning. Our first good morning.'

Her voice had broken into his waking dream. He didn't answer her, at least not in words. Her shoulders were broad, her thighs strong. Hers wasn't the body he'd dreamt of, it wasn't the body he wanted, but it was his to take. A few hours before she'd wondered whether he'd do it again tomorrow night. She realized now how little she knew. Did he always wake like this? Or like her was he driven by the need for them to be one. She gripped him close, her hands on his buttocks, her nails digging into the flesh, her legs gripping him. She knew nothing of the art of love making, was driven just by the need to bind them together, one body, one spirit.

He was harsh, brutal – yet she believed his need was the same as her own. She couldn't guess at the anger he felt: at her, at himself, at the temptations he'd so willingly allowed to beguile him. Here in the luxury of the hotel suite his body found release. His heart was in a cottage in Tanner's Row.

'Give her a honeymoon to remember', Louise had told him and given him the wherewithal to do it. They went to the music hall, even to the opera; they strolled in the parks, took tea on a barge on the Thames.

'Tommy, you're spending a mint of money. We're having a lovely time, but you didn't dig gold out of the hills to let it slip away like this.' For she knew the wage he'd earned at Netherton's wouldn't rise to this week's entertainment.

'Fortunes aren't for hoarding.' He smiled. 'Where would you like to go today?'

'Could we go to see a play acted? I saw a poster downstairs about *School for Scandal*. But this morning I'd like to walk about again. In all the hustle and bustle I love it.'

A knock at the door and the maid appeared armed with cleaning material and a bucket of coals and tinder wood.

'Beg pardon, ma'am, I didn't know you were in. I'll come back presently to do the grate.'

'No, come in,' Tommy told her, 'get the fire going. It'll be warm then to come back to later. I'll go on down, Hannah, and see about this theatre. You get your bonnet on and I'll see you downstairs.'

Another day was starting, hours stretching ahead of them to be filled with pleasure seeking. Or so she thought. The maid spread newspapers on the hearthrug and knelt to her task, and it was a chance in a thousand that Hannah should look down. Or was it that the words sprang at her? 'Blaze' ... 'Europa' ... 'Lowden' ... 'five lost' ... She was on her knees, reading.

'Whatever's up, ma'am?' And well she might ask for Hannah was tearing the newspaper, taking half a sheet of it.

Down the stairs she ran, she must find Tommy! They must go home.

'Tommy! See, read this! It's Monday's paper, that's three days ago. We must go home this morning. See! It's Dan, the "Europa", there was a fire.'

He read the paper. 'That must have been where the lifeboat went.'

'But your father said it was nothing.'

'They got him off – see, it says Daniel Lowden and the remainder of his crew were brought ashore.'

'He's hurt. It says he's hurt. Tommy, I'm going to pack

our things. You see to things here, the bill I mean, and find out the times of the trains.'

He didn't argue. It was Thursday. The bag of sovereigns would still be half full even when the bill was paid. Hannah would be packing for a little while, he'd have time for a stroll. The shops were full of pretty things he'd like to take-home to Susie. He could imagine the excitement in her lovely eyes as she undid the boxes; she had so little. Last night at the opera he'd thought about her. All around him were ladies dressed with such opulence and not one of them could hold a candle to her. He couldn't buy her anything bulky. Hannah would want to know. 'What's in that box?' 'A fur wrap for my mist –' No, not his mistress, he couldn't think of her as that. 'For my lover, for my love.' He decided on scent, expensive scent, something she would never have had before. The corners of his mouth turned up in a secret smile as he carried it back to the hotel in his overcoat pocket; the smile deepened as he imagined her opening it, dabbing it on her delicate skin.

London with all its excitement, its noise and bustle; days of pleasure, nights of love. Eagerly Hannah climbed into the carriage that would take them to the station. She couldn't get to Deremouth fast enough.

Light streamed from the windows of Netherton Hall into the early evening dusk. Upstairs and down the lamps had been lit.

Beatrice saw the hansom turn in at the drive and opened the door of the gatehouse to call: 'Is something wrong? Why have you come home?' What could she be hoping?

'Stop a minute, will you?' Hannah told the driver, then waited while Beatrice came to the step of the cab. 'We only saw the newspaper this morning. What's happened to Dan, Beatrice, do you know?'

'I only hear bits of gossip.' Somehow Beatrice managed

180

to address herself just to Hannah, averting her eyes from Tommy as though he didn't exist. 'Mrs Netherton has had him brought from the hospital to the Hall, and there are visitors there. A lady with two boys, he must have asked for them to come, I expect. She's lovely, I don't know who she is but she is beautiful. He must have wanted her to look after him.' She felt she'd scored a point, made a dent in something between Hannah and Dan she'd never been able to probe.

'You'll get frozen out here with no cloak on, Bea. We must go and see Aunt Lou. Come to Vicary Terrace for lunch tomorrow, will you?'

'But it's still your honeymoon.'

'Nonsense.' And this time it was Tommy who answered her. 'I shall go to the yard for a while. You come and keep Hannah company. She's not used to being at home all day.'

Hannah laughed. 'She's not intending to get used to it, either. I've a job of work waiting. But come tomorrow, Bea. I shan't start back to work regularly until next week.'

'We'll have to think about that. Things must be different, you'll have new interests with a home to run.' And there in front of Beatrice Tommy made his next wrong move. Hannah wasn't the girl to be told where her interests must lie.

Despite the house being so brightly lit there was no sign of life as they went into the Hall. In the dining room the table was set for two; across the hall the drawing room was empty but the fire was piled high and flaring up the chimney.

'You have a glass of wine or something and read the newspaper, Tommy, while I go and see Aunt Lou. I expect she's still getting dressed.'

How far away that hotel suite seemed now, like another world. It was as if she'd never been away as she ran up the familiar stairs. Dan would be in his usual room – but there

181

was no sign of the lovely lady who'd come to look after him. She must see Aunt Lou, find out what was wrong with him, find out why Rosalind had come (for there was no doubt in Hannah's mind that that's who it must be, Rosalind, his brother's widow, with her two boys).

A light tap on her aunt's door.

'Who is it?' Then, seeing the answer to her enquiry: 'And what do you suppose you're doing back here?'

'What's happened to Dan? I only saw the newspaper this morning?'

'Running home from your honeymoon!' Her sharp eyes missed nothing, she gave Hannah a penetrating look. 'I'll not be fobbed off with stories. If something's not right I want to know about it.'

'Of course I couldn't stay gallivanting about in London, not knowing properly what had happened. Beatrice says he's here – and there's a visitor. Is it Rosalind?'

'Yes, Rosalind. That flipperty widow of poor Peter's. And her two boys. Hah! Good enough lads. Take after the Lowden side of the family, seem to have a bit of spunk about them.' She chuckled at something. 'That little one, Matthew, is a jolly young rascal. Stephen, ah well, you'll see them for yourself. Solemn he is – seems a bit of a namby-pamby but I shouldn't say it. Daniel has always spoken well of them both. No, not for me to judge.'

'Did you invite them? Did you send for Rosalind?'

'Fancy asking me such nonsense! As if I would! I wrote to Hilary, told him about "Europa", told him it's going to be a while before Daniel goes to sea again. To be honest when I went to the hospital to see him on Sunday morning I doubted if he ever would, lying there as if he'd already passed over. Had a crack on his head that knocked the senses out of him for twenty-four hours and more. That's when I wrote to Hilary. By Monday morning Daniel seemed to have decided he'd not done with life. Damaged both his legs, though. Bad job, the left one. The right is a clean break, they splinted it for him in the hospital. That'll mend. It's the left that's giving the concern, crushed when burning timbers fell on him. Much to be grateful for that he's here at all. They'd done what they could at the Infirmary and I had him brought here. A nurse has come to look after him. Wasn't going to have the boy left there. In his own room now. Hah! He'll mend quicker here, that's been his room since he was younger than little Matthew.' A glower at Hannah, just to make sure she wasn't giving the impression she was being sentimental. 'My duty to Charles to have him here. Charles thought a great deal of Daniel.'

'He'll be all right won't he, Aunt Lou!'

'I told you, Daniel's not done with living.'

'And Rosalind and the boys? When did they arrive?'

'Monday. Round about teatime. Great ringing on the doorbell – that young Matthew swinging on it I should think from the clamour of it – and there they were. They'd been to the Infirmary and been told he'd been brought here.'

'So now they're staying here, sleeping here?' The thought of two noisy boys at Netherton Hall took some accepting.

'Hah! And what else could I do? Tell me that. Poor, useless thing she is, not fit to be turned loose in Deremouth. Doubt she'd have the wit to find herself a bed. And there are the children to think of. Daniel sets great store on those boys.'

'So now I know why every room seems to have a lamp burning.'

'Extravagant nonsense! They'll have me in the workhouse! And there's you and that husband of yours wasting your time doing nothing. That won't put anything in the coffers. A houseful of visitors to be provided for!'

Hannah's wide smile was evidence that the old lady's grumbles had gone over her head. 'Two extra this evening,

Aunt Lou. But never mind that, it's Dan I want to know about, Dan and "Europa".'

'I've said – don't you listen? Daniel will mend though I don't mind owning it, I was frightened to see the state of that leg . . . flesh burnt from it, blood, bone . . . Dear Lord, I never thought to see a man in such a state. On the Sunday there was talk of taking it off. Nothing clean about what a burning mast can do to a man.'

'But they didn't. He's strong and healthy, Aunt Lou.'

'That's what Dr Roberts says. Nature is on his side.'

'And "Europa"? How did the fire start? Did they save her?'

'Never mind so many questions, child. Do something useful. See to the clasp of these pearls for me. And if I'm to waste time chattering to you then you'll have to take Gladys's place and see to my hair for me.'

'Sit down then. Let's make you pretty.'

'Stuff and nonsense! Pretty indeed! Just see to it that my hair's in place. Pretty! Sort of remark I'd expect from that empty-headed Rosalind.'

'Beatrice tells me she's beautiful.'

'Get along with your job if you expect to get any dinner this evening. Now, "Europa" you asked me. How the fire started I couldn't tell you. A lamp overturned so people are saying, but it's all rumour. The cargo was hemp and tar. No wonder there was a blaze! Because of the wedding he'd journeyed this way.'

'Hemp? Tar? But where had he come from? He said he'd sailed from Scotland.'

'That's it. A cargo transferred to him in East Scotland, been brought from St Petersburg. He was only on a short trip, just round the coast. All the thousands of miles the boy's travelled safely, then here on our own doorstep . . .'

'Let's be thankful he *was* here on our own doorstep, Aunt Lou. Is "Europa" much damaged?'

'She's been brought back to harbour, I've had her laid

in Netherton's yard. More than that I can't say. With you and Tommy off gallivanting, Webster's got better things to do with his time than run to me with every tittle tattle of news.'

'I'd have thought they'd have told Dan.'

'Just you mind what you say to Daniel. He's in no state to take in the full story, I'll not have him worried. You hear me! "Europa" has been brought home to harbour . . . Bailey, that's his mate, is getting Mr Hawkins to see if it's worth the money it'll take to put things right. None better than Mr Hawkins, at least Webster had the wit to recommend him. Costs enough to insure the ships these days. Let's hope Daniel gets fair treatment.'

'Dan won't accept anything less than fair treatment.'

'Well, that's for the future. Just now we'll say no more than that Bailey has it in hand and the crew have gone back on the railway train to Liverpool. The crew, mark you, no mention of any that took a jump to a watery grave before the lifeboat got to them.'

'Can I see him, Aunt Lou?'

'If he can put up with that Rosalind always hanging about him, I should think he can stand you. Two minutes though, and mind you don't say anything to worry him.'

'You know I won't. Hold your head still or I'll jab you, this is the last pin. There! Gladys couldn't have made a better job of it herself!' She smiled at the old lady's reflection and the eyes in the mirror probed her closely.

'This holiday you've run home from . . . nothing wrong you say? That's the truth, child?'

'Nothing wrong, Aunt Lou. It was all so good. But it was a holiday, it hardly seemed real. I'm glad to be home.'

'Hah! So long as that's it. Now go and see your precious Daniel and mind you don't make too much of your noise in there.'

This evening Dan's room must have been the only shadowy room in the house. In the grate coals burned, casting shadows on the walls for the lamp was so low it had no more power than the glow of a candle. The nurse had gone downstairs to have her supper before settling Daniel for his long night. He lay quite still. A cradle held the weight of the bedcovers off his legs, even in this semi-darkness the shape of it a reminder that he was set apart by illness. His eyes were closed. Hannah felt helpless. The sight of him caught her unprepared. How ill he looked! His face was deathly pale, his eyes seemed sunk in their sockets. A bandage was tied round the cut on his head but even in this light she could see the bruise that spread beneath it, yellow and blue.

He didn't stir, seemed not to have heard her. His breathing was shallow, she didn't think he slept. Bending over him she laid her lips gently against his cheek – and in a second his eyes were open.

'Hannah,' he breathed, 'I thought . . .' His words faded to nothing. She didn't know what he'd thought.

'Dan, I didn't know until this morning. I've been so worried.' She'd told Louise how good everything had been in London, yet because it had been a holiday it had had nothing to do with reality. Reality was Dan.

'. . . a week?' She could only guess at the question. He had lost count of time.

'No. We came back. I didn't want to be holidaying when I didn't know what had happened to you.' His only answer was to move his hand towards her cheek as she bent over him, then let it drop back to the covers. 'I'm glad Rosalind has come, Dan.' Even as she said it she knew from the way his brows puckered that it was a mistake. But why? She knew how fond he was of Rosalind, how much the boys meant to him.

'. . . so much to do . . .' She heard panic in his voice.

She must be the prop he needed. 'No, Dan, you haven't. You've got to let the rest of us do the worrying. Everything's being taken care of, Aunt Lou told me.'

'So much . . . want to say t'you . . . can't think . . .'

'Close your eyes.' She drew a chair close to the bed and sat down. When she took his hand in hers it was as if she was willing some of her own strength into him. 'Don't talk any more. Aunt Lou will say I'm not good for you.'

A smile tugged at his pale lips, but he didn't speak. It seemed he meant to do as he was told. She heard Louise come out of her room, heard her sticks and her shuffling step as she made her way down the stairs. No sign that Dan had heard. His breathing was steady, getting deeper, catching in his throat as he exhaled. This time she knew he slept. Another minute to make sure her movement wouldn't disturb him, then she released his hand. How strange that he could look so ill, so altered, and yet his hands remain as firm and strong as ever. Almost silently she crept to the door.

Outside in the corridor she came face to face with Rosalind heading for his room. A finger on her lips, she shut the door behind her.

'Asleep,' she mouthed silently.

She'd never had a clear picture of Rosalind in her mind, but because of her aunt's dismissive 'namby-pamby', 'feathery', 'flipperty', she'd felt an instinctive sympathy for the woman, even given her a shadowy resemblance to her mother. When Beatrice had said how lovely she was that had fitted the image.

'You're Hannah. You must be. You've come home early.'

She nodded and silently, in seconds, they sized each other up. Rosalind must have been more than ten years the elder but there was an agelessness about her. Was her hair very fair, or was it silver? Either way it would slip from one to the other unnoticed. Her face was lovely indeed, skin pale and clear as a child's, the web of lines around her eyes the only evidence of the passage of time. She was almost as fine-built as Beatrice, yet there was a difference. Rosalind's shoulders were straight, she held her head high even though her neck appeared almost too slender and delicate for the task. Beside her Hannah felt clumsy, she was ashamed to have been given such vigorous health, such good fortune, when this fragile creature had been dealt so much trouble. No home of her own, no husband, no father for her sons. Hannah's smile was wide, generous, she was honest in her welcome to Rosalind and her boys. Of course she was, they were part of Dan's life.

From downstairs came the sound of voices, mostly one voice, Tommy's as he regaled Louise with stories of what they'd done and where they'd been in London. At second hand the old lady delighted in the atmosphere he conjured up, he could see she did. He'd not been keen to come to the Hall this evening, although he'd not told Hannah so. Once here though he began to enjoy the challenge. The old lady could be a martinet, no doubt of that, she needed careful handling, but he knew how to deal with her. Louise was no fool and not for a minute did he underestimate her. 'Could charm the birds off the trees,' was her opinion of him. And already he believed her grip on the branch was loose.

To charm the ladies was second nature to him yet he hardly noticed Rosalind, something that was not lost on Louise. The four at the table divided into two camps. From the head of it Louise talked to Tommy on her right; from the foot, Hannah to Rosalind on hers.

'I came as soon as Mrs Netherton's letter arrived,' Rosalind was saying. Then, in a burst of confidence and after making sure the other two were engrossed in details of Tuesday evening's Music Hall: 'I had to get away, I would have waited for Daniel to get home, he would have seen to things, but when I heard he wouldn't be coming I had to get away. You see, Peter's father – Daniel's father, I mean, too – he's given us a home and I've been grateful. But I couldn't stay on after he's married.'

188

'Dan's father? But he's never said.'

'He doesn't know. They told me on New Year's Day. What a way to start the new year! Mrs Houghton, she's a widow, her husband died a year or two ago, is to marry him. I've known he's spent a good deal of time with her, sorting out her affairs. When a woman's left alone she needs someone. Daniel was so good to me and to the boys. His father gave us a home, but it was always Daniel we looked to. So when I heard Mrs Houghton was going to become mistress I was just waiting for him to arrive, I knew he'd look after things for us. Then I heard this. And – it sounds unkind, almost wicked you might think, but I don't mean it that way – when I heard that he was ill, I was thankful that at last I could do something for him.'

'Have you no family?'

'Only him, just him and the boys.'

From the other two came a most unusual sound – Tommy telling a comic story with the same gusto as they'd heard it on Tuesday, and Aunt Lou laughing aloud not so much at the joke as from delight at being included.

'I think he knows there's something on my mind,' Rosalind went on. 'I've not told him, I've tried not to let him see how frightened I am of what'll happen to the boys and me. When he's a little better I'll talk about it. Daniel'll sort it out, he'll know what I must do for the best.'

It wasn't fair. Hannah remembered him as she'd seen him lying there, eyes closed, feigning sleep. She remembered his: 'Hannah . . . I thought . . .' Now she knew what it was he'd thought, what it was he'd been hiding from. Dan, her prop and her strength, and Rosalind's too for so long. If she'd needed evidence of what the wreck had done to him she had it now.

And just as he'd carried the burden of her problems, so now she took on the responsibility of his.

* * *

189

Not for long could the truth about 'Europa' be kept from Dan. The assessor from the insurance company came to see him; Mr Hawkins, the shipwright came to see him. And only after that did Louise consider him ready for the next visitor, the one he'd been asking to see for days – Mr Bailey. That's when the full impact of the wreck was brought home to him and what he heard was worse by far than the assessor's opinion that 'Europa' was beyond restoring. 'The crew have been sent home on a railway train' he'd been told. From Mr Bailey he learned of the five who'd jumped overboard hoping to swim through the mountainous sea back to the shore at Deremouth. Four of them had sailed with him on every voyage 'Europa' had made, and one was a lad only weeks from leaving home. Men who had trusted him. He'd been responsible for them and for the ship. He thought of the families in Liverpool. Fear was the constant companion of the families at home, fear of just this. He'd seen it all his life. His depression, his sense of failure, reached its lowest ebb. Five men had put their faith in him, five men now lying out there at the bottom of the sea off Braggs Head.

And there was something else that bothered him: Rosalind.

From where he lay in bed in the room above the library he could see out on to the side lawn where the boys were playing cricket. They'd made a bat from a piece of driftwood they'd found when Hannah had taken them to the beach the other day. Matthew, blond and sturdy, well-made for his six years, was bowling, while Stephen's task was to hit the ball as far as possible and, even more important, to guard the trunk of the sycamore tree, their wicket.

'Here comes a beauty!' Dan heard the excitement in his merry squeak. 'Here 'tis.' He bowled fast. But then Matthew did everything fast. Stephen took a chance swipe at the ball and by good luck hit it, a hit that brought a

190

whoop of delight from his little brother and sent the ball hurtling across the grass to lose itself in the shrubs by the house. Seeing the surprise on Stephen's face Dan laughed. Then from the room beneath him came a sharp rat-tatting on the window. He couldn't hear what it was Louise called to them, probably they couldn't either, the glare that accompanied her words was enough to warn them off.

Matthew called that they were 'Sorry, Mrs Netherton.'

Stephen coloured and said nothing.

By silent mutual consent they left their bat under the tree and went off to the wood beyond the grass. Dan wasn't easy about them. This was no place for them and yet Rosalind made no mention of returning to Liverpool. He'd heard from his father that he and Mrs Houghton were to be married, but with no mention of that altering things for Rosalind and the boys. It was time they started lessons again. At home they went each day to Harold Miller, not a teacher but a one time bank manager who had had to give up work after he'd suffered a stroke and been left partly paralysed. Not a satisfactory arrangement, but he needed to earn the money, the boys needed a man's guidance. The problem of Rosalind and the boys cast its shadow across Dan's thoughts night after night as he lay here helpless. And perhaps too he grasped at a problem he acknowledged for other thoughts were too intolerable to face at all. Now he watched the boys shuffle through last autumn's leaves and frowned. There was something aimless in the way they walked. They were heading for nowhere.

'May I come and sit with you?' It was Rosalind.

'I was just thinking about you and the boys.'

'What were you thinking? I've brought my crochet work. Mrs Netherton likes the fireside to herself in the afternoon.'

'Good. Stay and talk to me.'

In the years she'd been a widow Rosalind had become

all too used to having nowhere of her own, nowhere she didn't have to make sure she wasn't in the way. And her ears had become used to listening for the boys, being sure that they didn't make a noise. 'Poor little souls, they were having such fun,' she'd cry silently. But always it must be silently.

'I'm worried about you, Rosalind. You've given up too much time to helping Nurse Grant, it's not right to keep you here. You ought to take the boys home, back to their lessons.'

'We're not going back there, Daniel.' As soon as she said it she was frightened she should have kept her secret to herself. 'You aren't to worry about it. Hannah knows I'm not going back there, but I promised her I wouldn't say anything to you yet. Now I have, you might as well know the rest. There's a house to rent at the corner of Queen's Street in Deremouth. Crown Cottage it's called. Hannah found it for me.' She put her crochet work down and turned to him, her blue eyes wide with sadness, her mouth trembling. 'Dan, I can't go back to your father's house, not with another woman as mistress. I'd be nothing. I'm nothing wherever I go – but, oh don't you see? We'd be in the way, all three of us. All along Father has been out so much, we've not been so aware of it. But with Mrs Houghton there – only she won't be, she'll be Mrs Lowden – I can't.'

'You should have told me all this. Rosalind, I thought all these years you'd been happy there.'

'Happy! I think I've forgotten what it's like to be happy. To be happy must be to be important to someone, to matter.'

'And so you do. You matter more than most mothers to the boys, you have to take Peter's place with them too.'

'To the boys, Daniel, I think it's you who do that. They never lack a father as long as you care for them.' Then she resolutely picked up her work and dug the hook through

192

the next loop. 'But about the house – Hannah told me not to say anything, she said you weren't to be told anything that would worry you. I'll tell you though, because I think you'll worry more now if I don't. She found it for me and she's arranging everything. So, Dan, you mustn't think your being ill has upset things for the boys. To be honest I'm thankful to have this chance of trying to care for you and I know they love being here even if they are only allowed to come in for a few minutes at a time. And Hannah is being wonderful, such a friend to me.' She noticed that hint of a smile playing at the corners of his mouth. 'Just imagine, a home of my own. I'll be the one to make the rules; I'll be the one to decide whether the boys are allowed to stay up to supper; I'll be the one to say whether it's a sin to take their shrimping nets on to the rocks on the Sabbath.' Such an outburst from the gentle Rosalind. He'd never fully realized how difficult her years must have been.

'Poor Rosalind.'

'Not now, Daniel. Not poor. It's a dear little house. And there's plenty of room for you to have a bed there.'

'But why Deremouth, Rosalind? It's so far from anyone you know.'

'I've no real friends in Liverpool. And I know it may sound silly, but I'm not strong enough to be on my own there. When you're not around I feel – crushed, frightened by everything. I might manage if I only had myself to think of but – ' she turned to him pleadingly – 'it really is a big responsibility bringing up the boys. I'm strong when I'm here. Hannah will see we're all right when you're away, she'll be my friend. She makes me feel capable, sure of myself.'

Dan nodded slowly. 'She'll be your prop, eh? She's mine too, Rosalind.' How easy it would be to tell her.

'I expect it's because she's so happy herself that she

hates to see other people not so fortunate. He's a handsome young man, isn't he, her Tommy?'

He didn't answer but it seemed she hadn't noticed. 'There's a school nearby. Hannah has a friend who used to help there. It's going to work out so well. We'll learn to fit in, the boys will make friends. And when you put in at Deremouth it can be your home, too, Daniel.'

It was a reminder that he couldn't 'put in' to Deremouth until he 'put out' from it; he couldn't do that until he replaced 'Europa'; and he couldn't do that while he was kept here with two legs he couldn't walk on.

'Oh look,' Rosalind stood up, 'the boys are coming back. I must run down and warn them to come in quietly. Mrs Netherton will be having a nap.'

Yes, it was time Rosalind and her sons had a home of their own. Dan realized that Hannah had recognized that something must be done – and being Hannah she had done it.

It was years since Rosalind had let herself indulge in daydreams, yet as she planned the little house on the corner of Queen's Street her future began to take shape. It must be right that some of the money Peter had left (and it hadn't been much) should be used to make a home for the boys. She even imagined herself taking in dressmaking, she was good at sewing, anything she could earn would help.

Louise hadn't wanted her visitors, yet it was she who was least happy with the idea.

'It's no use my saying anything to her. She'd look at me with those great woebegone eyes. She'd think I wanted to clip her wings. Hah! Wings! No chance of her learning to fly, that's the truth of it.' She sniffed, eyeing Hannah with much the same expression as she had on that first day. 'I'd have hoped you would have learnt more sense than to send her out into the world alone.'

'Aunt Lou, Rosalind isn't stupid.'

'Did I say she was? Not that I may not think so. But it's not just sense I'm thinking of, it's stamina. Can you see her up on a cold morning, getting the house warm and a good breakfast inside the lads before they start for school? Wood to chop, clothes to wash, floors to scrub, brass to polish. Well? Answer me that. Can you see her doing it? Hah!'

'She needs a home of her own.'

Louise's mood seemed to soften. 'I'm not pretending she doesn't. I dare say she deserves it too. A home and a husband to care for her, that's what she needs. Why the good Lord saw fit to take Peter away from them I can't think, though I suppose He had His reasons.' Then private memories made her chuckle. 'Hilary — you don't know him but he can be a tartar. Not the sort to suffer fools. And I suppose she can't help being what she is.' She drummed her long fingers on the arm of the chair. 'But it's not just that that bothers me. Peter was consumptive. Came from healthy stock — had to get it from somewhere.'

'Aunt Lou, you can't hold her responsible for that.'

'Just a thought. Just a thought. Hah! And the boys. Her for a mother, a father with consumption — they need good food, warmth, well-aired clothes, someone with a bit of spunk to look to them. That girl's not made for hardship.' Her eyes pierced Hannah. 'You, you're different. Ah, and me too. We can fight for ourselves. But Rosalind, she's got no fight in her. 'Tisn't fair on the boys. I'd talk to Daniel but he has worries enough. So just you see if you can't use what influence you have and persuade her to bide her time here.' Still her fingers drummed. 'Not to please me! Children underfoot, not a ha'porth of peace to be had. But make her bide her time till Daniel sees fit to take a look further than his own affairs, his own aches and pains. Shut away up there, what does he see? Nothing.'

But she underestimated him.

Lying dependent on a nurse he listened for the sound of Hannah's visits. He dreaded her coming yet he wanted her. Since her honeymoon he'd seen very little of her. He told himself he was glad. To watch her with Tommy turned a knife in the wound; to have her sitting alone with him, a Hannah so unchanged, was even harder to bear. There were even occasions when he'd hear her step and feign sleep so realistically that she'd creep away. Then he'd hear her outside, talking to Tommy, laughing perhaps as they walked across the side lawn to the stable yard. He'd know he'd had the opportunity of talking to her, seeing her smile, hearing her laugh – with him, not with Tommy – and he'd been too much of a coward to take it.

It was one evening when Rosalind came to see him after saying goodnight to the boys that he put his proposition to her. 'It won't make it any less your own home, you'll be the mistress. You used to have servants.'

'That was with Peter. It was different. We had income enough to run a house properly then. I'll manage, honestly I will. I'll do the cleaning while the boys are at school. I know you think I'm weak and useless, but I won't be. I'll see we eat properly. And in any case, by the time I've paid the rent I couldn't afford to pay for help.'

'Rosalind, you tell me I may have a corner of your house when I'm in Deremouth, although sometimes I'll come here, I always have, so I insist I take a share of the expenses.'

He was ready for her to argue but there was only silence. The ticking of the clock filled the room.

'Well?'

She sat on the edge of his bed, her back to him. It was a minute before he realized she was crying.

'Rosalind, my dear, I promise it won't take away your freedom. It'll be your own home, you'll be mistress. If you won't let me do it for you, let me for the boys.'

'It isn't that.' Such a wispy handkerchief to wipe her

tears more lace edging than middle. 'Daniel, night after night I've lain awake worrying. What if I got ill or something – who'd care for the boys? And perhaps I wouldn't cook properly and they'd be undernourished. I know what I just said to you, how I'd manage – but the truth is I've never cooked the meals nor laid the grate nor scrubbed the floor. You'll really pay for someone to help me? Truly I'll learn, I'll try. I was just so frightened if I didn't do well ... because of the boys. But if there's someone who knows – '

'It's all right, don't cry.' His grip on her hand was strong. 'You'll make a good home for the boys at Crown Cottage. You'll find someone you like to help you.'

'I'll ask Hannah. She'll find me someone.'

She put her problem into Hannah's hands and waited with the trust of a child. And to Hannah it seemed a heaven sent opportunity.

'It would be just the place for you, Beatrice. She wants someone who knows how to run a home, who would do things without being asked.'

'I've told you before, I can't leave them. Ma depends on me. I don't know why you ask me when you know why I have to stay and help her.'

'Won't you come just for a while. Please, Beatrice.' Earnestly Hannah pleaded Rosalind's case. 'The boys need a home – and so does she. You're my friend so that makes you the ideal person.' Beatrice didn't speak, her expression gave no indication that Hannah's avowal meant anything. Only metaphorically did she prick up her ears. 'Won't you do it, Bea? She's had such a sad time.'

'Why do you bother so much?' Beatrice clung to her arm. Hannah could feel her finger nails digging in.

'Beatrice, I've only known her a few weeks but she needs help so badly. You and I could give it to her.' The 'you and I' wasn't lost on Beatrice.

'She's lovely to look at, isn't she?' It was no answer.

'Yes, lovely. And lonely too.'

And it was that that tipped the scales. Beatrice knew all about loneliness. And she knew too that if she refused it would be Hannah, even though her own life was full and busy, who would find time to assuage that loneliness.

So much in life hinges on that word 'if'. If Rosalind hadn't been so dependent on Dan he wouldn't have seen to it that she had help in the house and another woman living there; if she'd been more able to stand on her own two feet she would have advertised in the *Deremouth Gazette* and found a housekeeper that way; if she hadn't been warmed by Hannah's friendship on that first evening perhaps she'd not have chosen Deremouth as the place to bring the boys to live; and if Crown Cottage hadn't had a stable and coachhouse at the end of the narrow garden for which she would have no use, then the future might have worked out differently.

CHAPTER EIGHT

During March Beatrice moved into Crown Cottage and, two days later, Rosalind and the boys followed. Fires were burning brightly to welcome them, in the kitchen, in the living room, in Rosalind's bedroom. Hannah was there to see them arrive but once they were safely in she left them to Beatrice's care. Over these weeks she'd given so much time and thought to helping Rosalind: looking for furniture, measuring windows, buying stores. Tonight she'd go home from the yard with an easy mind. Beatrice was released from the gatehouse; Rosalind and the boys had a home of their own.

These things were partly responsible for Hannah's cheerful mood as she strode home to Vicary Terrace, humming under her breath and stepping out in time to the silent rhythm. But she gave credit for her mood entirely to Tommy. Today he'd gone to see Mr Hawkins near Exeter. He hadn't intended to come back to the yard afterwards, so he'd probably be home ahead of her. She hoped he'd have brought the written estimate for work the shipwright was to carry out on 'My Queen'. In her mind she saw a picture of them, dinner over, the plans spread out on the table. Then another picture, the plans rolled away, and it was that that quickened her pace. She'd wear the deep lilac gown he'd told her suited her, she'd twist her hair into a thick coil. She imagined herself – no doubt with a degree of flattery. She imagined Tommy, his look of appreciation. 'My Queen' was forgotten.

Hannah was a happy bride of less than three months standing. Some of her impatience for the hours ahead came from his parting words.

199

'I wish I were coming with you,' she'd said when he'd come into her room at the yard to say goodbye. 'But I must finish these figures. I've been out so much lately trying to organize things for Rosalind, I'm running late.'

He'd kissed the back of her neck as she'd sat at her desk. 'I'll be home as soon as I can. And tonight I shall expect the whole of you – you and your thoughts too. No more worrying about your lame ducks.'

Up Quay Hill she hurried, then turned right into Waterloo Street. She had to walk the length of it, across Station Approach, then right again down Onslow Place to the road that fronted the beach and to Vicary Place. She was in Waterloo Street, coming towards the railway station. A group of people came out of the building, the train from Exeter must have just arrived. Surely that was Tommy! She started to run, a most unladylike thing to do but she was much too pleased to think he'd arrived so early to care about that. She put up her arm to attract his attention – then stopped quite still, her arm dropped back to her side. She'd been mistaken. The man moving away in the little group of people wasn't going towards Onslow Place. Already he was beyond that and hurrying from her in the opposite direction towards the east side of town. She moved on slowly now, disappointed. Then she laughed at herself. What a state she must be in if every young man looked like Tommy from a distance!

Once home she changed into the lilac gown, and spent twice as long as usual grooming her long hair. By now the next train would have arrived. Any minute she'd hear him coming in. Her eyes expectantly on the front door, she went downstairs. No Tommy. In the drawing room she waited. Instead of closing the curtains she stood at the window watching for him. Half-past seven. Eight o'clock. By now her imagination was working overtime. She had him under the wheels of a carriage in Exeter, slipped from the quayside and hauled from the water in the shipwright's yard . . . It was about half-past eight when she saw Alan hurrying towards the house and one look at his expression sent her to open the front door before he was up the three steps from the pavement.

'Where's Tommy? He's home safely?'

'Not yet. He must have been delayed.'

Alan put a hand on the newel post at the foot of the stairs, a hand that wasn't steady. 'There's an accident. Had to come to find out. Hoped he'd be early.' His sentences were disjointed, short, sharp bursts.

'Where? What sort of accident?'

'I was late home. Passing the railway station I heard some sort of commotion, a crowd of people, could tell something was wrong. Thought of the boy. Went to find out. Don't know if it's off its rails or if there's been a collision. Due in at ten-past eight it was.'

'I'll get my cloak. We must go to the station.'

Alan's face was white, even his lips had no colour. Did she look like that? she wondered, surprised at the thought, surprised that she could stand outside herself. She even had the forethought to send word to the kitchen to have a message taken to Alan's house that he'd been delayed at Vicary Terrace and might be late home.

The next hour was a nightmare. At the station they learned that two trains had crashed about a mile along the track. One had been de-railed and an on-coming one had hurtled into it. They weren't the only ones to make their way along the grassy bank by the side of the train lines. To go by road would be easier, but they couldn't be sure where the accident had been and, in any case, the track was more direct. Someone ahead of them was holding a lighted flare. The scene lay in eerie shadow, didn't look real, didn't feel real. Hope fought with rumour. Just behind Hannah someone was crying, a young woman dragging a child by the hand. For her, rumour had overcome hope.

The evening was very still; the rain started, a fine, steady drizzle, the beginning of a wet night.

At last they saw a glow ahead of them. Lanterns giving light to the rescue workers. Their steps quickened even though they slithered and slipped on the wet grass of the embankment. Rumour led to fear.

But once at the scene of the crash hope gained the upper hand. It was true the train travelling westward had been de-railed but rumour had made a mistake about the timing. The goods train approaching from the other direction had only just pulled out of Deremouth, it hadn't got up full steam; and the driver had caught a hint of something across the track ahead of him, a glow from the fire of the on-coming engine. He'd braked. He must have believed in those seconds that he'd come to the end of his own particular track as he came closer, closer. But he wouldn't die of the cuts and bruises nor even the broken wrist he'd received.

And the passengers on the westbound train, Tommy's train, had none of them been seriously hurt. There were the two great engines, carriages that in this light looked like a child's broken toy. Hannah had never known joy so great. He hadn't been hurt. He wasn't even here amongst the group of shaken passengers waiting for a horse-bus to pick them up from the nearest point of the road. He was safe! 'Thank you, thank you.' She looked at the cluster of passengers huddled together, most of them with a journey further than Deremouth ahead of them for this was the train from Paddington to the west.

'He must have climbed up to the roadway and walked. He'd not have waited for the transport. Takes a lot to upset Tommy.' In his relief Alan took out his handkerchief and wiped it across his brow. Relief, no doubt; that and, now that the anxiety was lifted, a sudden awareness of just how wet they all were. 'Do you want to wait for the ride back?'

'No, I want to get home. A bit more mud isn't going to matter.' All the way she'd been haunted by the image of him lying maimed, perhaps crushed. But he was safe! By now he'd be waiting, watching for her at the window. 'I'm going to run on ahead.'

'It's dark. If you wait a minute they'll be coming with the lantern.'

'My eyes are used to it now. I want to get home.'

There were some who'd gone out of curiosity. If they could be any use to the rescue party one or two offered to stay, but mostly there was nothing they could do and they gathered together with the man who carried the lighted torch ready for the walk home. But Hannah was ahead of them. Once or twice she slipped. The ground was rough and the bank steeper in some parts than others. Her lilac gown was soaked, the hem coated with mud. Her hands were wet and dirty where time and again she put them down to save herself a fall. The hair she'd spent so much care on had lost its glory, some in the coil, some not. It wasn't what she'd expected of the evening but her bubble of happiness held.

Tommy was home ahead of her. He heard her come in through the front door. Madge, the maidservant, had told him that his father had called to fetch Hannah out. That must mean trouble at the yard but he'd had no intention of going down there to find out what it was. He'd had quite enough of Netherton's for one day. He'd hear soon enough. So he'd taken up *The Times* and started to read while he waited.

The door burst open – and the greeting he had ready for her died on his lips. 'What in the world have you been doing? You're drenched. Look at your shoes, they're ruined.'

'Tommy, you're back! Was it dreadful? Are you hurt? I ran all the way home.'

203

He was at a loss. 'Hurt? I've not been to the yard. I told you I'd come straight home.'

His answer made no sense at all. 'What train were you on?'

At her question an inner voice warned him: 'Careful what you say.'

'I've only got in just a minute ago. I was about to come down to the yard to see what the trouble was. What happened?'

'At the yard? Nothing. The train, Tommy, the ten-past eight at Deremouth. Your father and I have been along the track to Westley Junction. We thought ... Tommy, you weren't on it! Thank God, you weren't even on it.'

He did the right thing; he held her close. She'd rushed home to care for him but it was he who comforted her. He drew her towards the fire, chafed her hands in his although she was more wet than cold. This was a new Tommy, gentle and caring. She gave herself into his hands. Her questions were forgotten and he gained precious minutes to decide on his story.

The doorbell told them Alan had arrived. They drew apart and Hannah anchored her fallen hair with its pins.

'It seems I've alarmed you both.' Tommy smiled his close-lipped smile, sure of himself now. 'I'm sorry – and about the de-railment too. As you see I wasn't on it. Rather than go right back to the city for a train I waited for a ride with someone from Hawkins. He was coming right through Deremouth, it seemed the obvious thing to do when he offered.'

'Good man, good man ...' Alan burbled in his relief. 'I'll get straight on home. Thank God there's no bad news to carry to your mother. Good man.'

So he left them and the evening that was already nearly over looked at last like taking the shape Hannah had planned for it.

'I'm glad you didn't have time to go back to the yard,'

she told him later when, their dried up supper eaten, they came back to the drawing room. 'Pull the little table to the fire, Tommy, and let's look over the estimate. If you'd been in time to go to the yard we should have had to wait until the morning.' Wasn't this all part of her dream.

'Tomorrow's soon enough. It seemed satisfactory.'

'Oh, but let me see it. Come on, Tommy, let's go over it. Get the papers, let's look at them together.'

He fetched them for her and threw them on to the table she'd set in place then sat down with *The Times*. 'You look if you want to. I've had my fill of "My Queen", that's not my idea of a way to spend the evening.'

She laughed. Not for a minute did she take his words seriously. He'd read the paper, but she was confident enough that after a minute or two he'd be at her side. She spread the plan on the table and with it the details of the work to be carried out, happy at the job ahead of her and happy at the hint in his voice that he too was looking ahead to what would come later. To her the two moved hand in hand, both shared with Tommy.

'The sailmaker is charging £220, Tommy, that's a lot. Top sails, fore sails, main sail . . .' She was talking more to herself by now. *The Times* must be particularly gripping today. 'Main and mizzen sails . . . nearly 3000 yards of canvas, a complete re-fit. Replacement timber £286.13.4½d., carpenter's wages £41. Rope – did you see that, Tommy? . . . ropes to cost us £300. Did you know as much rope as that had to be replaced? It's costing us a lot of money altogether. What did you think of it? £848.8.4½d. Was that more than you thought?'

'Seemed all right to me.'

'I'd expected about a hundred less. I'd not expected we'd have to renew all those ropes, but Mr Hawkins – '

'Hannah, I met a man today, a first-rate seaman name of Ted Sharples. I told him we'd have a place for him. When "My Queen" is ready to put to sea again – and

205

Hawkins promised her for the end of next month – I want us to give her to Ted Sharples.'

Suddenly the evening was all that she'd hoped for. Tommy not simply doing a job but thinking ahead, caring about the company just as she did. She rolled away the plans and came to sit on a stool at his feet, leaning against him. Her hand was on his knee, her fingers caressing. He took hold of it and moved it higher. 'Up a bit,' he said. She oughtn't to have to be told. That dark-eyed ghost was there again, her hands teasing, egging him on. No, Hannah oughtn't to need guiding, prompting, hadn't she learnt anything! Who the hell cared how many yards of canvas the damned ship needed.

She realized he'd unbuttoned his trousers. Just for a second she hesitated as he steered her hand – but only for a second.

'Out of the way a minute.' And he got up to cross the room and turn the key in the lock. 'Now we can relax.' But it was evident he hadn't.

The fire was bright, the heat of it fierce sitting as near as she was. She was strangely excited at what they were doing, something they'd never done before here in front of the flaming coals. She longed for him to make love to her, knew it was what he wanted too. But she was hampered, stockings, corset, long drawers . . .

'Tommy, let's not stay up, let's go to bed.' Sitting in front of him on her footstool she bent forward, her head rubbing against his knee.

Bed! How often he and Susie had found their pleasure on the rug in front of the kitchen range. Thinking of her now he came near to hating Hannah.

"Bed!' There was no love in his voice. At the sound of it she seemed to recoil. 'Bed! God save me from puritanical women.' He meant it to hurt, and hurt it did.

Her lilac gown, dry now but still dirty from the mud of the railway track had a low neckline, buttoning down the back. As she bent forward he made a single movement, ripped undone the buttons and pulled both gown and chemise from her shoulders, down to her waist so that the only way she could free her arms would be to ease them out of the sleeves. The fire was warm on her naked breasts. Why did he look at her like that? Why had he suddenly changed? It was as if what was happening to his body had nothing to do with loving her. Only a minute ago she'd been moved with excitement as strong as his own but now as he bent over her, eyes closed, breathing heavily, he was a stranger.

'Damn you, do something,' she heard him hiss at her between gritted teeth. Then, pulling her forward, he pushed himself between her breasts. Sitting on the edge of the chair, forcing her against him, his voice echoed in her brain "Damn you . . . damn you . . ." She raised her head. She felt she didn't know him. His expression was wild, his body jerked, rocking on his buttocks. Then it was over. But not before her excitement had given way to revulsion. "Damn you . . . damn you . . ." still she heard it.

He was gasping, lying back in the chair now. 'Here, clean up with that.' All passion spent, his handkerchief was thrust at her.

'You disapprove,' he said after a while. He sounded like a man who'd been drinking and was looking for any excuse for a fight.

She shook her head, struggling to get her arms back into the sleeves of her gown. 'It's not that.' She wanted to make him understand. 'Tommy . . .' But how was she to say it? He was a man of the world, he understood so many things she knew nothing about. All she knew was what these months with him had taught her. 'I don't disapprove, I could never disapprove. To start with I felt . . . I wanted . . .' She floundered, out of her depth. 'But then it was as if I didn't count.'

He shrugged his shoulders. He tried to hurt her, not

207

because of what she said but because she was here when it was someone else he wanted.

'I expect you'd rather we'd gone over Hawkins' figures. That's what you wanted, wasn't it?'

She didn't trust her voice to answer, her throat ached with disappointment. For the first time she saw them not as a partnership but as two separate people. She'd believed they'd shared the same dreams, the work they did something that bound them. What he said, and even more the way he said it, left her feeling confused and alone.

They both wished none of it had happened. The atmosphere between them was strained. Hannah was frightened of what might come out of an emotional scene. The evening ended in the silence of truce but between them was a void they couldn't bridge.

With the morning they were determined to make amends. No mention was made of the previous evening; it was better forgotten. But Hannah had learnt at any rate one lesson: work mustn't be brought into their home. In the office she could talk to Tommy of company business. At home, never.

There was one thing that gave her a great feeling of satisfaction over those weeks of spring, and that was the ménage at Crown Cottage. There was nothing new to Beatrice in chopping the wood, carrying coals, scrubbing, ironing, doing all the tasks Rosalind had been frightened of. These things had been the background of her life, but never done as willingly or as happily as here. Right from the start she and Rosalind were in tune – and being here she could make sure that Hannah didn't become too important to the lovely widow.

At Netherton Hall Dan, too, was making progress. He could not yet put his splinted leg to the ground, but he was able to sit out of bed and a table was brought to his room where he could work. Sheets of parchment were brought up to him, pens, drawing material. Dan's sights were set

208

on the future, a new ship was taking shape. There came a day when Mr Hawkins arrived to see him and the two men were closeted together all the afternoon.

'And what do you make of our invalid, Mr Hawkins?' Louise was waiting in the hall for him as he came back down the stairs. 'Getting fidgety to be off to sea again, I suppose?'

'He's certainly keen to know there's a ship under construction. I'll work on these plans, let him have them within a week, I've promised him that. It'll be a good many months before we can have the work done, though.'

'And a good many before he'll be ready too. Keen is one thing, ready quite another. Like all the young ones, he hasn't learnt the lesson of patience.'

'I fear it's a lesson he'll have mastered before he's fit to go to sea again, ma'am.'

'Ah, poor boy. It's been a bad business. He had such pride in "Europa", you know, Mr Hawkins.'

'And so he will have in what we've been planning this afternoon. A ship we'll be proud to build.'

And, good as his word, the scale drawings arrived less than a week later and it was on that same day that Hannah visited. She found Dan sitting at his table, the plans unrolled before him. Together they pored over them. A fine ship, longer than 'Europa' and sleeker.

'The mainsails are as far from the foresail as from the mizzen, Dan,' she frowned. 'Have they made a mistake in the measurements?'

'No, it's right. The mizzen topsail and the top gallants have the same dimensions as the fore rig, too. See, here.'

Louise was struggling up the stairs, drawn by their voices. His door was open but they were much too engrossed to have heard her. Their heads were close – and their interests too. Ships, the very essence of life! She'd join them, be a part of it.

Hannah was speaking now: 'Yes, I see that. A full rig. And, Dan, the bow's very narrow –'

'Speed. It's designed for speed.'

Their eyes were rivetted to the drawings. Louise stood quite still and watched them.

'It's the most exciting thing! Now I want to see the plans for the engine.'

It had been a struggle to climb so far, but the old lady turned back. There was something about them that bothered her, yet what it was she couldn't define. They'd been friends for years – so what was so different? It was time Daniel found himself a wife, someone to give him sons. No man could give his heart just to ships.

'My Queen' was back in service and Ted Sharples on the pay roll. Most of Netherton's skippers had been with the company for years and treated Tommy respectfully enough when they came in contact with him. After all, he was Alan Webster's son and married to the owner's niece. With Ted, his relationship was quite different. Watching them together Hannah was glad. This was what Tommy needed. Ted was here because *he'd* engaged him, a proof of Tommy's rôle in the business. It was good to see them getting on so well. Whenever "My Queen" was in port they were together, either on the quay or even 'having a jar together' as Tommy called it. Ted was just the beginning, she told herself. There would be others, Tommy's influence would grow and become more important as he became more involved.

Hannah's dreams were dying hard.

On a May day that seemed to be jumping ahead into full summer she drove out to the Hall. It was quiet in the yard, there was nothing pressing for her attention and when she called out to Tommy where she was going, he was far too engrossed in conversation with Ted to do more than give her a disinterested wave.

That was the afternoon Dan suggested: 'I plan to visit the yard next week. What about your being there too?'

'I'll be there, of course I will,' she answered, for to her 'the yard' was Netherton's.

'Hawkins' yard, I mean. I shall go by train. Edward Hawkins has promised to have me met at Exeter.' By now he was getting around on two sticks and that impatience Louise had talked of was getting the better of him.

'Dan, I'd love to come.' She'd been to Hawkins' yard to see the progress of repair work and to talk of 'Oberon' when she was being re-furbished, but to see the plans of Dan's sleek new ship coming to fruition was quite different.

'Love to come, indeed, m'lady! Just you ask Tommy's permission before you go trailing over the countryside without him.'

'What, with Dan?' Hannah laughed. 'Of course Tommy won't have any objection. Why ever should he?'

'As you say, why ever should he? Nonetheless, you're a married woman.' Today Louise was in a disgruntled mood. What was it Dan had said of her so long ago: 'Snaps and snarls like a bad-tempered dog.'

Nevertheless when the carriage from the Hall called at the yard to collect Hannah on the following Tuesday, Dan said to Tommy: 'You don't mind me borrowing her for the day, do you?' and only he knew the effort his jocular tone cost him.

'I doubt if she'd let you go without her. I insist I drive with you to the station, you'll need a hand into the train.'

On the surface the atmosphere was easy and cordial. Each believed himself the only one to be aware of an undercurrent; Hannah, in her excitement, didn't notice one.

211

The ship was to be named 'Louisah' Dan told her, as the train steamed towards Exeter. 'Conceived while I was cared for by your aunt, and each step shared by my friend Hannah.' He said it lightly, perhaps too lightly. But Hannah knew him so well. His words and, even more, his expression were the chink in his armour. In that second she saw clearly, vividly, something she'd never considered before. From the outset he'd treated her as he might have a young sister. They'd shared the same interests – ships, trade; they'd shared the same affections – Louise and, more recently, Rosalind and the boys. 'He understands things without being told' she'd said of him years ago. It was she who hadn't understood, and she'd believed she'd known him through and through.

'Almost there, Hannah,' he said now, passing over the awkwardness. Had she imagined it? Whether in her imagination or in reality made no difference; her own vision of Dan had taken on a new dimension.

She was the first down the step to the platform.

'Hand me one of the sticks,' she told him, 'now put your weight on my shoulder.' She was strong. When Dan needed help she gave it as unselfconsciously as, had the positions been reversed, she would have taken it from him.

Edward Hawkins' carriage was waiting and they were soon bowling along out of the city and towards the boatyard. Today every heady scent of summer seemed to be bursting into the air. Hedgerows, wild flowers, blossom, the sounds and smells of summer were all around them as they followed the lane towards the river. By tomorrow the gales might well be blowing the blossom from the trees, clouds hiding the sun. But tomorrow was a long way off.

If Dan had leant on her for support at the railway station, it was but the first of many times as they clamoured around the unfinished 'Louisah'. They went into the deckhouse between fore and mainsails; they went into the cabins on the poop, one for the Master, one for the Mate. They went into what was to become the engine room. They stood in the slender bow.

Then Edward Hawkins took them to lunch at the 'Ship Inn' where they ate mutton and caper sauce in the privacy of a small back room.

The afternoon was half over, the drive back to the railway station still ahead of them, when he said: 'If you're to catch the teatime train I think we should set out.' Then, to Hannah, laughing at the memory his words stirred: 'We don't want a repetition of the drive with your husband – the day he came to see 'My Queen', remember? We left it late in getting away. I drove with him. What a race it was! I can see him now, dashing on to the platform while the guard held the train. And a lucky thing he did too. The next one came to grief, as I remember.'

'Yes, wasn't it lucky?' Hannah heard herself answer.

But what she'd heard couldn't be brushed aside and it wasn't in her nature to live with suspicions or half truths. So that evening as she and Tommy sat at dinner she asked him: 'Why did you tell me you'd had a ride home in someone's carriage, you remember, the night the train was de-railed?' Even now she wasn't accusing him. He must have had a reason, but she couldn't understand it.

'It was Ted Sharples. You remember I told you I'd met him?'

'So?'

Tommy had foreseen that something like this might come out of her visit to Hawkins' yard, he'd had all day to prepare his story. 'I met him on the train. We got off together. We'd hit it off well, we still do, you know that. I went to have a jar or two with him.'

'But what was so secret about that?'

'I'm sorry, Hannah. Afterwards it seemed silly that I hadn't told you. But you and Father had been worried, you'd been out there in the rain chasing up the track – how could I tell you I'd been in the alehouse?' He smiled

213

his special smile. It made her ashamed to be questioning him. 'Forgive me? Such a silly little lie and told with the best of intentions. I'm sorry.'

Of course she forgave him. It even explained to her why he'd turned the other way when he'd come from the railway station. She could remember it so clearly, her hand half raised to hail him. Of course, she'd not known Ted Sharples, that must be why she couldn't picture him there with Tommy.

Looking back on that day with Dan, a day that had been touched with magic, Tommy's explanation struck the only discordant note.

When 'Louisah' put to sea it was from Deremouth. It was from there Dan took his crew, with the exception of Mr Bailey who still sailed with him. Deremouth became his home, his base, just as it had Rosalind's and the boys'.

Hannah smiled as she recognized the footsteps on the wooden staircase. It was a sound which was becoming increasingly familiar.

'We've come again. Mama said we could,' Matthew called, knocking on her door and poking his head around it in one action in a way that reminded her of Gladys in days gone by.

'Mama said we had to ask first,' Stephen corrected him. He was two years the elder but had none of Matthew's assurance. 'She said we could watch in the yard if you said so – but not if you didn't.'

'Of course you may. I used to love watching. Be careful not to go too near the edge.'

''course we won't. We're looking for Uncle Dan. "Louisah" is due back, you know.'

Watching for Dan had become as much a part of their lives as it had been of hers. In the months that 'Louisah' had been trading they'd followed Dan's routes, crossed off the days, just as she used to.

'Why don't you take off your overcoats and watch from up here? It's warmer and you'll have a better view too. Take turns with my telescope.'

'From up here you look down on them all,' Matthew chuckled. 'It's like at school. When we go out to play Miss Sherwood stands upstairs at a window, just like this. She doesn't miss anything, does she, Stephen? Taps on the window: "Boys! Boys!"' and he clapped his hands in the authoritarian manner of the school mistress. '"That's no behaviour for my little gentlemen,"' He fell about laughing. If Matthew didn't grow up to follow his uncle to sea, he'd find a place as a mimic on the music halls!

'Sshh, quiet,' Stephen mouthed, 'Hannah's busy. Mama told us – don't disturb her.'

There was little resemblance between the brothers. Stephen, tall for his nine years, was slim and dark with the longest eyelashes Hannah had ever seen. A beautiful child, it was hard to imagine him grown to be a man. What sort of livelihood would he make for himself? she wondered. At home he often shut himself in his bedroom, happy to be left alone to pipe on his flute. He had a true sense of rhythm and harmony. Whether he tried to follow the notes in his music or played simply what he made up as he went along, which was his favourite, he was a natural music maker.

Matthew was the complete opposite. For him life was fun, the world occupied by people he assumed were his friends. And although he was the younger, he saw it as his job to protect his brother.

'Look at the way they lift those sacks!' He watched the humpers, wide-eyed. He puffed out his chest, bent his arm and flexed his muscles. 'Feel that!' he said proudly to Hannah.

She joined them at the window. ' "Muscles Matt," ' she laughed, 'we'll have you out there helping in no time.'

She saw it was 'My Queen' the men were loading. Tommy was onboard talking to Ted Sharples. But Stephen's attention had moved on. He had the telescope fixed on the horizon. He wasn't honestly sure whether he'd recognize 'Louisah', but he wasn't going to say so.

'Look, Stephen, out there.' Matthew had noticed it too. 'Can you see?'

A minute ago and Stephen would not have been sure, he'd almost passed the telescope for Matthew's superior opinion. But a change of angle and he saw the boat broad side on. Two masts. A topsail schooner. He shook his head and passed the telescope over, pleased with the certainty of his answer. 'Yes, I see it. It's not Uncle Dan.'

Apart from that one ship the sea was grey and empty. The sacks being carried aboard 'My Queen' were more interesting. With their noses pressed to the glass the boys watched, while Hannah went back to her desk.

An hour or so later it was time for them to go home and she decided she'd walk with them. From the top of Quay Hill Matthew tried to pull himself up on the wall for a last look at the humpers. 'Must be a lot of room in that hold. I counted seventy-nine sacks before we left your window and they're still carrying them. There are a lot on the cart waiting. There must be a hundred at least!' His voice was round with respect.

'That's only part of the cargo,' Hannah told him. 'There's ball clay to go aboard yet.'

Matthew was impressed.

Later in the day, Hannah was in Tommy's office. Quite by chance she glanced down over his shoulder at the ledger still open in front of him, the list of items and the line he'd drawn beneath. The cargo going out on 'My Queen'. Idly she looked over it. Then, carefully, she read it again.

'Tommy, you've forgotten the grain.'

He frowned. 'Grain? Ah . . . ah, yes, so I have. I'll make a separate entry. Leave it now, tomorrow's soon enough. Time we put out the lamp and went home, Hannah.'

Something worried her. Was it because he didn't quite meet her eyes as he spoke? Was it the hurried: 'Leave it now'? Silently she pleaded: 'Tommy, tell me the truth. What are you doing? You and Ted Sharples. Something is wrong, I know it. But what? Why?' But she couldn't ask it. Tommy had always been sure there was an easy fortune waiting to be made. She didn't ask because she was frightened of what she might hear. Those sacks of grain must be his own, a personal stake, 'a bit of business' he'd call it, between himself and the grain merchant – and Ted Sharples too she expected. But why? His salary was good, she knew just how much he was paid and how it was used. She believed that was something in his nature she had to accept. He wasn't trading for the money it would bring him so much as to prove he could do it.

In the evening he told her he would be out for an hour or two. She asked no questions. She supposed it had something to do with this paltry transaction. She was sick at heart, ashamed for him – and yet she pitied him. Was it her fault? Was it because she cared so much about Netherton's that he couldn't find his independence there? But where did he think this sort of transaction could lead him? To buy a hundred or so sacks of grain, the profit he would make on selling them overseas surely wasn't worth bringing deceit into their lives.

When he came home they neither of them mentioned where he'd been. The shadow of that ledger hung between them but no word was spoken of it. He knew how to dispel her unease and desperately she clung to the remnants of her dreams. As he made love to her he believed he put an end to her suspicions – if suspicions there had been – just as surely as he'd drawn that line at the bottom of his list in the ledger.

Hannah had felt pity for him, been saddened by his need for such petty deceit, but a further discovery was to turn that pity into cold fury. Tommy hadn't bought the grain, taken the chance of making money on a deal of his own. An invoice had gone out to the merchant: 'For transportation of 110×2cwt. sacks of grain'. But there was no tallying entry in the books and the payment had gone straight into Tommy's pocket. She was shaken by anger that he could cheat Netherton's – the very pettiness of the amount belittled him even further! – and anger at herself that she could sink so low as to check the ledgers.

Her eyes were opened. When 'My Queen' returned from Oporto she watched, she actually spied! She counted the number of barrels off-loaded; she checked the books, disgusted with herself at what she did, and hating Tommy for forcing her into it. Nothing could ever be the same again. Whatever his excuses, whatever his lies, her hero had feet of clay. The very things she'd loved best in him sickened her most: his smile that didn't alter even when she knew he was cheating; the foppish elegance of his dress; the faint perfume of the oil he used on his hair; his confidence that he could always manipulate her to want his love.

'I'm always the same,' she'd said to Dan years ago. She'd believed it then, she still believed it. But Hannah was changing. She hinted to no one that her marriage was falling apart, never imagining that there were those who needed no telling.

'What are you suggesting? Do you suppose I'd make myself a thief for the few miserable shillings you seem to think I sometimes forget to write in the books?'

For weeks she'd said nothing. There was a lifetime still ahead of them, even now she couldn't lose all hope. Each month she'd expected evidence of a baby on the way, Kath found it easy enough, already she had two and seemed to anticipate more as if nothing were more simple, each month with the same regularity her period came. It rubbed salt in the wound of her unhappiness, evidence of her own failure. And this morning it had come again on the very day she'd found that, as usual, 'My Queen' had carried a cargo benefiting Tommy more than it did Netherton's.

'Why can't you be honest with me, Tommy?'

'Damnation, woman, would you have me sit with my head in your cursed books like my father does,' he blustered. 'Oh, he would never make a slip, never lose the firm a farthing. He'd check and check again, he'd think of nothing else. Well, I can't be like that! You knew when you married me that my life had never been narrowed down to what goes on in this bloody yard you're so besotted with!'

Silence. She daren't trust her voice. Neither of them had heard the step in the passage outside, so neither of them were aware that it had stopped and someone stood there statue-like listening. Tommy's tone changed. He took Hannah by the shoulders and turned her to face him. 'We're young, Hannah, we should be living. Come on. Forget this place, forget your books.' He smiled, a gentle, intimate smile. She couldn't bear to look at him. 'It's time we had a holiday. I know! We'll sail on the 'Oberon', have a few days in London, another honeymoon. What do you say?'

'This bloody yard' he'd called it. The rest had been salve to make her forget what he'd said, words to steer her mind away from the truth. She didn't answer him. She felt choked with emotions: hurt, anger, disappointment and, most of all, a sense of loss. She couldn't even begin to understand him. She turned away from him. A lifetime ahead of them, but she couldn't see the way forward.

For better, for worse, for richer, for poorer, in sickness, in health ... She put on her hat and jabbed the pin through it. Without a word she left him. Better, worse, sickness health . . . but nothing had prepared her for this. How could this be the Tommy she'd made those vows to? To love, honour, obey. Blindly she walked away from the yard, up Quay Hill. A holiday, he'd said, a second honeymoon. It touched a raw spot, brought memories of the first crowding in on her, the faith and trust she'd had in the future they would share.

At the top of the hill she stopped, gazing over the wall to the wharf below. Even now she wanted to think that her misery stemmed from her aching groin, heavy legs, a reminder of that other disappointment. Had it been like that for Aunt Lou? She and her Charles had been happy. Had she known this sense of failure as month after month she'd had to accept she couldn't give him the son he must have wanted? Hannah wanted to cling on to that as the reason for her unhappiness – but the truth couldn't be swept aside. Her mouth trembled, she held the corners of it between her teeth, biting hard. Love, honour. How could she honour him? She didn't respect him. And how could she love what she didn't respect? She took her hand out of her muff and held it against the stone wall. The feel of it, cold and rough, was part of the reality of life. And there was reality in the truth she was facing now. This morning's was no first quarrel. For months she'd watched the coming and goings of 'My Queen'. She'd looked for loopholes, tried to make excuses. She bit so hard on her lip that she tasted blood.

Turning away from the viewpoint where she'd spent so many hours before Aunt Lou had agreed to her coming to the yard, she made for Queen's Street and Crown Cottage. Not to the front door, but down the side path to the back, to the kitchen.

'The others are out.' Beatrice greeted her with outstretched hands. 'I'm glad they are.' Then, drawing Hannah in, 'What is it? Something's wrong.'

Living here had given Beatrice a new confidence. She was still as round-shouldered, still as sallow complexioned, there was no more flesh on her bones yet her manner had altered. She was no longer cowed, she wasn't ashamed of her existence. Here at Crown Cottage she knew she mattered.

'You've found out about him!' It wasn't a question. 'I ought to have been the one to tell you. I knew I should, but, Hannah, I was frightened. I thought you'd not want to hear the truth, you'd hang on to your illusions.'

'Tell me? But how could you know?'

'I've followed him. Not just once, but lots of times. For ages I've kept my eyes on him. I've seen them together.'

Ted Sharples! Hannah had been sure he must be involved somewhere. Anger got the upper hand again. 'And if you know, how many more do? Bea, I've been such a fool. There at the yard are they all seeing, talking behind my back, laughing that I'm not the businesswoman I thought – '

'They've been careful. They don't come near the yard. I doubt if any of the men know. Except that she doesn't pick her customers off the boats now that she's got him to keep her.'

Customers from the boats.

'Hannah, it had to come out. I knew it from the beginning. He was always wrong for you. Remember I told you about her when she lived in Merchant Place.'

Hannah turned away, facing the window, frowning out over the long, narrow garden and the coach-house at the bottom of it as if she was seeing it all for the first time.

'Ought I to have been brave and told you, Hannah? Please look at me. I've watched; I've waited. I've prayed too, truly I've prayed to do the right thing. I was so afraid that if I was the one to tell you, you'd hate me for it.' Her lips trembled. She stood there with her hands clasped, her fingers restless. 'Hannah . . . please, Hannah . . .'

'Beatrice, as if I could ever hate you.' Hannah turned to her friend.

'Don't stay with him. I lie awake at nights imagining him with you, touching you, coming from her to you.'

'I didn't know about Susie Syms and yet, looking back, I can see . . . Bea, let's not talk about it.' Hannah heard herself say. It was as if their positions had been reversed and it was she who must comfort Beatrice.

'Don't stay with him. I could easily leave here, we'd find a place together. Picture it, Hannah. I'd keep house for us, you'd have your ships. We'd be happy.'

Hannah didn't take it as a serious suggestion. 'Leave here, you say? Aren't you happy here, Bea? I thought everything was going so well.'

'Yes, oh yes. She's a dear and the boys too.' Then she smiled, a rare and unexpected smile, lifting the atmosphere and making her look almost pretty. 'But there can only be one Hannah.'

'Where have Rosalind and the boys gone?' Hannah asked after a pause.

'Out to see some friends the boys have made at school.' Beatrice settled down in the rocking chair with her basket of darning. It seemed she was content to change the subject. 'I went to see Kath when I was shopping this morning. Timothy is so sweet with his baby sister. She's five months, you know, five months today, baby Trudie.'

Hannah tried to listen, tried to stop her thoughts wandering.

Bea went on: 'Kath's very good, she never grumbles, but they're so hard up on what old skinflint Coldrige pays Richard. She says he's had several offers, jobs people want him to do in his spare time, you know. It would make such a difference to them. But there isn't a spare inch in that rabbit hutch of a house for him to work in. She's so proud of it all – and I expect before she's many months older she'll be sticking out her stomach with number three on the way. I can't understand her.'

'I wish we could help. Would she – '

'She certainly wouldn't! I'm making woollen combinations for Timmy now that he's clean in the daytime. But she's so touchy if she thinks we look on them as hard up.'

'Perhaps they aren't, Bea, not in the things that count.' And like a cold cloud her misery settled on her.

Beatrice was steadily weaving her darning wool, it was the only movement. 'Isn't this nice.' It wasn't a question, she didn't expect an answer. 'Water dripped into my room again last night. I put a bowl to catch it. I don't like to worry – '

'Wait and speak to Dan. He'll get it done. He'll be back soon.'

'Louisah' didn't make the long voyages 'Europa' had, at least not yet. Her maiden trip had taken her to Lagos; she'd carried granite and come home with mahogany. Dan had sailed with such confidence, sure that each day he would walk more easily. But it hadn't worked out like that. He'd arrived home looking ill, deep lines of pain etched on his face. Even Louise had had the tact not to voice her opinion. Fear had kept her silent. If Dan must go to sea then his voyages should be short, coastal trade and continental at the most. So now, never away for longer than a week or two, he'd become part of the household at Crown Cottage.

There had been a time, in the days when they'd lived at Netherton Hall, when Beatrice had dreaded his visits. There had been something in Hannah's affection for him that had frightened her. But now she welcomed him. Hannah was married, albeit to a faithless husband. It was Rosalind and the boys who looked to Dan to complete their family. So when Hannah said 'Dan will soon be home' she was content to leave the problem of the leaking roof until he was home to take responsibility for it. She would have been less happy sitting here putting heels back into small socks if she'd realized what those words meant to Hannah.

Dan, her dear unchanging Dan, her prop. If she remembered what she thought she'd glimpsed through that momentary chink in his armour, she didn't let herself admit it. More than anything she wanted to tell him . . . but to tell him what? About Susie? About those unaccounted cargoes? Talk about Tommy to someone else? 'My husband is cheating the company – so that he can keep another woman.' And what did she really feel, what did she want? If Tommy were to promise her he'd give Susie up, what would she feel then? She made herself answer honestly, and was shocked by the truth. Was she any better than he was? She'd made excuses, she couldn't love him because he'd lost her respect. But if she'd really loved him nothing he had done could have destroyed what she'd felt for him. She longed to talk to Dan, to tell him everything. But she couldn't. And sitting half listening to Beatrice talking about the boys she faced another truth. It wasn't because of Tommy she couldn't take her unhappiness to Dan. It was because of herself, and of him, because of something she ought always to have realized.

Beatrice was tidying away her mending. Rosalind and the boys were due back. Without waiting to see them today, Hannah went home.

She hated subterfuge. But if she faced Tommy with what she'd been told she'd hear excuses, lies, perhaps even promises. She couldn't bear to hear him trying to talk his way out of the truth. Even in the beginning, when she'd hung on his every word, watched for his smile, how much truth had there been in his love? She'd trusted him, that was what hurt, and all the time he'd been running to that pretty little tart. Uninvited she heard the echo of his voice, the evening of the train de-railment: 'God save me from puritanical women.' Was that how he'd always seen her, even while she'd struggled to find that perfect moment when she'd believed their spirits had fused, their bodies and their spirits?

All her instincts told her to be honest. If he preferred Susie Syms then tell him to go to her. But she couldn't bring herself to speak any of it, she didn't want to trust her voice. As it worked out, though, she found herself alone. He'd sent a message that he would be late.

'In that case I won't wait.' Hannah showed no surprise when the maid gave her the message. 'Serve dinner at the usual time Madge.' With or without him the thought of food held no attraction. But to eat it was a challenge. She dressed, she sat alone, and she went steadily through the meal. At the end of it she felt better, she had scored a point.

It was late when he came home. With raised brows Hannah eyed him coolly. Consciously she stood tall, to her full height, chin up; the action seemed to set her apart from his pretty little strumpet. She wasn't aware of it but just so might Louise have faced Charles had he ever kicked over the traces. There was almost a 'Hah!' in her expression.

'I hope you didn't have them keep dinner for me. I have fed,' he told her.

How dared he look at her with such assurance. Fed! In that hovel in Tanner's Row. His face wore the smile she'd fallen in love with. He held her gaze. It was as though he were laughing at her.

'I hadn't expected to stay so long, but I could tell she was glad to have me there.' How dared he! Hannah could hardly believe what she was hearing. His smile held a look of triumph, he must have followed her thoughts. 'The faithful Gladys appreciated it too. When the old girl gets the hump it's always Gladys has to bear the brunt.'

* * *

225

'Tommy not in yet, Hannah?' Alan asked next morning.

'No. I came on, on my own. Is something the matter?' There was something in his manner that told her all wasn't well, he looked worried, tired.

'No, no. I just looked in to say good morning.' And that in itself was unusual. Even so she didn't realize just what it was that worried Alan – and yet she knew there was little went on at Netherton's that he didn't know about. Her own problems were making her blind to other people's.

It was a relief when the boys arrived to take up position at her window. Water was high. When 'Louisah' appeared round the headland and their whoop of excitement told her what they saw, a wave of relief surged through her. Dan was home.

As the ship moved towards the wharf the boys ran down the stairs to wait just outside Netherton's gate on the public quay. They knew the rules. They weren't allowed up the gangplank, they must wait for him to come ashore. Hannah had never waited. Now from her window she watched, remembering the joy, the importance, of what she'd always taken for granted. It had always been just the same, she'd rush on board the moment the gangplank was in place; whatever Dan had been doing his arms had been ready. His homecomings had been the high points, her life had been marked by them. 'That was while we were waiting for Dan to get home from Buenos Aires.' 'It was just after he'd sailed for Lima.' Or Gibraltar, or Calcutta or Trieste . . . Even when she'd fallen in love with Tommy: 'I wish Dan would get home so that I could tell him.'

Now she could no longer rush up the gangplank, hurl herself into his arms. From her room she watched. Was he remembering too?

Matthew's excitement was getting the better of him. Every now and again, his hands flat, he'd rub his palms together, then he'd jump, once, twice, three times. That was his way of letting off steam, saving his boiler from bursting with excitement. And when finally Dan came ashore, Matthew was the first to rush to him. But Dan had an arm for each of the boys.

Hannah's attention was diverted by the sight of a pony and trap coming along the quay towards Netherton's. Like her, Dan recognized the driver and opened the gate for him to drive through, following him in. Harold Thurlston! Seeing him here, against a background so unfamiliar to him, could mean only one thing. Hannah sped down the stairs and out to the yard as he lowered his great frame from the trap.

'Is it Aunt Lou?'

''Fraid so, m'dear. I fetched Dr Roberts first. Now I've come for you.'

CHAPTER NINE

The day had started badly for Louise.

'Silly blessed bones, giving me jip this morning – ouch – where's that stupid Gladys? Never on hand when she's wanted.' Then, steadying herself and standing straight, gripping the end rail of her brass bedstead: 'Come on now, Louise Netherton, pull yourself together.' It was coming to a pretty pass if she couldn't walk from her bedroom to the lavatory without an arm to lean on. 'Hah!' she muttered half under her breath. 'Once I can get to that stick . . . Steady now.' She stood still, head high, one hand on the bedpost. 'No one's watching – and old fool they'd think you if they were. Look at you there in that mirror. One leg at a time.'

'Ouch,' she whistled through stiff lips, 'bend the knee, that's it, bend it. Ouch! Bend it . . . Now the other . . . up . . . bend . . . Blessed joints!' A moment's rest, then the whole procedure again. Standing on one leg, the other bent, she caught sight of her reflection. There wasn't much mirth in her laugh. 'Look at you! What a sketch. Can you see me, Charles? What a business.'

Determination brought her to her stick, and with its help she managed the corridor to the lavatory. Determination or just pride? This morning it was a battle, but she'd not pull that bell cord and let everyone in the kitchen know what she'd come to. Gladys was a different matter. 'Taking her time down there – gossiping. She knows I feel better when she's on hand. And if she doesn't know it, then I'm not telling her!' The corridor seemed to have grown longer in the night, but she managed and her success gave her added confidence as she made her way back to the bedroom. Her grip was never too secure; it wasn't the first time she'd let her stick slip from her grasp.

No one heard her calling and she couldn't get to the bell rope. Couldn't? Whoever heard such talk. Who had ever gain-said Louise Netherton?

It was fortunate that at the moment she fell, Gladys was crossing the hall bearing her large enamel jug of water. Never had she got up those stairs so fast as she did now, the jug left behind on the hall table. She thought to help her mistress to her feet and get her back to bed, but one glance and it was apparent something was very wrong.

Harold Thurlston was sent to bring Dr Roberts. A broken leg could have been put in a splint – although at her age it would have been no certain cure. For a broken hip he could do nothing. Like a bird with a broken wing, Louise's mobility was over.

While Dr Roberts had got her back to bed and sent for a nurse, Harold had put the pony at a brisk trot down the hill to Deremouth and Hannah.

'I'll come,' she said without waiting to hear the story of the accident, 'you can tell me what's happened as we go along.'

'Can I find your husband for you while you get your cloak on?'

'He's out.' Out? she remembered his cool words at breakfast: 'I'll probably not be at the yard today.' 'I'll leave a message with his father.'

Only then did she realize that someone was beside her, gripping her hand.

'I'm coming with you,' Dan told her. 'Get your cloak and bonnet, there's a good girl.'

She nodded and turned back into the building like an obedient child. Dan was here. Her momentary panic was over.

All that day shock and pain combined to keep Louise in a state only bordering on consciousness. By her bed

Hannah and Dan kept vigil but she gave no sign that she was aware they were there. It was late in the afternoon when Tommy came, but she didn't know that either.

'I shall stay here. While she's like this I won't leave her,' Hannah told him.

'Yes, you do that. I'll look in tomorrow but there's no point in my staying now. She doesn't know.'

They spoke politely, almost like strangers. Yesterday hung between them and they were relieved to be apart.

That night Louise hovered on the brink between this world and the next. And from the look of her she was sorry when morning came to find that she'd fallen back on the wrong side. Today her mind was clear, and she had no illusions about what she could expect from life.

'Hah!' For a long time she did no more than repeat that one sound. At first it was hardly more than the hint of a sigh. Then, as she took stock of her situation, her voice grew stronger. There was fight left in her yet.

And in the next few days as Hannah sat hour after hour at her side, seldom speaking, they grew closer than they had ever been.

'Ships,' Louise mumbled on one occasion and Hannah bent close to hear her. It wasn't easy to catch her words. '. . . can trust ships, child. Wind in their sails. Hah!'

'If we could get your bed to a window in the opposite bedroom you could see the estuary.'

'. . . see it . . .' she tapped her forehead '. . . in here. Yard. . . . boats . . . Charles . . . in here.'

Hannah held her hand. She felt choked with affection.

'Aunt Lou.' But how do you tell a dying woman how dear she is?

It seemed there was no need. 'That's 'nough. I know, child . . . good child . . . I know . . .' Her eyes closed. Sleep was never far away. Yet when she spoke next her voice was almost normal. 'That young rascal – when's he coming? Young Tommy. Charm the birds . . . off the trees

230

. . . always said so. Birds off the trees. Hah!' And again she slept.

Tommy visited Netherton Hall each day. He never stayed more than a minute or two, but if Louise could be said to have smiled it was on him. No one else would greet her with: 'And how's my favourite aunt today?' or 'I'm not going to stay and tire you but I had to check that you're behaving yourself.'

For a week or so she lay helpless, drifting ever further from them. Dan spent hours with her and from his presence too they knew she derived comfort. He'd talk to her, of ships and voyages, her only sign of awareness the occasional grunt. But her expression was peaceful. There was no doubt that even if she didn't follow all he said she enjoyed the atmosphere he conjured up for her.

Her room was hot, the fire never allowed to burn low and the smell of lavender thrown into the flames wafting out into the corridor. How was it, lying in that temperature, she could get pneumonia? For that was what Dr Roberts told them it was as the fever raged.

'I'm sorry, my dear,' he said to Hannah, confirming what she already knew, 'but you must be prepared for the worst. We can't move her, her lungs are full of fluid.'

'She's always been tough, except for her "silly bones". Don't you think – '

They were standing just inside the hall and at that moment the front door opened to admit Tommy for his flying daily visit.

'Ah,' Dr Roberts greeted him, 'I'm glad you've come. I've just been warning your wife, Mr Webster. Things are grave, very grave. You must console yourselves that Mrs Netherton is beyond knowing. It can't be long now. No more than hours, my dear.' He put a hand on Hannah's shoulder. 'Send for me at any time, any hour. But Nurse Dodds will be here and she's a tower of strength. She'll be with you when the end comes.'

After he left, Hannah and Tommy were alone, facing each other in the large, still hall. For a moment neither of them spoke. Hannah's thoughts were upstairs with Louise.

'She didn't know I was here yesterday. If she's not going to notice I think I'll not disturb her. I'll get back to town. He seems to think she's not going to hang on for long.'

Hannah went back up the stairs. She felt no anger at Tommy that he could speak like that; anger would have been a call on her emotions. For him she felt nothing. In the bedroom she gazed down at Louise, a figure so different now from the proud woman who'd never let herself stoop even though she forced herself straight with her two sticks. It was less than two weeks since her fall but in that time she'd aged years. Her hair was in two thin plaits, her thin face had unnaturally bright patches accentuating her cheekbones, her eyes were sunk in their sockets, her mouth open. Only her hands were unchanged, those long boney fingers. Kneeling by her side Hannah took one of them in hers and lifted it gently to rub her cheek against it. Each breath rattled in Louise's chest; the sound hadn't altered all day. Seconds ticked into minutes.

Dan's step could be heard on the stairs. Hannah recognized it, the uneven tread a legacy from the wreck. A light tap on the door and he came in.

'No change?' he whispered.

She shook her head. Then, tucking Louise's hand under the covers, she sat on the bedside chair where she'd spent so many hours. He drew a second one to the opposite side and the silent vigil went on. Neither knew the other's thoughts, what ghosts from the past were their companions. Nurse Dodds returned from downstairs where she'd been having her meal. She had things to do for her patient.

'If there's the slightest change I'll call you,' she promised. 'Go and have your supper and a breath of air outside. I can't be doing with more than one patient on my hands!'

She spoke with all the brisk authority of ladies of her calling.

Downstairs Hannah and Dan faced each other across the dining table. The empty place at its head seemed to dominate the room.

'I remember my first meal here,' Hannah muttered. It had been difficult to swallow then, and so it was now. Memories of the past were everywhere just as they were when, the pretence of a meal over, they went into the library.

'This is where I first met you – a friend come to visit Aunt Lou. Do you remember, Dan?' But she knew he did.

What was there about this evening that made him say what he'd never have said normally? Hannah, married to Tommy, making a life which as time went on would have no place for him. Yet tonight none of that was important. When he spoke, it was from his heart. Upstairs Louise lay dying; between him and Hannah there must be truth.

'I remember that first day, and all of it through the years. The child I loved, the woman I've no right to love.'

Hearing his words she wasn't surprised. They, and somehow that third upstairs, were in a world of their own. It was Dan who'd shown Hannah the path to find the real Louise. Not a living soul – not even Gladys – knew her as they did, and it was right, it was the only way, that as she came to the end of her life there was nothing but honesty between them.

'Dan.' Hannah took his hand in hers and carried it to her cheek, pressing it hard against her. 'Why couldn't I have seen it.'

'If you'd known how I felt it couldn't have altered things. It was Tommy you fell in love with.'

'That was the child, Dan.' She shook her head from side to side. It was as if she wanted to free herself of something. 'Such a mess.' He heard the croak in her voice. She was crying silently, with no harsh sobs. Her face twisted. Already her eyes were reddened as the tears came.

'Sweetheart, don't, don't.' Tenderly he pulled her into his arms, holding her head to his shoulder. 'You're dead tired, you're upset. She'd not want you to cry.'

She sniffed, rubbing her face against him. 'It's not just for Aunt Lou. It's everything.' But after another sniff or two she began to recover. She'd longed to pour out her troubles to him; for weeks, months, as she'd suspected and spied on Tommy she'd imagined the relief of being able to talk to Dan even though she knew she could never do it. But now none of that mattered. Enough that he held her, that her head rested against him. 'The child I loved, the woman I've no right to love.'

In the grate coals slipped, sending a burst of sparks into the chimney.

'Say it again, Dan. That you love me.'

She thought he wasn't going to answer. But in this hour of truth and honesty there could be no pretence. 'I love you, my Hannah. Did I really need to tell you? Didn't you know it?'

'Oh, Dan, what have I done? I love you. I loved you when I was still a child.' She looked directly at him, holding his gaze. 'But I'm a woman now. In my heart I must surely always have known that I could never be whole without you.' She touched her lips against his. And then he kissed her, at first gently then crushing her to him as if he were starved of her love. It seemed they couldn't draw apart. Holding each other they rocked gently, face rubbing against face. Then again his mouth covered hers. This moment was their own. Later the reality of the situation would topple their dreams, but nothing could take this from them.

'That first day here in the library,' she whispered, her fingers caressing the back of his neck, 'do you remember, there was a poem?'

234

'Your father's. Yes. Not all the words, perhaps, but I haven't forgotten the meaning. You said you didn't understand it.'

'I do now. *"To love but once and once for all, In unity and truth delight, Where'er that love's long shadow fall is blessed in His sight"*.'

'Once for all, my Hannah.'

Her fingers on the back of his neck were still. He didn't kiss her. The moment touched them both, held them like a benediction.

Footsteps came running down the stairs. 'I think you should come,' they heard Nurse Dodds call as she crossed the hall.

Louise had never been dictated to in her life and apparently she meant to die in her own time too. For nearly three hours Dan and Hannah sat by the bedside, their chairs close, her hand in his. The rattle from Louise's chest had quietened. Indeed her breathing was shallow, her mouth slightly open, her eyes closed. The clock in the hall chimed each quarter, struck each hour.

It was as it struck the single note of one o'clock that her eyes opened, almost as if the familiar sound had penetrated her consciousness. She stared hard first at Hannah, then at Dan. It was as if her vision and her reason was suddenly clear. Hannah leant forward, opened her mouth to speak. But Louise seemed to be looking through her and beyond, a faint smile on her lips.

'Aunt Lou.' Hannah wanted to hold her back, to tell her. She raised the hand still linked with Dan's and held it to her aunt's cheek, 'Aunt Lou, Dan and me . . .'

Louise's mouth opened. They thought she meant to speak. But whether or not to Hannah they would never know. She was beyond words, perhaps she was beyond understanding, but her head nodded – nodded and flopped forward. Whatever it was she had understood, whoever she had seen in her final minute, Louise had found peace.

There were few hours of night left by the time Hannah got to bed and yet it seemed that dawn would never come. One ghost after another chased through her mind. Louise . . . She pictured her aunt stomping into that 'better land', her sharp eyes taking it all in, making sure things were up to standard! But, of course, she wouldn't stomp in on those sticks, not to Charles. She'd be the Louise he'd known, the Louise who, to him, would never have grown old and tired; the woman Dan had talked about who used to play cricket on her side lawn, the bride who'd walked up the aisle so long ago. That wasn't the Aunt Lou Hannah had known though, and in the stillness of that night other thoughts, other memories, crowded in.

Her own parents, the child she'd been as she'd grown up in that little house in Hastings . . . Would they see her as changed? For, she had changed, she knew, in these years at Deremouth. Or was there something, a core, a spirit, call it what you will, that never alters? So that whatever happens, however long you have to wait, one day you'll be together and things will be just as you've always expected. She knew where her thoughts were taking her. Her and Dan.

Was it her own fault that she was married to a man she didn't love? Was it her fault he'd not been faithful to her? He might have found reasons enough to lay at her door; her own only feeling of guilt came from knowing that all those dreams she'd started out with, all the fight she'd made to hang on to them, meant nothing now. Yet she was married, her life pledged to his, a prisoner to the vows she couldn't un-make. Her mind was back with Dan: 'And once for all, my Hannah.' Then to Aunt Lou, to the Charles she'd never known . . . round and round it went, but always back to Dan. At last daylight broke, the long night over.

Gladys had seemed ageless, the same yesterday, today and forever; never young, so with no youth to lose. But the morning after Louise died time had caught up with her. Suddenly she was an old woman, her plain face blotchy with weeping. It had been she who'd so often been the butt of her mistress's ill-humour, but she'd known she was needed. Now the voice was silenced and Gladys was lost. And there was something more than grief behind her tears. For more than fifty years she'd served Louise Netherton. They'd aged together, accepting each other. But who would want her now? Never until today had she spoken to Hannah with such deference. 'The mistress wants you – and best you get a move on she's not expecting to be kept waiting.' The echo of Louise's voice seemed to hang between them but today it was 'Mrs Webster, ma'am' from Gladys and nothing could have brought home to Hannah with more force that Louise had gone.

'A most straighforward will dated April 1853, invalidating the previous document we'd held. Changed by codicil at the time of your marriage, Mrs Webster.' Mr Clutterbuck of Clutterbuck, Christy and Clutterbuck looked at Tommy and Hannah over his half moon spectacles. All that Louise had was to pass to Hannah. So far straightforward indeed and reason enough for Tommy's tight-lipped expression. Netherton Shipping Company was entailed for her eldest son: 'And in the event of my said niece's demise without male heir, the Company shall pass to Daniel Lowden for his lifetime and thereafter to his eldest male heir.'

No legal document is simple. It was some minutes before Mr Clutterbuck folded away the papers and turned to smile benignly at his young clients.

'We've handled Mrs Netherton's affairs for many years and her late husband's before that. The business, of course, is an open book to you, sir, but there are other investments. We've managed them for her. Now, of course, in the happy event of your wishing the arrangement to continue, there are various papers for signature.'

'You'd like me to come to your office?' Hannah offered.

'Not a bit of it. There's no need for you to trouble yourself. I shall, of course, need your husband's signature but that will suffice.' He beamed on Hannah as if he were bestowing a favour on her.

'But things are in my name.' Hannah frowned.

'Indeed, yes. And from the way some of the politicians would have us think the day may come when the ladies will have to be called on regarding the management of their affairs.' But he laughed as he said it; such newfangled nonsense wasn't to be taken seriously in his opinion. 'However, as long as the law stands as it does today, the estate is controlled by your husband. Head of the house, sir, eh, what?' He chuckled, despite the solemn occasion.

Tommy had heard the will read, surprise and disappointment giving way to anger. He and the old lady had got on he'd been sure. He'd half expected that any alteration she'd made would have been to name him as sole beneficiary. Failing that he'd been confident they would have been joint inheritors. Now, listening to Mr Clutterbuck's parting words, his spirits rose. It seemed that all Hannah had was, to all intents and purposes, his.

Expectations of wealth are one thing but, the will read and explained, he found the reality very different. He looked at the elegant Adam fireplace – his! He opened the door to see Mr Clutterbuck out, a heavy door, solid, a heavy and solid brass handle smooth to his touch – his! A new assurance was born in Tommy, and with it a thankfulness that Louise had timed her departure when she had. For Hannah had found out about Susie and that house in Tanner's Row. And she'd found out about more than that, too. Now that his future was safe Tommy could look back to that day a couple of weeks or so ago, the morning when she'd faced him with accusations about what was going on

238

on 'My Queen', then the evening when he'd returned from seeing the old lady to be confronted with what she'd heard about Susie. He'd blustered, he'd known he'd walked a tight-rope: 'I suppose your girl friend has been whispering her slanderous lies in your ear – wanting you to herself again. Is that it?' Wordlessly Hannah had turned and left him. And in the morning his salvation had come; Louise had fallen.

Since then Hannah had been living at the Hall, their paths had hardly crossed. Now, as he came back from seeing Mr Clutterbuck to his carriage, she said something about 'things to sort out here'. A feeble excuse, but he made no objection.

'So I shall stay on here,' she told him.

His lips curled into a smile. 'You won't need me. The yard has been closed all day. I'll call in there on my way home.' His yard, his ships! If Hannah needed to be alone, so too did he.

But the following morning she was back in her office. If Tommy saw it as 'his yard' she certainly saw it as hers, a place that never changed. Years ago she'd felt it was the centre of the universe, and she still did, the hub of life. It had become the hub of hers, and the more confused and troubled she was, the more she needed the challenges it brought her.

Each evening she returned to the Hall. Tommy didn't suggest he should join her, nor yet that it was time she came back to Vicary Terrace. But the way they were living couldn't go on forever. Always like a wall in front of her there seemed to be something that prevented her looking into the future, prevented her even wanting to probe.

'I suppose one of these days we'll have to give up the house in town,' was the first mention of it from Tommy.

'No rush. It's convenient to have somewhere near the yard.' Her voice gave nothing away. She held it steady, listened to herself speaking the words.

'Yes, yes,' he agreed all too willingly, 'plenty of time. I really ought to help you there, it's my job as much as yours. But I don't want to intrude in a lady's personal things.' Such solicitude, such understanding. Nothing to suggest he was enjoying his freedom.

Alan watched. He was worried. It wasn't right.

'It's not fair on the boy, Em,' he grumbled to his wife. 'Her place is with him, whether it's in their own home or at the Hall. They should be together. It's not as though she's distraught with grief, she works like a demon. Not the way a marriage should be.'

'You worry too much,' Emily answered, practical as always. 'Tommy doesn't seem put off by her staying at the Hall, nothing of the neglected husband in him. He was here this morning, you know, on his way back from seeing the solicitor. Papers he had to sign, he said. Tommy's a man of substance these days, just take heart from that, a man of property. No matter about Hannah.'

But Alan still frowned. Things weren't as he'd imagined they'd be. But even to himself he didn't want to admit what was wrong. For years he'd managed Netherton's, always dreamed of the day when he'd give up and Tommy would hold the reins. Yet he'd never expected to feel like this, as if already he were a back number. To be fair – and Alan always tried to be fair – it wasn't Hannah who'd changed.

'Never comes here these days.' Now it was Emily who was airing her misgivings. 'I must say I'd hoped for – oh, I don't know – affection. Or was that too much to hope for? She used to come in. I suppose it was a novelty, dare say she wanted to be seen as the good daughter-in-law. It's weeks, months, since she's just popped in for ten minutes on her own. Lose a son and gain a daughter they say – not with that one.'

'Be fair to the girl, Em. She works hard at the yard and then there's a lot for her to see to for her aunt.'

'Humph. Time she gave up the yard, interfering in Tommy's affairs. Time she gave her mind to giving him a son. That'll be the day, Alan, Tommy's boy.'

'If it's a grandson you're hoping for, you're not likely to get one the way they're living. I tell you, it worries me.'

Kath had been giving her parlour its weekly 'turn out'. Each picture had been taken down from the wall, each ornament off the mantelpiece. Now, everything sparkling to her satisfaction, she was re-hanging the pictures, climbing on to the kitchen chair to reach to slip the hooks over the rail. Meanwhile Timothy trundled up and down the narrow passageway on the hobby horse Richard had made for him, and in the kitchen Trudie, now seven months old, was asleep in a wooden crib – something else Richard had fashioned. And, just as Beatrice had prophesied, Kath's figure bore evidence of her further fruitfulness.

Richard was late home for his dinner. He always came in at five past one and just before that she had strained the potatoes ready. Now it was nearly a quarter past. As she worked she listened for his step. When she recognized it, hurrying along Merchants Place, there were still one or two last ornaments to be put back and the last picture to re-hang. But without hesitation Kath turned her back on the unfinished parlour. She'd put the finishing touches to it this afternoon. Here was Richard, hungry for dinner and late into the bargain. So she carried the kitchen chair back to its place, then hurried to 'dish up' on to their plates. Kath prided herself that she never kept him waiting.

'Here's your Pa,' she called to the galloping Timothy. 'Have you done a pee like I told you? Then climb back into your chair.'

The routine never varied, neither did the food. Their palates had become used to boiled mutton, thin gravy reinforced with barley and potatoes and mopped up with bread to give it substance. Occasionally, as today, carrots added colour and interest. On the range the saucepan lid bobbed up and down; the windows were running with steam. Boiled mutton was to be followed by suet pudding, a round and shiny football to be smothered with the homemade jam that was already put to warm.

'It's all ready.' Kath beamed her regular welcome. 'Arms up, Timmy, there's a love, let's get your pinny on. You're late today,' she said to Richard. 'I was just putting the finishing touches to the parlour while we waited.'

All her life Kath had found happiness was hers for the taking in the everyday things around her. She'd never craved what she knew was out of reach. The sun slipping behind the moor in a glow of evening glory might move Beatrice almost to tears — and for what she'd never understood — but to Kath it had meant another fine day tomorrow. So now living on Richard's meagre wage might give them a diet that was monotonous, but her family had enough to eat and she found her satisfaction in eking out her money to last each week and never being beaten.

Now she served the food and took Richard's pewter tankard to pour his cider from the barrel. It was a luxury left over from Christmas when Harold had had it delivered to them; each day it had been doled out like a ration at mid-day. Today saw the end of it, thick and cloudy, no more than two inches up the tankard.

'Hey, Kath, it's half empty.'

'Drink it slowly, love, make it last. It's half full — and that's the last.'

Half empty — half full. Either way there was no more to come.

'What made you so late for your dinner? Ten minutes late you were.'

'I met that Mr Lowden, lives at Crown Cottage, you know, friend of Hannah's. All very well for him, he doesn't have a guv'nor watching him in and out. Get me my

242

pudding, Kath, before you finish your dinner. I haven't time to sit around while young Timothy chews.'

'Yes, of course, I'll see to it.' Richard had his job to do, she had hers. She untied the suet football and tipped it from its greasy cloth to slither on to a dinner plate. A large lump of it for Richard, blackberry jam, hot and sticky, smothering it. 'Careful with your mouth. That jam's been heating a long time, it's pretty well bubbling.'

He blew on it, an irritable frown etching deep lines between his brows.

'What did Mr Lowden want with you? Nothing wrong with Beatrice is there?'

'Didn't mention Beatrice. I'll have to scrape this jam off Kath, I've not got time to wait while it cools. Can't think why you got it so hot. Ten minutes and I've got to be back there.' Then unexpectedly he smiled, something that happened rarely these days. 'It was about the stable at the cottage. I'll tell you this evening.' And with one eye on the clock he shovelled the un-jammed, palid pudding into his mouth. With the last spoonful he stood up. In her crib Trudie stirred, sucking hard on her fists as she realized she was hungry. Kath guided Timothy's spoon into his mouth; she mashed potato and carrot into the gravy for Trudie; she piled her own fork with the fast chilling mutton stew and, with her mouth full, raised her face for Richard's farewell salute. Here in the bosom of her family Kath was content. 'Hard up' Beatrice had said. But to Kath their perpetual shortage of money was a small price to pay for all this – her home, her family, the flutter of that new life within her, a good husband. What if she had a struggle to manage on the few shillings he brought home each week? At least it was regular, it sufficed. The children grew healthy.

With a few crystals of soda to help her get rid of the grease on the dishes, she washed up. If she looked slippy she could give the parlour windows a good shine while the sun was high enough to see the smears. Dan Lowden and the stable were forgotten. So, too, although she didn't realize it, was Richard.

Today there was no reception committee waiting on the quayside, the boys were at school. Hannah had meant to stay in her room, watch from her window. But how could she? There he was! Since just after Louise had died Dan had been at sea. Now he was home! How could she wait and watch from up here?

Tommy was at the end of Netherton's wharf talking to Ted Sharples. He saw her run out from the sheds, bareheaded and with no cloak, hurrying to be ready when the gangplank of 'Louisah' was put down. He saw her board the ship and then, only feet away from Dan, suddenly stop quite still. Until that moment the thought had only been half-formed in his mind, hardly even that. Hannah with a lover! Hannah committing adultery! The idea was scarcely born when it died. Wishful thinking. Hannah hadn't rushed to Dan's arms as she used to. He was an old friend, not just of hers but of her aunt's. Nothing more than that. He turned back to Ted Sharples. What he was proposing was far more interesting.

Today Dan didn't take her into his cabin as he used to. But it didn't matter. Standing here on deck, rocked by the gentle motion of the water, she asked for nothing more. She hardly noticed the bustle all around them.

'I've thought about you.' To see him no one could guess at his words or at the depth of their meaning.

She nodded. 'I know. Dan, I'm staying at the Hall.'

'You mean just you?'

Again she nodded.

'Hannah, have I done this to you? Have I spoilt what you had?'

'No, you know you haven't. Dan, that night I only told

244

you half of it. I told you about me, about us. That was all that mattered.'

He forced tobacco into the bowl of his pipe with exaggerated care, anything to occupy his hands. He wanted to reach out to her, his Hannah. Half the story, she'd said.

'And there's more?'

'So much more, but none of it's important. That's how I knew I'd made such a dreadful mistake. None of it seemed to touch me.'

Mr Bailey was coming near, not to join them but moving to where he would have a better vantage of what was being brought up from the hold.

For his benefit Hannah said: 'Dan, I've been so busy at the Hall. Aunt Lou wanted you to have some of Uncle Charles' books. Can you go through them sometime?'

'I'll come up this evening, if that's convenient.'

She nodded. Convenient! 'I'll expect you for dinner.'

Had there been no ears but their own to consider their talk would have kept to narrower lines. As it was he asked her about the family at Crown Cottage, listened to her talk of the boys. And so it was the conversation came round to Beatrice, and from her to Kath.

'I wish there was some way I could help. She's such a dear, she never complains, and Richard is a splendid cabinet maker. Beatrice says people often ask him to do work for them, take orders on his own, and I don't wonder. But there's no room for him to do it. Dan, I've been wondering whether I should offer him part of the coachhouse at the Hall to use as a workshop. What do you think?'

'What he needs is somewhere in town. By the time he's walked right out there, he'd have so little time.'

All that happened at about half-past ten in the morning. And that's how it was that Richard came to be late home for dinner and had no time to cool his jam. At Crown

Cottage they had no carriage, the stable and the coach-house at the end of the narrow garden stood empty. But Rosalind was mistress of the house, Dan had promised her she always would be. So before he suggested what he had in mind to Richard he had to talk to her, to steer her thoughts into the right channel so that the idea seemed to come from her. And only then did he stop Richard in the street as the men filed out of Mr Coleridge's workshop.

That same evening, dinner over, Hannah and Dan were in the library. She'd had the fire lit as soon as she arrived, and banked high. Although it was spring the evenings were cold and even with the blaze that roared up the chimney the room still felt un-aired. It had hardly been used at all since Louise's death. With the door closed they were left alone, no one would disturb them. They'd come to sort Charles's books. In a minute. There was no hurry. Not yet. They moved towards the hearth.

'Only half the story, you said?' Gently, he held her chin in one hand, his gaze holding hers. 'Tell me, Hannah.'

'It's none of it important, Dan. It wasn't, even when I heard about it. Tommy has a mistress.' A slight change in his expression: a tightening of his mouth, a narrowing of his eyes. She could have imagined it. 'Perhaps she's not really that. She's – she's a prostitute, that's all I know. She used to wait around on the quay. A pretty prostitute. She doesn't go there anymore, she hasn't for ages. I've been told she has a house in Tanner's Row. Tommy rents it for her.'

'Who told you this?' Anger blazed in him. At Tommy for treating his beloved Hannah like it, letting his infidelity make of her marriage a subject for gossip and speculation; at the malicious tale-bearer; at himself that he could do nothing.

246

'Bea. She'd known for ages and not wanted to say. Poor Bea.'

He drew her into his arms. Then, sitting on the swivel chair at the desk, he pulled her on to his knee, holding her close.

'Dan, I wish I could just sail away with you. Sail the seas, share your life. Lots of masters take their wives.' She sat up straight, turning to face him. 'It's only a word – "wife". They might as well say "chattel", "possession". But I'll never be that to him again, never! Dan – ' and only to him could she bring herself to say this – 'he doesn't care about Netherton's. He cheats, and for such paltry sums. Time and again I've come across it. I tackled him, I had to. Not because of the money, but I had to know, to bring it out into the open. For him to do it to Netherton's, to Aunt Lou, and all the time fawning around her, flattering her – and tricking her! I think that's what gave me such contempt for him. After that the business of a mistress didn't count.'

'You accused him?'

'Well, yes, of course. I had to. It was the day before Aunt Lou fell. Mistakes, slips, that's what he said. One mistake perhaps, one slip, but it had been going on for ages. And what was so degrading – so demeaning – was what it had done to me. I'd been checking his ledgers without telling him, waiting until I knew he was out and then going to his room, being careful to leave it as I found it . . . I'd watched and counted the cargoes. I was cunning, sly. Suspicion warps you. And I knew even then that if I'd loved him, I couldn't have done it.'

'You should have told me.'

'I'll never live with him again, Dan. Never!'

'No, my Hannah, by God you won't. You'll live with no one but me. And I took you up the aisle and handed you into his keeping.' He spoke quietly, but something in his voice frightened her.

'Sailing away with you – that's just a dream,' she said presently as she slipped down from his knee to sit on the stool at his feet. It might sound romantic to sit on a man's knee, but Hannah was a realist, a tall realist, nothing of a feather weight. And Dan hadn't the advantage of two good legs. 'Aunt Lou made me responsible for Netherton's. Tommy may think of me as no more than a chattel, but that wasn't her idea. He used to have her eating out of his palm – but it was me she really looked to.'

'I know she did.'

'If he cared about the company I wouldn't mind so much. But I've got a feeling, a premonition . . . No, Dan, I'll never be a wife to him, not any more. I couldn't.'

There were long pauses, long silences. For so long she'd wanted to tell him everything. How right it was to have shared it all with Dan, to have no secrets.

'That night Aunt Lou died, you know now it was with us. I tried to tell her. I wanted her to know, remember?'

His hand covered hers, holding it to his knee. His brows lifted and his voice teased: 'You think I might forget?'

'Dan. I'm serious. She wasn't really part of our world by then. Do you know what I believe?'

'Tell me.'

'I believe that her spirit had gone already, she was free, unfettered. Remember how happy she looked, hopeful somehow.'

'I hope you're right, Hannah.'

'Yes, but more than that. If that's true then her spirit would already have know about us. And, Dan, I believe that's why she stopped fighting, she knew she was free to leave us. She knew we had each other, everything was right.'

Wherever Louise's spirit had been that other night, it was with them now.

'Hannah,' the tic in his cheek belied his quiet voice, 'I love you very much, so very much.'

* * *

248

Richard worked every waking hour. There had been nothing to clear out of the carriagehouse to make room for him, the accommodation was heaven sent. The building at the end of the narrow garden wasn't approached from Queen's Street but from Cleggs Lane that ran along at the back. So he came and went without disturbing anyone in the house.

His first commission was well received and quickly led to others. Word passed and there was no better recommendation than the evidence of the quality of his work. Soon his order book began to fill.

It was too soon to think of throwing away the security of those few shillings Albert Coleridge paid him each Saturday, but there's no greater incentive to a man than to work for profit that lines his own pocket. So as the days of spring lengthened he put in an hour or two before he went on to his day's work; then as soon as he was free he hurried back to Cleggs Lane. At the little house in Merchants Place there had been a change of diet for now that Richard left at five o'clock each morning he had to carry his victuals for the day. Mutton stew was a thing of the past. Pasties, bread pudding, crusty bread and cheese, food that was easy to eat in his fingers, was packed each morning in his tin.

By May the evenings were long. Hour after hour he was in his workshop, his own workshop, king of all he surveyed.

'There's no one home.' Beatrice's voice surprised him from the open doorway. 'I've brought you a jug of tea.'

'Are you supposed to help yourself to the tea caddy?' The last thing he wanted was trouble that might cost him his welcome here.

'I'm not like a servant.' Beatrice looked sullen. 'I suppose you think that's what I am, but I'm not just that. She — Mrs Lowden — Rosalind — said I must see you have everything you want. She and the boys have gone off to the beach with their shrimping nets, then they're going to listen to the band.'

'I could do with a proper hot cup, that's a fact. That tin of cold stuff isn't the same. I won't come up to the house, though, I want to make the most of the light. Do you mind pouring it and bringing it out to me?'

That was the start of the bait. Sometimes she stayed with him while he drank it, then sat quietly and watched him work. She didn't talk, just watched, finding satisfaction in seeing such craftsmanship. She knew each piece he made, came to recognize each different wood: elm, sycamore, walnut. Richard was a perfectionist and she found infinite pleasure in the beauty he created.

'You and Kath aren't a bit alike, are you?' he said one evening as he bit into his last piece of seed cake and washed it down with the tea Beatrice had brought out from the house.

She felt her face grow hot. What had Kath been telling him?

'Kath's always been the jolly one,' she mumbled.

'Ah, she's that. But, Beatrice, she doesn't see things. Not like you do. That chest, I reckon it's about as ready as it'll ever be, can't do anything more to it. What do you think of it, eh?' And his voice told her of his own pride in what he'd made.

She ran the flat of her hand over it. 'It's beautiful – so smooth. Look at the sheen on it in this evening light, Richard.' She opened one of the drawers, handling it lovingly. 'You can run the drawer with one hand, smooth as silk. Don't you feel sad when what you've made goes off to someone else? You put so much of yourself into it.'

He laughed. 'Sad! Not if they line my palm well.' He slid the drawer in and out. 'Umph. Like satin.'

The boys liked to see what he was doing, but Matthew's visits were brief. It wasn't in his nature to sit and watch. Stephen came often and Richard was glad to have him

250

there. He liked company while he worked. But it was Beatrice who surprised him. Living at Crown Cottage had changed her, he thought, brought her out of her shell. At the gatehouse she'd seemed to have no personality, no warmth, her thin, hunched body a reflection of a thin, hunched nature. Yet as he watched her carry his mug back to the house he saw something pathetic in her bearing. He imagined Kath, her strong, frizzy hair, her cheery face always ready to smile and show the wide gap between her white teeth. He imagined her body, a body that hadn't found its shape from having Trudie before it had blossomed again. And Kath had never been less than plump. Poor Kath, her ankles were swollen now. But Kath never complained, just loosened the lacing of her boots. How tiny Beatrice's ankles were . . . And her wrists.

They were walking on the grassy clifftop together when Beatrice told Hannah: 'She's gone from Tanner's Row. I was passing there yesterday and I saw the house was empty. Shuttered.' She waited a few seconds to let the dust settle on her announcement, then went on. 'So I pretended I was a friend. I knocked next door and asked, "Can you tell me where Susie's moved to?" The woman looked me up and down. I felt she was thinking if I was a friend of Susie's I wasn't worth the knowing. Of course I don't know how well her neighbours knew her, whether they –'

'Gone where?'

'She said she didn't know.' Another pause. 'I'll tell you what she said. This was it Hannah, just her words. "She never told me, but I'm not blind. Wanted to get settled somewhere before the baby arrives, I expect." There! Doesn't that prove what I've been telling you.'

From the cliff top they looked down towards Deremouth and beyond the town to the estuary. 'Hannah,' Beatrice slipped her hand into Hannah's, 'face up to it. For months

251

you've lived at the Hall and he's been at Vicary Place – or more likely at Tanner's Row. You don't live with him.' Hannah only half-listened. A baby. Was that what turned him away from her, that she couldn't give him a baby? She remembered how each month she'd felt that sense of failure. Silently now she sent up a prayer of thanks that she hadn't borne his child. 'You don't live together and he doesn't even want you. Leave him. Leave all of it. I'd run the house, I've said so before.'

'Beatrice, if I were free of my marriage – ' But not even to her could she say what she'd do. 'I'm not though. And I'll never leave Netherton's.'

'Money isn't everything.'

'Netherton's is more than money.'

Beatrice still clung to her hand. Hannah found herself wishing she wouldn't. From the cliff top the path descended steeply. It led to the eastern end of Deremouth, the Market Square, the poor end of town. Beatrice was talking now about Richard, extolling his talents. Hannah tried to listen; at any other time she would have noticed how unusual such enthusiasm was. Today she was simply glad of the chatter, it needed no contribution from her. Her thoughts were far away from the coachhouse at the bottom of Rosalind's garden. All these years she'd been close to Beatrice, knowing her every mood, every thought. How could she not recognize that this exuberance was an attempt to hold her attention, to arouse her jealousy? But her answers were automatic; Beatrice's words washed over her.

Hannah wanted to get away. She knew just where she was going and already her imagination was rushing ahead of her. When she and Beatrice parted she hurried on. She didn't look back, didn't see Beatrice wave, didn't see the dejected stoop of the rounded shoulders.

At the yard she went straight to Tommy's room. It was empty.

'Where's Tommy?' She put her head round Alan's door and enquired.

'He went home ten minutes or so ago. I understood him to say something about going out early this evening – er – both of you, I took him to mean.'

'I must have just missed him. I'll catch him,' was all she told her father-in-law.

Alan watched the door close on her with a satisfied expression. So they were off out somewhere this evening together. He'd tell Em, that would please her. Perhaps an evening out then Hannah would go home with him where she ought to be. Yes, that'd please Em. It might well be the beginning of getting down to a proper life together again.

Hannah let herself into the house that had been their home. There was no sign of Tommy downstairs, so she went to their bedroom.

'Well, well.' He turned to her, the close-lipped smile almost a sneer, 'If it's not Mrs Webster, the girl from the next office.'

'I didn't come to listen to jokes.'

'Could you have come because you live here, perhaps, because you remembered you're my wife.' He knew that whatever she'd come for, it certainly wouldn't have been that!

'Yes, because I'm your wife and I mean to put an end to it. Tommy, we haven't got a marriage. Perhaps it's partly been my fault – '

'What do you mean, "partly"? Have I left you?'

'Don't play games with me. That woman, that tart, she's having your child.'

He frowned, looked puzzled, even hurt. 'I don't follow – '

Hannah had a way of pulling herself very straight, her eyes almost level with his and before them he lowered his glance. Her words cut into the silence. 'I shall go to a solicitor. For the child's sake I should have expected you to be glad.'

'You can't use gossip as evidence. You need proof.'

'Don't pretend you believe I don't know who she is. Susie Syms. You took her out of Merchant Place and set her up in Tanner's Row. Now she's having a child, your child.'

He stepped close to her, his face only inches from hers. 'I went to another woman, you say. And what when I tell them how long you've refused me?' Even nearer he came, his manner menacing. She moved backwards, another step and she'd be forced to sit on the bed. But she wouldn't sit, she wouldn't let him tower over her. In a falsetto voice he mimicked, ' "Please, sir, my husband's been to bed with another woman," is that what you'll say? "Oh, no, sir, I don't have him in my bed. He does nasty things – he expects me to open my legs." And what comfort do you expect from the solicitor? "We'll send the wicked fellow away," is that what you think he'll tell you? What is it you're after, Hannah? Your girlfriend, is that what you want? I shouldn't tell the solicitor about her if I were you. Nice girls don't – '

'How dare you! I won't stand here and listen to your filth. Go to your whore, she probably speaks the same language.'

'She probably does. And you go to your solicitor and see what sort of language he speaks.' The smile left his face. With no warning he was holding her, his mouth covering hers. She toppled backwards, lost her balance and was on the bed just as he intended.

Perhaps she'd never understood him, she thought, as she fought to push him off her. The more she wrestled, the more his passions were aroused. After saying the things they had to each other, how could he be ready, wanting her, fighting for what she had no intention of letting him have? With one hand he'd pulled his trouser buttons undone, all the time holding her firmly down. Excitement seemed to have given him strength, and the softness of the

254

bed robbed her of a firm base to fight from. Her hat was knocked over one ear, her skirt was round her waist, her silk drawers torn down to hang from one ankle.

'No! No!' She pounded his shoulder, bit his mouth as it tried to cover hers. But he was strong and the battle was adding to his passion. Brutally he entered her. His strength didn't lessen but by now the conquest was over. Hannah or any other woman, it would have been all one to Tommy. She was a female body. And she recognized that this was her moment. Hate gave her strength. As his breathing quickened she used all her force to roll him from her and on to the bed.

'No . . . no . . .' Now it was his turn to shout. 'You bitch! You cow!'

There was no way of regaining her dignity. She stepped back into her drawers and pulled them up. Her hair was hanging in long loose strands, her hat hanging over one ear, still attached to her hair by its pin.

So this was marriage. She felt sick.

Next morning, instead of driving herself to the yard in the trap she was taken to the railway station. When the London train pulled out of Deremouth Station at five minutes to nine she was on it. Paddington – London . . . an anonymity she couldn't hope to find in Deremouth, nor even in Exeter.

CHAPTER TEN

She had no appointment. Perhaps she'd not find anyone who could talk to her today. 'If I can't, then I'll buy some night things and stay here. I'm not going home until I've found someone to take my case. When Dan gets back I'll be able to tell him. I'm going to be free.' A husband finding his pleasure with a prostitute was one thing, a husband with a mistress who was having his child was another. She felt that today was the beginning of a new life and, as if to confirm her faith, she found a lawyer to talk to her; one at the top of his profession, a Mr Archibald Lessingham.

It was like living a dream to be sitting facing this stranger across his desk, in the large room with two walls panelled in polished oak, the other two lined with leather-backed books – with the exception of the fireplace, a mean and out of character grate in a room of such proportions. In surroundings so unfamiliar she heard herself set out her case: the date of her marriage; when it was she'd first learnt of her husband's unfaithfulness; the coming child. Then there was the inheritance, his handling of her estate. From beginning to end she spoke clearly and unemotionally. Mr Archibald Lessingham listened, wrote the occasional note or two, but mostly just listened. His expression told her nothing.

When she came to the end she waited. There could be no doubt that with evidence like this there would be a simple way out. That her search had brought her to a man so eminent added to her confidence.

Then he spoke. 'In the last years there has been reform. You may already be aware of the new Matrimonial Clauses Act, passed only as recently as 1857. Under this, in certain circumstances, dissolution of marriage may be obtained.'

Hannah nodded. She always read her *Times*. Well, she'd told him the circumstances, now it was up to him to explain what the next step must be.

'Mrs Webster, are you able to produce visible evidence – or alternatively can you bring a witness prepared to testify – that your husband has treated you with physical cruelty?'

'Hit me, you mean? Good heavens, no. But what I just told you,' – and yesterday's scene had been the most difficult to phrase while she'd kept her voice steady – 'of course there were no witnesses. You mean I'd have to stand up in Court and . . . But what proof have I? I swear I've told you nothing but the truth.'

'Indeed, I'm not doubting your word, Mrs Webster. I understand you to say that you and your husband are living apart, both in properties belonging to yourselves. And it would seem that you were the partner to remove yourself from the matrimonial home to return to the domicile of your spinsterhood?'

'Yes, I went to be with my aunt.'

'And continued to live in your aunt's home after her death. Am I correct?'

'Yes. But I already knew of his unfaithfulness –'

'We can only work to the law, Mrs Webster. Believe me, if it is within my power, within the law . . . For instance, have you suggested that you should return to the matrimonial home?'

'I couldn't.'

'Have you invited your husband to join you at, er –' he glanced at his notes – 'Netherton Hall? And has he refused?'

'No.' Her confidence was badly dented.

'Then, my dear lady, I fear you haven't the grounds on

which to petition. Even *I* cannot hope to gain your divorce.'

'You mean that unless Tommy beats me or runs away — and he won't do that, he has too much to lose — we have to continue this pretence of marriage while he fathers a bastard.' She heard the spite in her voice. She knew it wouldn't help her case but she couldn't hide it.

'One must work to the letter of the law, Mrs Webster. Now, should the adultery be committed by the wife — and believe me, this is not a personal inference, I am merely explaining the legal grounds on which divorce might be sought — so, as I say, if the wife is the adulteress, it is much more straightforward. That in itself is sufficient grounds for her husband to petition.'

'You mean that if Tommy had evidence of my adultery he could divorce me?' she clutched at the ray of hope, visibly brightening. 'Well, the end result would be the same.'

Up to that point the lawyer's manner may not have been encouraging but at least she'd felt she had his sympathy. Now his face took on a closed-in look. But he was a fair-minded man; in his profession he must be no less.

'Your financial circumstances make for certain complications. Under your aunt's will you have been the beneficiary of a substantial inheritance. As you are aware under the law your husband is endowed with your properties and estates. Should you give him grounds to seek divorce brought about by your adultery — or serious misconduct — then he would have every right to bring a case to disinherit you in his favour.'

'You mean take everything of my aunt's for himself! For himself and his strumpet!' Hannah sat very straight in her chair. Her eyes blazed across the desk. 'Hah! I'll not have it!'

* * *

It was late by the time her journey was over and she climbed down from the train at Deremouth. She remembered waiting on the platform only this morning, so confident, so sure of the light at the end of the tunnel.

The one and only cab was outside hoping for a fare from this last train of the day, and fortunately she was the only traveller to need it. She wanted to get home, to shut out the world. All the way from London, rocked by the steady motion, she'd felt numbed, hopeless. But already Deremouth was putting the fight back into her; the yard and the wharf were lost in the blackness of night but she felt their nearness, knew every cobblestone, knew each boat tied up there. Her determination was rekindled, her spirit rose. Somewhere there must be a way – and she'd find it. She'd not be beaten. She had a childish faith that once she was indoors, imbibing the atmosphere of the Hall, she'd see what it was she had to do.

She went straight to the drawing room. It was as if she called Louise for help. Purposely she sat in her aunt's chair, very straight, her hands on the arms. Just so must Louise have spent many long and lonely hours.

She remembered the day she'd announced that she wanted to work at the yard. 'It's what's between my ears that counts,' she'd said. But the world thought differently. And people talked of justice. There was no justice! A woman must always expect to be inferior, must hand the reins to her husband and master. That Hannah never would. If the law considered her less able than a man, then the law was an ass!

Did Tommy know that a man might disinherit his wife? Was that what he was hoping for? Perhaps he was waiting his opportunity. Well, she'd see he didn't get it. Had this been what he'd wanted right from the beginning? His affair with Susie Syms was no new thing so had he just used his marriage to her, was she a means to an end, she and Aunt Lou too? The thought added to her fighting spirit. Netherton's would never be his, she vowed. It was hers – and one day it would be her son's.

Ah, but there was no son. All the time she'd hoped, believing that if only she could have his child they'd find what they'd seemed to be losing. She'd never have a son. What was wrong with her? Aunt Lou had never had children; maybe she was like Aunt Lou. No son. If she had no son then Netherton's would pass to Dan's eldest. She closed her eyes, her body slumping back in the chair. Her marriage had failed and as the seconds ticked by Hannah touched rock bottom. She took the full burden of failure on herself. She could never give Dan a son. She'd be like Aunt Lou. She'd grow old alone.

At last she went to bed, but not to sleep. There seemed to be no way forward. Her only comfort came from the knowledge that even now Dan must be coming nearer with every minute. He'd been gone a while, this time to Boston, his first long voyage. Given fair wind, in another week she'd be watching out, scanning the horizon. She'd imagine that moment and not look beyond. Anguish and misery had kept her awake but with a picture before her of 'Louisah' inching to the quayside, she slept.

Hannah looked up from her desk as her door opened. In front of her were the ledgers prepared for the auditor. They made disturbing reading. No wonder she frowned.

'Hannah, it's time we talked.' Tommy closed the door behind him. 'We can't spend our lives running away from the truth as you seem set on doing.'

It was the day after her trip to London, but he knew nothing of that.

'Indeed we can't.' She tried to sound calm, composed, sure of herself. But what Tommy said could only mean one thing. Her tired eyes couldn't disguise her sudden hope. Tommy wanted his freedom! Her heart was banging. Together they'd find a way that was acceptable to the law.

'I've been to see Mr Tozer, he's the agent for Lord Hunter, you know. I've decided to give up the lease on Vicary Terrace, it's an unnecessary expense to run two houses. The furniture can be sold – unless there are any items, ornaments or anything, you want. There's nothing of it we need.'

'What about you?'

'I told you, there's no point in running more than one house. I shall move to the Hall.'

She clenched her teeth. She was trapped. 'Speak up, girl,' she told herself. 'No wonder women get credited with having no gumption. Say what you mean. Tell him.'

'I can't stop you moving in. As my husband that's your right. But,' she glared, determined that he wouldn't see her fear, fear born of the memory of his strength as he'd forced her to the bed, held her there, 'I won't go to bed with you. I mean it, Tommy. I won't.' She bit her lip. She was concerned. How still he was, his smile never changing, a smile that curved his mouth but didn't reach his eyes. Like a cat with a mouse, keeping it covered, waiting, delighting in tempting it to move then dabbing with its paw. 'I mean it. I'll move into Aunt Lou's room.' Even in her own ears her voice was shrill. His lips curved a little more. He didn't take his eyes off her, just stood there, silently mocking her. 'Do you hear me?'

'Oh yes,' he spoke softly, 'I hear you. They must have heard you from the yard too. Hannah, even you admit I'm within my rights to live there. And remember too that if I desire you – *if* I say – that's within my rights too.' No cat could have delighted more in its cruelty than he did as he watched her. 'Of course, if we're to follow the terms of your aunt's will there's the matter of a son.' He shrugged. He'd known the regularity of her disappointment, delighted in the sudden hot colour that flooded her face now. He imagined he'd played the trump card. 'I fear Aunt Lou will never get her heir that way.' Then, with a laugh, 'But there's not much you wouldn't do for Netherton's eh, Hannah? Of course, if you refuse me ...' He left the sentence unfinished.

The next day he arrived at the Hall. His portmanteaux were carried upstairs. Hannah felt sick with shame and fear. In the evening he viewed her speculatively down the length of the dining table. He seemed to be weighing up whether she was worth the effort of a fight. To have him decide against it might not have been a compliment but it was a relief.

Once safely inside Louise's room she locked the door. Time and again she looked at the handle, waiting, dreading, expecting a movement. Not that he'd get in, but there would be a scene. She wanted just to be free of Tommy and all he threatened. Her fears were groundless; he didn't come.

They both lived under the same roof; they both worked at the shipping yard. Yet it seemed by mutual consent their lives didn't touch. She was conscious of curious glances from the maids, even from the gardener's boy, but none of that mattered. She didn't care what gossip and speculation she'd given rise to when she'd moved her things into Louise's old bedroom. Tommy hadn't once rattled the door handle and with each day her confidence grew.

'When is the furniture coming up for sale?' she asked him a week or so later.

'Oh, I decided not to put it under the hammer. Found a private buyer. It's all settled.'

She eyed him coldly. So Susie Syms sat at the dressing table that had been hers, slept in the bed she and Tommy had shared, hung her clothes in the wardrobe where her own used to hang! He read her thoughts, saw the icy glare. With brows raised he smiled, silently taunting her.

* * *

262

'There, I've finished it. Look, Beatrice.' Rosalind fastened the last loop into a knot and spread out the collar of delicate lace with satisfaction. On the back of the parlour door hung the gown she'd been stitching, finished now except for the hem and the neck, a gown of silvery blue, quite unsuitable to life at Crown Cottage. But wearing it Rosalind would look lovely.

'You ought to be going somewhere really special to show it off.' Beatrice rested her hand on the smooth silk.

'It'll be special wherever we are. You see, Daniel brought me home the silk a long time ago. I remember what he said when he gave it to me – that I should wear pretty things, try and look to the future. I'd been in mourning for Peter, you see.' And even now Rosalind never wore bright colours, only black, pale grey, slate blue, colours that befitted a widow.

'It must have been so dreadful for you, left with just the boys. Better than without them, though. At least, Rosalind, you've never really been alone.'

She nodded. 'He's been like a father to them you know, Beatrice.'

There was something in the way she said it that held Beatrice's attention. Why had she never considered that possibility? At the back of her mind she'd always been uneasy about Dan, about his long stay at the Hall after the wreck, about the hours he'd spent there when old Mrs Netherton had been ill. Even Hannah being married to Tommy hadn't laid the ghost of the jealousy she'd always felt. But this might be the solution.

She showed no surprise as she answered: 'I know he has. And of course, living here with you ... well, I've never repeated anything to you, I've thought of him as your brother almost. But, Rosalind, some people do have such cruel minds. He's exposing you to all kinds of unpleasant rumour.'

'You mean you've heard things? But from whom?'

263

'I couldn't tell you just who. Sometimes it's no more than knowing looks, you know what some folk are like. I remember one day in the grocery shop, I'd handed in the order and there were some women gossiping while they waited to be served. Such a look they gave each other and they whispered something about it being a big order, and "she's got the master in port". It was the way it was said, and the horrid suggestive snigger.'

'But, Beatrice, of course Daniel stays here. Why, I came down from Liverpool so that I could be near him when he was hurt, to care for him.'

They stood still, looking directly at each other, neither putting words to the plans that were forming.

'I'll stitch the hem for you if you like,' Beatrice offered.

'I'm going to wear it his first evening home. Men are so funny, aren't they! You never know whether they remember things like we do.'

'About why he gave you the silk, you mean?'

'That's right. Telling me I should look to the future. For ages I couldn't, I really couldn't, with Peter gone. But coming here I feel I've got a life again. You're happy here, too, aren't you, Beatrice? You won't leave me?'

Beatrice gave that rare smile that lit up her thin face. 'Your life may be changed once you start looking to the future.'

'Goose!' Rosalind chuckled. 'Daniel won't be home very often, and you and I do run such a happy home for the boys.'

So as 'Louisah' set her course towards Deremouth, battling with gales that whipped the waters of the North Atlantic to a fury, Hannah wasn't the only one who watched and waited. But she was the first of them to have sight of the 'Louisah' and, as it approached the estuary, telescope to her eye, she scanned the deck. She could see Mr Bailey giving the orders as the ship came towards the quay – but no sign of Dan. She couldn't wait at her window any longer. As the gangplank was put down she was ready to hurry aboard.

'Welcome home, Mr Bailey. Is he below?'

'No, ma'am.' The mate had dreaded this moment, she could see it in his face. 'Had a bit of trouble on the outward run . . . Just one minute, ma'am.' And he left her standing while he went to watch the men tying up.

'What sort of trouble? Where is he?' she shouted into the wind, coming close after him.

He couldn't put it off. She had to be told. 'Was his leg, you see, Miss Hannah. Going out we had a bad time, storms enough to toss the steadiest of men – and the master wasn't as steady as he liked to think.'

'But where is he now?' Her mouth was dry, she felt sick. She was frightened of what she would hear. Dan not here. Trouble.

'He told me to bring 'Louisah' home. They had to take him into the hospital when we got to Boston.' She leant against the rail. Hannah never did have sea legs. She put out her hand to hold steady a world that gently rocked. He was in hospital. But that was nothing to the dreadful fear . . . She closed her eyes.

'Mr Bailey, sir,' one of the men was calling him.

'Come and see me in my office when you're finished here,' she told him, 'I'll wait for you there.'

In the afternoon she had to carry the news to Crown Cottage. No one answered her knock, so she walked down the side path to the narrow back garden. Sitting in the shade of the solitary tree, a sycamore, Rosalind and Beatrice were sewing. Two pairs of eyes looked up at the sound of Hannah's step.

'Oh, it's you, Hannah. I thought it might be Daniel arrived home.'

'It's about Dan I've come, Rosalind. Hello, Bea.' For it would never do not to give Beatrice a greeting of her own. 'He's in hospital. They had to leave him behind in Boston.'

'My poor Daniel! But why? What's wrong with him.'

'It's his leg, the old wounds. They had a dreadful crossing going out, Mr Bailey said the storms were fearful. Dan was thrown about, his wounds opened again.'

'Oh, but they should have made him come home. Mr Bailey could have brought the ship home, Daniel could have rested. He'd get well so much quicker here.'

'Of course he would,' Beatrice added her weight, 'there's nothing like your own folk around you. You could have cared for him here in his own place Rosalind.'

Rosalind's face flushed a becoming pink. 'Indeed I could! And so I shall when he's well enough to make the journey.'

'He couldn't have been brought home. Mr Bailey said the wounds weren't healthy. He was dreadfully worried going out, he said he'd never been so thankful to reach land. By then Dan had a fever – '

'Hark, I hear the boys coming in the gate – they always come home along Cleggs Lane and through the back way.' Rosalind held her hand up to check Hannah. 'Be careful what you say in front of them. Just that Daniel's leg was being troublesome, no more. Children worry more than we give them credit for.'

Beatrice nodded in agreement, folding away her mending. 'Stephen is always a worrier – and they both would be about Mr Lowden. He's the nearest to a father they know, poor mites.' And it was true, Hannah knew it was.

It was later when she walked to the gate with Hannah, that Beatrice said: 'The boys took their disappointment well. Rosalind was wise to see they weren't told anything to worry them. She is a dear soul, isn't she, and how bravely she heard what you had to tell her.' She knew that Hannah was listening with the whole of her attention now. 'Just between you and me, Hannah – not a word mind – I expected that this visit things would have been settled between them. For the boys' sakes it'll be a good thing if she marries him, won't it? He's been almost their father

266

for so long. Well, he's been *her* support too. I must go in, she'll be feeling wretched.'

Hannah had certainly listened with all her attention and what she'd heard worried her. Was Rosalind living in a fool's paradise? She hoped it was all in Beatrice's imagination. Losing Peter had been sadness enough for one life without building hopes on such an impossible dream. Today though Hannah had more on her mind than Rosalind's aspirations, true or imagined.

'Don't wait up for me, I'm sure to be late, Kath.' Richard packed his tin of food into the canvas bag he carried, then slung it over his shoulder.

'Again tonight? That'll be every night this week I'll have been in bed when you come home. It's no life, Richard. You work every waking hour.' But it wasn't on her own account she complained.

'It's a good life, Kath. The way things are going I'll soon be making enough without old Colderidge's pittance.' The clock struck five. Richard's routine might have altered but the new order was becoming as regular as the old had been. During the long summer days he meant to make the most of every daylight hour.

Kath's days had altered too. First to get up, half-past four saw her downstairs in the kitchen; first to bed, before nine o'clock she'd plod wearily up the narrow stairs. By now she was cumbersome, heavily pregnant, but still just as content. She scrubbed, she polished, she played with Timothy, she dandled Trudie. Shopping had to be done when the day was young for later on, even if she loosened her laces, she couldn't get her boots on. Early nights suited her. Almost as her head touched the pillow she slept. Usually she didn't even hear Richard climb in beside her. With a baby on the way she accepted a good night's rest as her due. Making love for the sake of it had never been part of Kath's scheme of things. Later, when the baby was here, she'd never dream of being unwilling; like all her wifely duties she would make herself available whenever Richard wanted. A good wife, that was Kath, and a good mother too.

As far as Richard was concerned Merchant Place was becoming no more than somewhere to sleep. His life, the part of it that counted, was at Crown Cottage. Hour after hour he worked. And during the summer evenings it had become part of the pattern that some of the time at least Beatrice would be there with him.

But while she mended holes in stockings and sewed on shirt buttons it wasn't Richard she thought about but Hannah. Something was wrong. Tommy was back at the Hall, but surely the gap between them was too wide to bridge. Hannah wasn't happy, of that she was certain. Hannah needed her.

Hannah was alone in the drawing room at the Hall. Today when she'd arrived home she'd found a letter from Dan waiting for her. She'd read it so many times she must have known it by heart, but still she looked at it.

'A visitor come to see you, ma'am.' She was elevated to 'ma'am' but Gladys had relaxed back into the habit of putting her head round the door to speak to her. 'It's Thurlston's girl. The eldest one.'

'Beatrice? Let her come in, Gladys.' She put her letter in the bureau. What she'd read couldn't be shared, she couldn't bear to say the words – and least of all to Beatrice. Dan had long been the one person she knew she couldn't talk to Bea about.

'I haven't seen you for days,' Beatrice said as she shut the door behind her.

'I've been very busy, Bea. The boys were on the quay for a while at teatime.'

268

'Anyway, I'd rather see you here. I suppose *he's* out?' Beatrice always spoke softly but there was no doubting the hatred she felt for Tommy. 'It's better here. Back there either one or other is always popping in and out. I wanted it to be just us, no one to disturb us.'

Not a rustle stirred the leaves on this perfect summer evening. The light on the headland emphasized the brilliance of the colours, red cliffs, green grass, and sea calm, shimmering. Already the first hint of sunset was turning the river to burnished gold. The sight drew Beatrice to the open window, yet Hannah saw it but wasn't aware of it. The words she'd read filled her mind.

'Hannah, you look dreadful. My poor Hannah. Why did you have him back? You know you don't love him, you don't. How can you live with him?'

With an effort Hannah pulled herself together. 'With Tommy? I share a roof with him, that's all. I'm married to him, I have no choice. Don't you see? Everything – all this – everything that was Aunt Lou's is Tommy's because he's my husband. I have no rights.'

'It's wicked, it's monstrous. Hannah, each night I pray you'll be free of him.'

'Each night I pray it too, each night, each day. I was such a fool.' Hannah's voice broke. She held her jaw tight, stiff. She wouldn't cry. If she started she'd never stop.

Joy flooded through Beatrice. All the way here, as she'd hurried up the long hill out of Deremouth, she'd felt that this evening was important. But her joy was short-lived, dashed by what Hannah said next.

'My rights or his – as if any of it matters now. I've learnt that.' She'd thought she couldn't talk about it but she found she couldn't stop herself. 'Bea, I've never talked to you about Dan. I'd thought of him always as so much a part of myself that I hardly thought of him at all. Bea – ' her long fingers gripped her friend's small hand – 'you say you pray, then pray for that: that there'll be a way for Dan and me.'

'No! No, Hannah, I don't believe it! All this business with Tommy has upset you. You're unhappy so you've let yourself believe you're in love with someone else. Dan's always been your friend – I've thought of him as a sort of uncle to you. Hannah, don't let him see you make a fool of yourself. And there's Rosalind, have you forgotten her? He's part of their home, he's only waiting to get back to them . . .'

Her words raced on but she might as well not have spoken for all the notice Hannah took.

'I've had a letter from him, Bea. They couldn't save his leg. The wounds that Mr Bailey said weren't healthy . . . there was some sort of poison, Dan calls it gangrene. There's no way of curing it.' Desperately she was trying to keep the emotion from her voice, to hide the aching pity she felt for him. But she couldn't hide the bewilderment and hurt in her dark blue eyes.

'I'm sorry. For him and for Rosalind and the boys too.' But Beatrice wasn't sure Hannah even heard her.

It was with a heavy heart that she went back down the hill to town. It wasn't quite dark but the lamp was alight in the coachhouse. Richard was still there.

'Where've you been?' Briefly he looked up as she came to the doorway.

'Just walking. You missed your tea. I'm sorry.'

'Never mind the tea. Aren't you coming in to keep me company?'

He tried to say it casually. It was easy to frighten her off and something had upset her this evening he could tell. The look of her sent his mind back to childhood, to Shaggy, a dog they used to have. Shaggy, cowed and shivering in a corner, tail between his legs and ears down when he'd had a hiding for some misdemeanour or other.

But who could have hurt Beatrice? Richard pulled her

stool towards where he was working at the bench. It was meant as a sign of welcome, a hand held out in friendship – for a sister-in-law? Is that why he did it, because she was Kath's sister?

Beatrice was a mystery to him but this was no moment to solve mysteries. Enough that he recognized a need in her. If Kath had been less satisfied with her daily round, if sometimes she'd let him feel that he was the pivot on which her world turned, then in Beatrice he wouldn't have seen a reflection of his own isolation.

This evening her dreams had been dashed. If ever she'd needed friendship it was now, and yet kindness was more than she could bear. Her bottom lip quivered. She turned her head away from him.

'Come on, Bea. Here's your stool by the bench.'

A hiccough as her breath caught in her throat. As if to hide the misery within her she kept her back towards him, her round shoulders pulled forward, her head low so that her chin was almost to her chest. She felt his arm around her drawing her gently but firmly inside the coachhouse and away from the open door. Then he turned her to face him, lifting her chin. She had nowhere to hide.

What's up? That's what he meant to say. Isn't that what any brother would ask? But at the misery in her eyes the question died before it was spoken.

Never before had any man, not even Harold, held Beatrice in his arms. And certainly she'd never wanted one to. Richard was strong, he was gentle. For years she'd loved no one but Hannah, she'd wanted no one else. Hannah, her body so beautiful, statuesque, as a woman should be, everything that she herself wasn't . . . and yet always a mirror of herself. They'd had no secrets, or so she'd believed. Always it had been Hannah she'd turned to. Of course she had; their very sameness was what had held them. Tommy had cast a temporary shadow, but in her heart she'd known he could never divide them. All she'd needed was patience, love and patience. Yet all the time Hannah had been hugging the secret of Dan to herself. Beatrice couldn't face the truth. Later she'd think things through, find the way to make Hannah see . . .

She was pulled close to Richard, her tears warm on his chest. Here she was safe, she could hold the truth away.

His first reaction was to protect her, poor, hurt little Beatrice – like Shaggy, beaten and not understanding why. Until now the passing of a mug of tea had been the only physical contact they'd had, no more than a glancing touch. His hands moved up and down her back. He wanted to comfort her. He could feel each vertebra of her spine, her shoulder blades stuck out like wings. So tiny . . . so thin . . . His touch moved to her waist, he imagined his hands encircling it. Round-shouldered and flat-chested would have been his description of her not so long ago. Flat-chested? But was she? He'd known no breasts but Kath's, always well endowed and in the years since marriage perpetually enlarged either by pregnancy or nursing her young.

It surprised him – shocked and excited him, too – that in a moment when Beatrice turned to him for comfort his imagination should be doing this. Her skin would be white, her body thin. Ah, but she was a woman for all that. Her breasts would be small, firm. He pulled his thoughts up short. Beatrice, his sister-in-law, was turning to him for help.

'What happened, Beatrice? Where did you go? Did some wretched chap frighten you?'

She shook her head. 'No one.'

And perhaps that was the answer to her sadness. No one. She had no one. The light wasn't good enough to do any more this evening. Even the lamp didn't make it much easier to work but threw shadows. But he didn't want to pack up and go home, leaving her like this.

'Dry your eyes, then come and see what I've done this evening, eh?'

She blew her nose, ran her hands over her hair to tidy it and made an attempt at unhunching her shoulders. Here in Crown Cottage, in the middle of town, there was no glorious twilight. The last of the day was fading with no aura of beauty. But the coachhouse had its own power of healing and she smoothed the flat of her hand over the wood, sniffed the scent of it.

It was only later, alone in her bedroom at the top of the house, that she faced the emptiness of her dreams.

Always at the forefront of Hannah's mind was Dan. Anxiety coloured every thought of him. What was happening to him? News was old before it reached her. Work had to be her lifeline. And, as if to strengthen her purpose, Netherton's gave her more than enough to fill her time. She'd known the annual figures would be down; only now did she study the books, analyse the profits and losses, work out which routes were no longer viable. She'd known that for years the coastal trade had been losing ground. Whatever Tommy's petty transactions had cost was but a drop in the ocean, she couldn't hold him responsible for the general slump. In fact, she wanted not to think about him at all, not him, not the girl who was to have his child. She didn't want to connect him with life here in the yard. Certainly he spent less and less time here. When Ted Sharples and 'My Queen' were at sea, he hardly appeared at all. And as if by common consent neither she nor Alan commented on his frequent absences.

One thing was apparent. 'Oberon' was a success story, the profit constant. In home waters it paid better to carry passengers than freight. So the idea was born in Hannah of a paddle steamer service across the Channel. These days foreign travel to the Continent was the fashion amongst those who could afford it; services ran regularly from ports along the south coast, Newhaven to Le Havre, Dover to Calais, Weymouth to Cherbourg; from the south east they carried passengers to Dieppe, Hamburg and Ostend. But nothing sailed from Deremouth. Yet the railway came here from London and from the Midlands. The idea was taking shape. Netherton's would lead the way.

The 'Oberon' had grown out of what she and Tommy had planned, they and Louise. This time she'd say nothing to him, nor to Alan. For years all Netherton's affairs at the bank had been handled by him, and recently Tommy had made a point of visiting Mr Habbins, the manager, believing it behoved him well for them to be on good terms.

Today, for the first time, Hannah faced him. In her mind she'd built a picture of him, tall, white-faced, thin-lipped. But the man who stood up to greet her as she was ushered into his presence was none of these things. She liked what she saw. Her smile was spontaneous, an expression of her relief. There was nothing certain about the outcome of her visit, she wasn't even sure of how to conduct the interview. But Hannah liked honesty above all else, and here was a man she knew she trusted.

Perhaps it was Mr Habbins' size that sent her memory back through the years to her meeting with Harold Thurlston, and perhaps it was something to do with that memory that set her at her ease. Tall, broad shouldered, his ruddy complexion made even more fiery by his ginger side whiskers, this man might have been a seaman or a yeoman farmer. She had no idea what his first impression of her was, the thought didn't enter her head. Had she known she might have been surprised.

'Mrs Webster, I'm delighted to meet you. Your husband isn't here yet? Do take a seat while we wait for him.'

'I'm here on my own, Mr Habbins. I want to talk to you about something that I'm attending to myself.' She sat tall in her straight-backed chair, her hands clasped in her lap.

274

He couldn't see just how tightly they were clasped and there was nothing in the firm, determined voice to hint of the daunting echoes of Mr Clutterbuck's words or Mr Archibald Lessingham's. Neither man had left Hannah with any illusions about her status, but she must make Mr Habbins feel she knew what she was doing. Chin high, she began: 'You may know that I came into the business as soon as I was old enough. I wanted to and it was my aunt's wish that I should learn the business, be able to take control when the time came.' (Silently she sent an apology to Louise for this necessary fabrication.) Almost without a pause, she went on: 'The management remains with Mr Webster, my father-in-law, but I've played an active part for a long time and intend to continue to do so.' How bright his eyes were, he watched her without so much as a blink. 'A few years ago we converted the 'Oberon'. That was my idea, I drew up the original plans and worked out the costings. My aunt gave me her support; she could see that Netherton's had to accept change, look to the future and be ahead of the next man.' Then, with a smile that was hardly less than a grin: 'She loved the work. I can see her now – poring over the drawings, wanting to know every last detail, welcoming the challenge.' She drifted into silence realizing she'd strayed from the point. Mr Habbins would see that as a feminine failing, no doubt, letting herself be swayed by affection, not being able to concentrate her mind on business.

'She was a very great lady. I first saw her more than fifty years ago when I was a lad at the counter.' And like Hannah, Mr Habbins took a jaunt down memory lane. And that was the end of her prepared speech and her attempt to create a good impression. She relaxed.

'I've brought a lot of figures to show you. Can you spare me the time? You'll see how the coastal trade has been declining, not suddenly but for years, so Netherton's must put something in its place.'

She showed him the figures for 'Oberon'. Next came the outline plan she'd drawn up to take to Mr Hawkins. She told him the route she expected this new ship to operate and set before him what she'd drawn up of the passenger figures of other companies sending package steamers to the Continent. Mr Habbins was impressed. This young woman had done her homework and done it well.

'And now we come to the crux,' he said, and Hannah took heart from his smile. 'What is it you're wanting of the bank? Netherton's accounts are healthy enough, for all your talk of decline in trade.'

'I know that.' She bit her lip. For a moment her confidence deserted her. This was a man's world. She was conscious of her vulnerability now, and yet as she'd set out her scheme she'd forgotten everything but the challenge of what she proposed. Honesty had always been her only way so she told him straight: 'You see, Netherton's may be mine, but I can't do anything on my own. It's always my husband's signature, or else his father's.'

'What is their opinion of this new project?'

'I've not told them.' She had to fight with every weapon she could find. 'My husband very seldom comes in to the business – and his father has always been against change. He didn't want the 'Oberon' to run a passenger service, but he couldn't do anything about it. Aunt Lou was so keen you see and he couldn't go against her. So I haven't said anything to either of them. But, Mr Habbins, I know it'll make a profit. We'll see our money back and a good return too. I have it in mind to sell off 'Polly Anna' and 'Alberta', they run between Deremouth and Cork and Deremouth and Liverpool, never full and both routes already covered. I may have a battle on my hands with Mr Webster – and Tommy too if he backs his father – and even if I don't there will be shortfall. May I have your backing when I pay the shipwright? If you want security all I can offer you is my aunt's jewellery, silver, pictures perhaps, just things I can carry away. The house, the business, all her investments — he has control of everything.'

'Mrs Webster, why don't you talk to your husband? When you travel in harness, it's easier if you can move in the same direction.'

She stacked her papers. He wasn't going to help her. It had been as useless to talk to him as it had to Mr Lessingham. 'Talk to your husband.' She felt rebuffed and the disappointment was all the greater because he'd seemed interested in the figures she'd shown him.

'I've been wasting your time, I'm sorry.' She tried to sound composed but how hard it was. He watched her, the tilt of her chin, the long fingers that neatened the sheaf of papers. And not for a moment did she suspect what it was that tipped the scales in her favour; not her accounts, nor yet the information she'd gleaned of the trade of other shipping companies along the coast — much as he respected the way she'd presented her case — it was the likeness to the woman he'd watched with boyish adulation more than fifty years ago. And where was the risk? Netherton's was one of Deremouth's oldest established firms and one of its biggest employers. Woman or no, it was to this young creature that Louise Netherton had entrusted it.

'Go ahead with what you want to do, my dear.' His words were totally unexpected. Hannah had been holding herself ready for refusal and now it was all she could do to hold her bottom lip steady in her relief. 'If Mrs Netherton saw fit to have faith in what you suggested for 'Oberon', then I believe she'd want the bank to be behind you in this venture. But it may not come to that. Mr Webster senior is an astute businessman, even if he doesn't approve of change,' Mr Habbins added with a conspiratorial twinkle in his eye.

'He is. We couldn't have a better manager. But he's also my husband's father, don't overlook that.'

'Umph.' Certain whispers had come Colin Habbins' way about young Tommy Webster, but he'd discounted them until now.

'I'm more grateful than I know how to tell you, and I won't let you down,' Hannah promised.

'If I thought for one moment you would I wouldn't be asking for the specimen of your signature I might require. I have a responsibility to the bank. I wouldn't be guaranteeing you support if I had doubts.'

What it was that had privately influenced him Hannah knew nothing of, and gave herself full credit for the faith he'd shown in her. Once outside in Waterloo Street she gave a threepenny bit to the lad she'd left holding her pony then climbed into the trap. The euphoria of success reinforced her determination as she took the reins and drove towards the quay.

Never one to let the grass grow under her feet, the next day she took her outline plans to show them to Mr Hawkins. A rough working sketch, enough to start discussions. For two hours they talked, then he took her to the 'Ship Inn' just as he had before.

'I'll have it drawn up and costed, Mrs Webster. Then perhaps you or your husband will come again.' Did she imagine it or did he say it intentionally, watching for her reaction? 'Or would you prefer me to come to Deremouth, see you both together?'

'No. I shall come here. How soon can you have it ready for me? And, Mr Hawkins, I know I'm asking you to do extra work, but when you draw the plans could you have an extra copy done so that I can take two.'

'A good idea, let you have one each.' That belied the tales he'd been hearing. 'No trouble at all.'

They were in that same back room having lunch. What a lifetime ago it seemed since that happy day when she'd been here to see the work on 'Louisah'. As if the shipwright was following her thoughts he said: 'Bad business that, with Mr Lowden. Great tragedy.'

She nodded. 'How did you hear?'

He frowned, trying to recall. 'Now that I can't be certain. There's nothing goes on amongst the shipowners but word of it gets passed around. What one doesn't know, another does.'

He took her to Exeter just as he had before and promised that when she came again in a fortnight's time he'd have the drawings and the estimate ready.

That night she shut herself in the library and wrote to Dan. A long letter, it told him the reasons for what she meant to do and all about her day with Mr Hawkins.

'We'll call her "Futura", she wrote, "The Future", our future. This is why I want to get the work started now, while we are having to wait. Something we can both look forward to, something we can plan together, a kind of promise of our tomorrow. One day we'll have that future and, because you're you, you'll learn that life still holds so much that is good. It must do, Dan. Dan, my beloved Dan, if I could spare you one moment's pain or unhappiness, if I could bear it for you – but what can I do? I feel so helpless, so useless.'

Her pen flew, words tumbled out. And when he read the letter he knew from her writing just how full her heart had been as she'd scribbled. And he knew too that she'd pulled herself up, brought her racing thoughts under control, as she'd started the next paragraph. His lips twitched into a smile as he imagined her sitting straighter, making a fresh start, determined to keep her thoughts from rambling.

'She's to have a length of two hundred feet, a width of thirty-five feet. She'll be a beauty, Dan. Mr Hawkins is excited, too. We discussed the paddle. He says a wheel thirty feet diameter, just imagine it, with twenty fixed floats. Of course I can't tell you anything exactly, not until he's done his drawings. But he reckons we shall have space for a hundred, or perhaps a hundred and ten, passengers. The other companies better look to their laurels! We went to the "Ship Inn" to have lunch, you remember that little room at the back?' And her writing wavered as the words dashed across the paper. 'Sitting in there you seemed so close. You're always close, Dan . . . '

Fourteen days later, before that first letter had even reached him, another followed it with a set of drawings of 'Futura'. And her anxious query: 'If you were here you'd be able to go over it all with Mr Hawkins. You know so much more than I do. What do you think of it, Dan?'

By the time his reply reached her and she heard what Dan thought about it many weeks had passed. Indeed it was already six months since Mr Bailey had brought 'Louisah' home without him.

'I think "Futura" is a fine boat,' he wrote. 'She is worthy of going further than Cherbourg. Why not Spain, Gibraltar? A route of, say, Cherbourg, Vigo, Lisbon, Cadiz, Gibraltar, Tangiers. And have you considered the possibility of carrying mail? The Post Office is handling less of its own overseas mail now, giving subsidies to shipping companies who take the work. If you cover a regular route to the Mediterranean, the subsidy would be a benefit – and no great space required.' Dan's writing was regular, slightly slanting, each letter the same even height.

'I've read your letter so many times. "Futura", our future. May God grant that it is so. I am proud of you my Hannah, my very dear Hannah, proud of all you are and of your love . . .' And at that point his hand lost its copyplate perfection.

Down in the yard Tommy was with Ted Sharples. There was something in their manner that drew Hannah's attention, not just theirs but the group standing apart from them, the crew of 'My Queen'.

That Ted should hang about on the quay once they were ashore didn't surprise her. As far as she knew he had no family waiting for him. It was the group of seamen she wasn't easy about, their heads together. Men home from the sea didn't stand talking at the water's edge! Now they were moving off, coming towards the building, making for Alan Webster's room to collect the pay due to them. She heard their heavy boots on the stairs, then a minute later one by one going back down again. Yet they still waited outside, seeming undecided. By her open window she listened. A low murmur of voices but she couldn't hear what they said. Ah, they were going.

'We'll leave it to you then, mate.'

'That's it. If they don't want to take my word, if one of us ain't enough, then I'll let you know.'

'Buggers!' that's what it sounded like, but she couldn't be sure and it made no sense. All together they went out of the gate and off in the direction of Quay Hill. Then home, she supposed.

She soon forgot about them for it was Saturday, a feeling of weekend was in the air. According to the calendar summer should be over but today was probably the warmest of the whole season. She'd promised to call at Crown Cottage, then with Rosalind, Beatrice and the boys to take a picnic to the beach.

CHAPTER ELEVEN

The sun beat down relentlessly. The bathing machines were busy and Rosalind, clad in a frilly, long-sleeved, long-legged bathing suit, took a deep breath then stepped down into the water. Oh, the joy of it! A joy not so much in the feeling of the water, indeed that took her breath away, but the sheer sense of freedom. Here she was, dipping in the sea, the boys a little further along the beach with Hannah having a swimming lesson. Once undressed Hannah had stepped down from the machine and immersed herself then waded off to join them. It was lovely to see how she could look after them; Rosalind watched admiringly. To swim was a rare feat and Hannah had proudly demonstrated her ability – seven strokes! These months had been happier than Rosalind had ever expected. What had happened to Dan was the only cloud and even that had a silver lining for when he came home he would be dependent on her care.

'Fancy Beatrice not coming.' Hannah waded back to her. 'Was she out? I didn't even see her when I called.'

'I ought to have let you go and talk to her, try and persuade her to change her mind. No, she was in, upstairs in her room. It was only at the last minute that she said she couldn't come after all – so I guessed why it must be.'

'Shame. She could always have watched from the beach if she couldn't come in. Matthew's almost swimming. He took both feet right off the bottom just now. By the time Dan gets home we'll have something to show him!'

'By the time Dan gets home.' How often Hannah said it. Rosalind shivered. 'I'm going to get my clothes back on. I'll be happy waiting on the shingle, no need to hurry.'

'When Dan gets home.' But she wouldn't let her mind wander down that path. She'd hang on to the facts, not worry about Hannah. And the facts were that Dan's home in Deremouth was at Crown Cottage, with her and with the boys. Hannah had a husband – not that you'd think so sometimes, she never so much as mentioned his name.

The late summer sun was bright, the shingle warm to her touch as she spread her rug and settled to wait for the swimmers. There was nothing to hurry home for, they'd carried their tea in a hamper. A rest would do Beatrice good.

But her picture of Beatrice lying quietly in her bedroom, curtains drawn against the sun, couldn't have been further from the truth. There had been two things that had decided Beatrice not to accompany the party to the beach; ever since that evening at the Hall she'd tried to avoid Hannah, but how was she to know whether Hannah had even noticed? That was the first thing. The second was Richard.

Saturday was his half day, he came to the coachhouse straight from work. She watched from the back window for him to arrive, then took him his mug of tea.

'Here's your drink. Have it with your dinner.'

'Thanks, Beatrice. Sweltering, isn't it?'

'We're going to the beach. Into the sea.' And at that point she'd still supposed she'd go with the others.

'You are? You mean you won't be here?' She heard the disappointment in his tone.

'I don't particularly want to bathe, but I said I would. Rosalind's taking their tea, making an outing of it. Summer can't last much longer.'

'Stay here, Bea,' he persuaded. She smiled to hear the wheedling note in his voice as he went on: 'Leaving me all alone.'

If she stayed behind Hannah would notice, would miss her. She told herself it was that that decided her. But it wasn't the whole truth. There was something in Richard, a loneliness, something she'd been conscious of for weeks. She'd worried about it, had even been to see Kath. Not to mention it, of course, but keeping her eyes and ears open for signs of trouble. But Kath, her merry face red with the heat, had been the same as always. A little shorter of breath but nothing that another few weeks wouldn't put right as her time drew nearer.

'Oughtn't you to be home now on a Saturday? Kath's not got long to go.'

'Your Ma's coming today for the whole day. They won't notice whether I'm there or not.'

'Well, eat your dinner and drink your tea. I'll tell Rosalind I'm not going with them. I'll make up an excuse.'

His eyes met hers. They were conspirators. Just for that second Beatrice was too honest to believe it was solely because of Hannah that she was staying at home.

The afternoon temperature soared into the unseasonal eighties. No wonder the bathing machines were busy. In the coachhouse it was too hot to work. Sweat was running down Richard's face, the chisel was slipping in his wet hands.

'Come up to the house and have a nice cold wash. You'll work better if you cool down.'

And how was it she could look so unaffected by the heat, her face just as pale? Her only concession to the temperature was that the top button of her grey cotton dress was undone. Then, as he followed her up the brick path to the kitchen door, Richard noticed something else. She wore no stockings! He could see the pale skin of her ankles, so slender, the bones sharply pronounced. It wasn't the first time she'd stirred his imagination, it wasn't the first time he'd felt this twinge of excitement at her nearness.

'I'll go and fetch you down a clean towel,' she told him and left him by the sink running cold water into the bowl. By the time she brought the towel down he had his shirt off and was splashing cold water in his cupped hands over his body. Richard was well-built and proud of his physique; there was still that excitement nudging at him, enough that he wanted her to admire his body. But she seemed not to notice, just said something about going to do some work in the garden and left the towel on the back of the kitchen chair. He didn't think she'd so much as looked at him!

He was partly disappointed, partly relieved. He could relax, he was safe. She was Kath's sister, he didn't intend to let himself forget it. It was obvious Beatrice hadn't realized the way his thoughts had been turning. So with renewed vigour he threw cold water over his face and chest, towelled himself, then put his shirt on again. He wore no collar or tie, and rolled his sleeves to his elbows.

Then, refreshed and determined to work, he went outside.

Kneeling on the brick path Beatrice was scratching weeds from the rock hard border with a hand fork. He'd meant to go straight back to the coachhouse but he found himself stopping by where she gardened. She didn't look up, just went on digging her fork into the ground and one by one prising out the weeds. Yet, even though she worked, there was a stillness about her that held him. On her knees she was bending forward, her back curved. The cotton dress clung to her, he could see the shape of her spine. Bare ankles ... now this. And as if he'd willed that she should, she sat back on her heels surveying the patch she'd cleared.

There was nothing accidental in the direction his glance fell, he knew just what he was looking for as he craned his neck forward. With the top buttons undone – both of them now – he had a bird's-eye view. Not stockings, no chemise, nothing ... the sun beat down, heat prickled on the back of his neck.

He should work. That's what he'd come here for. 'I oughtn't to have persuaded you to stay behind, you could

285

have been dipping in the sea. Why don't you go and join them?'

She didn't answer. Her face took on what her mother always referred to as 'that hang dog look'. Again he remembered that evening when she'd cried. And now it was he who'd hurt her.

'Beatrice, it's because I want you to stay that I say you ought to go.'

'We'll see.' She turned back to the weeds. 'Anyway you'd better get on, standing here in this sun you'll be no cooler than before your wash.' Still she knelt at his feet. For a moment he believed she knew why he stood above her, that she knew his gaze was riveted on her white flesh. But that was impossible.

Without answering he went on down the path. He was tormented by his thoughts. He had a wife and two children; any day he'd have a third. No one had listened to Harold when he'd told them to wait. Perhaps he'd been wiser than they knew. Even now Richard was barely twenty-one. The responsibilities of a family had turned his youth into a battle for existence. In the coachhouse he sat on Beatrice's stool. He'd thought that by running away from her, by hiding in here, he'd escape his own desires. After the brilliance outside it seemed dark, the air still, the smell of wood sickeningly strong. A trickle of sweat ran down his chest.

She was his sister-in-law . . . he lusted after his wife's sister. It was a sin, and a sin against Kath too, dear jolly Kath. And it wasn't that she'd changed, she was just as affectionate and good-humoured. Through all their hard times – and thank goodness there was a bit more coming in now – she'd never grumbled. She never refused what he wanted, except when she was pregnant. 'It can't be right,' she protested, 'not when there's a babe growing in there.' But soon she wouldn't be pregnant. She never refused, she

286

never shirked her duty. He ran his fingers through his hair. God, but it was hot! He looked out of the window just for a sight of her still kneeling there. She'd gone. She must have followed the others to the beach. He ought to be glad. Except for Kath he'd known no other girl, and found himself on strange ground. It must be the heat that made him feel like this, that and all these months with Kath saying it wasn't right because of the baby. Yes, a good thing if she'd gone off to the beach. Hadn't he told her to go?

Alone, he stripped off his shirt, he wouldn't be so sticky without it. No stockings, such boney ankles, legs that would be long and thin, thighs he'd be able to encircle with his hands. No chemise, nothing under the bodice of that cotton dress, perhaps nothing under it at all ... He must work. He took up his chisel. It must be the heat.

But Beatrice hadn't followed the others. Up in her attic bedroom she sat on the edge of her narrow bed. Hannah was on the beach. She could join them, watch the boys at play, listen to their talk. Dan this, Dan that. She shut her eyes and lay back on the bed. To love as she loved Hannah left no place for reason. She'd only known how Hannah felt about Dan for a few days and yet in that short time it seemed to her that they had grown apart. Reason would have told her differently. As long as she'd known her there had been Dan – 'a part of myself' – reason would have told her this was nothing new. But reason had no place in Beatrice's heart.

There was something else, again only half understood. Richard. Kath's husband. She'd seen the way he'd stood above her just now, she'd known how he looked at her. Because there was a loneliness in him that touched a chord in herself she hadn't been repelled. That surprised her. 'I'll never love any man like I love Hannah.' How could she? Every urge and need in her was a reflection of what Hannah knew and understood. How could she know what

a man felt? Her small hands rested on the barely perceptible swellings of her breasts, then moved down her body,
the material of her dress unfamiliar against her nakedness.
'Hannah, my dear, beautiful Hannah, why don't you care?
Dan, always Dan.'

The coachhouse was shadowy. Looking in from the
open doorway as she stood outside in the brilliant sunshine
it seemed almost dark. He looked up as her shadow fell
across the threshold. Involuntarily he held out his hands
to her.

Long before dusk Richard went home. He wanted just to
get back to Kath. He thought of their little kitchen,
washing always steaming on the high fireguard around the
range, the pulley adorned with airing clothes, the lid of the
big black kettle bobbing up and down as it constantly
boiled, always ready for a welcoming cup of tea. This was
home, this was safety, security. Kath's smile never failed
to greet him. Her body sturdy, thick, her thighs dimpled
with fat. He wanted to run from the afternoon, from that
cool passive body. Only now did he realize just how long
the thought of Beatrice had haunted him. A body everything that Kath's wasn't. He'd push it from his mind, from
his memory. Partly what repelled him now was the very
thing that had attracted him: her coolness. If what he'd
done had brought her any joy then the chauvinist in him
would have been satisfied. But had it? She was an enigma.

As he turned the corner into Merchant Place she was
forgotten. The doctor's trap was outside his door. Richard
broke into a run.

Upstairs in their little bedroom Kath worked at what
she prided herself she was good at. A good wife didn't
scream as her body was torn in labour. Kath bit into her
lips until she tasted blood, she pushed, she strained – and

just before midnight on that day, the 18th July 1859, their second son was born, Harold George.

Weak from her hours of struggle Kath held her son in her arms. Was ever a woman so happy?

The next time Richard let himself into the garden through the gate in Cleggs Lane he looked uncomfortably towards the house. Much had changed in the three days since that hot Saturday. A son had been born to him; the heatwave had broken with a tremendous thunderstorm that had put an end to summer. Today it was more like November, a grey drizzling mist hung low over Deremouth. Last week – its heat, its clear sky, its passion – might have all been a dream.

Richard didn't look forward to his first contact with Beatrice alone. He'd seen her at Kath's bedside, a mousey and withdrawn Beatrice, the girl he remembered from the days of the gatehouse. On this Tuesday it took all his determination to undo his box of tools and set to work. Minutes passed. Half an hour. An hour. Ah, she was coming, the steaming mug of tea in her hand. His mouth was dry as sawdust, he had no idea what the next few minutes might bring. However she pleaded, he had to make her understand it was a mistake. But supposing she clung to him, supposing she cried . . . He didn't want to touch her, shrank from the memory of her knobbly spine under his hand.

'There's your tea.' She put it down on the bench. 'I shan't stay out here, I'm going to make some jam. The boys have been berrying.'

'Beatrice, about Saturday – '

'Can't we pretend it didn't happen? I'd rather forget it.' And she was gone.

Well, at least she wasn't going to make trouble! His first feeling was relief then he felt rebuffed. Almost angrily he watched her walk back to the house. 'Who the hell does she think she is! Three pen'north of scrag!' It was hurt pride that spoke. Sneering at the little round-shouldered figure helped restore his unappreciated manhood.

Work started on the building of 'Futura'. Alan had disapproved of passenger trade right from when plans for 'Oberon' had first been mooted. He couldn't dispute there was money in it, but Netherton's had always been a cargo carrying company and, as Hannah had told Mr Habbins, Alan hated change. Especially he hated it this time. Wasn't it proof if he'd needed it of just how little his opinions counted for these days.

'What you do here is for you to decide,' he said, cornering Tommy on one of his increasingly rare visits to the yard, 'but couldn't you have had the courtesy to tell me, even if my views count for nothing any more?'

'It's not me you want to tackle, Father, it's Hannah. It seems she means to ride roughshod over both of us.'

'You mean she didn't ask your advice! But this is disgraceful! Where's your authority, man? You're her husband. I've never heard such a thing. It's time you settled her at home with a family to fill her time with. Business is no place for meddling women.' He blustered, his anger at Hannah going far deeper than the package steamer in Hawkins' yard. No wonder the boy was never here. Who could blame him with a wife who'd disregard him in front of the staff? And if the rumours he'd half-heard had any truth in them and there was a bit of fluff Tommy amused himself with, well, what else could be expected? A man should be master. She was too much like that arrogant aunt of hers!

Alan had accepted Hannah under sufferance when she'd first come to sit with Albert Tyzack and learn his job. But that was long ago. Nowadays she had her finger in everything that went on. He'd learnt to respect her judgement, been proud that Tommy was married to her. He'd tried to foster some sort of affection even, but his success must have been superficial for in a moment it could die.

On that particular morning when he spoke to Tommy, 'My Queen' was setting out, this time to New Orleans. Watching the crew Hannah was reminded of that other morning recently. She was reminded of it because even now there was something about them that made her uneasy. Wives and families were gathered on the quayside, on the surface there was nothing out of the ordinary. And yet she sensed a difference. She noticed Mr Binns, the mate, signal to one or two of the men; she noticed the way they stood, heads together, voices low. Scheming, she was sure of it. Yet she'd watched the cargo go aboard, she'd checked the record; she could swear that this time everything was accounted for. Yet she smelt trouble.

'Imagination!' she told herself, and tried to believe it.

Netherton's yard stood empty. A single beam of light shone into the darkness from one upstairs window. Hannah's window.

By the light of her lamp she was reading the notes she'd made today on her visit to Edward Hawkins. Hark! She raised her head and listened. There was someone in the yard. Would Tommy come here at this time of evening? Careful not to let herself be seen or her shadow fall across the window she moved away from the lamp, edging her way around the wall to try and peep out without being seen. But it was dark out there, the shaft of light from her room only deepened the blackness around it.

That wasn't Tommy's step but a stranger's. Her first panic that he might have come purposely, knowing she was alone here, gave way to fear of a different kind. Not many minutes ago as she'd walked from the station she'd noticed a group of seamen, some more drunk than others, at the top of Quay Hill. They must have noticed her, followed her, realized she was alone!

It wasn't in her nature to be nervous, evenings enough she spent here when everyone had gone home and the yard was closed, but there was something sinister in the intruder's step. He was uncertain, groping his way. She pictured him feeling for the latch on the door of the sheds, shuffling on the uneven ground. What a fool she was, she thought. But it was too late, whoever it was was inside now. A stranger, she could tell that from the uncertain tread in the darkness down there. She could walk anywhere here blindfold.

She'd turn out the lamp. In the dark he wouldn't know where to come. She'd have the advantage.

'Hannah!'

Her fright was gone. She felt empty, light, as if she were made of cotton wool. Dan! 'Dan! Dan!' And instead of turning out her lantern she carried it with her, lighting her way down the wooden stairs to the store below. And there he stood, at the foot of the stairs.

Whatever happiness her past had held there had been nothing to compare with this. Joy, relief, and now that he held her close against him, an awareness of the fear she'd never dare acknowledge. Suppose he'd died in hospital.

Sacks of grain stood stacked, tomorrow they would be put aboard. Now they half sat, half leant against them.

'Things must be different.' Was he asking her or telling her?

'Yes, they must be. Dan, there's one thing I've learnt – and you know this too – we have to be together, we have to share whatever is ahead of us. I don't care what Tommy does. I'll fight him in every court. But we have to be together. Whatever I lose, I shall be the winner.'

Dan's throat was tight. Did she know what she was saying? Suppose Tommy divorced her, disinherited her, stripped her of this place she so loved, of the home her aunt had given her? Suppose he let that happen to her, and him hardly fit to take a ship to sea.

'Don't look like that Dan.' She knelt down on the stone slabs of the floor, her cheek against his thigh, her hand gently touching his severed leg. If he shut his eyes he could imagine himself whole. The ache in his thigh went far beyond the wound. It tingled in the ankle and the toes he no longer had.

'This can't come between us – not us, Dan.'

'It can never come between us but it must make a difference, Hannah.'

'You're the same man you always were, the same you always will be.'

'I'm not the same. If I were whole – if you were free.'

' "Whole" you say! Dan, you are whole.' And now she stood up, her eyes almost level with his as he stood leaning against the sacks, her hands firm on his shoulders. 'When Aunt Lou died, I remember lying in bed that night, picturing her stomping in through the pearly gates, her Charles waiting for her.'

His mouth twitched into a flicker of a smile. 'Hah!' he mimicked affectionately, remembering too.

'Then I realized she wouldn't be stomping in on her sticks, not to Charles. The fundamental her, the core, the spirit, whatever it is that makes us what we are – oh Dan, I'm saying this so badly, but don't you see? The things that happened to her here, as her body grew old and crippled, none of it altered the fundamental her, nothing could.' Even if she were saying it badly, her meaning was clear.

'My Hannah.' He pulled her back into his arms. She buried her head against his neck. She didn't see the way his mouth worked, but when she raised her face and rubbed her cheek against his she knew the tears weren't just hers.

'We can face anything, Dan, you and me, so long as we

293

can share it.' She looked at him as she spoke. In future they'd hide nothing from each other.

'I have no words' ...' His voice broke. 'Just – ' his hands, his dear, unchanging strong hands, held hers tightly – 'I thank God, Hannah.'

She nodded wordlessly. The lantern flickered, casting long and weird shadows on the warehouse walls.

'Louisah' had been tied up in Netherton's quay since Mr Bailey had brought her home. The crew had found work on other boats, the mate had gone back to Liverpool, his home port. Perhaps even he hadn't much faith in Dan's future as a ship's master.

It had been Hannah's idea that they should come aboard, she who pulled the gangplank into place. Now, their eyes gradually becoming attuned to the night, they stood on deck, feeling the gentle rise and fall from the wash against the harbour wall.

'Now I know I'm really home.' He spoke softly, his hand rubbing against the rough canvas of the furled sail.

'Let's see your cabin.' She whispered too. The stillness all around them seemed to demand it. 'I'll go ahead and light the lamp. Can you get down there do you think, Dan?'

'You go first.' Then, with a laugh that tore at her heart: 'Stand by to pick up the pieces.' But still she hovered, hating the forced bravado. It seemed to put a barrier between them. Perhaps he sensed what she felt for when he spoke next there was no doubting his sincerity. 'I have to learn to manage, Hannah. It's not easy – it's the hopelessness of it. With an illness you can look forward to recovery. But with this ... Still, I'm not the first man. Others have managed, and so shall I. You find your way down and get a lamp, there's a good girl.'

She nodded. Now she could leave him.

The lamp lit she came to the foot of the ladder. She took his sticks as he passed them down to her, then braced herself to be ready should he slip. But he didn't. Somehow he got to the bottom.

'There! How's that?' And his smile had all the pride of Matthew's when he'd managed to swim two strokes with both feet off the bottom. 'We did it!'

She didn't answer, her heart was so full.

His cabin. Everything just as he'd known it. A little empty and unlived-in, no water in the tall enamel jug, no towel, no charts spread out on the desk. He sat at that desk now, his hands feeling the familiar wooden top. She perched on the bunk watching him, saying nothing. These moments belonged just to him.

'God carry you safely.' She heard the echo of so many partings. And now, looking at him, she sent up a silent thank you. There was no doubting what he'd been through. Lines of suffering were etched on his face, his brown hair changed to grey at his temples. But he was himself; he'd come home.

Not a sound could be heard, not a movement save the gentle rocking of the boat. To move across the cabin to her he needed sticks to give him balance – not at all the thing for a swashbuckling sea captain. As he came near Hannah her hands reached up to him, pulling him to her side.

He'd had such resolutions. He'd vowed he'd never let Tommy be able to accuse Hannah of breaking her vows. Yet now, in the dimly lit cabin, their world had no place for Tommy, no place for anyone but themselves and each other, the rightness of being together. There could be no other way for them. Hadn't Hannah always known that this was what love should be?

And afterwards, still lying close in each other's arms, they knew a peace untouched by earthly things. The months that had gone had been a purgatory for them both.

Now the misery was wiped away, their souls were cleansed. Whatever the future brought, it was theirs together. Like a ship coming to the haven of her home harbour, Hannah knew no doubts in those hours of night. This was where she belonged, this was her purpose for living, this was fulfilment.

Alan wasn't given to premonitions. Yet that evening he was uneasy. It might have had to do with the gossip he'd overheard that afternoon – and not for the first time – amongst the humpers. Not that he believed it! Why, the boy had moved back to the Hall! All the worrying he and Em had done over these last months was over. And yet . . .

'I think I'll get a breath of air before I turn in, Em. Don't wait up for me.'

'You're going out? But, Alan, it's not a bit nice. The mist has come in. It's gone right into winter. You'll catch your death after sitting by this fire.'

'Just a quick walk. One or two things I want to think over . . . can't sleep with the job on my mind. Never could. You know that.'

'I'd expected by now you'd have let Tommy do the worrying.'

Alan didn't answer, just patted her shoulders as he passed her. 'Get along to bed when you're ready. I'll come in quietly, I'll not disturb you.' Poor Em. Today hadn't been the first time he'd heard whispers that Tommy was carrying on with some woman or other. Plenty of men looked outside marriage, but he was a fool for all that. Later, when he'd got a son, when the future was set fair . . . but why couldn't he look further afield than his own doorstep if he couldn't wait? What if Hannah heard the talk? Now that Tommy was living at the Hall he and Em had supposed everything was rosy again. He knew his wife was only waiting now for news that a grandchild was on the way.

Perhaps the rumours were wrong. Perhaps the men in the yard had just got word of something that was already over. And if Tommy had been finding a bit of comfort somewhere else when Hannah had left him all by himself in Vicary Place, who could blame him for that?

The night air was clearing his mind. His confidence was returning.

Whenever Alan walked, instinctively he made for the estuary and the wharf. At the top of Quay Hill he stood by the wall, but tonight the masts of the boats moored at Netherton's were lost in mist and darkness. He wasn't a fanciful man, yet he felt uneasy, he had a premonition that all wasn't as it should be. So what more natural than that he should go down the hill, along the public wharf, through the gate into Netherton's yard.

The lamp had long been turned out. Everything was still.

So what was it made him try the door of the shed? Open! Someone must have broken in! Hadn't he felt that something was wrong! He went inside, stood quite still and listened. Like Hannah, Alan could walk anywhere in here blindfold, so as quietly as he could he went up the stairs. His eyes were getting accustomed to the dark, one by one he looked into the rooms. His own room shared with Tommy, and then Hannah's. There were signs that someone had been recently working, her desk was covered with papers. The feeling that all wasn't well grew stronger. Hannah would never have gone home and left her papers out and the doors unlocked. He crossed to her window and looked out. It was then that he noticed a hazy glow of light coming from 'Louisah', tied up at the end of Netherton's quay. The ship had been here ever since Mr Bailey had brought it home. Netherton's had been taking charge of it. Alan saw that someone had gone aboard, and felt responsible. Back downstairs he went, this time making sure that the sheds were securely locked, then quietly across the cobblestones to where he found 'Louisah's' gangplank in place. He could see that the light came from the porthole of the cabin. He'd creep down and catch the intruders redhanded.

Neither Hannah nor Dan heard anyone coming.

As Alan came near the cabin door he halted. A woman! Was she crying? No ... And if his first thoughts flew to Tommy it couldn't be wondered at after the gossip he'd so recently heard. No doubt what was going on in there. He ought to fling open the door and catch them! Some men might have been able to – but not Alan. He swallowed his suddenly large Adam's apple. Supposing it was young Tommy and this woman he'd heard about? Well, if it was he didn't want to know. He certainly didn't want to walk in on ... Oh dear, oh dear. Alan hated his role of peeping Tom. These were things that should be private.

He had no business to be listening like this but he had a duty. Alan put out his hand to stave off the rocking of the boat. He thought of home, Em going off to bed. Yes, it was his duty to apprehend whoever had broken in to Mr Lowden's boat. But he wished he'd stayed at home.

Voices crying out, the woman's and now the man's too, then silence. Alan ran his fingers around his stiff collar. It seemed to be sticking to his neck. If that was Tommy he didn't want to know. He'd creep away. But who was to say that it *was* Tommy? It might be strangers, waiting for high water so that they could sail away. Netherton's had been made responsible for Mr Lowden's ship, Netherton's responsibilities were his responsibilities.

'Hannah ... Hannah ...'

Whatever Alan had imagined it hadn't been this. Not easy to anger, now he was shaken by hatred. And people were talking of Tommy, giving the boy a bad name. The bitch! She with her airs and graces! What ought he to do?

298

He thought of Em. He couldn't tell her, she'd had such dreams for Tommy. Somehow he groped quietly away from the cabin door, feeling his way in the dark. The water was hitting against the wall, rocking the boat with more force now. He was used to terra firma, gratefully he found his way back up the ladder and across the deck to the gangplank. On the quay he was on his own ground. He must think.

Already he could stand outside himself, overcoming the anger that had consumed him only minutes before. Hannah and Daniel Lowden . . . How long had she been making a cuckold of Tommy? And, if what he heard was the truth and Tommy had found himself a bit of fluff somewhere else, who could blame him?

But what about Em? He imagined himself carrying the tale home to her. He couldn't do it. He was torn in two directions. To expose Hannah and old Mrs Netherton's precious Daniel Lowden, or to protect Em from the hurt Hannah's unfaithfulness to their Tommy would inflict. No, he couldn't do that to her. The girl had known Lowden for years, this was probably no new thing. How often he'd seen her fling herself at him. If he brought it all out into the open, where would that leave Tommy?

If Alan had expected a walk in the night air to clear his mind he'd been mistaken. His night was restless, short snatches of sleep haunted by dreams so lurid that he woke confused at the imaginings of his subconscious. Long before it was light he was wide awake, anxious to find forgetfulness in work.

Morning showed no signs of life aboard 'Louisah'. Had it not been for the gangplank still in place Alan would have wondered if the whole thing had had no more substance than the rest of the fantasies of his broken night. No movement there, and no sign of Tommy nor yet of Hannah.

When he did hear a step on the stairs it was Tommy's.

'Hannah not in this morning?' Alan greeted him. 'Nothing wrong? She's not unwell?'

But Tommy didn't seem to be listening. He was peering out to sea, where a ship was approaching the estuary. Alan followed his gaze, then took the telescope from Tommy's desk and held it to his eye.

'It can't be. Here, take a look through the glass. If that's not 'My Queen' then I'm a Dutchman. When's she due? Not for weeks.'

'That's impossible!'

'See for yourself.'

Tommy focused on the advancing vessel; Alan focused on Tommy. Had it been Hannah watching him she would have put a very different interpretation on the wariness that changed his expression. But then, she would have been on her guard, ready to expect that something was afoot not likely to bring credit to Netherton's. Alan saw fear but read it as hurt. Today he was father first and manager only second. Something was very wrong, he could see clearly, and after what he'd heard last night he was sure it had to do with Hannah.

In those seconds as he looked at Tommy all his resolutions to say nothing vanished.

'It's Lowden – that's what's troubling you. Oh dear, oh dear, what a business.' His words tumbled out unplanned.

'What do you know about Lowden?' Even confirming whether or not it was 'My Queen' coming towards the port was of secondary importance to this.

'I'm sorry, son. We had such hopes, your mother and me. You knew he was home?'

'He came to see me, this morning.'

'Trollop! She with her airs and graces! I'd no idea what I would find, just saw that someone had come aboard 'Louisah'. Netherton's had charge of the boat, so of course I felt it my duty – '

'A-ha!' Tommy beamed triumphantly, a most unusual

300

expression. 'You mean you caught them! Father could you testify that that's what they were doing – actually at it?'

Alan tut-tutted. 'What a business. Your marriage to come to this! All our hopes for you here at Netherton's.'

'Netherton's you say? Not for much longer. Webster's! And I'll tell you something else while we're on the subject. She's no loss. Cold as ice. You call that marriage? And where's this son the old woman has entailed the business to? I'll tell you. There'll be no son, not mine and hers – nor yet her precious Lowden's. She's as barren as the old woman was before her.'

'Dear, oh dear.'

As if to shelter behind something he could understand, Alan took up the telescope again. In his excitement Tommy seemed to have forgotten the incoming boat.

'No doubt about it, that's 'My Queen'. She's coming in.' Tommy with a lady friend at a respectable distance he could accept, even if he might not condone it. Hannah with a lover, the intimate affairs of their marriage aired for all the world to know . . . No wonder Alan concentrated all his attention on what was going on in the approach to the estuary.

Who was that on deck? Not Sharples, nor yet Binns, the Mate. It was a man in uniform. 'What do you make of . . .?'

But Tommy had gone.

'But, Tom, I don't understand.'

'And I don't want you to understand. What you don't know, you can't tell.'

'Tell? Tell on you! You think I'd ever do that?'

'No, Susie, I don't. But if you don't know the answers you don't need to lie.'

Susie's black eyes never left his face. The baby at her

301

breast sucked steadily. Thomasinna with her mother's olive skin, her father's gingery brown eyes.

'What is it we gotta do, Tom? I dunno what trouble you're in, but we can move on easy enough if that's what you want.'

Tommy looked around him. At last he'd given her a comfortable home, a few miles out of town where no one knew her. A home that was paid for and furnished thanks to the Netherton estate. Not for the first time in this last hour he cursed himself for being a fool. Things could have been so easy; things were already easy as long as he kept a low profile. Now, with what he knew about Hannah, the way would have been open for him. Yet what Ted Sharples had whispered in his ear had seemed too good a chance to miss. The first trip had come off well, given them a nice profit too. So how could things have gone wrong this time?

What Tommy had seen aboard the approaching 'My Queen' had spelt clearly that his time had run out.

For more than twenty years it had been illegal to bring slaves to England, or for an English ship to deal in the slave market. He'd known it; Ted Sharples had known it. But trade that is legal can never pay such dividends. Temptation had been too much for either of them.

The first trip had worked according to Sharples' well laid plan. Instead of sailing directly to New Orleans he'd taken 'My Queen' to West Africa and picked up his shackled cargo. A fine profit for Tommy, and for himself; they'd believed that even the crew had been silenced by their sovereign or two. But then they hadn't had the view of them that Hannah had from her window, they'd been much too busy whispering together about their success to notice the disquiet amongst the men.

So on the next trip he'd walked – or rather, sailed – right into a trap. Mr Binns had taken 'My Queen' from Lagos to the appointed rendezvous some twenty miles into the Atlantic where she'd been hailed by a ship of Her

Majesty's fleet and where the boarding party had taken away Ted Sharples' command. Return to Lagos to put the 'slaves' ashore, then home to England under naval escort.

At first sight of the uniformed officer on deck, Tommy had known exactly what must have happened. He had no illusions about Ted Sharples, either. If Sharples sunk, then he'd be sure Tommy went down with him.

'You'll be all right here, Susie, but I'll have to clear off, there's no doubt about that.'

'Tom, just tell me one thing. Have you got the law after you for something? Or is it just Hannah?' Tommy's lips were tight, he didn't answer. 'Come on Tom. It's the law, isn't it? Whatever it is you've been tinkering in, it can't change things for me, you know that.' She stood up, Thomasinna over her shoulder, her breasts bare. So might Kath have walked across the room towards Richard, her work reddened hands thumping up Harold George's wind. Yet Richard would never have been moved by the sight as Tommy was now.

'Susie, I'm in a mess. I've got to get away.'

'Money, you mean. Because of what you got from the yard for me and Thomasinna?'

'Worse . . .' And so he told her.

She heard him through and knew it was the truth, the whole truth. Only when he came to the end did she speak.

'Hold her, will you, Tom?' She passed the baby to him. 'Can you stay here for a bit? I know a man. I promise I won't tell him anything, just that we're after a passage, want to make a new start together.'

'Mind you don't tell anyone where I am. Don't tell him who it is you want to run off with. Promise me.'

'Don't you trust me, Tom?'

He was ashamed.

So she took his pony and trap and set out on the road in the direction of Plymouth. Her destination was about an hour's ride, and all the way she silently prayed that she'd

303

find the man she sought, that he'd be at home on his own. If having a past like Susie's has one advantage it's that somewhere she could usually find a man who owed her a favour.

'I've told Tommy, and now I've told you. We want no whispers and innuendos and, Rosalind, I know you'll help us. Whether or not people approve can't be helped, but come what may we're going to be open.'

While Tommy raked over the ruins of his marriage with his father, Dan told Rosalind the future he and Hannah intended to build together.

Word had already reached her that he was in Deremouth. The postman had helped him into the cab at the station, so what more natural than that this morning when Beatrice had seen him go by as she'd polished the brass knocker he should have called: 'Glad to see the Captain's safely home.'

'Home' and yet he wasn't at Crown Cottage. To Rosalind that could only mean one thing. She thought of Hannah's constant 'When Dan gets home', and Beatrice remembered 'Then pray there'll be a way for Dan and me'. Both of them took comfort in the thought of Tommy, the ties of matrimony.

So when Rosalind heard the news that he was back she dressed carefully in her silvery blue gown and when she saw the carriage from the Hall stop outside her gate she was ready with her welcome. Now, though, that 'special' gown seemed to taunt her. She felt over-dressed at eleven o'clock in the morning in the cottage parlour.

'Tell me you wish us well, Rosalind.'

'I always wish you well, you know that. But, Daniel, what good can there be in it? Tommy isn't going to let Hannah turn him out of his home to put you in his place just because she's changed her mind. She made solemn

304

vows to be faithful to him.' Her great blue eyes were turned on him, full of innocence. The world had used Rosalind cruelly they silently said, but still she could understand only what was good. 'Where is Hannah?'

'She'll be here soon. I left her at the Hall.' It had been Hannah's wish that he should talk to Rosalind without her. Even if those things Beatrice had said had never been taken seriously, she had a suspicion that Rosalind might have had ideas of her own.

Neither Rosalind nor Dan heard the movement in the passage outside the parlour door. Beatrice had listened long enough to know all she needed to. Upstairs in her attic bedroom she put on her bonnet and tied it firmly, then fastened her cloak. It was a wintry morning, the wind strong and from the east. Holding her cloak about her she crept back down the narrow stairs, out through the kitchen and down the brick garden path to the gate into Cleggs Lane.

This was her chance. This was her last chance.

She reached the top of Quay Hill and stopped to peer over. Would she be able to see Hannah's trap? Would she have gone there before coming to Crown Cottage? What Beatrice did see riveted her attention on the yard and sent her down the hill and to the public wharf where already a crowd was gathered. Uniformed men were in Netherton's yard; they had brought a boat in. A man was being escorted off, held in custody.

'Whatever's been happening?' Beatrice forgot her shyness and spoke to no one in particular in the crowd.

'They've brought the ship in. They'd had African slaves aboard. Caught 'em red-handed. Someone's going to be for the high jump.'

'Netherton's. Oh, no.'

'That young Webster, him what married the Netherton girl. That's who it is they're after. Not a sign of 'im here.'

305

'Nor often is, from what I've heard,' someone else put in.

'Slippery customer, that one.'

'Ah, always has been trouble. Gone to earth somewhere you may be sure. His sort always knows how to sniff a hole.'

''Tis the old man, his father, that's who I feel sorry for.'

'Aye, he can't win, the old man can't. If they catch the young bugger or if they don't, bad outlook for the old chap.'

Beatrice turned and hurried back up the hill. She'd never realized before how steep it was. By the time she got to the top she was fighting for breath. But she didn't stop. Round the corner and towards the long hill towards Netherton Hall. What she'd heard must be her trump card. She didn't know how she'd play it, but that she had it gave her confidence as she saw Hannah's trap coming towards her.

CHAPTER TWELVE

'Are you off to your mother's?' Hannah drew in the reins as she came level with Beatrice. 'I was on my way to Crown Cottage, but it's mostly you I want to talk to. Hop up Bea.'

'I'm not off to anywhere. Only to find you.' Her answer could only mean one thing.

'You've seen Dan?'

Beatrice nodded, then climbed into the trap. 'Yes, I saw him. And I heard what he was telling Rosalind. Please, Hannah,' she turned to her, desperately seeking words, yet all she could say was, 'please, don't do it, please.'

They were sitting in the trap, the pony standing with a bored and disinterested air until the jerk on his reins would re-call him to duty. But Hannah made no attempt to move. Here beyond the outskirts of town they were alone. To their right the grass sloped gently down to the cliff's edge on the southern side of Braggs Head. Today there was a wildness in the scene. Beyond the cliff white horses galloped on the sea.

'Hannah, say something.'

'What is there I can say? Beatrice, you know about me and Dan. How can you tell me not to do it. We are as we are. I wish you could understand.'

'Men! They're all of them the same. There's Tommy, he's never been faithful to you. So what makes you think Dan'll be any different?' She didn't quite look at Hannah as she went on. 'I've lived in the house with them, with him and Rosalind. You know what it is, don't you? You know why he pretends he wants you? Just the same as Tommy – they want you because you're rich. Dan must know he can't take his boat to sea. Both of them – ' Her voice had risen, it was shrill, hysterical.

'Stop it Beatrice.' Hannah shook her shoulders. 'Anyway, if Tommy has his way I shan't be rich, I'll have nothing. But, Bea, I don't care. I'll be with Dan. I won't be living a lie.'

'Is that what it would be living with me? Would that be a lie?' Beatrice held her face close to Hannah's, contorted by tears.

'Don't cry like that, Bea.' Hannah took her in her arms. 'Try and understand.'

'No man can ever love you like I do, Hannah.' Just for a moment Hannah still heard it as the cry of the lonely girl Bea had always been. But only for a moment. Then: 'Hold me, hold me.' Beatrice burrowed her tear-drenched face against Hannah's neck.

'Hush, Bea, don't cry, Don't . . .'

It was then that Hannah felt the mouth on her neck. Instinctively she pulled her head away, but Beatrice was too quick for her. She felt her mouth covered with kisses that bore no relationship to their friendship of so long. In a flash she remembered that other occasion, long forgotten, Bea guiding her hands to press them against her breasts.

'No, Bea! Sit up.'

Like a rebuffed child Beatrice moved away and wiped the back of her hands across her wet cheeks.

'Tommy's no good. I knew he'd not make you happy. And your Dan, he's no different. He's grown tired of Rosalind and the boys, I suppose – and he'll grow tired of you, your turn will come. I never will, though, Hannah. The sort of love you want is the sort of love I want. We could give it to each other. For always Hannah. You're all I love, all I want.'

'I'm going to drive us home – back to town. Wipe your face, Beatrice.' She felt repelled, shocked – and out of her depth. She and Bea had been so close, as close as only two girls growing through adolescence together can be. Yet now that very closeness set them apart. Beatrice's words hung between them. She seemed a stranger.

'If it had been you who'd had Tommy's baby instead of that Susie Syms, you wouldn't have imagined yourself in love with Dan Lowden. That's all it is. It's because you're disappointed, you feel you've failed. But Hannah,' like a conspirator she leant closer, 'see – look.' She took Hannah's hand and held it against her. 'Can you feel how different I am? I did it for us. We'll share it. We'll have everything.'

'What do you mean, different?'

'No one's noticed. Not even you. But – see.' She pulled her cloak back and stuck out her chest.

All Hannah's revulsion melted. She understood now what had made Beatrice talk so wildly. She was pregnant! Bea, of all people. But who was the man? And where was he? She'd sounded demented just now as she'd clung to Hannah, but who could wonder at that? Hannah took hold of her hands in a firm grip.

'Tell me about it. Who is he? You must love him, Bea, or you'd not have let it happen? Is he a seaman, has he gone away? He'll come back.'

'He doesn't matter. He's not important. I'll tell you one thing about him, though – ' and again she leant close, her face next to Hannah's – 'he has a wife. And she's like all of you, believes he's faithful!'

'You won't be alone, Bea. We'll look after you. We'll have to tell the others, but we'll work it out between us. We'll face it together.'

'"We!" You and him, I suppose you mean. "We'll look after poor Beatrice."' But she clung to Hannah's hand all the same. 'All that – men – what they want – it's so hateful. They don't understand, not like we do. I can give you all the love you need, just let me be with you. We'll have the baby, we'll have each other.' She tugged Hannah's hand. 'Feel me . . . touch me. Growing . . . all the time.' Again she was crying, her voice out of control. It was hard to hear all she said.

'Stop it, Bea, you don't know what you're saying.' Purposely Hannah spoke sharply, anything to bring reason back again.

And stop it Beatrice did, just as if Hannah had touched a switch. For a few seconds they sat still, not touching each other now. Hannah was trying desperately to see her way towards the next move.

'Let's walk on the cliff top, just for five minutes before we drive home.' It was Beatrice who spoke and her voice sounded so normal Hannah looked at her in surprise. 'If Dan's to have you for the rest of your life, you can spare me that much.' It was that last sentence that warned Hannah. She must tread carefully. She tethered the pony to the branch of a tree and they walked side by side silently down the slope towards the cliff edge and the headland.

'Remember, Hannah, when we first came to know each other, properly to know each other. It's so bitterly cold today, not like that day. The boulders were hot to lie on. Do you remember? Not that it means anything to you any longer.'

'Of course it does. And all the years since then too. But, Bea, we're not children, we're not young girls, feeling our way, wondering together, finding out. We're women.'

They'd come to the cliff edge now, not a sheer sandstone drop as it was on the estuary side of the headland. Here the red earth was dotted with bushes and brambles, looking for all the world as if they'd slipped over the top and were hanging precariously by their roots.

'You drive on to town, Hannah. I'll walk. I don't want to talk anymore.' Rain had begun to fall, a cold, driving, fine rain. Beatrice held up her face, her eyes closed. 'Go on, please. I'd rather just walk back, let the rain wash my face.' And seeing her swollen, reddened eyelids Hannah supposed she wanted to hide her tears from Rosalind. On impulse she leant forward towards her, poor bedraggled little Bea, and kissed her forehead. What happened then was so sudden that she could never quite be sure. She felt Beatrice pull her in an instant she understood just what she meant to do. That's all it took for that other occasion to come alive in her memory, an evening years ago when Kath had become betrothed to Richard. They'd stood by the gate at the top of the garden and Beatrice had wanted to carry them together through that shaft of golden light, to lift them away from all that their lives were. Cold rocks and a swirling and angry sea or a golden glow of evening sun, the end result would be the same.

She was caught off her guard in that first second. But she was the stronger, and she grappled with Beatrice. The edge of an overhanging clifftop is no place to struggle.

Had there been no pony and trap to be noticed unattended in the lane who can say how long they might have lain where they fell, Hannah halfway down the cliff where she'd been hurled against a gnarled and bent elder tree and Beatrice spreadeagled on the shingle below? Had no one stopped to look for the occupant of the trap, shouted in the wood to the left of the lane and finally searched from the edge of the cliff, the rising tide might have carried away Beatrice's body and Hannah might have died from exposure to the winter elements.

She remembered nothing of being hauled to safety; she saw nothing of the group of men who approached the shingle beach from the other side of the headland. Here they could follow the beach to the mouth of the estuary and then clamber across rocks and boulders until they came to where Beatrice was lying. On an improvised stretcher they carried her back. Then came the journey to the Hall and to the gatehouse.

311

Hannah had made her mark on Deremouth; Beatrice had lived there all her life. There was no problem in recognizing either of them. News was carried to the quay, then to Crown Cottage and from there to Kath in Merchants Place.

Beatrice had held no importance at the gatehouse, she'd always known it. Today, though, all that was changed. Carefully the stretcher was eased up the narrow stairway and her broken body laid on the bed in the tiny room that used to be Algy's. The doctor pronounced her dead; it didn't take much knowledge to do that. Then, between them, Kath and her mother put her into a clean white nightgown.

'Poor Beatrice,' Kath murmured, looking down at her sister, 'not much of a life, Ma. I think she was happy with Mrs Lowden and the boys. Never said much, but she seemed more content. Filling out too.' She sniffed. Not like Kath to cry.

'Umph,' Sarah agreed. Neither of them wanted to talk. Filling out, Kath had said. 'If I didn't know her better I'd think – ' But even in Sarah's mind the suggestion was impossible.

So the following Thursday Beatrice's secret was buried with her. The doctor had seen no reason to blacken the girl's character, nor add to the family's grief.

Hannah hadn't been severely hurt, but the knock on her head left her concussed. Back at the Hall she was put to bed in the room she used these days, the room that had been Louise's, the room where she and Dan had shared that other vigil. Now he watched over her and it was he who answered that question: 'How's Bea? What happened to Bea?'

'She fell right to the bottom, Hannah.' He held her hand firmly, but he told her no lies. 'She couldn't have known anything.'

Hannah closed her eyes. Beatrice gone, never to be with

312

her again. 'To be lifted away, through that golden light. Not just me, you too, Hannah.' But Hannah was still here. Her fingers gripped Dan's. 'Not just me, you too, Hannah.' Now Bea had no one. She'd even lost the baby before she'd known the joy of loving it. Yet nothing could hurt her now, she was beyond hurt. Those last moments together in the trap came back to her, but now there was no revulsion, only a sense of relief.

Peace enveloped her. It had to do with Bea and with the certainty that now she'd know no more loneliness. She'd understand now what no words could ever have made her see. And if words had been needed Hannah wouldn't have known how to find them. It was something her heart knew, and so too did Bea's there beyond the shaft of golden light. Whatever it was in Hannah that had been Bea's was hers still, would be hers for ever.

Watching her Dan saw her smile. Her eyes were still closed.

And there was something else that fell to Dan to tell her. As she lay between sleeping and waking she must have been the only person in Deremouth not to know how 'My Queen' had been escorted home. Even Tommy's disappearance was common knowledge. The journalist from the *Deremouth Gazette* had had a field day. No scouring the town to scrape a story out of nothing; this week he was spoilt for choice. As if the cliff accident, the young heiress from Netherton's being hauled up unconscious and Beatrice Thurlston killed weren't scoop enough to cover the front page, there was the even more exciting story of Tommy Webster being mixed up in slave trading, and a warrant being out for his arrest.

Notices were pinned on the walls of coaching houses and railway stations in the district. 'Have you seen this man?' and a drawing of him. 'Wanted in connection with trafficking of slaves to North America.' It spread further afield than Deremouth, for by now it was evident he wasn't to be found there. While Ted Sharples languished behind bars at Deremouth Police Station, Tommy was free.

And Alan knew there was nothing he could do to keep it from Em. Almost he relished bearing the news of what he'd stumbled on in 'Louisah'. Any wrongdoing by Hannah seemed to him to ease the blame from his boy. 'Whatever he was driven to, I blame her.' Tight-lipped and red-eyed Emily was ready to fight for her young. But she had no need to fight Alan.

Any other man would have turned his back on Netherton's but Alan's sense of responsibility was too deep a part of his nature. So as Hannah regained her grip on her intelligence – bumps and bruises would take longer but she could live with those – Alan still held the reins in the yard.

For a few days the wharf buzzed with gossip of 'My Queen' and then something else took pride of place. Alan stood by his open window staring unseeingly out to sea. For four days Tommy had been gone. But gone where? Was the boy safe? Someone must recognize him. Wherever he was there'd be someone ready to give him up. Those drawings about the town bore a remarkable likeness. What must his life have become, to be hunted and hounded, no one to care, no one to help. Young Tommy, his boy. And poor Em, she'd done nothing to deserve the misery. He'd never seen her like it, so changed. Under his window men were talking as they loaded sacks on to a trolley but his thoughts were far from what was going on in the yard. 'Help him, I beg of you, help him. There's nothing I wouldn't do if I could. But what? He's not an evil lad. You know that. He's just silly.'

And it was at that point that he heard two things. One was Hannah's step on the stair. So she'd come back! She'd dared to come back! Somehow as he'd come and gone over these few days he'd not visualized her ever returning

314

here, he'd tried not to think of her at all. And there was a second thing that broke into his consciousness.

'Good luck to 'em, that's what I say,' one of the humper's voice carried up to him.

'Wouldn't say no to her myself. She could warm my bed any night of the week,' another put in, a younger man, not long with them.

Then from Ben Brooks: 'Enough of that! I'll not have that kind of talk. If what we hear is the truth, you may be sure it's not some flight o'fancy. We've all seen the way she watched out for him, been the same since she was no more than a child. And I remember Daniel Lowden when he was a youngster, used to come here with the old guv'nor. Thought a deal of him, did the guv'nor. Some of you must remember, same as I do. If you ask me that's the way things should have gone for her from the first instead of tying herself up with young Webster.'

Now they had Alan's full attention. He leant nearer to the open window. So even the workmen knew about her! Bitch! What would they say about her and her precious Lowden if they knew the real truth, just how she'd been behaving. Alan was an even-tempered man. Never in his life had he been so shaken with anger and hatred as he was now.

'One thing's certain,' the voice wafted up, 'she's well shot of that young bugger. How many sacks, Phil, is this the last load?'

'Ah, this load should do it. Wonder whether she'll give the old man the boot now she's back.'

'The old chap? Oh, I dunno. Reckon she'll feel as sorry for him as we do ourselves. Bad enough having a bastard like that for a son. This the last one? Right, all on then.'

The trolley rattled across the cobblestones towards the boat they were loading. Still Alan stared out, seeing nothing. Anger and hatred had left him drained. His shoulders drooped, his arms hung limp at his sides. He

315

knew he should do something, but how can a man look to the future when he is stripped of hope?

Ahead of him was no more than a stretch of time, days to be lived through. He thought of Em, at home alone, her future as empty as his own. Days to be lived through. But not here. Not where he had the men's pity – and Tommy their contempt. He'd always had such pride in Netherton's. Their voices echoed in his mind, what they'd said turning like a knife in his heart and their pity robbing him even of the pride he'd had in the job he did.

Blindly he turned to his desk and slumped in the chair. All around him were ghosts: Tommy standing in front of himself and Em, head high, shoulders back, as he recited his first poem; Tommy in his best velvet suit walking between them as they took their Sunday afternoon stroll; Tommy playing cricket; Tommy in his first wing collar, his first love pipe hat. His boy, his pride. Times enough there had been scrapes, failed ventures. But always he'd been able to come to the lad's rescue – and usually had him on the carpet too! But always there had been faith, always he'd believed that next time would be different. With marriage to Hannah there had been such hope. All this to Tommy, then to his son. It had never been for his own sake Alan had wanted it, only for the boy's.

Sitting with his head in his hands he muttered to himself: 'Don't know what to do . . . don't know . . . don't . . .'

How long he sat there he had no idea, but gradually his way became clear. The idea of staying here where Tommy was held with scorn was impossible. His next move seemed to him a way of showing his faith in his son.

'I've come to tell you you must manage without me. After what's happened you can't expect me to serve you.' He spoke as he flung open Hannah's door, for once without knocking.

'No, don't let it come to that. You weren't involved – '

316

'Not involved! My son driven away and you tell me I'm not involved!'

'You know that's not when I meant.'

To keep his hands from trembling Alan pressed his weight on them as he leant across her desk, his face coming close to hers. Never had she seen him show any emotion. All her sympathy reached out to him now. His eyes were bloodshot and weary.

'When he can he'll get word to you and his mother, you know he will.'

'Oh yes, to me and his mother,' his answer was a sneer, 'not to his wife. And you think I don't know why? You slut! You and your fancy man, it's the talk of the yard, the talk of the town I dare say.' He ran his hand over his thinning hair. 'I suppose you mean to bring Lowden here, put him in Tommy's place? Well, you can do it without me.'

'If you feel like that, of course I can't try and persuade you not to go.' She stood tall, the slight inclination of her head so like the dismissal he'd always received from Louise at the end of his monthly visits to the Hall. 'You'll clear any personal things from your room before you leave.'

He turned and left her. He'd been a man of honour, he'd cared for Netherton's as if it had been his own. She heard him moving about in his room and was torn with pity for him. She tried not to listen, not to think about him. The future was hers and Dan's. But it was no use, she put down her pen and went in to him.

'Why don't you change your mind? Surely there's no need for this. You've worries enough, at least hang on to something. I'm sure Tommy's mother would agree with —'

'Tommy's mother! You honestly think she'd want to have me here serving you, you who couldn't keep your vows and make a marriage for our boy? Oh no, madam, whatever he's done the responsibility for it lies at your

317

door. If you'd kept your nose out of affairs here he would have known himself to be master. None of this would have happened.'

'You're upset by – '

'Don't tell me I'm upset! Who are you to know how I feel – or his mother either? Now if you'll step out of the way I shall leave.'

And without a backward glance he went. His hopes had been dashed, even his memories were too painful to contemplate. And there was no future to hope for, even dreams need substance to build on.

They wanted no whispered hints, no innuendos. That's what Dan had told Rosalind. So it was that, the same morning that Hannah made her first trip to the yard since her fall, he stayed at the Hall knowing just what he meant to do.

'Gladys, I want to talk to all the staff,' he said as he and Hannah were at breakfast. 'Can you see they all come upstairs at, let's say, half past nine. The outside staff too. I'll see them in the morning room.'

'All of them – stable lad and all?'

'That's it. What I have to say will concern everyone.'

Gladys looked from one of them to the other, that old fear stabbing at her. Downstairs everyone knew that Tommy Webster had turned out to be a bad lot, the whole district knew it; for herself it hadn't surprised her. She'd watched the way he used to fawn round the old lady, so sure of himself. Ah well, he'd kept her amused. But Gladys knew what went on in her mind better than he had, the young bounder. Now, over these last few days since all the trouble, no one had been surprised if he'd stayed in town and left Hannah to face her distress alone. Things couldn't go on like this, though. Gladys's hands were unsteady as she started to stack the tray. He'd go, then the young missus would be on her own. Perhaps that was it. She'd remembered her aunt, the lonely life she must have had here all those years. She'd decided to sell the Hall, go and live in the town somewhere. Gladys thought of her savings, pictured the old handkerchief sachet where she hoarded her money in between the horse-hair mattress and her feather bed. Of all the servants she was the only one to know the warmth of such a resting place, passed on to her by Louise a few years back. Kind words had never been part of Louise's make-up; the nest of feathers had been the only evidence of her concern for her ageing and loyal servant. The tray was stacked. Gladys would send Dolly up to carry it down to the kitchen. Her mind was still on the future, a future that had no shape. No one would take her at her age. She couldn't hear like she used to, couldn't remember things for five minutes at a time. What happened thirty years ago was as clear as day, what happened thirty minutes ago was lost. For all that, what she'd been told now wouldn't be forgotten. That had made its mark on her mind right enough.

'Gladys, I shan't be here. It'll just be Mr Lowden,' Hannah told her as she went towards the door.

And if that wasn't a sure sign of what they'd hear, Gladys didn't know what was. Couldn't blame the girl if she wanted to get away from it all, make a clean start. Downstairs they'd all known for months the miserable lonely life she must have had with that rascal. Him with his soft voice and cunning smile!

So, ready for the worst, she marshalled her troops, and sharp on half-past nine Mrs Hall, the housekeeper, led the way up to the morning room. Gladys brought up the rear and, feeling as wretched as she did, she had to hit out at someone. So it was that Harold Thurlston's men came in for the brunt of her fire.

'Just you scrape that mud off. Thinking you can come up my stairs with boots straight from the garden!'

'Leave it to me, I'll see they're all clean, Gladys m'dear,' Harold answered. He saw the boots were all free of the red earth from the garden, and he saw much more as he looked compassionately at the old servant. 'Poor old gal, it's all got too much for her. Naught else to look forward to.' His ruddy face gave her a look of encouragement – and that he could take time to bother about her when his girl had only been put under the ground twenty-four hours heartened Gladys as she followed the little troop up the back stairs.

'We want no whispers and speculation.' Dan told them. 'You'll all have heard what's happened recently but I want you to understand that that has made no difference to what I'm going to tell you. While your mistress has a husband we can't marry. We all try and abide by the laws – of the land and of the Church. You must each of you act as you feel to be right about the life we shall be leading here together. Perhaps you'll see it as sin. Believe me, we feel no sense of wrong. That's why I'm telling you this. There shall be nothing secret.'

Mrs Hall was looking with fixed concentration at the wall somewhere above his head, a red patch on her neck a tell-tale sign of either embarrassment or disapproval. Gladys's plump old face was set in a smile, not at him, not at anyone. She was safe! Dolly the under-housemaid gazed at him wide-eyed. Fancy! Them two were going to be living in this great house in sin!

'I hope we may have your support and understanding. I hope nothing will change for anyone – except for Hannah and me,' he ended with a smile that seemed to unite them, with him and with each other, all part of the new order of things at Netherton Hall.

'For myself – and I'm sure for all of us – I wish you well, sir,' Harold spoke out loud and clear.

But it was soon evident that he hadn't spoken for everyone. Mrs Hall packed her bags that same day and went to live with her sister until she could find a place where 'folk lived by good Christian rules'. Dolly went home for her half-day brimming over with the excitement of such a romance. She didn't return. A note from her father told them that he'd not have his 'dorter waiting on people wot served the devil'.

A new housekeeper was engaged, Mrs Trump, whose motto was to 'live and let live'. Netherton Hall suited her well enough, the mistress occupied herself outside and wasn't forever breathing down her neck. Granted there was that old Gladys, she seemed to think she ruled the roost. But, poor old girl, give her a friendly word and she was as good as gold.

Rosalind found another helper, Ben Brooks' daughter, Florrie. A young widow with a two-year-old daughter, Rosie, she came to Crown Cottage thankful that life was giving her a second chance. Two widows, three children. Rosie sufficiently young that Matthew and Stephen treated her like a pet to be protected.

At the bottom of the garden the lamp burned on the cold winter evenings. Florrie regularly took Richard his mug of tea. A friendly word, a smile, but never any suggestion that she might stay and talk. Now it was winter, his fingers red with cold. But spring would soon come, and still he'd be alone. In the corner stood Beatrice's stool, empty now; come spring and summer, empty then too. Florrie and Rosie had brought happiness and laughter into the house. Sometimes Rosalind would think of Beatrice and feel ashamed that her gentle presence could so soon have been erased.

Of them all it was Richard who carried the most memories of last summer, her little hands caressing the smooth surface of the wood. That other ghost, scrawny body submitting itself passively to his, was only a part of the Beatrice he remembered. Not so long ago he'd shied away from the thought of that hot afternoon but now he could think of it without distaste. The man in him was glad it had happened. At least she'd not died never having known. Sometimes, as he worked alone, the door of the coachhouse closed against the wintry evening, he could feel her presence still there with him, sitting on her stool, steadily threading and weaving her needle as she put a heel back into a stocking for one of the boys.

Beatrice had gone. The gap she'd left in the house closed over. Yet in that workshop the spirit of peace she'd brought with her still lingered.

'Futura' lay moored at Netherton's wharf. Today the traffic that made its way down Quay Hill was very different from the drays that were the customary sight. The railway station's one and only cab was running a steady service backwards and forwards to the ship for those who travelled to Deremouth by train; its driver had never known trade so brisk. Even so most of the passengers to set out for the Continent were arriving in their own carriages. Such a to-do there was at Netherton's on this third Thursday in May, 1860.

The *Gazette* had given half a page to a description of the ship – its cabins, the table it promised to set – and given the space gladly too for Deremouth had little else of excitement to report. 'Futura' was opening the gateway to the new fashion of foreign travel to people from this part of the country. To be truthful there were precious few in working Deremouth likely to be able to indulge in such luxury and adventure; but a pennyworth of reading, for those who were able, could spark off many a fantasy.

What he read evoked no fantasy in Alan, it wasn't to the faraway places his thoughts turned. But he couldn't put the news from his mind. Such a perfect spring day, so when Em suggested they might take a turn in the sunshine he knew where his steps would lead them. For weeks, months, he'd not been near the quay. Even now, while he had no power to resist the temptation of watching what was going on, he knew it would bring him pain. Almost, he wanted the pain. This was something Hannah – ah, Hannah and that paramour of hers – had done over his head, and over Tommy's head too. He needed to watch her in her triumph, to suffer it for himself and for Tommy.

Arm in arm he and Emily walked to their vantage point at the top of Quay Hill by the low wall – 'Paupers' Gallery', where those with no hope of travelling could enjoy the sight of the flurry and bustle of fashionable society below. Portmanteaux, boxes, baskets, all were carried aboard.

'Up, Mama, please. Up me.'

They moved further along to make space for the young mother. Kath, with Trudie perched on the end of Harold George's bassinet and Timothy clamouring to see. The Websters didn't know who she was, but she recognized them.

'Thank you.' She turned her ready smile on them, then squeezed her portly self into the space they'd made. 'There, Timmy love,' she raised him in her arms, 'now you can see.'

Down on the wharf the Deremouth Brass Band struck up, individually rather than collectively, but by the time they'd played a few bars they'd got into formation. 'Hearts of Oak' rang out loud and clear, bringing them triumphantly to the winning post all together.

Finally 'Futura' got up steam. Her siren blasted, and slowly she slipped her mooring and inched away from the quay.

'Never thought to see . . .' Alan blew his nose. 'Just look at my yard. My yard, Em.'

Today it was a colourful sight, crowded with friends

and well wishers who'd come to watch the 'Futura' set out on her maiden trip. The band, having planned their programme around music of the sea, was now playing a hymn tune so well-known that it needed no voices to bring the words to everyone's mind. 'We cry to Thee for those in peril on the sea.' Hardly aimed at boosting confidence in Netherton's new pride!

Emily glanced anxiously at Alan. She wished they'd stayed away. But it seemed that having felt the sharp sting of pain he couldn't draw back, he must have more.

'I'm going down there. Just for a quick look.'

'No, Alan, let's just go home.'

'I want to see it, Em, just to see it.' She recognized the danger in his quietly spoken words. If she argued he might lose his grip on himself. She must help him, get him away from this crowd of gawping people. For one terrible moment she imagined that he might break, he who never let emotion show. He'd wept over these months; she'd wept too. And who could wonder at it? But not here, in the street. She knew she had to fall in with what he wanted, stand back and let him indulge in the suffering. And she was angry. The thought of Tommy never left her. As if she hadn't enough to bear without Alan wanting to turn the knife in the wound. Kath moved to one side to let them move from their vantage point. To Emily she was just a mother, a young mother with her little boy. A little boy . . .

But loyal to Alan she walked by his side down the hill. By now the carriages were coming away, the bandsmen had packed up, the show was over. One or two men who'd watched from boats moored on the public quay recognized Alan, called a greeting – and no doubt whispered amongst themselves that he should be here. There was dignity in the way he lifted his hat to them.

Then there was nothing between them and Netherton's. The gate was still open but he made no attempt to enter.

Work was starting again, already the humpers were lifting sacks from the sheds on to a trolley. This was the yard Alan knew but the sight brought no comfort. Emily wasn't watching the men, she had her eyes on Hannah.

Talking together by the water's edge, she and Ben Brooks were obviously delighted with the way things had gone. One last word with him, something that made both of them laugh (their unknown joke somehow cutting Alan and Emily off even more completely), then she walked back to Dan. It was half a year since Emily had seen her, five months since Tommy had gone. There was no mistaking the evidence of her eyes. If they hadn't lived such solitary lives over these months of winter and spring the gossip would have reached them long ago.

Where was her modesty! Coming here amongst all that crowd in her condition! Em had suffered grief, and anger too, but she'd never known such spite and hatred as she did as she looked at Hannah. All her dreams, all her hopes of being told Tommy was to be a father! Dan put an arm lightly around Hannah's shoulder, a Dan who walked confidently now, hardly needing the support of his one stick.

'Look at her!' her mother-in-law hissed to Alan. 'Disgusting! Flaunting herself in front of all these men in that state – his bastard child.'

Neither of them wanted to stay any longer, this had brought them to their lowest ebb. Without a word they turned away. Alan had never realized how steep Quay Hill was, such a short time ago he could have taken it in his stride with hardly a puff. But then life had been full of interest, his mind on other things. Today they stopped halfway up to get their breath.

'Third Thursday in the month, Em,' he said as they at last turned in at their own front gate, 'my afternoon for taking the report to the old lady.'

She didn't answer him. They ate a silent tea then she

cleared away, spending longer than she needed to in the kitchen. Busy hands kept thought at bay.

'No good you reading that silly newspaper article over and over,' she said, when she came back into the parlour. 'Why you can't find something to do with your time I don't know. If you let M'lady Hannah see you so down in the mouth, she'd put the blame for it on Tommy. If you can't put up a show for your own sake – I wouldn't ask you to for mine! – then you might try and make an effort for his.' She straightened a picture that hadn't been crooked.

Alan folded away the paper. Poor Em. He was wise enough to know when not to let her see his sympathy. Compassion for her was what gave him the courage to face each empty day.

CHAPTER THIRTEEN

There had been other changes over the months as well as the one so cruelly evident to Emily. At the yard Alan had been replaced by Cedric Marshall, a man as unlike him as one could find, at least in appearance. He had the look of a seaman, but then for years that's what he'd been. An invalid wife had kept him on dry land and he had all the experience behind him that Netherton's wanted. Dan had advertised the post in Bristol and in Plymouth; they knew there was no local man with the background they looked for. Cedric appeared to be a find, about forty-five, with a wife keen to be in Deremouth where she would be within visiting distance of her sister. That was change number one.

The second appeared in a notice in the *Deremouth Gazette* – and in *The Times* – announcing to whom it may concern that Hannah Webster (neé Ruddick) of Netherton Hall, Deremouth, owner of Netherton Shipping Company, would in future be known as Hannah Lowden. Hannah and Dan were only too conscious of the narrow conventions of the age, indeed they accepted them as part of life and they knew that what they were doing would be condemned. But there was no other way. Tommy might be on the run from justice but that gave Hannah no grounds to seek her freedom. Full of hope they'd been to see Mr Clutterbuck but he'd made the position painfully clear.

'So all I can do is have my name changed? Is that what you're saying? That unless Tommy comes back I can never be free?'

'And even then, the fact that he has – or we assume he

has – broken the law, gives you no right to seek your freedom from him.'

'Then a legal change of name must be our answer,' Dan had tried to bolster her disappointment. 'You can arrange that Mr Clutterbuck?' They wanted everything settled as soon as they could. Hannah, who'd believed herself to be as barren as her aunt, was more sure with each passing day. She was to have Dan's child, their child. At that time they'd been together for less than a month. Life with him had already erased all her bitterness, and that she should bear their child so soon was, to her, evidence of the rightness of what they did. So she heard Dan ask Mr Clutterbuck to start proceedings for her name to be changed. The vows that went with marriage were between themselves; this was an outward sign, a protection for their child.

Mr Clutterbuck ignored Dan, indeed it was almost possible to imagine that he turned his shoulder to him, speaking just to Hannah.

'I fear, Mrs Webster, that without your husband's written consent a legal change of name is not possible for you. Even with it – and in your particular case there seems little chance that you could obtain it – still it's a complicated business. As I say, without Mr Webster's agreement, you have no case.'

A notice in the newspapers was all they could do. Legally she must remain Hannah Webster.

All that had happened months ago, at the turn of the year, when events arising from Netherton's and from the Hall were keeping local gossip well supplied. Interest that wells up suddenly is as suddenly forgotten. Before many weeks no one had spared them a second glance as they picked up the threads of their lives. Certainly Mr Habbins at the bank lost some of his friendly manner and Mr Clutterbuck's cherubic smile seemed to be a thing of the past. But in the town the dust soon settled.

328

The day 'Futura' sailed they rode home in a glow of accomplishment. Their ship. The first mark of success on what they would achieve together. In the shade of a tall elm, beyond the edge of town, Dan drew in the reins so that they stopped, looking across the grassy clifftop and out to the open sea.

'A day we'll remember, Hannah.'

'Umph!' She took off her hat and rested her head against his shoulder, nuzzling her face to his neck. As if a cold shadow fell over her she remembered that other day on this very lane. Beatrice's mouth on her neck, on her lips ... Not for the first time she felt a flutter inside her, a movement hardly more than a tremble. That other image was still there. Beatrice pulling her cloak open, wanting her to see ... Beatrice who'd loved her. Hannah clung to Dan. He was her whole world, and yet this feeling of guilt haunted her, jabbed at her, making her ashamed of having so much. Dan felt her teeth nibbling his neck. He might not know the ghost that whispered to her, but he felt her need of him. Hadn't she said to Kath so long ago: 'He knows things without being told.' Her mouth moved to seek his, his hand needed no guiding as he tenderly caressed her enlarged breast, a silent expression of love and of desire. The shadow of Beatrice vanished. 'Futura', too, was forgotten.

The moment passed, it had to out here in the May evening. The afternoon had been evidence of the success, of their union; these minutes were the culmination of that afternoon.

Then Dan took up the reins, Hannah re-tied her bonnet and the pony was recalled to his task of pulling them up the hill and home.

'It's funny isn't it, Dan. Wouldn't you think that when two people have wanted to be together, and then they are, wouldn't you think the very beginning would be the best time of all. Wouldn't you expect that?'

329

He smiled at the earnestness of her tone. For all her shrewdness in business, for all the maturity of her loving, there was still so much of the child in Hannah.

'You're telling me, my Hannah, the beginning wasn't all you'd hoped?' But his voice teased.

'You know that's not what I mean. It's just that every day I think life is better and better.'

He took her hand in his just for a second.

'Every night,' she went on, sitting straight, somehow feeling that by keeping her tone serious and untouched by emotion, he would understand how sincerely she meant what she said, 'every time we make love, it's more meaningful. Does that sound silly?' She turned to him, but she didn't touch him. 'Every time, afterwards I'm sure I love you more.'

'And so you should.' His words teased. His eyes gave her his answer.

They turned in at the gate of Netherton Hall.

'"Mr and Mrs Daniel Lowden"', she read as she picked up the letter that was waiting for them. 'It looks like your father's writing, Dan.'

She left him to read it while she went on upstairs to change for the evening. Phyllis Bentley's needle had been flying lately trying to keep pace with Hannah's fast changing figure. Here, in the south-facing room they'd taken over, she changed into a maroon gown. Until now this had never been anything but a guest room, with its view of the rose garden and Mann's Wood beyond. Her old room had looked towards the estuary, but that belonged to her past, just as the one Dan had always used belonged to his. Louise's had been her retreat from Tommy but not the place for her to start her life with Dan, it held too many memories.

She heard him climbing the stairs, not a thing he found easy but as the months went by his confidence was growing.

330

'You must read this, Hannah.' He put the letter on the dressing table. 'He wants us to go up. You'll see what he's suggesting.'

Even then she didn't hurry. She finished pinning her hair, shook some toilet water on to a clean handkerchief, slipped her feet into the maroon slippers that matched her gown. Only then, as Dan sat on the edge of the bed, feeling his way into fixing a fresh wing collar on to the back stud at the neck of his shirt, did she unfold the letter from her 'not quite father-in-law'.

In silence she read, only muttering the occasional word more to herself than to him. 'Emigrants . . . sixteen thousand in one year he says.' When she came to the end she turned back to the beginning, this time she was prepared for what she'd find. It was when she came to the point of Hilary Lowden's letter where he'd quoted those figures that she stopped, her brows puckered.

'Dan, he says they could carry about sixteen thousand a year. Imagine all those people going. At six guineas a head, what's that?' She shut her eyes to help her concentrate.

'It's ninety-six thousand guineas. That's a lot of money, Hannah. But that's Liverpool. They carry the Irish traffic, a great deal of the Scottish too. And of course there's already Plymouth here in the south.'

'It's interesting though, isn't it?' She sat down by his side, still absorbed in the idea. 'Dan, it's exciting. Thrilling! Just think of it. We live in such wonderful times don't we! What would our grandparents have made of a letter like this?' She looked hard at him. 'It is interesting, isn't it, what he says?'

'It's more than interesting, Hannah.'

To both of them it seemed auspicious that the letter should have come today of all days, just as their plans for 'Futura' had seen fruition. His arm around her shoulders, his neck-cloth still hanging unknotted, they re-read his father's closely written pages. The clock in the drawing room struck seven, time for dinner. They hardly noticed.

At that time the clock in Websters' parlour chimed, then struck the hour. Emily heard it as she busied herself, picking up a piece of her jig-saw puzzle, fixing all her concentration of it; anything to keep her mind occupied, to stop her imaginings of what Tommy's life must be.

Kath glanced at the clock on the wall too as she rolled out her pastry, stopped to give the fire a rake and add a shovel full of coal to make sure the oven would be right, then started to cut up the vegetables for Richard's pasty.

How strange that in that moment Hannah's mind should turn down a path it so seldom went, bringing to her a picture of Alan and Emily. Perhaps it had to do with the letter, with Alan's years of loyalty, his mistrust of change. Or was it because of that sudden and stronger movement that fluttered within her, the reminder of the life she and Dan had created. She shut her eyes, scarcely breathing. Was this the son who would one day be master of Netherton's, the promise of their tomorrow.

She shivered. It was as if icy water had trickled down her spine.

'I take it my letter must have interested you – at least enough that you wasted no time in coming.' Hilary addressed himself to Dan as they gathered in the drawing room waiting for the dinner gong.

'Ships! Hardly in the house and Hilary thinks he wants to talk ships!' Ruby – the erstwhile Mrs Houghton who had frightened Rosalind southward – peered into the large gilt-framed mirror above the fireplace, adjusting the neckline of her gown. 'Come and sit down, Hannah. Try not to listen to their chatter.'

'Oh, but I want to hear. What Mr Lowden has proposed –'

332

'What's this "Mr Lowden"!' The first thing Louise had told her about Dan's father was that he didn't suffer fools. She would have known it now if she hadn't before as he turned his attention to her. From head to foot he looked at her, missing nothing. She felt he knew her every thought. 'If I'm your father-in-law, young Hannah, you'd better get used to calling me something better than Mr Lowden. Father – Papa – '

'Dan calls you Father – but I'd rather say Papa. My own was Father, Papa.' She smiled at him. 'And thank you – for talking about it, for saying that. You must be disappointed that Dan hasn't brought you home a proper wife.'

'Disappointed nothing! You'll do me very well as a daughter. You put me in mind of your aunt, as she was when I first knew her – and that's praise, I can tell you. She thought very highly of you.'

'Aunt Lou did? You mean, she said so?'

Hilary laughed. 'Now, just you think about her. Would she have told me a thing like that, girl? It was because of what she didn't say that I knew it. Lou didn't suffer fools.'

It was plain he and Louise had shared a mutual respect for each other. Remembering her aunt, Hannah settled down to enjoy her 'almost father-in-law'. Already she looked on him as a friend, ever after these few hours.

As the evening went on the conversation found its way back to where their interests lay. Lowden Shipping Company had moved into the trans-Atlantic passenger trade. Their packet boat 'Precedent' made regular crossings to Boston. It was the pride of their fleet, its cabin accommodation as comfortable as cramped conditions could allow, the grand saloon furnished with easy chairs, settees, even providing a harmonium for the passengers' pleasure. No sea crossing could ever live up to the boasts the shipping line made of its comfort for there was no way of holding the vessel steady as it pitched and rolled on the ocean. For all that, Hilary Lowden was honest in his belief that

'Precedent' was unsurpassed. Anyone travelling in her expected to pay a fare commensurate with her luxury.

His eye now was on a different standard. Those setting out to seek a new life couldn't afford 'Precedent' and neither could it accommodate the numbers he had in mind.

'The emigrants go out steerage. For some of them it's as much as they can do to scrape together the £3. 10s. for their fare and enough food to keep them alive for the voyage, poor devils.'

'That's under sail,' Dan answered. 'There are plenty who would pay a bit more, still to travel steerage but faster. What we must aim for is speed.' Hadn't that always been Dan's belief? 'Think of the weeks in a sailing ship, the malnutrition, sea-sickness and disease in the insanitary conditions they're confined to. Father, the answer has to be in steam.'

'Indeed yes. "Precedent" travels under steam. I've no argument with that. That's what I set out to you. Many would pay six guineas willingly to cross under steam.'

'We have to move forward. We have to look to screw propulsion.'

'An iron-screw vessel. I don't know . . . even 'Precedent' is paddle driven. I haven't your faith in the screw type – it's said they haven't the strength. And there's a risk of their falling off.'

On and on they talked. Hannah listened, asked occasional questions, soaked up their words and felt wrapped in a cocoon of well-being. The train journey had been long, the day full of excitement. Physically she was weary, yet she didn't want to end the evening. She had a sense of belonging. The voices talked on, Dan's, his father's while Ruby played endless games of patience, occasionally dipping her hand into a jar of fondants. Hannah's eyelids were heavy . . .

'Let her sleep,' she heard Ruby say to the others, 'she's had a long day.' But she didn't sleep – or so she thought –

she knew just where she was. 'Hah!' she heard a familiar voice. 'Just listen to them! Boats, the sea, nothing better. Hah!' No wonder she smiled.

For four days they stayed in Liverpool and by that time the plans were laid. And those plans were to take Dan to Boston on the next sailing of 'Precedent' towards the end of June. Edmund Rochester was the man he meant to see, a man ahead of his time when it came to the combustion engine, an Englishman who, like so many, had gone to make a new life in America.

They knew what they wanted of this ship they were to build. An iron hull, four blades to its screw propellor, it would travel fast and carry five hundred passengers. Because of the number of fares they would cut their steerage rate to five and a half guineas, half a guinea less than they first estimated. Because there would be less days at sea they would feed the emigrants, who wouldn't have to carry their own supplies.

In Deremouth the emigrant trade would never play a major role; those setting out for the New World were mostly from Ireland, Scotland or the Midlands. But the future of Lowden's and Netherton's must make them as one; already they were entwined.

By mid-June Hannah and Dan stood together on the railway station at Deremouth waiting for the train from Plymouth that would take him northwards. Already in Liverpool 'Precedent' was loading the victuals necessary for the comfort of her passengers.

'I hate leaving you.'

'It'll be no time at all, Dan. Why, you'll be home again in a few weeks.'

'If it weren't for the baby you could come with me.'

'What nonsense you do talk!' then she laughed. 'Did you hear that? I sounded like Aunt Lou. The baby isn't going to rule my life when he's here, so he certainly isn't now. If I weren't such a bad sailor I'd not let you go without me. But I'm that with or without the baby.' She felt hollow in her misery at the thought of his going. This was such a step forward for him, though, and for that she was thankful. Granted he was to be a cabin passenger, not the ship's master, but it was a Lowden ship. He'd be with men who talked his language. Did he imagine she hadn't known how he'd craved for the sea?

They heard the whistle, saw a thin trail of smoke heralding the approach of the engine.

'God bless you, my Hannah.' With his hand under her chin he turned her face up towards his.

'And you, Dan. And carry you safely.'

As long as she'd known him their lives had been made up of partings, partings and meetings. But these last months had been so different.

'I'll see to your luggage, sir,' the porter's voice cut in on them. 'She don't wait here more than a minute.'

She took his stick, felt his weight on her shoulder as he climbed aboard. Then it was over. There was nothing left but a lingering smell of smoke, an empty platform, and the desolation of being without him.

It's doubtful whether all the passengers considered the crossing so easy. To many it was their first time on the water. 'Precedent' kept a steady twelve knots; the Atlantic threw no dirty weather at them. The wind was against them, but it was gentle. Ten days after facing the open sea, they were within sight of land.

In Boston Dan spent hours with Edmund Rochester – and while the engineer worked on the plans, he spent hours on his own. It was about halfway through July. He'd not seen Rochester for a couple of days and had no appointment until the end of the week. Like a magnet the docks drew him. He enjoyed the atmosphere there, the noise, even the smell of the waterside.

'Cap'n Lowden, sir,' he heard a voice hale him. 'It is Mr Lowden, isn't it?'

'Yes?'

'You don't remember me I don't expect, sir, not after all this time. Jim Tucker, sailed with you on "Prince Rupert". First ship I took.'

'Yes, I do remember you. A little scrag of a lad in those days. I'd not have known you. I recall the time we rounded the Horn, you were pretty well iced up, more or less fell into my arms. You'd been aloft in that wind, do you remember it? Snow enough to cut your skin, ice coating the ratlines. You'd gone aloft without your oilskins.. . .'

'That's it. As I slithered down my legs seemed to give way. Like you say I more or less fell at you. The Horn's no place to be in those July storms. Thought I was a gonna, truth I did. You rubbed snow into me to get my circulation going. Gor! Hurt worse than being frozen when the life came back again. What a way to have to bring the roses to your cheeks!' It was easy to laugh at this distance.

The common bond of that journey held them. Dan puffed at his pipe, Jim Tucker took his from his pocket and started to push tobacco into the bowl.

'You were a game youngster all right,' Dan said. Then, trying to picture the boy: 'But you weren't with me on the "Europa"? Where did you go?'

'I met a girl in Deremouth, when "Prince Rupert" put in for a few days. After that I got taken on with Netherton's, sailed for them.'

'Netherton's! Well I'm damned! But you're not with them now. I'd know – '

'No. Me and the girl – she's my missus now – we came out here last winter. Doing pretty well, too. Don't go to sea these days, I'm working at the chandlery just near the wharf here. Usually come and have a look at things most days.'

'You miss it?'

But young Jim Tucker wasn't prepared to admit to having any regrets.

'Can't have everything, have to chose what you think matters. I'm all right as things are. A grand country, this, a man's what he is here, not what he has.' And his expression defied sympathy for the passing of his sailing days. 'Looks like you've had a bit of trouble. First thing I noticed. Sorry to see that, sir.'

'Could have been a lot worse, Tucker. As you say, no one can expect everything to go right for them. I'm not complaining.'

Leaning against the rail, they stood idly pulling at their pipes.

'Yes,' Jim picked up the conversation where it had been a few minutes back, 'I was with Netherton's. Funny the way that worked out. That girl who tried to stow away on "Prince Rupert", she belonged there you know. Later on she married the manager's son. I never had much to do with him, hardly saw him. But she was usually about when we landed.' He followed his thoughts, didn't seem to notice that Dan was saying nothing. 'Yes, like I say, she married this chap Webster. Then last year, just about the time I left Netherton's it must have been going on, he got himself in some sort of trouble so I've heard since. Didn't know anything about it at the time. Well, I'd already packed it in and me and Dolly were ready to come out here.'

'The end of last year you say?' Dan felt he ought to make some contribution. It was unbelievable, standing here three thousand miles away from Hannah and home listening to gossip about the trouble Tommy Webster had got into.

'That's it. December. Hardly saw him, but on the boat coming out I recognized him straight away. He sort of stood out.'

'Coming here? You say Webster's here?'

338

'No. I'll tell you what happened. I never spoke to him, but there was no doubt that's who it was. God, what a journey. I've sailed in all weathers and in some pretty rotten conditions but that took the biscuit. The stench! God! Turns my stomach to think of it even now. Couldn't get away from it. Not enough water, not enough food, and what there was most of 'em were too sick to eat.'

'What about Webster? He was a seasoned traveller I believe.'

'Maybe he was. I wouldn't know about that. Made his last journey now, poor bugger, whatever it was he was running away from. Cholera. You ever seen cholera? One after another we had to get rid of the corpses overboard. They'd come away so full of hope – whole families. The youngsters died before they got here; husbands and wives, or one or the other, ended over the side. What a start.

'You're telling me Webster died?'

'There was him and his girl – I remember her at Deremouth. Not the girl from Netherton's, this was his fancy bit I suppose. They had a baby with them. You'd have thought he'd have stood more chance than her with the baby to suckle, wouldn't you? He got ill after about a week out at sea – him and plenty more. For some it was nothing more than the journey. Once they got out here – well, like I said, this is a fine country.'

'And he never got here?'

'Lasted till we were only a few days from journey's end.' Jim forced more tobacco into the bowl of his pipe as he talked. 'His woman – Susie her name is, Susie Webster she calls herself but she's no more Webster than she's my Aunt Flo. Common tart, just living with him. What is it they call 'em, "common law wife"? Some would say she's got her just dues, breaking up a marriage. I dunno.'

'Did she go home?'

'Got herself taken in at a boarding house for seamen.

Works there.' Then with a chuckle that was as good as a nudge: 'What work she might be doing is anyone's guess.'

'Tucker, I need to talk to her. Tell me where I can find her.'

The young man raised his eyebrows. 'Wouldn't have thought Susie was much of a one for talking, not from what I heard say back in Deremouth.'

But he told Dan where to find the boarding house.

'Look, Grandpa,' Timothy shouted, attracting Harold's attention away from the yew archway he was clipping, 'you see what me can do! Whheee . . .' And screeching with glee he hurled his chubby body to roll and tumble over and over down the grassy slope of the garden.

On the cast iron seat Hannah and Kath sat idly chattering on this September afternoon, summer still giving no hint that it would soon be gone. Today the sky was high, so clear one felt one could see forever.

'I often think of Bea, don't you, Hannah?' That translucent sky had something to do with their thoughts. Hannah nodded. The silence between them was comfortable. 'She missed so much.' Minutes must have passed before Kath picked the conversation up where she'd put it down. 'I could never picture her growing old, standing up to making a life, being just Aunt Beatrice . . . Every family needs a maiden aunt, they're very special sort of people – but they're not Beatrice.'

'I hope she knows about everything here. I hope she understands.'

Hannah had never seen Kath's face as serious as it was as she answered now, her brows drawn together, choosing her words carefully. 'I'm sure she does. We are as we are Hannah – us and Beatrice too. We couldn't have made things different for her.'

In silent understanding of all that was left unsaid they

340

turned to watch the children, Trudie trying to copy her brother's antics on the slope. Hannah shifted her position, nowhere was really comfortable.

'You keep well, Hannah?'

'Oh yes, I'm strong as an ox. Oh but Kath, I feel like a baby elephant and I've over a month to wait yet. I'll be thankful to have my body to call my own again!'

Kath smiled indulgently, but to be honest she couldn't understand how Hannah could say it. To her pregnancy had always been such a happy time, she wore her bow-shaped figure like a badge of success.

'How will I know when my time comes, Kath? There's no one I can ask but you.'

'Oh, you won't need to ask – you'll know right enough!'

'Is it very awful?'

'Of course not. It's what we're here for, isn't it? I remember when I was having Timothy – and I didn't know what I was expecting that time either – I thought of Ma's cat, you remember Tibbles? Regular as clockwork she has a litter of kits. Pa has to put them in a bucket except just the one each time. I thought to myself, well, if she can do it all alone I'm not going to be beaten by a mog!'

Hannah laughed, somehow feeling less frightened by the unknown.

'When's Dan expected home?'

'He should get to Liverpool more or less any day, and he won't stay there any longer than it takes to talk with Papa.'

'I wonder he went. Couldn't they have sent someone else.'

'No. It was right for Dan to go. Engines are Dan's love.' She laughed, so many memories giving her voice that note of affection. 'This project is important, it's the first ship that will come out of both companies. We shall still keep the same name on the wall in the quay – so will they in Liverpool – but Netherton and Lowden is to be one.'

341

'Pity it had to be now, though. Once you've got the baby you'll have enough to fill your mind.'

'I've enough now, believe me. It's just my cumbersome body hampers me.'

'You are funny,' and Kath meant it. Not for a second did she take Hannah seriously. 'We must make tracks. Richard will be wanting food for his box tomorrow and the cupboard will be empty if I don't get a move on. It won't be long now before the evenings are useless to him and he'll not be able to work. Come on you two, home time.'

At the gatehouse old Mrs Thurlston watched them come down the slope. Kath would have to come back to collect Harold George and the bassinet.

'I wonder you don't speak to that girl, Sarah.' Her voice grated even though it was always quiet. 'She ought to know better than to hang around with Mrs Webster. Webster I say – and I'll say it again – Webster! A woman with a husband and calling herself by a name that'll not be her own.'

'Hush, Mother, do. Just remember she's Harold's mistress.'

The old woman cackled. 'Harold's? She's that Lowden man's mistress, that's what she is. Can't expect you to know right from wrong, but I wonder Kath behaves like it.'

Sarah went indoors without answering. Her mother-in-law's jibes had lost their sting long ago. But she was glad to see Hannah wasn't coming right back to the gatehouse. The old woman could say what she liked amongst themselves – and if she wasn't grizzling about one thing it was the next – but it wouldn't do to let Hannah hear. Ever since Harold had fetched her from Hastings they'd looked on themselves as her friends, but for all that she was indeed Harold's mistress. One word from her and then where would they be?

342

The weather held, making Hannah's frustration at being at home even harder to bear. It was two days after that talk with Kath that she decided to spend the afternoon at the yard.

'Shall I bring the carriage to the door, ma'am?' Harry Gibbons had been engaged years ago as the coachman, but small chance was there of him getting behind the reins. Old Mrs Netherton had seldom gone anywhere in her latter days and, as for this one, she was too independent by half. It did look as though today he'd be able to enjoy a drive out. His hopes were dashed.

'No. Just the trap. I'll drive myself.' And he knew he was destined for another afternoon edging the grass for Harold Thurlston.

The outcome of her trip might have been different had she had the protection of the closed carriage. It was as she came into the town, past Miss Sherwood's school, that it happened. The children were tumbling out into the freedom of the afternoon, one small boy too eager to realize the danger as he bowled his hoop down the steep drive to the road. It seemed to appear from nowhere right in the pony's path. The animal shied, then bolted as if all the devils in hell were after him.

Through mists of pain Hannah surfaced, but pain took away all power to reason. Where she was, how she'd got there, she neither understood nor questioned. Out of control her pony had bolted down Waterloo Street, beyond the railway station; there, where the surface of the road suddenly changed, the trap had rocked wildly then tipped, throwing her to the ground. Once the pony slowed down, someone was able to catch him but by that time Hannah knew nothing. People appeared from all directions, some to help, some being sure they didn't miss anything that hinted of drama. The lad from the butcher's shop was sent

343

to run to the Infirmary and when the wagon arrived for her she was still unconscious. So she was never to know how she cried out as pain took hold of her. Another month and nature would have been on her side; but there was nothing natural in this.

For the second time in less than a year word of an accident was taken to the yard and to the Hall, and two cablegrams were despatched in the same day to await Dan's arrival in Liverpool. From Cedric Marshall: *'Return immediately. Wife taken Infirmary.'* And from Harold: *'Come home. Miss Hannah Infirmary.'*

For Hannah there could be no thinking of Tibbles and gritting her teeth. Pain broke the barriers of consciousness, imprisoned her, cut her off from all reason and understanding. It was some kind of purgatory and she had no power to help herself, she could only suffer it.

Then there came a point when she believed she saw Dan, yet even then she wasn't sufficiently aware to realize it, just to feel that she wasn't alone. She'd believed herself in hell but she wasn't, she knew that now. Her hand gripped hard on what? On whose? It was held firmly. Strength and purpose flowed into her, but still no clarity of reason. Contractions tore her. With all her might nature made her strain. Her finger nails dug into whoever it was she clung to.

The doctors had hoped they could prevent her from going into labour. Premature babies had little hope even when nature brought them. As she lay unconscious all through the first evening and night they heard her unknowing moans, but still they hoped. There had been no visible signs then that the pain came from anything more than her fall. By morning they stopped hoping. Labour had started, a long, difficult labour with a child not yet in a position to make a natural birth. But there was no turning back.

When at last Hannah opened her eyes to a world she felt part of, it was to see Dan at her side, a nurse busying herself at a crib, and the vicar standing at the end of the bed.

'Dan?'

'Thank God.' His answer told her the story.

But the vicar? Why was the vicar here?

'It's a boy, Hannah. Reverend Meaking has just baptized him. Charles Netherton Lowden.' And again his words told the story.

'Dan . . . want . . . see him.'

They looked at the nurse who'd been putting the bundle into the crib. She wasn't at all sure that it wouldn't be kinder to the poor woman to leave him where he was. But she propped Hannah up on her pillows, then carried the baby carefully and put him in her arms.

'We'll leave them.' Her voice held authority. 'Give them a minute or two.' She ushered the vicar to the door. He was undecided. He'd baptized the poor scrap of humanity but what of the mother? Hadn't he a duty – but the nurse had him out of the room and the door closed behind them.

So tiny, so helpless. 'poor little boy . . . poor little boy . . .' Dan could hardly hear Hannah's words. Her face crumpled. Like a child, she cried. Tears of exhaustion; tears of love. Her son, hers and Dan's, given to them. 'Don't take him away,' she sobbed, 'please God, don't take him. Our boy . . . small . . . poor little boy . . .' Dan's arms were around her, around her and the boy. Silently with all his heart he too prayed. They were a family, he, Hannah and little Charles. He and Hannah must give strength to Charles; he must have enough courage for himself and Hannah too until she found her own. He held his hand behind the tiny head.

Hannah wasn't crying now.

'Our boy, Dan. Ask it together – for him.'

With all their strength they willed Charles to live. He weighed less than four pounds, he hadn't been ready for life's rigours.

345

In those minutes they saw themselves not just as two people but as a family. They wouldn't consider doubts. What sort of faith was it that pleaded and then doubted.

The nurse opened the door a crack, peeped in unnoticed, then shut it again.

'I never thought it would be like this, that I'd feel like this ... so small.' Then, and perhaps no one but Dan would have recognized the new determination in her voice: 'But he'll grow into a boy, a man. You hold him, Dan.'

He took the child, the miracle of life. It opened its eyes in an unfocused stare and its mouth in a yawn. Hannah sat up straighter, it was only now that earthly things were coming back to her.

'You're home, Dan.'

'I'll tell you everything by and by. But not yet. You've got a lot of resting to do. Oh, Hannah ...' He couldn't say it. He set his jaw tight. She knew just how frightened he'd been.

As the days went by even the nurse, who'd seen the sadness of premature births plenty of times, began to hope. Hannah had prided herself on being as strong as an ox. The nurse knew that so many of the women who didn't carry their babies full term and who stood no chance of saving what they gave birth to were undernourished, overworked, with too many mouths at home already waiting to be fed. Hannah was healthy, well able to provide for Charles and give him a fighting chance.

In those first days, as they picked up the threads of life – threads into whose pattern another was now woven – Dan told Hannah about his talks with Edmund Rochester. He drew sketches for her of the engine Rochester had designed; he told her about his journey, the cabin accommodation, the catering on 'Precedent'; he told her of the ship Netherton Lowden were to have built, a ship that would eat eighty two tons of coal a day as it steamed steadily across the Atlantic. But it wasn't until Charles was more than a week old that he considered her ready for the emotional strain he knew what she would hear must bring. Only then did he tell her about his meeting with Susie.

'I brought home a letter for you, Hannah.'

'Fancy forgetting to give it to me all these days. Who's it from?'

'Hannah,' he took her hand in his, still not producing the letter, 'Tommy is dead. I heard about it in Boston.'

She was silent. At her breast Charles sucked loudly. A tear spilled down her cheek. She turned her head against the pillows.

'It ought to have had a better ending. I'm sorry, sweetheart.'

'Now they'll have no hope, nothing.'

'They?'

'His people. He was everything to them. What he'd done wouldn't make any difference, he was everything. Like Charles . . . he was little . . . theirs . . .'

Perhaps he should have waited longer before telling her. She pulled his handkerchief from his breast pocket and mopped her face. 'Tell me,' she said. 'What happened?'

So he told her the whole story and it was only at the end he took Susie's letter from his pocket. Writing didn't come easy to her.

'It ort never to have been like wot happened. Tom and me were together before you came and took him. If he'd married me instead of you he woodn't have got in all that bother. He would have kept strate with me, I wood have made him happy, he was always happy with me, he knew I loved him.

'Your Dan will tell you about wot happened. We were going to have a fresh start out here, me, Tom and Thomasinna. Things were going to be orite, I never been so sure of anything as I was that things would be orite once we got away on that boat.

347

Wonder if you hate Tom for marrying you when he knew he'd never love you, not like he did me. Well, if you do you wood have been satisfyde to see him so ill and I coodn't help, no one cood help him in that hellhole of a boat.

'The lor man is giving your Dan a paper saying that Tom's name was one of those we had to bury in the sea. Just becos him and me lost our chance it doesn't seem fare you have got to lose yors. Susie.'

After Dan had left her, and the nurse had settled Charles, she lay in her bare room at the Infirmary. When she'd been Tommy's wife she'd scarcely given his parents a thought. She'd known pity for Alan certainly when she'd seen him so broken by Tommy's going, she'd believed she'd understood. She knew now though that she hadn't. Until she'd held Charles, until those blue eyes had gazed emptily up at her, she'd not started to appreciate what their suffering must be.

Over these last months with Dan she'd woken each morning knowing a sense of anticipation for the day, eager to live every moment of it. But what about the Websters? To open their eyes each morning and be faced with the void, Tommy gone, not to know where. To fill their hours until they went to bed at the end of another day, to be haunted in the darkness by fears for him. Never to know . . .

Next morning a messenger knocked on the door of Alan Webster's house. 'Letter for you from Mrs Lowden.' The boy who brought it had heard all the gossip. He couldn't resist watching to see the effect of his words. But he was disappointed. Alan took the letter with a nod and closed the door on him.

'It must be right to send this letter I've had on to you – to know anything must be preferable than just nothing. As Susie says, it ought never to have happened. We were both to blame, Tommy and me too.'

She was still at the beginning of the road to understanding. She believed that the letter would at least bring them the comfort of grief; a grief they could share with no shadow of fear. She thought they must find solace in knowing that Tommy had never been alone, always he'd had Susie, loyal and loving. Even now, that love she felt for little Charles, didn't teach her the next step.

Alan had vowed that he'd never again pass through Netherton's gate, but that afternoon saw him climbing the familiar stairway to the room that used to be his own.

'Mr Webster?' Dan stood up as he saw his visitor in the open doorway.

'I've come to ask you about Susie — Susie Syms.'

'Susie Webster. I met her in Boston.' Dan pushed a chair towards Alan. 'Someone told you.'

'Hannah sent us a note this morning — sent us a letter she'd had from Susie.'

'I'm so sorry.'

But Alan wasn't ready for sympathy. 'It's about Susie I've come — about Thomasinna, the daughter, Tommy's daughter.'

Dan smiled. 'I saw her. A grand little girl. Dark curly hair, pretty too, big eyes — Susie says her eyes are Tommy's.'

'Mr Lowden, do you think she'd bring her home? She doesn't say where she's living, just that she has found work and has a place. Do you know where I can get a letter to her? I'd make the journey myself if I thought it would do any good. It's the little one, you see, Tommy's — our granddaughter.' And he spoke with a note of pride this time. 'But would she make the crossing again? Would it be right to try it with the child? Hell-hole, that's what she calls the boat.'

'And so they are, some of those sailing ships they take them out on, but all crossings aren't like it. Mr Webster, write her a letter. If you can persuade her to come, I promise you she and Thomasinna will have a comfortable cabin and be well cared for on 'Precedent' They'd come in at Liverpool.'

'Em and I would go up. We'd be there to meet them.'

'Write to her at this address.' Dan wrote something on a piece of paper and passed it to Alan. 'Tell her to contact Lowden's office in Boston and they'll give her details of the sailing. I'll instruct them from this end.'

But would she come? Dan suspected there was a strong streak of independence in Susie. As Alan walked out through the yard he watched him go; saw him stop, take the paper out of his pocket, read the address, fold it and put it back, then with his shoulders somehow straighter walk briskly along the public wharf. Home to his Em, with hope in his heart. And seeing him, Dan understood. His own understanding must have already moved further along the road than Hannah's.

Little Charles – he seemed to be taking a firmer hold on life with each day. But still weighing in at only four pounds. It would be a long time before their fears were behind them. Watching Alan, and remembering those long hours at Hannah's bedside, he knew that hope and fear must always go hand in hand, both of them born of love.

Fontana Paperbacks
Fiction

Fontana is a leading paperback publisher of both non-fiction, popular and academic, and fiction. Below are some recent fiction titles.

☐ FIRST LADY Erin Pizzey £3.95
☐ A WOMAN INVOLVED John Gordon Davis £3.95
☐ COLD NEW DAWN Ian St James £3.95
☐ A CLASS APART Susan Lewis £3.95
☐ WEEP NO MORE, MY LADY Mary Higgins Clark £2.95
☐ COP OUT R.W. Jones £2.95
☐ WOLF'S HEAD J.K. Mayo £2.95
☐ GARDEN OF SHADOWS Virginia Andrews £3.50
☐ WINGS OF THE WIND Ronald Hardy £3.50
☐ SWEET SONGBIRD Teresa Crane £3.95
☐ EMMERDALE FARM BOOK 23 James Ferguson £2.95
☐ ARMADA Charles Gidley £3.95

You can buy Fontana paperbacks at your local bookshop or newsagent. Or you can order them from Fontana Paperbacks, Cash Sales Department, Box 29, Douglas, Isle of Man. Please send a cheque, postal or money order (not currency) worth the purchase price plus 22p per book for postage (maximum postage required is £3.00 for orders within the UK).

NAME (Block letters) _____

ADDRESS _____

_____

_____